Praise for

The Beast's Heart

"I stayed up until the small hours . . . what a delight! This is a beautifully . . . retelling of the fairy tale. Leife Shallcross opens a brand-new window onto the old story, creating a cast of engaging characters whose fates we really care about."

—Juliet Marillier, author of the Blackthorn & Grim series

"A glorious debut from Australian author Leife Shallcross, *The Beast's Heart* retells 'Beauty and the Beast' in a compelling and surprising novel filled with peril, darkness, romance and beauty. An utterly enchanting fairy-tale retelling that breathes new life into a beloved classic."

—Kate Forsyth, author of *Bitter Greens* and *The Wild Girl*

"Leife Shallcross weaves her words like a fairy-tale enchantment. *The Beast's Heart* is like nothing you've read. Welcome to a glorious darkness."

—Angela Slatter, World Fantasy Award–winning author of
The Bitterwood Bible and Other Recountings

"I might have a new favorite 'Beauty and the Beast'! Five out of five stars to Leife Shallcross's utterly beautiful retelling, *The Beast's Heart*. Gorgeous writing, magical romance at its best. Absolutely loved it."

—Sam Hawke, author of *City of Lies*

"A lush retelling of my favorite fairy-tale classic. Beautiful, poignant and enchanting . . . Leife Shallcross's Beast shines."

—C. L. Wilson, *New York Times* bestselling author of
The Sea King

The Beast's Heart

LEIFE SHALLCROSS

ACE

NEW YORK

ACE
Published by Berkley
An imprint of Penguin Random House LLC
1745 Broadway, New York, New York 10019

Copyright © 2018 by Leife Shallcross

Library of Congress Cataloging-in-Publication Data

Names: Shallcross, Leife, author.
Title: The Beast's heart / Leife Shallcross.
Description: First edition. | New York: Ace, 2019.
Identifiers: LCCN 2018023812 | ISBN 9780440001775 (trade pbk.) |
ISBN 9780440001782 (ebook)
Subjects: | GSAFD: Love stories.
Classification: LCC PR9619.4.S534 B43 2019 | DDC 823/.92—dc23
LC record available at https://lccn.loc.gov/2018023812

First Edition: February 2019

Printed in the United States of America
1 3 5 7 9 10 8 6 4 2

Cover art by Lisa Perrin
Cover design by Katie Anderson
Title page photo: rose © Kyselova Inna/Shutterstock
Book design by Elke Sigal

To Dennis, my one and only

And in loving memory of Marguerite,
the best of grandmothers

CHAPTER I

*E*nchantments and dreams: I suspect they are made of the same stuff. They each beguile the mind and confuse the senses with wonder and strangeness so all that was familiar becomes freakish, and the most bizarre of things intimate and natural. For the longest time after the curse fell, I did not know if I was a beast who dreamed of being a man, or a man who dreamed he was a beast.

There are moments I recall with clarity from that dark stretch of years in which I lost myself. In remembering them, though, the real is indistinguishable from the phantasm. My initial flight in abject terror from my home is as sharp and shapeless as a shard of glass. I know it happened. Everything since has unfolded from it. The details, though, are the stuff of nightmares.

I have tried to string my memories together to make some sense of those years. But living under such an enchantment is akin to being trapped in the grip of a restless slumber, fighting toward wakefulness and finding only dreams locked within dreams.

The first moment I felt as though I was awake, in all those years, was the first time I saw Isabeau, standing in a fall of golden light, hesitating on my doorstep in her poor, patched gown. The sun flooded in, spilling across the flagstones and lighting up the very air around her. It was too bright for me. Her radiance dazzled my sleep-blighted eyes and I crept away to hide.

Everything before that has faded into shadow, or taken on the livid shimmer of a half-remembered delusion. The decades I spent haunting the wild, wild forests my fair lands had become, terrifying people and savaging any livestock foolish enough to stray within its bounds; the starvation years that inevitably followed, as the forest emptied of all living creatures save vermin and the occasional watchful raven; the shatteringly lonely term of my imprisonment in the home I eventually returned to when my misery finally crushed my rage and I remembered what I once had been.

If it was a living nightmare that took me into the forest, it was most certainly a dream that brought me out of it, and back to my ancestral home.

Since I had forgotten myself, my dreams had been wild, primal things, a reflection of the savagery that filled my days. But, as the skin sank deeper into the hollows between my ribs and my empty belly cleaved to my spine, I lost even the strength to run and hunt in my imagination. Now, each night found me limping through the endless, empty forest in my mind, searching and searching. I had no clear idea of what it was I searched for, except that, unlike during my waking hours, it was not food. My memories of those bitter dreams are of hunting through dark, shadowy trees for something hidden in the heart of the forest—something I feared to discover, but I feared more I would never find, and would be lost to me forever.

One grim night, as I was nearing the end of my strength, I fell asleep upon a bed of pine needles, curled against the rain soaking through the branches above. At once my mind found itself slinking between the measureless ranks of phantom trees. As I dragged my paws forward, I saw ahead a glimmer of moonlight. I lifted my weary head. The moon never pierced the canopy of this unending nightmare.

As I looked, the pale gleam began to move. I followed. I was so far behind, and so weak and sore of foot, it was all I could do to keep the errant moonbeam in sight. But eventually, I began to draw closer and I could see I was following a woman. She was dressed in the most exquisite finery, such as would not be out of place at the royal court, and she moved as lightly through the trees as if she were stepping across a dance floor. Her pale skirts were long and trailing, and shone in the gloom. She wore a tall, old-fashioned, horned headdress, from which a gossamer veil floated, dissolving behind her into drifting motes of silver light that sank away into the dark soil of the forest path. She was a vision so rich and rare, I could not help but follow along behind.

I soon realized we were walking upon a road that wound through the forest. It was ancient and much degraded, its cobbles displaced by roots and covered by moss. Indeed, parts of it were in danger of being entirely reclaimed by the creeping wood.

Eventually she stopped ahead of me. I came as close as I dared. She was standing before a ruined gate. It had once been very grand indeed, but now ivy twisted through its rusted ironwork, and the stone columns supporting it were crumbling and broken. I did not like to look at the gate; to do so made me feel miserable and afraid. So instead, I looked at her.

Now that I had come upon her, I saw her dress was not, as I had thought, a sumptuous court gown of satin and brocade.

Up close, I could see it was constructed of clotted cobweb and the velvet wings of dead moths. It was not embroidered with pearls and diamonds, but decorated with the tiny bones of small animals and glittering with spiders' eyes. The veil was no veil, but a drifting cloud of tiny insects glimmering with their own milky iridescence. I hunched down, my hackles rising in fear, and she turned to look at me.

I could not see her expression, but her eyes gleamed in the darkness, green as a cat's. Terrified, I hid my face.

When I looked again, the gate was open and she was some distance away from me, walking between the cracked columns. I did not want to put my paws through that gate, but as my eyes followed her, my gaze fell upon the dark, jagged shape of a ruined building far ahead. Something about its lightless, misshapen hulk called to me and I crept forward.

I lost sight of the woman for some minutes, then, as I slunk along the overgrown path, I spied her again. She was no longer ahead of me, but walking far away, to the side of the ruin ahead. I hesitated, unsure if I should follow her, or my growing compulsion to see what lay amid the broken walls. By the light of the ghostly glimmer she cast about herself, I saw her walk beneath an archway in a tall hedge. I could see nothing but trees beyond. My heart quailed. What could lie through that portal, but the forest? I did not want to go back there. I turned away from the fading smudge of light and started again toward the shattered building looming distantly against the night sky.

The path twisted to and fro among strange, dark shapes vastly different from any forest tree I had seen, and yet eerily familiar. With every step I took, a sense of creeping unease grew in my breast. Then the path made another twist and before me lay the ruined château I had seen from the gate.

Within its roofless, crumbling walls, burning brands illuminated a scene of the basest debauchery. Bodies writhed and danced and crawled around the figure of a man, who stood among them, his shirt open and his hair wild. In his hand he held a bottle glinting amber in the firelight. His eyes shone with a mad light, and his face was gray with the ravages of illness.

Pain lanced through my heart.

I knew him. I hated him. The anger I thought had died erupted into incandescence within me and I sprang forward, snarling.

But my claws and teeth met with nothing. I crashed heavily upon the stone floor and lay, writhing and alone, amid the cold, dark ruin of the house in which I had been raised.

Memories came flooding back. A confused and bitter cacophony, with rage and hatred at its heart. I threw back my head to howl, but the sound that came out was a human scream.

I jerked awake.

I was in the forest. My hairy paws scrabbled in the sodden mulch as I heaved myself upright.

Nothing had changed. Everything had changed.

I was still a broken, starving beast—but I remembered now. I remembered what I had been, and how I had been transformed. I remembered the Fairy's cold, green eyes. *Let all who look upon you see the nature of the heart beating in your breast,* was the curse she had laid upon me. And only now, with my arrogance crushed and my rage exhausted, could I begin to see the truth of her words.

But what good was any of it now? I was alone and close to death.

I hung my head. At my feet, a pale, wet rock glistened in the darkness. It was a curious, regular shape. Not far from it lay another, so similar as to be identical. I looked around. A short distance away, the rain had washed a film of dirt and mulch from the ragged edge of a ruined, cobbled road. My hackles rose as fear gripped me.

Was I still dreaming? I was so sure I was awake.

I stepped forward, sniffing. There was an odd tang in the air. It took me a few moments to place the scent. Magic. I don't know how I knew it, but I realized now the scent had pervaded the forest as long as I had lived in it. Until now, however, the magic had been old and settled. This was fresh and new.

With sudden clarity, I knew I was not dreaming. The road was real, and I knew where it would take me, if I chose to follow it.

I could, of course, choose not to. I could slink away into the forest and ignore it. Without a doubt, that would have spelled my death. I did not feel ready to take the path. I did not feel ready to return. But with death as the alternative, my formless fears were no longer of any consequence.

Not knowing what else to do, I stepped onto the path and began to follow it home.

CHAPTER II

$\mathcal{M}$y return was a bleak event. The gates were rusted open, the gardens overgrown and tangled. As I came to the château I saw crumbled walls and broken windows and exposed beams like shattered ribs where the roof had fallen in. The elements, the animals and insects had all found their way inside. The furniture, fine tapestries and luxurious carpets were rotting away. Expensive baubles had been scattered and broken and the colors of valuable paintings washed away by rain. If I had not known, I would never have recognized my beautiful home. But I knew now. The moment I put my hairy paws through the gates, I knew it all again.

That night I crept into the entrance hall, through the drifts of decaying leaves and piles of rubble. My arrival disturbed a veritable horde of verminous beetles, black and glittering, that fled at my approach, scuttling away into cracks in the broken stonework. I lay down before the fireplace. I could not light a fire, but I had my accursed fur. Weary and sorrowful beyond belief, I followed the example of the dogs I had owned, many

years before, and laid my great, shaggy head upon my paws and
fell asleep.

When I awoke—seemingly but a moment after I had closed my
eyes—it had all changed.

It was the fire that woke me. The instant I felt its glow on
my flank and heard the quick snap of wood, I was roused. At the
sight of the flames dancing brightly in the grate, I sprang violently back, hurtling into a chair. I knocked it over, scrambled
up and backed away. The chair was upholstered in wine-colored
velvet and familiar to me. It had been a favorite station by the
fire once, long ago. Warily I looked about and saw my hall as I
remembered it. But to my beast's nostrils, the air stank of magic,
recently invoked.

As I stared around myself, a movement caught my eye. An
earwig crawled over the velvet brocade arm of the fallen chair and
disappeared. Then, before my eyes, the chair righted itself and
moved back into place. I had been a beast for many years and had
only just remembered myself. For longer than I had lived as a
man I had let wild instinct govern me, and it governed me still.
I fled. The great doors were shut fast, so I bolted up the grand
staircase, only to be halted at the halfway landing. Here was an
elaborate Venetian mirror; taller than a man, it dominated the
landing where the staircase branched. The sight of myself in this
mirror brought me up hard. I was frozen. I could not run. Not
from myself.

I was no pretty creature. Not built like a wolf or a bear or a
lion; yet, a little of each. I had the lion's mane—a mass of dark,
dark hair growing about my face and neck and over my shoulders. I was massive, my paws armed with long, sharp talons I

could never sheathe, and crowning my head was a pair of gnarled and twisted horns. But my eyes—oh, my eyes! They were unchanged, as blue and human as the day the curse had been laid. No wonder people ran in terror from me. To recognize my eyes and know the horror and corruption I had become—how they must have feared me.

Now my own eyes held me. I stared into them; they stared into me. Around them, instead of a nobleman with elegantly clipped hair and clothes of velvet and satin, was a beast with tangled, matted fur and slavering jaws, groveling on all four feet.

After the first shocked moment of realization, such despair and anger surged within my monstrous breast that, snarling, I hurled myself at the mirror.

I met the cold, implacable glass with such force it cracked in two. I fell back. What I saw only enraged me further. My hackles rose. Each half now reflected back to me my image. Two sets of shocked, blue eyes now stared at me from within the broken frame. I gave a roar and threw myself forward again, one thought in my brain: *No mirrors. I will not abide any mirrors.*

Again and again I attacked that great slab of mocking, silvered glass. Each time it cracked, a new set of glaring, human eyes would be there, staring out from the abomination of my face. I tore at it with my claws and blindly pounded my horns against its surface. Shards of glass began to fall around me, smashing apart on the marble floor. Finally, the entire thing shattered, cascading to the floor in a thousand fragments. I stood on my four feet, swaying with exhaustion, surveying the destruction I had wrought. It was enough. Nowhere could I see a sliver large enough to show me what I had become.

What little strength I had left now deserted me. I collapsed, exhausted from my frenzy and torn and bleeding from my work.

* * *

When I awoke the next morning, I was sprawled upon the bed I had used when I was human. The room was hung with cobwebs and thick with dust, but the dirt and tangles had been combed from my fur, the insidious splinters of glass removed and my gashes dressed and bound.

On a chest at the foot of the bed was a tray upon which sat a most unappetizing breakfast. Stale bread, withered fruit and a thin, greasy gruel. Still, I was hungry enough to eat anything. A tarnished spoon lay beside the food: a utensil I had no hope of being able to use. In bitter humiliation I ate by thrusting my blunt nose into the middle of the meal, tearing at the bread and gulping down the gruel as though I were a dog.

The very act of eating exhausted me, but the room was so cold and drear, I could not bear to stay. I slunk out the door and down the corridor, back toward the entrance hall in search of the fire that had roused me last night. Despite the ministrations of whoever had tended my wounds, I hurt all over. A deep cut on one of my hind feet reopened, leaking blood through the linen bandage and leaving a trail of crimson paw prints across the bare stone. At the great staircase I stopped, wary of subjecting my lacerated paws to the gauntlet of broken glass I had created in my distemper. But I could not see even the tiniest glittering fragment amid the ruins of the rotting carpet and dead leaves clogging the stairs. The only remaining evidence of the existence of the great glass was its ghostly outline on the wall.

I limped cautiously down the stairs, sniffing at the air, trying to catch the scent of whoever had cared for me last night and left me food this morning. I had no coherent thoughts in my head as to what I would do when I met them, just an instinctive yearning for warmth and more food. All I could smell, however, were the myriad, musty odors of decay underpinned by the now-familiar tang of newly awakened magic. I breathed deeper. I could not even detect the smell of wood smoke. As I reached the bottom of the staircase, the reason for this strange absence became apparent: the hearth was empty. Not just cold, but utterly bare. No charred remains of last night's fire, not even the tell-tale, ashy coating of a hearth swept clean. Indeed, the soot stains in the fireplace were so faded it looked as though it had not been used for years. There was nothing here but cold stone and mildew.

Not far away was a pile of weathered sticks and disintegrating fabric. I crept forward and sniffed at it: woodworm and the faintest vestige of mouse. A few stray strands of horsehair quivered in a draft. *My chair.* Or, more correctly, the remains of it. The skin across my shoulders prickled with unease. *Did I dream the fire and the chair?* I was so sure I had not. I nosed around the floor and found one of my own bloodied paw prints. *How could I have possibly dreamed up broken glass that cut me?*

A new scent reached me, the merest thread of warmth in the vast, gray chill of the abandoned château. I turned to follow it. I padded lamely up the stairs, along halls, until I came to a long, empty gallery. It was so desolate I did not immediately realize where I was. Shutters had fallen away from a series of large windows that showed countless gaps where the panes had cracked and shattered. Part of the roof had collapsed and, beneath the rubble that had descended from the breach, the floor was sagging dangerously. It was not until I saw the splintered frames, torn canvases and warped boards still adorning the decrepit walls that I recognized this was the gallery in which had hung portraits of my family, dating back many generations. I had little care for these ruined heirlooms now. I was exhausted and in pain and entirely focused on tracking the tiny point of heat I had detected. The scent of it was not wood smoke, but something else that spoke of warmth and light and comfort—something I had known in another life. Memory tugged at my brain like a snarl in my fur, but I could not place it. I picked my way along the gallery beneath my obliterated ancestry, following the enigmatic trace. At last I saw a tiny, winking light.

Of course. Candle wax.

Visions of tall tapers burning in silvered candelabra washed through my brain, of people and dinners and dancing and church, and all the things candles meant to me once upon a time. Instinctively I looked all around for the person who must have placed the single, jewel-like light, twinkling in a glass upon a shelf. There was no one about.

Then I saw it.

Amid all the destruction wrought by time and neglect, one portrait remained untouched. It hung above the candle, the rich gilt of its frame intact and reflecting ruddy glints. It was a portrait of a woman of middle years in a russet brocade gown with a starched ruff, smiling gently, if a little sadly, down upon me. One hand rested upon a ruby droplet depending from a strand of pearls about her neck; the other clasped a posy of wild flowers in her lap: white daisies, red carnations, forget-me-nots, celandine and purple fritillaries. The strength left my legs and I sank to the floor, staring up at her. Every line of her kind face was intimately familiar. My heart broke open and memories spilled through me, sweet and piercing.

Grand-mère.

A miserable whine rose in my throat. *Why must I see her now?* I'd never felt my wretchedness more keenly. She was the only mother I had known, for mine had died when I was very small. She had understood all too well the failings of her son, my father; it was her life's sorrow. She had doted upon me, perhaps hoping I might choose a better path. *But look at me now,* I thought, bitterness stopping my breath as though I had swallowed thorns.

I dragged myself up, too ashamed to remain here under the benediction of her painted gaze. But as I took a faltering step I heard the ghost of her voice again. *Chéri, you must be the best man you know how to be.* I stumbled. She had said this to me so often in the last years of her life, always with a gentle touch and a smile, trusting me to choose the right path and not lose myself to the course of corruption chosen by my father. I hung my head, staring at my bandaged, bleeding paws.

I am not a man.

Yet someone had cared for me. Had left me food. And however pitiful that meal had been, it had been a human meal. I twisted to stare back at the candle. *Someone else* was here in this ruined château and whoever it was knew me for being more than just a beast. Perhaps they could help me . . . I limped off in search of my mysterious benefactor.

I found no one.

It's true; I was ill and injured and could move but slowly. It would not have been a difficult task to avoid me. Even so, if there had been someone to find, eventually I must have discovered some sign of them. But there was no one. I searched for days. Weeks, even. Every night I returned to my dreary room and every morning a meal was waiting for me beside the bed. Sometimes there was even a meager fire burning in the hearth, or in the hearth of the entrance hall. At long last I came to the uncomfortable realization I was entirely alone and that whatever food or fire or light appeared in this desolate place was a result of the magic that seemed to have sunk indelibly into the very walls. There was no one to help me. If there was to be any change in my pitiable condition, I would need to work it myself.

The morning after this epiphany, as I was finishing my paltry meal, a basin of steaming water appeared on a table nearby. I cannot describe how wholly disconcerting this was. It simply materialized out of nothing. I flung myself away from it, snarling. When it did nothing more remarkable than send up gentle curls of scented steam, I gathered my courage to investigate it. Circling the table upon which it stood, I recalled the way my fireside chair had picked itself up after I knocked it over the night I arrived. Indeed, the water smelled of chamomile and pine and the faintest whiff of magic. I knew what it was for. I remembered it from my previous life. It was as though, now that I had accepted any change in my situation was mine to make, the magic inhabiting this place was offering me a challenge.

I could only reach it by standing on my hind legs and my only means of cleaning my face was to submerge it in the water and shake it about. By this method I ended up with half of the basin's contents up my nose and the other half down my front. Still, most beasts will wash themselves with their own tongue, and I had done it with a bowl of hot water. An unfamiliar feeling of warmth gathered in my chest. It caught me by surprise when at last I recognized the foreign sensation for what it was. *Pride*, I realized wonderingly. I honestly could not have said when I last did something I felt proud of. This was such a simple thing, it seemed ridiculous. But it certainly wasn't the last simple thing to challenge me.

Thus began the process by which I learned anew how to be a man. At the start, it was almost as miserable as the existence I had just escaped. Many, many times I tore outside and threw my body at the iron gates, trying to force them open so I could run back into the forest and be a beast once more. It seemed, however, that having accepted the house's hospitality in my darkest hour, I would not be permitted to return to oblivion.

The house was not the crumbling ruin I had first encountered on my return, but it was little better. It was rank with neglect and inhabited by every pestilential creature imaginable. The strange forces that had cared for me and brought me food on my return were erratic. One day I might find a feast awaiting me in the entrance hall, another I would be served nothing but rancid cheese and spoiled meat. There were occasions when I did not eat for several days together. Even so, with the relics of my old life constantly before me, I began to try to reclaim what dregs of it I could.

And it seemed to me the magic now pervading my house rewarded my efforts toward this impossible goal.

Over time, the rooms I used most improved and became comfortable. The invisible servants inhabiting my house became more reliable. I found it easier to pretend I was a man. I would shake off the drowsiness that dogged me and walk around on two legs. I would dress in a fine linen shirt and velvet doublet and dine at the table.

It was not easy. Eating with any appearance of civility was ever difficult; that never changed. Always I had to allow the magic to help me dress, or the velvet doublets I wore became torn and the fine linen ruffles at my wrists frayed and unraveled. I found it almost impossible to draw on my own boots, even after my hind feet grew more human in shape. Yet it was of immediate concern to me that, in every possible respect, I appear as noble as I had been born. I knew all the conventions of civility; they had been ingrained in me as I grew. I had practiced them in empty pride, a mere exercise of righteousness. But now, in absolute solitude, I made them the mark of my humanity.

Progress was achingly slow and each milestone I achieved was a thing to be treasured. It took years before I could walk unaided down the grand staircase on my hind legs, and many more hours of effort before I could do it easily. And, of course, some conquests cost me more than simple physical exertion. There was the day, before ever I thought to stagger about on two legs like a parody of a lady's lap dog begging for treats, when I wandered into the room that had once been my study. It was a decrepit mess. Not wholly derelict, perhaps, but close. The curtains over the windows hung in rotten rags, mildew bloomed across the walls and the books piled upon the desk had swollen with damp and burst their spines. Several had come apart entirely and spilled their pages across the floor. I looked down at the water-spotted piece of paper at my feet . . . and discovered I could read.

Why should I have been so surprised? It was something I would not have thought twice about in my previous life. But here I was creeping about on four paws, my body clothed in nothing but coarse fur, looking down at words scrawled across a page and *reading*. I think that was the first time I knew for certain I was no mere beast. I stood there, transfixed by those faded words, trembling with the import of this revelation. *I could read!* What beast can read?

The onslaught of grief this presaged, as I realized anew what had been done to me, was difficult to weather. I finally understood what was lost to me and what must lie ahead. But, even so, after that, the study became a favorite haunt of mine. Even before I could sit in an armchair, I would sprawl on that threadbare hearth rug, a book open beneath my animal paws, my phantom servants turning the pages as I found refuge from my unbearable existence in the words and knowledge of other men and women that those precious volumes contained.

Another incident stands out in my mind. On this occasion I was prowling through the upstairs portion of my house, shambling along on two legs as elegantly as any bear, when I passed a gallery that had once been used by the men of my family as a sort of *salle d'armes*. Every other time I passed it, it had been a shell of its former self, reduced to warped floorboards and damp-streaked walls. But on this day the door was open and through it I glimpsed an apparent mirage: the room, set up as it always had been, as neat and tidy and impeccably maintained as if my fencing master had only just that moment stepped out to run some errand.

What was this? Why this room? Why now? The hallway I stood in was as rank and neglected as ever. But inside the gallery . . . There were the leather dummies, set at one end of the room, presided over by a wooden manikin with one outthrust arm surmounted by a battered saber. There were the hooks upon which hung thick leather jerkins and a heavy canvas jacket. There was the rack of shining weapons, some among them intimately familiar. I crept forward, hardly daring to breathe, feeling as though I were trespassing on forbidden ground. *Why should this disconcert me so?* I shook my head to clear the anxious buzzing in my ears. My heartbeat was racing itself, tripping against my ribs.

The art of fencing. Surely the mark of a civilized man. I had known how to handle a blade. I had been very good at it. I had learned and practiced and honed my skill in this very room. *Was this a sign?* If I took up my sword and proved my skill, would I likewise prove my manhood? Would I be free of this stooping, hulking, hateful form? I edged closer to the rack of steel. *There. That one!* My own saber rested there, gleaming.

I reached out one beastly paw and wrapped it around the hilt, lifting it from its wooden rest. At once I was assailed by memories, rushing through me as though a river had suddenly burst through the walls and was carrying me away. My nostrils filled with the remembered stink of blood and smoke and burning steel. For a moment it seemed my paws and blade were drenched in scarlet. Screams of pain and cries of "*Beast!*" echoed in my ears. Memories of a wall of spears and flaming torches rising up before me sent me stumbling to my knees. I lost my grip on my blade and it clattered to the floor.

Slowly the darkness obscuring my vision began to clear and I could see the whitewashed walls of the *salle d'armes* again. I gasped in clean, untainted air.

"I am not a beast," I croaked in protest, the sting of tears rising to blot out the room anew.

"Not a beast," I said again.

And then I heard it.

Not the suffocating silence that usually filled these lonely halls, but the words I had spoken to break it. *Words.* No inarticulate whine or anguished howl, but human speech. My first words in a century, or perhaps more. If I had not already been on my knees, I probably would have fallen then.

It was this, more than anything else, that taught me to keep striving to regain those things I had thought lost. To keep trying to walk upright, though I felt as though I were performing a foolish trick for an unresponsive audience. To do what I could to regain my skill in fencing, though at the start my ungainly paws could barely grasp the hilt. To take up what other pursuits I remembered from my life before, though my clumsiness made me grind my teeth and my solitude mocked me at every turn. And to read aloud a little, every day, so that my voice might strengthen and lose its beastly growl, and I might hear something to break that frozen silence.

Still, there were times when I raged about the house, or ran to the rooftops to howl curses at the night-time skies with their cold stars. For, as I tried vainly to regain my humanity, I began to feel, more and more keenly with each passing year, each day and hour, the one basic need that makes every person truly human.

My invisible servants were by no means physical beings. They did as I bid them, but aside from that, talking to them was like talking to the wind. There were no replies. I could still feel the forest around me, and no one ever came into it now. Even though I no longer haunted its shadowy ways and mysterious groves, the miasma of my anger remained. I had passed into myth, but the taboo persisted.

My sorrow was loneliness. My craving was for human company. Often I pondered the bitter irony of my situation. Before, I had been a man locked in a constant struggle with the monster within. But the Fairy had torn me open, exposed my most shameful secret to the world and ensured I would only ever be recognized for what I had tried to hide.

Despite this, when the chance came to see and speak to another human being, I grasped it without thinking twice.

CHAPTER III

Who knows how many years I spent there alone? A lifetime? Half a lifetime? I never counted. Indeed, time seemed an unreliable, mutable thing. It stretched and contracted with dreamlike unpredictability, while the rest of my world remained utterly static.

It was early one evening, in the depths of midwinter, when I became aware someone had entered my forest. I always knew when some creature had broached my borders. For many years it had only been the occasional goat or cow that strayed too far. But this was no dumb animal; this was a man. Cold and hungry and possibly near death.

I laid aside the book I was reading and sat for a few moments concentrating on the presence of this solitary traveler. He was indeed exhausted, and so was his poor horse. But he seemed driven onward by some burning need. I had the strongest sense he *refused* to die, that he knew if he let himself or his horse rest for even a moment, they would never leave the forest. The poor fool. I could tell that unless both he and his animal got food and rest in the very near future they would not see morning.

My strange connection with the forest did not end with my capacity to sense intruders. I had long been able to shape it to my will, to somehow change the course of the pathways winding through its green heart so, if I chose, the lost might wander forever without once catching sight of a break in the trees. Now, though, I made sure he found an overgrown path that led straight to my gates.

I did not know if they would even open for him. I merely hoped. My joy, when he finally rode through, was unutterable. I could only imagine his amazement when he saw what lay on the other side. For, within the tall hedge that kept me from the forest, my lands in their previous entirety could be found.

This was not all. My ability to manipulate the forest outside was multiplied a thousandfold within the confines of my prison. Even before I learned again to eat with decorum, or read, or fence, or shoot with bow and arrow, or do any of those things that are the mark of a civilized *man*, I found solace in shaping my gardens. In them I could use the enchantment binding me to create something of refinement and beauty.

I had not been able to resist a certain measure of exotic variety that could only ever exist by magic. It took time (of which I had eons to spare) and much careful experimentation, but at last I had gardens straight out of the pleasantest dreams. Winding paths twisted past flower beds permanently in their prime, flourishing with springtime blossoms and fragrant herbs growing together with delightful untidiness. I had orchards both in fruit and in flower and lawns ornamented with ancient yew trees trimmed into fantastic shapes and hedges. Sometimes the lawn and yews were cool and green and sometimes they were covered in a blanket of clean, white snow. Another lawn was set with bosquets of different varieties of trees, all in glorious autumnal colors. Tended by my unseen servants and pampered by magic, my gardens flourished, even as parts of the house persisted as a ruin.

This, then, was what greeted the lost traveler as he rode through my gates. How his amazement must have grown, as the world around him melted from winter into spring and summer. I lit lanterns along his path, so he could better see the nodding blooms and ground free of frost, and I made sure every window of my house was ablaze with welcoming light.

I led him first to the stables where the doors swung open to reveal fresh hay and warm oat mash. He dismounted, but did not directly lead his horse inside. This puzzled me until something registered in my mind. Something I had hitherto overlooked. This man was afraid. He had come from a winter forest steeped in a legend of terror, to a springtime paradise exhibiting magical opening stable doors.

The man hesitated for some few minutes, but was eventually decided in his course of action by his horse. As the seconds trickled away it became obvious they were in no immediate danger. At least, the horse thought so. To it, the smell of oats became more important than the smell of magic, which, although strange, apparently offered no real threat. And after a while it began to demonstrate its interest in what lay beyond the threshold of the stable door. This must have made the traveler realize that, trap or no, his only alternative was the forest—which offered certain death. He eventually relented and led his horse inside, where it very sensibly went straight to its stall and began to consume the oat mash without even waiting to be divested of its livery.

The man dithered awhile with his animal, making an attempt to care for it. I say attempt, for he had hardly touched the girth strap before it became unbuckled. And by the time he had taken the saddle off and placed it on its peg, the saddle blanket and bridle had also mysteriously found their way to their places and his pack and bags were nowhere to be seen. He only conceded defeat and left the horse to its mash after he discovered that, while he picked one of its tired feet clean, the other three had been done and its coat curried to perfection.

As he left the stables, a series of well-placed lamps lit to show him the path to the entrance hall where a marvelous feast awaited him. And as he made his way through the garden, I left my library and also went to the entrance hall. I was excited beyond words and could no longer satisfy myself with the vague sense of him in my house. I had to see him with my eyes.

I did not go down into the hall, but rather to one of the curtained galleries overlooking it. I intended to watch him as he ate, and measure the kind of man he was. I would let him eat his meal and then I would come down the staircase, and we would sit by the fire and talk as men should. I expected him to be afraid at first, but, I reasoned, after a good meal he would be more relaxed. He would find me fearsome, but he would have already experienced my hospitality and good care and surely that would reassure him as to my good intentions.

I waited in darkness, peering through the gap in the velvet drapes. The seconds passed me by and I felt each and every one, like single drops of water falling into a crystal bowl. Then he entered. Even allowing for his exhaustion, his gait and posture were not those of a young man. He stopped when he saw the table laid out before him and was so taken with it, he did not notice my unseen servants remove his cloak. His chair slid out from its place and turned invitingly toward him, and a flask arose from the table and poured him a glass of wine. His mouth gaped open and again he just stood and stared.

"Sit!" I growled in frustration, as his astonished, lack-witted response began to grate on my nerves—and was astonished myself when he started, looked fearfully around and quickly seated himself. I, too, glanced around. Perhaps it was echoes or perhaps it was magic, but if I was to frighten him as little as possible I would have to be more careful.

I watched him eat with interest. He ate quickly as a hungry man would, but he did not gobble his food. It became obvious he was a man of some breeding—or at least his table etiquette was excellent and seemed unconsciously so. He ate a lot, but did not gorge himself, and when he was done, he folded his napkin and pushed back his chair and stood up. He cleared his throat uncertainly and began to speak.

"I do not know if there is anyone to hear me or not," he said loudly, "but if there is, I thank you for your hospitality. You must forgive my hesitation. I am by no means ungrateful, but this château is a strange place and I have had a very hard journey."

I sat motionless. His was the first human voice I had heard in perhaps a century and to me it sounded as beautiful as the finest music. But what held me frozen in my chair was the quaver of uncertainty the man had not been able to keep from his voice. He was still afraid. All this—my forest, my lands, my house, my servants—perhaps it was all too much. When I had lived in the world, magic was certainly rare. I had been living apart for so many, many years. What if, as was inevitable, the world had changed? What if magic was unheard of? I leaned forward and peered again through the curtains. The man had seated himself on the edge of one of the chairs by the fire and was twisting his hands nervously.

My courage failed me. I was a beast and not fit for him to look at. If I went down he would try to run, or to kill me, or he would faint with fright. I could never have a conversation with him as I had wished. I fell back into my chair with my hairy, taloned paws covering my human eyes. Below me the lights in the entrance hall dimmed, and lamps leading up the stairway and to a bedchamber flickered alight. I did not watch him go.

That night, in my own rooms, I tore off my costly garments, shredding the fine cloth and gilt embroidery with my claws. Clothed only in my own dark pelt I ran from the house and out into the night. I was a beast again, and my strange body flowed back into the shape of a creature for which it is natural to prowl on four legs. I roamed my gardens and roared in anger and disappointment at the blank face of the moon. Until, through my howls, I heard the screams of my guest's terrified horse. I hadn't wanted to frighten it, I had only come out to indulge in my own bitter rage. Ashamed, I slunk away to my old haunt among the rooftops.

As I lay there, subdued and humiliated, I noticed something new in the magical fabric of my house. I closed my eyes and lay my shaggy head on my forepaws and tried to concentrate. Within moments I realized what it was. My guest was dreaming.

And such dreams! There was never anything new in my life, so my dreams were always the same. But this man had a life, and a family. Three daughters. He must have loved them very much for their faces kept on appearing in the unfolding images of his dream. A thin current of worry threaded the flow of his reveries, however, and the youngest daughter kept asking him for roses. Every time her sweet face appeared, she said, laughing, "Bring me a rose, Papa!" and a wave of unhappiness swept through the dream.

I cannot tell all the emotions that arose in my breast as I eavesdropped on my dreaming guest. The warmth of his love for his children first suffused me, then became a bitter ache as I realized I could never hope for such. My heart soared at the tenderness in the youngest daughter's eyes, and shriveled as I ground my teeth in rage at the remembered image of my own face, covered with fur and crowned with twisted horns. Eventually, I shut my mind to his sleeping visions, unable to bear them any longer.

I lay on the rooftops, exhausted by the ordeal I had put myself through. I felt as though my heart were breaking. I even fancied I heard a noise that sounded like the shattering of glass. I could not summon the energy to rise and howl to the heavens as I had first sought to do. The hopelessness of my situation consumed me and I lay with my muzzle on my paws, too sick at heart to even move.

I slept, and I dreamed. But this time I did not dream of forests and terror and painted gardens. My sleeping mind plucked images from the traveler's dreams and wove them together anew in my head. Now the youngest daughter was smiling for me, and not with the eyes of a daughter, but those of a sweetheart, a lover, a wife.

Her hands were full of roses, in every color, and they were woven into her hair and strewn about her feet. She plucked one from her breast and lifted it up to her face. As the creamy white petals touched her lips, they blushed. First a delicate shade of pink, then, as she presented the flower to me, the petals darkened to a vibrant crimson. Unable to resist her gift, I reached my hand out and, with a shock that jolted me awake, saw human fingers, a human palm, and a hairless, human wrist.

CHAPTER IV

I could barely breathe for wanting.

I had never seen a woman smile at me that way. I had never wished to. I had been witness to the misery and terror my father visited upon the objects of his ungoverned lusts, and I had eschewed the company of women for fear of treading in his footsteps. But at that moment, still reeling from my dream, it seemed as though my whole existence depended upon this man's daughter.

Dawn was not far off, but even in the graying light I could see my hairy paws. A pale ray of sunlight broke over the distant hills and speared the ragged clouds gathering at the edge of the sky. As I watched it grow and produce more pale shafts of light, an idea unfurled in my mind. I could not stop it. I saw it for the canker it was, God help me, and I trembled as I realized I did not know how to withstand the temptation of it.

I will not! I staggered to my feet in horror. *I will not become the jailer in this prison!*

But, even as I struggled to banish the hateful idea, a plan was taking shape in my head.

I just want to meet her, I told myself. *Just speak to her.*

My head spun at the enormity of the wrong I knew I was about to commit.

I should do nothing, I thought. *I should not move from this rooftop. I will stay here and when it grows light, he will leave and never even know there is a beast here.* But even as I formed this counsel in my mind, I saw again the vast stretch of years I had lived here alone and my heart quailed at the prospect of the next incalculable eon of isolation I would likely face. I could not go back to my solitary life. I would rather die.

I took a step toward the edge of the roof.

A sudden sense of movement dragged my eye down to my gardens below, still lying in deep shadow. A ripple of fear ran down my back, lifting my fur. Something huge was stirring there. Something indistinct and spreading that reached and thrashed. I strained my eyes against the gloom the new sun had not yet dispelled. My sensitive snout caught the diamond scent of new magic a moment before my senses were overwhelmed by the perfume of roses.

It was happening. Exactly as I had wished, even though I had tried my hardest not to.

I turned away from the edge of the roof and began to make my way back to my quarters. Already the path from the front door of my house to the wrought-iron gates wound past a walled garden, grown out of nothing in the moments between dawn and morning. But not just any garden—this one overflowed with glorious roses, the door tantalizingly ajar. If he wanted roses for his daughter, he would have his choice; but at a price. And just in case he did not venture into my rose arbor, plenty of perfect blooms spilled generously over the stone wall to hang nodding above the path—at exactly the right height for a man mounted on horseback.

I walled off my trepidations from the rest of my mind and dressed with care. *I just want to meet her!* Most likely her father would see only a fearsome beast, but on the slim chance he would look past my savage face, he may see I dressed as elegantly as any man. Would it make him think better of me? Would he relay this to his daughter? Might it ease her fears a little?

Guiltily I caused his deflated saddlebags to be filled with all manner of fine things, including a parcel of good food appropriate to eat while traveling, a flask of wine and a jeweled goblet to drink from. It was a small reparation for the distress I was about to inflict upon him and his family. *Perhaps if she sees I am generous . . .* I included a great deal of money and presents for all three daughters. I had his clothes replaced with much finer apparel, and his horse's livery improved upon. His own clothes gave me cause for speculation, as they were poor, simple garments that had obviously seen much wear. This was at odds with his behavior of the previous evening.

When I was ready, I made my way to the curtained gallery overlooking the entrance hall. My guest was still fast asleep in his chamber, clearly exhausted from his ordeal, but it was not long before he awoke to find a steaming bath and his new clothes laid out ready for him.

Eventually he appeared at the top of the staircase, and slowly made his way down. He was wearing his new clothes, but still looked nervous and uncomfortable. The chair at the head of the table drew itself out to welcome him and he went to it, and put his hand on the high, carved back. Before he sat down to the meal awaiting him, however, he turned and said to the room, "Again, I thank you. You have been more than generous and I am sure I would have died last night had you not brought me into your home. I am overwhelmed by your gift of clothing." He stopped and looked confused for a moment. "I have no way of repaying you. You have my most sincere thanks."

He took his seat and I sank back in my own chair feeling guilty and dishonorable. My guest had had little alternative but to accept my hospitality. Now I would take advantage of his love for his daughter and his desire to bring her what she had asked for.

My guest ate hurriedly and soon finished his meal. I silently wished that after his encounter with me, luck and good fortune would follow him for the rest of his days. I was surprised then by the scent of new magic drifting past, and I sincerely hoped this meant my wishes would become reality. I left my curtained gallery to the sound of my guest expressing more thanks, and taking his leave of the empty room.

I made my way to the rose arbor and waited.

It was not long before I heard the brisk sound of hooves on the path: why would the traveler not be eager to return to his family as quickly as possible? When he came around the bend and saw the roses, however, the hoof beats slowed to a walk. I could see him now from my hiding place. He rode past me, and reined in the horse at the door to the rose garden.

"Oh my," he murmured, so quietly I could barely hear him. "I had given up hope."

He rode forward, until he was level with a spray of perfect crimson blooms growing from a branch overhanging the path. He reached up and pulled them toward his face, breathing in the rich perfume. The horse was agitated, having picked up my scent, and fidgeted, blowing nervously. The traveler was too enraptured by the roses to pay it much heed, however. I held my breath as, smiling softly to himself, he searched through the spray of heavy blooms until he found one not quite open. Gently his gloved fingers found the base of its slender stem, and snapped it away.

With a deafening roar, I leaped into the middle of the path behind him. The horse spun around and, confronted with the sight of me, reared up, screaming in terror. The man, taken by surprise, was thrown from his seat and fell to the ground. The rose fell onto the path between us. The man looked up and turned white when he saw what had frightened his animal.

"Ungrateful wretch!" I cried. "I take you in and provide you with shelter and food, and this is how you abuse my generosity? By stealing my roses?"

"Sire! Lord!" he stammered, scrambling to his knees before me. "Forgive me! I did not mean to offend you! I did not realize—" He threw himself forward onto the path. I had to give him credit. He had not fainted away, or jabbered incoherently at my monstrous appearance.

"All I have given you, and this is how you repay me?" I growled.

"Please," he gasped, "do not hurt me. I intended no disrespect. I only thought to take it as a gift to my youngest daughter. If you kill me I do not know what will become of her and her sisters."

"Perhaps," I said, folding my arms, "I will not kill you for this."

"Thank you, sir!" he cried to the ground.

"On one condition!" I snapped. "You bring me your youngest daughter."

"No!" he cried in horror, lifting his face to me. "You cannot ask it!"

"I promise I will not hurt her," I said, trying to sound imperious and not desperate. "I just want to meet this connoisseur of roses."

"Never!" he cried, beginning to anger. My desperation swelled.

"I will kill you now, unless you promise to return here with your daughter, within a month," I growled. My words horrified me. Had I really just threatened his very life? To my ears my voice shook with a craven tremor that spoke of everything I feared in that moment—that I found myself capable of such contemptible threats and that he would recognize my bluster for what it was. But he, at least, seemed to believe my tone was one of implacable fury. He rose up from the ground, paler than ever and shaking.

"I promise," he said bleakly. "In one month I will return."

I realized immediately he was lying.

He had no intention of bringing his daughter here. He would travel home to say good-bye to his family. Then he would return, alone, to meet the death he now imagined awaited him. I was rendered speechless by his courage.

I stood, frozen, as he backed away from me and turned to look for his horse. The unseen forces tending my grounds had stopped the horse from fleeing in terror and it now stood, some distance away, trembling and rolling its eyes, its sides heaving. The moment he was in his seat the horse sprang away, bolting toward the wrought-iron gates, which swung open as they drew near. I stood and watched them go. Out in the forest I let the path he needed to follow unfold before him. It was a long time before the horse began to tire and slow down.

CHAPTER V

*W*ith the traveler's departure I was left to contemplate the consequences of the morning. For the barest moment my heart soared in hope. *Would he bring her?* Of course not. He had—quite rightly—refused to even entertain the thought. But then why agree to return in a month? A chill settled over me. *He believes my powers extend beyond the reach of the forest and I can claim what I want whether he promises or not.*

I staggered back against the wall of my new rose garden. *What have I done?* The first person to brave my cursed forest in a century would return to civilization with tales of a vicious monster demanding the sacrifice of young women. My knees gave out and I sank down. *Why did I not have the courage to go down and meet him last night?* Now he had no cause to remember anything but the wild beast I was trying so hard not to be.

I closed my eyes and let my head sink into my hands, blocking out the unbearably brilliant morning sunshine. There was nothing else I could do. I would just have to wait to see what would happen.

*   *   *

I barely slept in the month before the traveler returned. The days were endless, and the nights worse. I could not concentrate on anything. The weather around my house responded to my agitated mood by becoming blustery and unsettled. Clouds scuttled across the sky so fast the sunlight flickered. Brief cold showers came and went, and the wind was relentless.

My guilt over my unworthy deception gnawed at my gut and warred with the unbearable suspense I found myself in. What would I do but send him away again when he came on his own to meet his death? I had no hope he would bring his daughter. But, if he did, what then? The days passed. The moon grew from a sliver to a perfect pearl, then shrank to a sliver again.

I could feel her from the moment she entered the forest. As soon as she came beneath the canopy of the vast, dark trees, I knew it. The sun had not yet showed itself above the horizon and I was still in my bed. I leaped out and rushed to my window, although there was no hope of seeing anything yet.

She rode quickly and, I realized after the first few breathless minutes, she was alone. Where was her father? Or was I mistaken? Was it someone else? I leaned my forehead upon the chill glass of the window and concentrated all my focus on the person riding full tilt through the trees. No, it was most certainly a young woman upon a horse. Making straight as an arrow for the heart of my forest.

For an hour or so I watched her ride with my strange sixth sense. Then a second person burst through the edge of my forest, riding hard along the path to my gate. There was no doubting who this was: the traveler. With a cold, crawling sensation, I understood what must have happened: the girl had clearly left without him, hoping to reach my domain first and save him from the nameless doom I had promised.

But her father was riding fast. Faster than she. What if he caught her up? She had a significant head start, but her horse had slackened its pace and I was not sure she was traveling fast enough to stay ahead of him. What could I do? I wanted so desperately just to meet her. I could slow him down. Just enough to allow time to . . . I hardly knew. The ruined road she traveled began to twist and wind and stretch behind her.

I did not know where to wait. Despite their speed, they had several hours of travel ahead of them. I paced through dusty, unused hallways and prowled through the library. I spent an hour half-heartedly fencing in the upstairs gallery, stopping every few minutes to monitor the two people racing through my forest. I remembered I had not eaten properly for days and summoned a meal, but finally sent it away, merely picked at. I went out to walk in the rose arbor.

Closer she came. And closer and closer he came behind her.

The midwinter sun had climbed to its paltry zenith, and had begun to descend again, when she finally reached the iron gates. Despite my efforts with the road, her father was not far behind her at all. Another minute and he would be upon her.

I stepped carefully out of the rose arbor to where I had a view of the gate, trying to gather my courage to go and greet her. She slid down off her horse, but did not come any farther toward the gates; she simply stared at them as they swung slowly open.

A moment later I heard a faint shout. Her father had arrived. Without thinking I moved to where they would not see me. The girl glanced over her shoulder and ran forward. When she stepped over the line marking the limit of my lands, I felt it as though I had been struck by a thunderbolt.

As her father pelted up on his foaming horse, the girl stumbled farther into my gardens. Slowly the gates began to close. The girl put her hands over her mouth as her father reined in his horse sharply and threw himself from the saddle. He stumbled across the overgrown gravel toward his daughter, but the iron gates met with a resonant *clang* just as he stretched out a hand to halt them.

In that moment I knew something close to panic. The movement of the gate was none of my doing. It had never opened for me and I did not know how to make it open again now. What had just happened?

Father and daughter stood on opposite sides of my gates, staring at each other in dismay. There was some argument and I found I could not bear to be where I could hear his desperate cries. I turned tail and crept away, back to my study, where I waited anxiously, unconsciously reducing the covering of the arm of my chair to shreds with my claws. The two of them stayed together at the gates for some time. Finally something was resolved. The girl turned away and began to walk down the path to the house. Her father stayed watching at the gate until she reached the doors of the entrance hall.

As she came away from the gates, I panicked. I almost wished for a mirror in which to check my appearance. My invisible servants reacted to my agitation, grooming me again and again, until I growled at them to leave me alone. The meal in the entrance hall was assembled with more fuss and clatter than I had ever experienced before. I forced myself to breathe slowly and calm down, and eventually the invisible servants followed suit.

I went to the gallery overlooking the hall to wait and watch for my new guest. The door swung open and she stepped inside. A wide ray of golden sunshine shone in through the door, and she stood in the center of it, looking about the room. Of course she was lovely, I knew that from her father's dreams, but I was not prepared for the effect her beauty had upon me. She stood there, not in any of the fine clothes I had sent home with her father, but in a plain, homespun dress, holding a small bag and looking cautiously about the room. The light shining in around her burned away all the dregs of drowsiness clinging to my poor brain. I felt as though I was awakening from some dream filled with immeasurable sadness and I began to weep. I had not wept in all the years I could remember, before the curse or after. But now an overwhelming grief gripped and shook me until something cracked and broke free. I had to drag my velvet sleeve across my face to mop away the tears spilling down the fur on my cheeks.

I cannot meet her like this!

I stumbled out of the gallery, choking back sobs I did not want her to hear. I felt strangely light-headed, as though I had been shaken untimely from a deep slumber. I just wanted to meet her, talk to her. *Then . . .* I did not know what then. I could not think. It was hopeless—I could not meet her. I turned tail and ran.

I ended up in my study: a small, safe, familiar room where I could close the door and hide my beastly self away. However, as I sank down into the armchair by the fire, something caught in the corner of my eye. There, in a recessed corner of the room, was a place where long ago I had wrenched a mirror from the wall and dashed it to the ground. Now something hung again in the empty space, covered with a drape of red cloth. I moved across the room and pulled the cloth away from the object. It was a mirror. The sight of my reflection drew a snarl from my throat, but as I lifted my arm to smash the offensive glass, it clouded, then cleared to reveal a view of tall, oppressive trees. A path wound through the trees, and on the path was a man on a horse. He was leading another horse, decked in saddle and bridle, but riderless. I recognized my traveler. He was moving slowly, and weeping as he rode. I snatched my hand away and the drape fell back. He had not stayed. He was returning home and leaving his daughter here. He did not expect to see her again.

I did not know what to do next. Now that she was here, I was terrified of finally meeting this girl. I did not know what I feared most: her reaction to my beastly countenance, or her denunciation of the bargain I had forced upon her father. Would she give me a chance to explain before she left? I went to a chair and sat, and a goblet of wine appeared at my elbow. I drank it down gratefully and watched as it refilled itself. I drank the next glass more slowly, and this time it was not replenished. I did not want to compound her ill feeling toward me by being affected by drink at our first meeting. I had to laugh at this—as if I could make things any worse!

I sat in my chair, rehearsing speeches, apologies, compliments and pleasantries in turn until the sunlight outside had darkened and faded to a dull orange glow. A fire sprang up in the hearth and candles lit themselves around the room.

Then, I heard it, clear as striking crystal.

"Beast!"

I looked around in a panic, expecting to see her at my study door. But there was no one and I realized she was still in her chamber, in another part of the house entirely.

"I am ready to meet you now." Her voice was clear, but very

soft, as though she half thought she was talking to herself. I found myself grasping the arms of my chair in a death grip, and released my hold slowly, so I would not tear the fabric again. I rose unsteadily, and heard the blood drumming in my ears loud enough to drown out the crackle of the fire. On the other side of the house, I knew her bedroom door had opened itself, and lamps were springing into life down a hall. I retreated into the darkest part of the room, near the window, and all the candles were snuffed, save one on the table by the empty wine glass. She arrived at my open study door, to a darkened room smelling of warm wax and candle smoke.

"Are you in here?" she asked, and I could hear the nervousness in her voice. She stood with her hand on the door handle, leaning forward to look inside. The lamps in the hall lit her from behind, and turned her hair into a golden russet halo. Her face was partly in shadow, but where the light touched her cheek, it made her skin glow with a rosy hue. The lamplight also picked up the golden glints and rich red brocade in her gown—a very different dress to the one she had arrived in.

"I am," I answered as softly as I could, trying to keep the beastly coarseness from my voice. She stepped inside the room and the candles closest to her sprang into life. I frowned in consternation and they guttered, but did not go out. I could see her peering into the darkness shrouding my corner of the room and had to stop myself from shrinking from her gaze.

"Won't you come where I can see you?" she said.

"You are not afraid to look upon me?" I asked her.

"My father said you promised not to harm me," she said bravely. I could see her left hand clench nervously, heard the way her voice tripped when she mentioned her father. I took a deep breath and stepped forward into the dim light. Her gaze traveled up from my chest to my face, but when her eyes met mine they skittered away, and she looked down at the floor. I noticed she was trembling only a heartbeat before I apprehended that so, too, was I.

"Please"—I indicated the chair opposite mine, with only a flash of curved talons under my ruffled cuffs—"won't you have a seat?"

She sat, poised on the edge of the velvet cushion, her hands clasped tightly in her lap, and I sat, too, trying to appear elegant and unbeastlike.

"You are wearing one of the gowns from your wardrobe," I said carefully, trying to strike up a first conversation. "It becomes you."

She darted a look at me that was almost outraged.

"They"—she waved a hand to indicate the invisible servants—"took my other clothes. I had no choice."

"Don't you like the clothes I've provided?" I asked in consternation. The dress *did* look odd. It was cut low, exposing her shoulders, and the sleeves were loose, voluminous swaths of fabric that left half her arms bare.

"My own were more comfortable," she said, then looked up, stricken. "Not that I'm not grateful," she gasped, "this is beautiful."

I tried not to mind that she feared an angry and possibly violent reprisal for her criticism.

"You should wear what pleases you," I said, more roughly than I had intended. I took a breath to calm myself before I continued. "I won't be angry if you wear your own clothes. I'm not going to eat you, you know." I added this last with a bitter twist of humor, hoping to make light of her apprehension.

"Forgive me," she said, looking at the floor, "but I would

like to know why I am here. You don't need a servant, and you don't want to . . . eat me . . ." She blushed and looked uncomfortable.

Now it was my turn to look at the floor, as the misery of my condition threatened to overwhelm me.

"I have been alone a long time," I said, my voice reduced to a hoarse whisper. "I just wanted to meet you. To talk to you."

"Is there no one else here?" she asked, her voice straining against some strong emotion.

"No," I admitted, "your father was the first person to enter my forest in a century, I think."

"And you forced him to bring me here—his youngest daughter!" Her voice was full of rage and grief, and when I looked up at her she returned my gaze unflinchingly. She stood up quickly. I did not know what to say and sat before her in miserable silence.

"Excuse me," she said, turning away. "I must bid you goodnight." She left, and the candlelight seemed the poorer for her absence.

I realized, then, I had not even asked her name.

CHAPTER VI

I spent another sleepless night after our first meeting. Even so, the knowledge of her presence, as I watched the first rays of sunlight striking through my bedroom window, was one of the most intoxicating sensations I had ever felt. I spent a strangely conflicted morning. My guilt over the trickery I had resorted to in order to bring her here nagged at me and I was terrified of confronting her unhappiness again. Yet I felt such a sense of anticipation over meeting her once more, I barely touched my morning meal.

I fretted over my clothes. The garments laid out for me that morning were of a strange, unfamiliar cut. The coat and pantaloons were longer and looser than I was used to wearing, and my shirt had sprouted a large collar, ornamented with lace. I growled in disapproval and stalked over to one of the chests where my clothes were kept. But when I threw open the lid to get the clothes I wanted, all the elegant doublets in my wardrobe had disappeared. I turned around to stare at the empty room in anger. *What was going on?*

With a subdued roar, I snatched up the shirt with the preposterous collar and was about to tear it apart when I remembered the unfamiliar style of the dress the girl had worn last night. How long had I been here? Suppose the clothes I had been wearing were ancient? Ridiculous as I thought this attire looked, did I risk looking almost as ridiculous if I insisted on wearing the clothes I was used to? I dropped the shirt quickly and flexed the tension from my claws. I had to trust the magic knew better than I this morning.

I let myself be dressed with bad grace, irritated at the way the lace caught on my talons. Once finished, I left the house to wander my gardens. She had not left her rooms and I thought perhaps it would be best if I allowed her to seek me out in her own time. Moments after I decided upon this course of action, I had a sudden, panicked fantasy that she would never be able to bear to look upon me again and I would have to hide myself away from her until she left. This had such a powerful effect upon me, I had to pause on the threshold of the great staircase in the entry hall and steady myself against the banister. With the weight of this new fear now firmly settled over my shoulders, I stepped outside.

I knew when she entered the gardens and while I could not help but know where she walked, I stayed away from her. Following her, perhaps, but at so great a distance she could not have had sight of me. She walked slowly and I vacillated between hoping it was because she took joy from my beautiful grounds and despairing that her pace reflected a sense of oppression in being imprisoned here. Eventually, of course, she came upon the walled rose garden. She stopped for a few moments then turned and walked inside. I found a bench in a nearby shrubbery and sat myself down to wait in an anxiety of apprehension. I resolved

I would meet her when she left the garden, even if only to bid her good morning and leave again. Perhaps she would even allow me to walk with her awhile.

She spent some time in the garden and I was daydreaming almost happily when I was surprised by the sound of her voice calling me. Again, my hearing her must have been the result of some magical echo, as her voice was barely above a speaking tone. This time, however, she sounded as though she expected to be heard.

I rose and went to the arched doorway leading into the rose garden. I stood looking within for a moment before I entered. My heart was pounding and my mouth suddenly dry, but the rose garden before me remained tranquil as ever. The mossy paths were dappled with fallen petals, yet not a one was bruised or brown. The way before me was lined with roses that tangled over my head in a cool green tunnel. I walked slowly down the covered avenue toward the heart of the garden.

At the center of the rose garden was a small pavilion. We came upon it at about the same time, she from a different path. I was a little closer, and saw her before she saw me. I stopped, my breath caught in my throat. She walked with her head bowed and her hair glowed like honey in the morning sun. The clothes she wore today were far simpler than those she had worn the night before, the soft tones of the plain cloth echoing the roses surrounding her. She looked as though she had been born out of the garden that very moment. As she came toward me, a small breeze breathed petals from the arching cane of a wild rose. They flew up into the air and caught the sunlight for an instant, glowing pink and gold. It was then that she looked up and saw me.

She, too, stopped, but if she caught her breath it was because

I had a vastly different effect on her than she had on me. Still, she came toward me again with a resolute air, and I am certain she was by far the more composed of the two of us.

"Good morning," she said politely, in the manner of one determined to be pleasant.

"Good morning," I replied, suffused with relief at the change from the previous night. "I trust you slept well?" I asked, and then wished I had not. How could she have?

"Tolerably," she answered, with a tight smile. I looked at her and saw her eyes were red, and darkly shadowed underneath. I turned away.

"I'm sorry—" I started to say, but she interrupted me.

"No, please." She put out a hand as though to detain me but then drew back with a start. Embarrassed, she made a fist and hid her hand in her skirts. "It is I who must apologize for my behavior last night. I was rude, and ungrateful. *I* am sorry."

I turned back to stare at her in astonishment.

"Please don't think of it," I growled, embarrassed at her belief that she had anything to apologize to *me* for. "You were distraught. It is nothing."

"You have been nothing but hospitable," she replied, addressing the lace on my collar as though she had been rehearsing this speech all night. "And I thank you for that hospitality."

There was a moment's silence.

"Ah, I'm afraid I don't know your name," I said. I wondered whether I could induce her to look at me again, but an overwhelming consciousness of my hideous face crushed the impulse to try.

"Isabeau de la Noue, sir," she said, and dropped a brief curtsey. Her next question caught me unprepared.

"And what am I to call you, sir?"

"I am . . ." I started, and then paused. I felt a rush of shame. How could I even think to tell her my name? For so long I had thought of myself only as the Beast.

"I'm just the Beast," I said.

"Very well, Lord Beast—" Isabeau started to say, but I interrupted her.

"No! Not Lord or Sir, just Beast. That is all."

"I'm sorry," she said, sounding distressed and frightened. I was instantly contrite.

"No, please forgive me," I said, trying to make my beastly voice gentle. "I've been alone for too long. My manners were never good and I have not used the little I have for many years."

Isabeau nodded, but did not look up. She appeared to be chewing her lip. We stood in silence for a few moments.

"Have you been here very long?" she asked eventually.

"Yes," I replied, watching for her reaction. "I don't know exactly how long. As long as the forest."

She looked straight at me for a moment, too startled to be shocked by my appearance.

"Then it *was* you," she gasped. My confusion must have shown upon my face, for she hurriedly explained. "The people in our village warned us against going into the forest."

And look what happened when your father did. The words hung between us, unspoken.

"Is your village close to my forest?" I asked tentatively. Instantly her face clouded over and she looked away.

"Yes," she replied shortly.

Despite my oppressive size, beside her I felt small and mean. I wanted to turn away from her and howl. Again the silence fell.

"Will you tell me about your sisters?" I asked after a few minutes had passed. She shook her head and it was evident she was finding it difficult to retain her composure.

I turned away, toward the pavilion. What more did I want of her? I had met her twice, spoken to her twice. Even if I wanted to argue that her family owed me something for sheltering her father from that bitter winter night, she had more than discharged the bargain I had forced upon him. I could not entertain the thought of holding her a prisoner further against her will. She had shown me her courage and compassion in being courteous and civil to a ghastly creature she must surely view as nothing but her jailer. I had to show myself worthy in some way of the effort she was making.

"I am sorry," I said. "I am sorry that my actions have separated you from your family. From your friends. Perhaps from a suitor."

She gave her head a brief shake. "There was no one like that," she said without looking at me.

Some tiny knot, hidden within me somewhere deep and ignoble, loosened.

"Isabeau," I said, "will you grant me a favor?"

"What favor?" she asked, half turning to peer into the shade of the pavilion.

"Please, come and sit with me?" I asked. She quickly wiped her eyes, then came and sat opposite me, looking down at her lap. I sank onto the wooden bench.

"You must think me a monster—from my actions, not just from my appearance," I started, and plowed on before she could respond. "I offered shelter to your father, without which he would have died. Then I forced him into bringing you to me."

Isabeau made a small noise, but I did not look at her.

"I confess it was nothing but trickery. Had he not brought you, I would have done nothing. I . . ." How could I tell her about my dreams that night? It would only embarrass us both. "I only wanted to meet you."

She drew in her breath sharply and I looked up to see her staring straight at me. I looked down again.

"I cannot leave here. I have tried. The magic here bars the gates to the forest against me. They won't open for me. Your father was the first person I have seen in many, many years. You were the second. I saw you in his dreams . . ."

I dared to raise my eyes again. She was still staring at me, her face a picture of shock and surprise.

"Isabeau, would you stay?" I paused. "I have no right to request this of you. I can only beg it as a favor. Would you stay and talk to me, and teach me about the world?" I spread my hands helplessly. There was much more I could not ask for.

"Stay?" she echoed. "But, I thought . . ."

I watched her realize she was not bound to spend the rest of her life imprisoned in this lonely place with only a beast for company.

"Would you think on it?"

"For how long?" she asked. It sounded as though she found it as difficult to breathe as I.

How long? How could I set the term of my one chance of respite from the endless solitude of this curse?

"A year?" I blurted out, my mouth dry.

"But I can leave now if I wish?"

I nodded, unable to speak. I could not say any more. I heard my heart beating in my ears again and I heard her draw in her breath and, for the briefest moment, I thought I heard something else, but it was too vague and quick to put a name to.

Eventually I rose and bowed briefly. It occurred to me she was only waiting for my absence so she could run to the gates. I turned away from the pavilion as though sleepwalking. I was so blinded by despair, I almost stumbled into the reaching branches of a large rose bush, as unyielding as my iron gates and full of cruel, hooked thorns. Utterly bewildered, I plucked uselessly at the canes tangled in the lace of my collar and cuffs, trying to free myself.

There was a soft cry of "Oh!" from behind me, and a moment later she was there, pushing between me and the rose bush, unsnagging the delicate cloth with nimble fingers. When she had freed me, she guided me onto the path and stepped back, looking up at me in consternation.

"You have truly been alone all this time?" she asked.

"Yes," I said hoarsely.

"You must be so lonely," she said.

I could only nod. I could not look at her. I could only stare at my feet and will the humiliating tears filling my eyes not to fall. She backed away from me. I thought she was twisting her fingers together.

"A year is not so long," she said, almost to herself. "They hardly think to see me again at all. Very well."

I held my breath, my heart suddenly thundering so hard against my ribs I shook.

"Beast, I'll stay for a year. I will."

I went to my study after I left Isabeau. All at once the world seemed too bright for me, and I needed somewhere quiet where I could reflect on this turn of events. The incandescent joy flaming in my breast was overwhelming—I was almost too afraid to contemplate it too closely lest it somehow burn me up. Why would she choose to stay with me? I could only assume she pitied me—which showed a certain greatness of heart after the way in which I had brought her here. A glass of wine appeared by my chair. As I picked it up, I noticed my hairy hands were shaking once more.

A year; she had given me a year of her life. And after the year was up, what then? Banishing visions of my vast, empty house was easy when for now I could see it filled with the sunshine of her presence. Who knew what would happen in a year, in this place where magic hung thick in the air? I had determined to walk like a man, and my very bones had shifted and stretched, so now I stood upright with no trouble. Perhaps there were other changes awaiting me.

CHAPTER VII

I took up a book I had been reading, and tried to concentrate. Naturally it was difficult, with my thoughts continually flying away from the dry, printed words and toward the living, breathing woman who was somewhere in my domain. I made little headway and was reading the same page for the third or fourth time, when I was once again distracted, this time by a dancing glimmer of light in the corner of my eye. I laid aside my book, a little more tattered around the edges than it had previously been, and stared at it. It was a winking gleam on one wall, obviously a reflection from some shining object. I turned to find the source, and noticed the draped mirror that had appeared on the wall the previous evening. A sliver of the glass stood exposed where the drape did not fully cover it. A sunbeam, glancing in from the window where the curtains were only partly drawn, struck the silver edge and brought its ghostly twin to life on the opposite wall.

Nothing in this place was random, so I rose and went and stood before the crimson drape. I took a breath and carefully pushed it aside. For a moment I saw my own flinching reflection, then again it clouded. This time, when it cleared, I was looking in upon a small parlor room, sparsely furnished and looking somewhat gray. There was no fire in the grate, only cold ashes. A young woman lay in the one comfortable chair, her hands over her face. As I watched, her shoulders heaved and shook, as though she was weeping silently. A door opened and Isabeau's father came into the room. He stood, looking at the young woman for a few moments, with a curious expression on his face, part grief and pity, and part bitter frustration.

"Where is your sister?" he asked, and his voice, while clear, sounded hollow and far away, as though I were listening to him speak from the bottom of a well.

The young woman raised a wan, tear-stained face to look at him. Her skin was very pale, almost blue, and there were deep shadows under her eyes. She looked thin and ill, wrapped in a thick shawl.

"She is still abed," replied the young woman, in a weak, petulant voice. "There is no fire, and I have not eaten. There is no breakfast." Isabeau's father closed his eyes and pressed one hand to his forehead.

"Isabeau is gone," he said in a voice flat with grief. "We will have to shift as best we can, and you and your sister will have to learn to do the tasks that fell to her."

"She looked after me!" said the young woman tremulously. "She knew I was too ill to do housework." She turned her face away and her father sighed. He left the room and for a few minutes I stood watching Isabeau's sister staring into space with her cheeks damp from crying. A hollow shame crept over me. Had grief at Isabeau's departure injured this woman so? Or, worse, had she been an invalid, possibly dying, and Isabeau her chief nurse? Would Isabeau's absence leave her comfortless and speed her death?

The young woman gave a loud groan.

"Gilles!" she sobbed and put her hands over her face, beginning to cry in earnest. My horror at the possible consequences of my actions gave way to a new confusion. Was she grieving over Isabeau or someone else?

Isabeau's father came back into the room, followed by another young woman. She was older than the first, yet clearly young enough to be another of Isabeau's sisters. Indeed, both had something of her in their faces. The oldest sister was darker than the others, her mouth set in a hard, bitter line.

"Make a fire," said Isabeau's father, "and see what you can do about some food for her." He went then, leaving the two women staring at each other. The middle sister gave a quiet sob and looked piteously up at the elder.

"*You* will not show me kindness, even now," she said wretchedly, shrinking into her shawl.

"I cannot see you ever needed it," said the elder sister. "And you will find none while you lie on your couch and continue to whimper about what is gone and cannot be regained." The middle sister sprang up from her couch, the movement belying her apparent lack of strength.

"*You* do not know what it is *like* to have your heart broken," she cried furiously, more tears spilling angrily over her cheeks. The older sister pressed both her hands to her forehead, the gesture making her look very much like her father.

"No, I do not," she said in a dry, resigned voice. "But the fact remains, Isabeau has gone, and now we two will have to stir ourselves or we will freeze, starve and die in stinking, unwashed clothes. The Beast's money may buy us the services of a tire-woman, but we still cannot pay enough for someone to do all the things Isabeau did for love of us. I do not even know where to start." She looked at her sister. "Pick your chores. I do not care what I do."

The glass began to cloud over again and I was left looking into my own eyes. I hurriedly pulled the cloth to and went to sit back by the fire. My wine glass was full again and I sipped it gratefully. What did it mean? At least I knew Isabeau's father was now safe at home. But her sisters? Was I really the cause of their unhappiness? Neither had demonstrated the profound grief their father had shown, although the middle sister was obviously deeply sorry for herself. There had not even been any particular disgust in the elder sister's voice when she mentioned my name.

I uttered a half-frustrated, half-amused sigh. This family had afforded me more diversion in the last few minutes than I had ever found in this empty house in the last however-many years.

Isabeau stayed almost all day in the gardens. I stayed inside, out of her way. If she changed her mind and decided to run to the gates, I did not want to see it, even though I resolved she would find them open to her. I was almost certain she would—for who would scruple to keep a promise made to a beast? But she stayed away from the gates, remaining all day in one of the walled or-chards. By the late afternoon, I began to be afraid she had devel-oped a horror of my house.

I noticed the light from my window was turning thick and golden at the same time I became aware she was returning to the house. I resolved to meet her and thank her for agreeing to stay. *Perhaps I should ask her if she would dine with me,* I wondered. I rose, took a deep breath and straightened my jacket, and stepped out into the hallway. The lamps and candles were only just kindling into glimmering life as the shadows deepened.

I reached the doorway of the entrance hall just before her and stood to one side as they swung open. She was deep in her own thoughts, walking with her eyes down and her hands clasped about her arms. At my first attempt to speak my voice failed me, and I had to cough. The sound brought her instantly out of her reverie. While she flinched again on looking at me, and her eyes were very red, she seemed relatively composed. For all my attempts at elegance, however, my first words were clumsy.

"You stayed," I said, my voice catching.

She nodded. "A year," she said, "and then I will return home."

There was another moment of silence as we looked at each other in the dying light.

"Thank you," I croaked. "Would you . . ." I cleared my throat and started again. "I wondered if you would do me the favor of dining with me tonight?"

"Of course," she replied politely. "I would be pleased to."

"Thank you," I murmured. "Please come down whenever you are ready."

I bowed again and in response she dropped a neat curtsey. Again I found myself wondering at her family's background. She and her father showed a distinct gentleness of breeding and her sisters were obviously unused to ordinary housekeeping.

"If you have any preferred dishes," I suggested, "you only have to make them known to . . ." I gestured helplessly at the air.

"Thank you, sir," she said, not raising her eyes. "I will."

"Until tonight," I said. She nodded and I moved aside to watch her walk up the staircase. She moved slowly and I was relieved she had not been too anxious to hurry from my presence.

I dressed as carefully this night as I had for my first meeting with her, even though the unfamiliar clothing now filling my chests still irritated me.

Eventually I heard Isabeau's voice calling quietly, but clearly, "Beast! I am ready!" Almost, for a moment, I wished for a mirror in which to check my appearance. I instantly squashed the impulse—a momentary glimpse before and after my observation of Isabeau's family was more than enough for me in one day. But I was comforted to feel a few last tweaks and plucks from my invisible servants as they straightened my collar and smoothed back my thick, black mane.

I had decided to abandon the cavernous entrance hall for a smaller, more intimate dining room. It overlooked a terrace that would be the perfect place to meet Isabeau. Here the walls of the château were purple with the blossom of an ancient wisteria vine and my magic weather was warm enough for it to be quite pleasant in the evening. I arrived to find the terrace softly lit with tiny lanterns; crystal glasses and a flask of wine were standing ready on a small table. The sky was ablaze with winter stars and all that was wanting were perhaps some unobtrusive musicians to complete the scene. But musicians had I none, and there were never even any songbirds in my garden.

I forgot all thoughts of music as a door opened farther down the terrace, and Isabeau stepped out. She, too, had dressed for dinner, and while the dress she was wearing was not as rich as the one she had worn last night, it was very fine. It was made of some pale, gleaming fabric, and in it she held herself like the lady I was sure she had once been.

"Good evening," I said, bowing low. She dropped another elegant curtsey.

"I thought perhaps the candles were leading me astray," she said, not quite looking at me, "but this is very beautiful."

"May I offer you a glass of wine before we dine?" I asked, suddenly nervous.

"Thank you," she said graciously and waited with her hands clasped in front of her while I poured.

"You did not mind dressing for dinner?" I queried, as I passed her the glass.

She glanced down at the fine fabric of her skirts and said, "No. I believe I had a choice tonight, but this was laid out." She darted a look at me. "You yourself have all your finery on."

I had never been one for glib flattery and smooth compliments, and now any words I might have said stuck in my throat. I barely managed some gruff, dismissive remark. There was an awkward moment, which I eventually dispelled by asking her how she liked the wine.

"Very nice," she said. "Is it your own?"

"A good question," I answered, relieved my person was no longer the focus of her attention. "I believe there was a vineyard on this estate once. I had nearly forgotten it."

She looked surprised.

"How large is your estate?" she asked.

"I think the forest covers what used to be my lands. However, within my gates they exist much as they once did. Although . . ." I paused, thinking of my unnatural weather, and the rose arbor grown from nothing in a night. "The magic that keeps this place has allowed me to make certain changes."

"I see," she said, and I could not tell what she was thinking.

"Do you like my grounds?" I asked, fishing for a way to continue our conversation.

"Yes," she said, turning to face me. "They are extraordinarily beautiful. I am afraid I have spent the entire day lying in the sun in your orchard and eating the fruit off the trees."

The picture this formed in my mind was entirely charming. My pleasure must have been evident on my face, for she smiled. A little tight at the edges, perhaps, but still, I had made her smile.

"I should thank you," she said. "Today, at least, was a true holiday for me. I have not had such time to myself for . . . many months."

I had to swallow my surprise. "I am glad," I managed to respond, "you found such pleasure in my gardens." I could not tell her how relieved I was she had not spent the day weeping in her room, or running from me in mortal terror, which is what *I* had feared would happen.

She seemed to notice my discomfort, for she placed her empty wine glass back on the small table, and said to me, "Well, I am hungry. Shall we go in to eat?"

I agreed, and would have offered her my arm, but I could not face the possibility of rejection in case she could not bear to be near me. I settled for holding the door open for her, and breathing in the scent of wisteria she carried with her as she brushed past me into the dining room.

The meal served up that evening was a little different from what I would normally have eaten and I wondered if this re-flected her preferences after all. I had momentary nightmares of lobster, still in its shell, but I was relieved to find none of it re-quired any unusual dexterity to eat.

Our conversation stalled for a while as we ate, but eventually when the silence grew protracted I asked another question preying on my mind.

"You do not mind the solitude?"

"No," she said, "not at all."

I looked at her in surprise. At this point, I could not imagine the kind of solitude I had to offer being anything but a burden. She saw my expression and gave a wry smile.

"As the youngest of three sisters, I have the ill fortune to combine the worst traits of both of my elder siblings, without any of their redeeming virtues," she explained. "Like my eldest sister, I am solitary, but where Marie is studious, I am idle. Claude is idle, but her pretty, open manners make her a delight in company and somewhat sought after." Isabeau laid her spoon down on her plate and stared at her meal in a way that made me think she had forgotten I was present.

"We used to live in Rouen," she said, "but it was too busy for me. I never felt at home, there." She blinked and came back to herself, snatching up her spoon and turning her eyes back down to her meal.

"You lived in Rouen?" I inquired. "You are not from your village?" For an answer she shook her head and quickly took another mouthful. I swallowed my curiosity; it appeared this was a tender subject. Still, she had given me several morsels to treasure: the names of her sisters and her descriptions of their personalities. None of which threw any light on what I had witnessed that morning.

I ate in silence for a few minutes, to allow her to regain her composure. After the dessert arrived I asked, "So if you are both solitary and idle, what is it you like to do?" She looked up at me and her mouth twisted into another brief smile.

"I read a little, but only for pleasure I'm afraid," she said. "I do not do critiques and translations and essays, and I prefer a good story to anything philosophical. I am fond of music and I play several instruments. But again my unstudious nature is against me and my talent is strictly mediocre." She sighed heavily, and I sensed she was used to comparing her own achievements and virtues against those of her sisters.

"I did keep several pets." She smiled at the memory, but my heart sank at this information, as I knew the only animals that dared to set foot in my forest or my grounds were the kinds of creatures one did not try to tame.

"In the city I had quite a collection. Two funny little dogs, a cat, a bird, even a darling monkey . . ." Her face grew sad again for a moment. "But I had to leave them all behind when we came to the country. I hadn't had time to make many friends at our new house." She smiled sadly. "I had begun to put seed out for the birds, and milk for the hedgehogs."

"I am very sorry," I said heavily. "You will find no other animals here. Only myself."

She frowned at me. "What do you mean?" she asked.

"A very long time ago," I told her, biting down on my shame, "I roamed the forest. I was a very angry beast and those animals I did not kill for food I terrorized. No animal has dared enter my forest or my grounds since. Even the birds shun this place. You will find only mice and crows here."

She looked at me thoughtfully and took another spoonful of sorbet. She ate it slowly, then said, "Well, your reputation wanes. I saw rabbits skipping on the lawns today. It seems they have followed my father's example and are returning."

My mouth gaped open and my spoon fell with a clatter into

the crystal dish. Before I could digest this news or compose myself, she asked another question that sent a new jolt of surprise through me.

"Tell me," she said, "do you really class yourself among the animals? Surely you believe yourself to be something more?" This question caught my heart painfully in my chest and the misery of my beastly form rose up and choked me.

"Can you ask me that?" I said roughly, unable to keep the pain out of my voice. It was her turn to look startled. In my distraction, I rose from my seat and leaned across the table toward her. "You can barely look at me. Tell me, Isabeau, could you pledge to spend your life with such a one as I? Could *you* marry me, Isabeau?" At my question she recoiled, shrinking back, away from me.

"Oh no," she said in the most horrified tone of voice. It was like a bucket of cold water over me. Instantly I remembered myself and backed away from her. In that moment she too realized what she had said and put her hands over her mouth. I straightened my jacket and bowed briefly.

"I am sorry," I said formally. "I have distressed you enough tonight. I beg you will excuse me. I will trouble you no further." I left the room, the image of her sitting pale and straight as a moonbeam locked in my mind.

CHAPTER VIII

After that unfortunate evening we avoided each other's company for several days. I kept largely to my study, although there were times when I could not help but follow the warmth of her presence into my gardens. I never came near enough to her to let her know I was there, however.

She spent a great deal of time rambling over the grounds. The rose arbor she avoided. On the occasions when I followed her into the gardens and skulked cow-heartedly in the shadows, I also looked vainly for a sign of the rabbits she claimed to have seen on the lawns. But I never saw so much as prints in the snow.

Even watching her family in my strange mirror did not divert me as much as I had anticipated. They had obviously lived a privileged life in the city, with servants to attend to all their daily needs. These next few days only showed me their miserable attempts to grow accustomed to doing for themselves. There was not much entertainment to be had in watching Marie grimly scrub floors and dust shelves, and Claude weeping into her mixing bowls and constantly burning her fingers as well as anything she tried to cook.

A kind of tension began to permeate the atmosphere of the

house. I was too cowardly to meet with her. I did not want to force my company on her and the memory of her shocked face still burned. She seemed equally as intent on avoiding me. As each day passed, the house itself grew more unsettled. My clothes chests became infested with a plague of tiny, black, voracious beetles and as I dressed each day, my hair was tweaked and pulled, as though a normally attentive servant had become cross and irritable. Clouds of moths began to inhabit the drapes.

It came to a head four nights after the dreadful dinner. I was in my study, trying to think of a way to pass the time. My books no longer held my interest. Indeed, when I tried to read, often as not I found the bindings had deteriorated and I would open a volume only to have the pages spill out across the floor. I had again tried to look in on Isabeau's family, only to see Claude flee, wailing, to her room with a burned hand (again) after dropping a hot dish. The sight of Marie and their father sitting down to dinner and poking unenthusiastically at the blackened scraps they had salvaged only deepened my gloom. I left the mirror and sat down in my chair, requesting a glass of wine. The wine splashed untidily into the glass, as I had never seen it do before. I drank it and requested another. This time the bottle upended itself over the glass, the glass overflowed and I was left staring as a great dark stain spread over the carpet. There was a deep silence, as of a servant shocked at their own outburst. I had a sense of someone holding their breath, waiting.

"Very well!" I said wearily, holding up my paw to placate the air. "I promise I will speak to her tomorrow."

The next morning Isabeau stayed in her room longer than usual and I wondered if she was growing bored of spending time in the gardens. She eventually emerged, however, and I contrived to meet her at the foot of the grand staircase in the main hall. She stopped halfway down the stairs when she saw me, then came on more slowly, her face flushed. When she drew close, I could see her eyes were reddened. She answered my good morning, then said in a low, troubled voice, "Beast, I must apologize for my thoughtless words the other night. I fear they must have hurt you terribly."

"Please do not think of it," I said, in a hurry to make my own apology. "It is I who must apologize. My manners have grown sadly lacking after all these years."

Isabeau managed a small smile.

"I will accept your apology if you will accept mine," she said. "Friends?"

She held out her hand.

For a moment I froze, staring at it. My first instinct was to put my paws behind my back where she would not see my terrible claws and be afraid. I faltered a heartbeat too long.

"Will you not shake hands?" she asked, a new note of uncertainty in her voice.

"Of course," I said in a rush. Tentatively I offered her my ungainly paw. She took it gently enough, but such a thrill ran through me as she laid her hand on the rough pad that served me as my palm, my very blood seemed to thrum in my veins and it was a wonder I remained upright instead of falling to my knees before her.

Could she know she was the first person I had touched in over a century?

If she felt any hesitation or repulsion as my great hairy paw enclosed her slender fingers, she hid it well. I fear I did not hide my own agitation so perfectly. As her fingers disappeared amid my pelt, my impulse was to clutch at her for dear life. Instead, I held her grip for the briefest moment, then relinquished her hand and bowed.

"You said you were fond of music," I said, putting my right paw behind my back where I could unobtrusively curl it closed around the precious sensation of her warm palm against mine. "May I show you the music room? There are a number of fine instruments there."

Her eyes lit up. "If you please," she said eagerly. "I probably will not do them justice. But what I lack in skill I can promise to make up for in enthusiasm."

"I've not heard any music for many years," I said gravely, "so I can promise you I will think your playing the finest I have ever heard. That is, if you will permit me the honor of hearing you," I added hastily.

She gave a self-conscious laugh. "Of course! It is the favorite wish of every player of mediocre talent to find an audience that can be guaranteed to think they are a great proficient."

She looked ruefully down at her hands.

"However, it is some months since I played any instrument, so I am bound to be rather scratchy at first."

I showed her the way to the music room, and once we arrived, I had to smile. Owing to my inability to use any of the instruments without seriously damaging them, I had rarely come in here. My recent memories of this room were of a dark place, all the furniture and instruments hidden under dust sheets. After the last few days, I had half expected it to be shrouded in an impenetrable curtain of cobweb, or find the instruments had rotted away. However, when I opened the door, it was as though my invisible servants had been preparing for this day a week in advance. The room was filled with sunlight and, to my pleasure, a number of sweet-smelling floral arrangements. Further, every instrument Isabeau ran a lingering hand over was beautifully in tune.

She inspected the harp in the corner, and after drawing from it a few notes of trembling sweetness, she stepped back and said, "Now I wish I had paid more attention to my music master." She selected a lute from a stand, played a few more notes and replaced it. Then she moved to the virginal. Here she stayed for an hour or more. After a few minutes I went and seated myself unobtrusively in a corner. Mostly she played various scales and arpeggios, and it is true, especially initially, her hands did falter. But I was disposed to be entranced. When she played some pieces she evidently knew by heart, I was transported, despite the scattering of wrong notes. Eventually she closed the lid and looked over at me.

"I'm afraid I am sadly out of practice," she said.

"It was beautiful," I said sincerely.

"How am I to believe that?" she asked, sounding amused. "I heard myself how poorly I played. And you had already promised to be pleased, so you can hardly renege on your word and give me an honest appraisal."

"Have you ever eaten a simple, coarse meal after being hungry all day?" I asked. "If you equate how good such a meal tastes to your playing, you can understand how I enjoyed it."

Isabeau grimaced.

"I am happy with the comparison between my playing and a meal of dry bread and salt pork," she said.

The next morning, I had to pause at my breakfast to listen to the thread of arpeggios winding its way up to my bedchamber from the music room. The day after that I rose a little earlier and went to stand at the music room door only a short time after she had started. She paused in her exercises when she saw me, and made a wry face at me, but then she returned to her playing without objecting to my presence.

After that, music echoed through the halls of the house every day. Either Isabeau had overstated her disinclination to apply herself to the study of music, or her new situation gave her cause to find in music a way to spend her time. I did not care. She seemed happy for me to sit quietly in a corner of the music room whenever she played, although she never sang if I was in the room. Consequently there were days when I contented myself with sitting in the parlor next door, and creeping quietly away when she finished, just so I might hear her voice. I had never made much time for music in my previous life; however, like so many other things, I welcomed it wholeheartedly when it reappeared in my world after such a long absence.

CHAPTER IX

$\mathcal{O}$ne afternoon, after Isabeau had retired from her initial musical pursuits, rubbing her aching hands ruefully, I returned again to my study. I was feeling as though a heavy cloud had lifted, and I remembered the breath of new magic that had followed my wish for Isabeau's father's good fortune. Was it too much to hope his family's situation had shown some improvement as ours had? I gathered myself and pulled aside the curtain shrouding the mirror. My spirits were not immediately lifted by what I saw.

Marie and Claude sat at the kitchen table in front of a dish of something unrecognizable and blackened. Marie had an arm around Claude and looked tired. Claude had her head buried in her arms and was sobbing.

"I cannot go on like this!" she wailed.

"I agree," said Marie wryly. "We will all of us starve."

"I was not meant for such work!" She raised her face from the table to stare pitifully at Marie and, despite her apparent misery, I noticed there was markedly more color in her cheeks than the first time I had seen her. Marie looked at her thoughtfully for a moment.

"Perhaps we should exchange duties?" she suggested. "I cannot pretend dusting and scrubbing will afford you any joy—they are odious enough tasks. But, at the very least, they do not offer the same opportunity for injury cooking seems to present you with."

Claude looked at her with tear-stained gratitude. "Oh, would you, Marie? But this is such a hateful job."

Again that wry smile crossed Marie's features. "I would not be sorry to never scrub a step again. At least with cooking one may create something others will enjoy, but no one ever notices a step."

While Marie had been speaking, Claude was eyeing the gently smoking dish on the table as though she could not credit cookery with being an opportunity to create something others would appreciate. When Marie had finished, however, she shook her head.

"On the contrary, sister," she said, as though Marie had overlooked an important point, "at least when you have finished your tasks the house looks nice. That is always a comfort."

At this Marie laughed. "Perhaps our own initial experiences with housework have made the other's duties seem more attractive. Let us see what we have to say about them when we have been at them for another week."

The mirror clouded and shifted, then cleared and I saw Isabeau's father. He was in his bedchamber, poor, bare room though it was. There was a simple wooden bed behind him, with only one thin blanket thrown across it. He himself sat at a small table that seemed to serve him for a writing desk, lit by a single, smoky tallow candle. Strewn across the desk were a number of letters. He was reading one and, as I watched, he appeared to finish it. He dropped it back on the table and gave a low groan.

"Nothing, not a denier," he whispered hoarsely. "What am I to do? What will become of us?" He put his hands over his face and said in the bitterest of tones, "What a worthy father am I! I should thank that terrible Beast for removing Isabeau from my care!" He swept up the letters lying on his desk and screwed them into a crumpled ball. Then he hit the table with his fist with such violence I jumped. He sat motionless for a few minutes further, then, with infinite weariness, pushed back his chair and rose and left the room. I was left peering into the dimness of his simple bedchamber. I noticed the saddlebags I had filled for him were lying under his bed, evidently still full. Only one had been broached, and I could see at the top of this bag were the pouches containing the money I had sent home with him. Again, only one of these had been opened, letting out a tiny gleam of gold. My heart grew heavy as I looked. He was a desperate man, but he would not stoop to using the gold I had sent him in place of his daughter. I had seen enough. Self-hatred burned once again in my breast as I stood before the mirror. All the grief I had brought to this family!

But the mirror had not done yet. The image of the father's room was now replaced by that of the kitchen again. Claude still sat at the table, but she was no longer weeping. She now leaned her chin on her hand and watched Marie move about the kitchen. Marie was opening all the cupboards and peering inside, looking in urns and generally taking stock of her new domain. She entered the larder, then came out a few moments later looking thoughtful.

"There are eggs, bread, a little butter and some ham left," she said, ticking them off on her fingers. "There is an assortment of vegetables as well, but I haven't the faintest idea how to cook them. I think I could manage to boil some eggs and we could toast some bread for our supper tonight. Then tomorrow for breakfast we could eat the ham on the rest of the bread." Claude wrinkled up her nose briefly, but said nothing, and on the whole looked relieved Marie had taken charge.

"Now, how long do I boil the eggs for?" Marie asked herself.

"I know that one!" said Claude, laughing delightedly. "Three minutes! Loussard always used to do three-minute eggs for me."

I must admit I was pleasantly astonished. After seeing her for the first time, I could not credit Isabeau's description of her middle sister. However, watching her face light up as she laughed, I found myself believing that Claude could be charming company.

"Yes, but do I put them in the pot when the water is cold, or when it is boiling?" asked Marie.

Claude shook her head. "I don't know."

"Well," said Marie, "it will be easy enough to find out. I will do one each way as an experiment. Do you think you could manage if I was away for most of the day tomorrow?" Marie looked across at Claude, who sat up straight in her chair looking curious and mildly alarmed.

"Where are you going?" she asked.

"I thought I might go to the inn tomorrow," said Marie, "and offer my services for the day if Madame Minou would teach me something of cooking. I can at least scrub pans."

"She has been very good to us," said Claude. "I think she would agree."

"However," said Marie in a more serious tone, "learning to cook will be of limited use if I have nothing to cook with. If only Papa would use some of the Beast's money. Lord knows we have nothing of our own left."

There was a short silence, as though Marie had said something very shocking.

"He says it is blood money," whispered Claude.

Marie considered this, and then shrugged. "Perhaps it is. But we need it," she said. "The landlord must be paid, and we must eat." She suddenly sat down opposite Claude and put her hands over her eyes.

"Oh, Claude, I have to believe he is an honorable Beast. I have to believe he is as good as his word. The idea Isabeau has gone to some horrible doom is too much to bear." She looked up and her face was stained with tears. "I must believe that, somehow, this Beast is our savior."

Claude looked at her gravely. "What else do you think he put in Papa's saddlebags?" she asked. "It cannot all be money. Papa said there was a little food, but there must be other things."

"I don't know," said Marie. "But we must ask Papa to let us open them."

"Open what?" Their father entered the kitchen and both sisters turned to face him.

"The saddlebags, Papa," said Marie, firmly. "We have so little food left, we need to buy some more. I know we cannot have any of our own money left."

"Absolutely not," said their father, his face darkening with rage.

"Very well," said Marie, and while her voice was completely calm and composed, there was an edge in it that said she would rise to any challenge. "Tomorrow I will go to the Crossed Keys and offer myself in service to Madame Minou. Perhaps I can at least earn enough to pay the landlord when he comes for his rent in a fortnight. If she has no need of me, she may at least know of someone who does." My heart swelled with admiration. I had no doubt that if her father did not relent, she would do as she said.

"You will not," he said.

"I will not starve and be turned out of *this* home. That is what I will not do."

At this her father flinched as though she had slapped him. Something in him seemed to crumple.

"Very well," he said bitterly, "do as you please." He turned to leave the kitchen.

"Papa," said Marie, in a much gentler voice, "please let us not quarrel. The Beast saved you from the storm. Perhaps he is saving us even now. Perhaps he took Isabeau to live with him in luxury because she has worked so hard looking after us over the last few months. Now it is time for us to look after ourselves."

"Very well," he said again, but his voice had lost its bitter edge. "Go into the parlor. I will bring the bags down. We will open them together."

The sisters went into the parlor together and a few minutes later their father joined them, dragging the heavy bags.

As I watched them I thought hard about the fine things I had filled the bags with. I now understood the clothes and jewelry I had thought would please them would be completely impractical. I wondered if, at this great distance, I could add to the bounty contained in the bags. *Blankets*, I thought, remembering the father's bed, *and linen. Wax candles, fine paper and pens and . . .* I waved my hand impatiently. *Whatever else they may need.*

Their father reached into the first bag, bringing out the leather pouches full of money. Six in total. Then came the fine clothes I was embarrassed about now. Silk, lace, velvet, spangles, feathers, gold and silver trim, exquisite embroidery soon spilled over the laps of the sisters and across the floor, making something of a mockery of the poor, simple furnishings. Marie turned her eyes to the sky in exasperated astonishment, but Claude looked at the finery with a tender expression.

"I had nothing so fine when we lived in the city!" she murmured.

"And where, pray, do you intend to wear it here?" asked Marie. "No one has parties and we would look ridiculous should we wear it to church!"

However, Claude was not deterred from lovingly caressing the fabric, and exclaiming over the decoration. *At least*, I thought, *this gift has warmed one heart*. Next came three caskets, each with a name wrought on the cover: Marie, Claude and Isabeau. Marie caught her breath when she saw Isabeau's and Claude put her hands to her throat, but their father put it aside on the mantelpiece, saying, "We will leave it for her to open when she returns to us one day." Marie and Claude then lifted the lids on their own caskets and both gasped in astonishment.

"Oh my," said Marie weakly, lifting out an ornate necklace flashing blue with sapphires. Wordlessly Claude lifted out a long rope of pearls with diamonds at the clasp, followed by matched earrings and a bracelet. More jewelry followed, until it lay in glittering heaps on their laps.

"Well, he is a generous Beast," said Claude, eyeing a golden locket as big as a goose egg.

"But not very practical," pointed out Marie, echoing my own misgivings. "What are we to do with all of this?"

"At least I will have something to wear if *he*—" said Claude warmly, but then she bit her lip mid-sentence and was silent. Marie and their father looked at her apprehensively, and she impatiently piled all her jewelry back into her casket and put it on the floor. As she bent down she surreptitiously wiped her eyes, but when she straightened up again, she only said, "Well, what is next? A gilded carriage and four? The keys to the kingdom?" Their father picked up the bag and peered inside it, then shook his head.

"There is no more in here," he said, "although I scarcely would have believed all of that would fit into this bag. We will see what treasures are in the other."

He loosed the ties on the second bag and thrust his hand inside. I could hardly breathe. When he pulled his arm out, he brought out a blanket of fine wool. Marie could not suppress a laugh.

"This is more suited to our needs!" she cried. "Generous *and* practical. Noble Beast!"

"I should not go so far as that," said her father, a warning in the tone of his voice. "You have not seen the awful creature."

"I'm sorry, Papa," said Marie, contritely. "I did not think. I'm sorry."

With a frown their father reached once more into the saddlebag. Five more blankets followed, then three sets of linen sheets. Then the candles I had thought of, two dozen in total, a roll of paper and a soft wallet containing a number of quills and a knife to cut the nibs, another bolt of fine linen, a bound book with blank pages and two more caskets, labeled "Marie" and "Claude." These caskets were much plainer than the first, which had been finely carved and inlaid. Claude opened hers first and found within skeins of colored thread of wool, cotton, linen and silk; needles, buttons and various other bits and pieces completely unfamiliar to me, but evidently essential to a fully equipped workbox.

"Oh look, Marie! Papa!" she cried. "Now I can make some

lovely things for the house!" She looked beseechingly at Marie. "May I have that bolt of linen? Then we can have a tablecloth, napkins . . ." Marie looked amused.

"What I would want with the linen, I do not know," she said. "You were ever the one who devoted hours to embroidery and the like. Of course you may have it. May I have the book? I can use it to write down everything Madame Minou can tell me about cooking."

Claude beamed. "Of course. Now what is in your box?"

Marie raised the lid and looked puzzled for a moment. Then she lifted out a few small linen bags and some tiny earthenware jars.

"What . . . ?" she said in a puzzled voice. Then she opened one of the jars and sniffed its contents. "Spices!" she exclaimed. A closer inspection of the linen bags proved they contained seeds for a variety of vegetables.

"Well," she said, "evidently we were destined to exchange our chores. Or at least the Beast thinks so." She turned to her father. "Is there anything else left, Papa?"

"I do not think so," he said, delving once more into the bag. "No, wait, here." He pulled out a leather workman's pouch and unrolled it. Inside it were a range of various tools, again, mostly unfamiliar to me.

"Ah," he said. "Now I can begin to make this house habitable."

The mirror began to grow dim again and I hurried to pull the drapes across before it cleared and showed me my own hideous face. The mirror had held my attention for the whole afternoon, and the last rays of the sun were painting my study window a glowing orange. I ached all over from standing motionless in front of the glass for so long. More uncomfortable were the varying thoughts and feelings surging through my brain. They liked their gifts. But I was embarrassed to think of them crediting me with the choice of all the items. Blankets and candles, yes, but all the other items? Still, I was relieved to think they would find them useful.

A glowing warmth spread through me at the memory of Marie calling me noble—she was better disposed toward me than her father, at least. But I winced at the memory of his anger. Could I ever make good what I owed him?

A note of curiosity remained regarding who might be the mysterious Gilles that was obviously very much in Claude's thoughts. What part had he played in their lives? Was he likely to come to Claude, as she seemed to very much hope he would?

Eventually my mind turned toward another, less comfortable matter. Uneasily, I wondered if I should show Isabeau this magic glass. Perhaps it would put her mind at ease to know that, while her family missed her, they were no longer adrift and helpless without her.

I stared at the velvet drapes uncertainly, my mind filled with the image of Isabeau's family gathered together in their parlor. What if, instead, seeing them made her more homesick than ever and shook her resolve to stay her year with me?

CHAPTER X

 few days after I showed Isabeau the music room for the first time, I was struck by a brilliant idea as I awoke. Or, at least, I was struck by an idea that, because of its potential to give Isabeau pleasure, I was disposed to think of as brilliant. I decided I would make her a present of some music for her instruments. After a hurried breakfast I repaired to the library, a vast room, or series of rooms, entered directly from my entrance hall. Its walls were lined with bookshelves and the uppermost shelves—two stories high—were approached from a balcony running around the top of each section of the library. The highest shelves below the balcony were accessed by a number of ladders on wheels—inanimate in my previous life, but now ensorcelled to trundle over to me obligingly if I so much as looked up. On the wall along the front of the house were a number of large windows. All these contained lavishly cushioned window seats and were delightful places to read, although a little cramped for an overlarge beast.

I soon found the musical manuscripts and extracted those I remembered as favorites. When I had done I turned to see them all neatly tied in a bundle on a nearby table, with paper and a pen beside them. It took several attempts to scratch out an appropriate note making it clear they were hers as a gift, but not (I hoped) sounding desperate for her gratitude, or implying her gratitude was required. I then threw my numerous failed attempts into the fire and sent the package off to be left in her room.

I had been aware for some time she had left the house, which was not unusual: she generally took a walk each morning. I went over to the window closest to me. I had a view down over the flower-filled parterres and lawns to the high dark hedge representing the limit to which I was allowed to roam. Only the great wrought-iron gate pierced it and the forest loomed over it on the other side. Standing in front of the gate, in a hooded cloak and looking small and far away, was Isabeau. I did not know whether she looked out longingly, or with curiosity, but she made a lonely figure against so many great, tall, dark things. I think that was what moved me to go and join her.

She was not by any means close to the house, and it took me some time to reach her. She did not turn her head as I approached, yet she must have heard my step on the gravel of the drive, for she raised her hand to her lips and indicated I should be silent.

I stood close behind her, staring where she watched, into the forest. I could see the road winding back and disappearing behind the fir trees. What few rays of sun penetrated the canopy looked like shards of glass hanging in the air. This close to the hedge, I could smell the forest, too, cool notes of earth and pine. It was very still.

After some time I heard a faint, far-off twitter, and she

turned to me, her face lit with triumph, and whispered, "There!" as though she had proved a point that had been in fierce contention.

"What was it?" I asked in a low voice.

"I'm sure it was a wren," she answered, peering out into the gloom once more. "But I think I heard a lark as well, a short time ago."

"A lark, truly?" I asked wonderingly. We stood there in silence for a few more minutes, but no more sounds came forth from the trees. "Have you seen the rabbits again?" I asked.

"No." She shook her head, then glanced up at me. "Although I can show you their tracks in the snow, if I can find them."

"I would like that," I said.

We left the drive and walked for some distance along the hedge. I could feel the forest breathing cold at us from the other side. All my grounds were in the grip of winter this close to the forest's edge, and we walked ankle deep in snow. Eventually Isabeau began to look around intently, and then to bend down and peer into the depths of the hedge.

"I'm sure they were around here," she said, and then, kneeling in the snow, "A-ha!"

I bent down beside her to see what she pointed at. Her finger, ungloved and rosy pink in the cold, pointed at a single clear print in the muddled snow. Beside it, caught on a twig protruding from the hedge, were a few fine, soft hairs.

"There," she said. "It would seem your realm is no longer shunned by—" And to my sorrow I fairly heard her swallow the words "other beasts."

"—the creatures of the forest," she continued. I tried to give no sign I had sensed the words she nearly said and we were silent for a few moments.

"Isabeau," I said cautiously after a while, "you are not still afraid of me?"

She turned to me with a thoughtful frown on her face.

"Afraid?" she asked. "No, I don't believe I am. I don't think I could play music with you by if I were still afraid." She hesitated, then said with more confidence, "No, Beast, you've given me nothing to fear at all."

"Thank you," I said gruffly. "You do not still resent the manner in which you came here? I am deeply sorry for it." The words caught in my throat and were difficult to get out. She turned to look up at me and gave me another thoughtful stare.

"I would very much like my father to hear you say that one day," she said. "I have given that matter much thought. No, I do not resent it anymore. Desperate men do desperate things."

I looked at her closely to see if this was her redress for almost referring to me as a beast, but she was caught up in her train of thought and quite unconscious of the words she had used.

"Take my father for example," she continued. "It was desperation that made him leave us to undertake such a journey at the beginning of winter. It was desperation that made him try to return in midwinter, and again to try to travel through your forest. It was desperation to save my father that made me come to this place. In your long solitude I do not doubt you had grown somewhat desperate."

This exchange formed the basis of my reflections for the remainder of the day. Of course, I found her utterly charming. Her slip of the tongue—or near slip—placing me among the beasts of the forest fell away into insignificance beside the fact that for the most part she spoke to me as though I were a man. Besides, I chided myself, I had asked her to call me "Beast."

As evening began to fall, I took myself for a walk through the portrait gallery, now largely restored to its former glory. I had not been in this place above three times since my return from the forest. One reason was that a portrait of me had once hung at the far end, and even though it had been consigned to a dim, dark attic room where I did not have to look upon it, even the blank wall on which it had been displayed recalled a painful comparison between my appearance then and now.

My other reason for rarely visiting the gallery was that the pictures of so many family members, so still and mute and entirely gone from me, made me feel my loneliness intensely. In particular, the portrait of my grandmother never failed to make my heart ache. Just like on that first day after my return from the forest, there were always fresh flowers in the vase beneath it and a candle burning in a glass beside them. Though I visited it but rarely, and had not consciously placed the flowers there, I was glad of the tribute, for her memory deserved much more than I could ever offer. It had always been difficult to stand beneath that kindly, painted gaze when I knew how her heart would break to see what I had become.

Now, with Isabeau in the house, the passing of all I could claim blood ties with stung a little less and I felt more able to gaze upon my ancestors and lost cousins. Indeed, that evening I believe I was seeking some sense of my place within their ranks, as Isabeau held her place in the hearts of her sisters and father, even in her absence.

My hope of finding such welcome was so strong that, as I pushed open the doors to reveal the long, stately room, I fancied

I heard a low, tender whispering, as of the murmured conversation between two intimates. There was no one there, of course, but a sudden draft shook the flowers beneath my grandmother's portrait, scattering rose petals and dried leaves across the floor and gusting past me in a summer-scented breath.

I did not find what I looked for that evening. There were so many faces, and so many of them handsome and beautiful, and noble and proud. In the end the thought of my own nightmare visage depressed me and I was weighed down by a sense I was committing sacrilege in thinking to place myself among them. Even when I thought back to the life I had lived before the curse, I recognized how little I measured up to most of those who had gone before me.

I shuddered again at the echoes that came back to me down the years. Voices of people trying to gain my favor or pleading for my compassion. My heart curled up in shame when I thought of how rarely I had ever truly bestowed either.

There was, of course, one among my ancestors who represented the very nadir of human baseness. I dearly hoped I was a better man than him. But then . . . I looked down at my beastly paws. No Fairy had ever appeared to curse him. I fought the sudden swell of anger rising in my throat. He was gone. I was the only remnant of him on this Earth. There was not even a portrait of him in the gallery. I had destroyed that painting many years ago.

My perusal of the gallery eventually brought me to stand in front of that blank, staring wall with its strangely prominent hook—a large, sturdy thing that looked as though it could only be removed if the wall was first demolished. As I stood there, I had a sudden urge to confront my portrait again. It was so strong, I instantly turned my footsteps toward the attic room where it now stood.

There was a staircase behind a door on the third floor—a small, dark door so slight I could not easily fit my bulk through the frame, or ascend the cramped, wooden stairs with any comfort. There were no elegant candelabra here, either. A few single candles in tarnished, sparsely spaced sconces lit my way.

As I climbed the steep, crooked stairs, I could hear my heart pounding as frantically as it had when I first met Isabeau. It was a similar fear that set my pulse racing: the fear of confronting someone, or something, that could pronounce me as being less than human. I remembered the face in my portrait as cold, proud and disdainful. No doubt my memory was colored by the bitterness of envy, but now I wanted to challenge that arrogant visage. To stand before it and, despite all appearances to the contrary, declare myself to be the better person.

At last I stood on the bare, dusty floorboards of the attic. Gazing about myself, I was visited by a renewed sense of how derelict my home had been when I first returned from the forest. All around me were stacked broken and forgotten objects, many showing signs of the ravages of time. Drifts of leaves had gathered here and there, and cobwebs veiled the exposed rafters. The occasional missing tile in the roof let in shafts of light from the three-quarter moon, now directly overhead and impossibly bright.

I made my way through this strange landscape, searching. I had no idea where it might have been placed. I had not gone far, however, before I stepped upon something that crunched faintly beneath the sole of my boot. I looked down and saw the desiccated remains of an ancient mouse. When I looked up, I saw the painting. Taller than I, in its heavy, gilded frame; draped in a cover and leaning against a far wall. The encroaching shafts of moonlight lit the pale sheet and turned all the surrounding jumble into shadows. I stood, barely breathing, and stared at the anonymous white shape. Then the dust sheet twitched and slowly slid to the ground. I found myself looking again at the likeness taken of me when I was a young man.

For all my nervous anticipation, the experience was quite different from what I had expected. The silver light leached the picture of all color, lending it a serious, tragic air, absent in daylight. The arrogant expression became haunted; the proud, cold features pinched and desperate. I was shocked. Although I thought I had grown used to my beastly countenance, I confess the face I saw in my portrait that night was the face I still somehow expected to see whenever I glimpsed a reflection of myself.

CHAPTER XI

$\mathscr{I}$ went back to my study and ate a late, lonely meal in front of the fire. Seeing my portrait again had stirred up complicated feelings in my breast and I found myself wanting a distraction. Naturally, my thoughts turned to Isabeau's family. As my empty plates were whisked into thin air, I hesitantly went over to the mirror and pulled the drapes aside. I did not know if I would find any of them still awake, as it was now growing late.

The glass cleared and showed me the kitchen. As I feared, all was dark; the only light in the room came from the fire. I could see Marie's book on the edge of the scrubbed table. A few loose sheets of paper had been placed inside the front cover and I remembered she had said she was going to spend today at the inn. I was about to redraw the drapes to cover the glass, when the room grew lighter. A moment later Marie walked in carrying a candle. She was treading quietly, as though she did not want to wake her father and sister, and she was wearing a nightgown with a shawl wrapped around her shoulders. She was also carrying a bundle of paper, pen and ink. She set the candle down on the end of the table closest to the fire and sat down herself and began to write. Her lips did not move, but as I watched, I could hear her voice as though she was speaking.

"Dearest Isabeau," she began, "I am writing to you because I feel that one day, when you return to us, you will like to know how it was for us from the very beginning. You may be worried we cannot do for ourselves all you did, and I want to reassure you we have rallied ourselves tolerably well." Here she paused and rested the pen against her lips for a moment. Then she began again.

"Of course, I have to believe you will return. Papa is very bitter and holds no hope, but the Beast has sent us such fine, thoughtful gifts, I cannot think he is so terrible. I imagine you living in luxury, with all the jewels and fine dresses Claude could desire, and a vast library of interesting texts to keep you busy.

"I must be honest and say that at first we did not do so well. Claude fancied the kitchen could be her kingdom, and I took on the responsibility of the remainder of the house. We were both as miserable as it is possible to be, although I will allow Claude was slightly more so, on account of her burned fingers. This unfortunate arrangement lasted only five days before we could tolerate it no longer. We gratefully agreed to exchange our chores and for some reason are the happier for it. Claude seems to think that by zealous dusting and scrubbing she can transform our poor, bare parlor into something like the grandeur of the salon in our old house. She has announced her intention to turn some of the plain linen gifted to us by your Beast into very fine furnishings.

"I, on the other hand, have spent an entirely profitable day with Madame Minou, learning the rudiments of household cooking. To think, I, who have spent so many hours studying poetry and the works of Greek philosophers, am now applying myself to measures of beans and goose fat. I will not say I did not utter a sigh now and then, but I confess it was better than lying in that uncomfortable bed staring at that dreary ceiling.

"Madame Minou was kind enough to give me an old pot to take away—filled with the stew that was the fruit of my first day's labor! You cannot imagine my triumph, walking home from the Crossed Keys, carrying a great sooty cauldron full of beans and vegetables. It is nothing like arguing about philosophy in an elegant salon, but I do not care how much my friends might laugh to see me, for there is something deeply satisfying in doing something as useful as feeding one's family. Papa and Claude were good enough to declare it delicious, and Claude even ate the whole bowl! I am returning tomorrow on Madame Minou's promise that she will teach me how to bake bread. I am told there is a knack to it.

"Claude tells me Papa has spent the day banging away on the roof with the tools sent to him by the Beast. She was terrified he would fall and be killed. However, on my return this evening Papa was very satisfied with himself, and less inclined to be gloomy than he has been. I hope this is a trend that will continue.

"My last bit of . . . well, I don't know whether it is really news, but it was very pleasant so I will tell you about it. I have made a new friend. You see? I am at last following your advice to try to settle into our new life and make this village home. Do you recall René Dufour, Madame Minou's youngest brother? I am sure we have encountered him once or twice before. He has a farm to the north of the village. Apparently he visits Madame Minou once a week to supply her meat. He came today, while I was there, and we fell to talking. He is very kind and chivalrous, and when I told him of my hopes to start a garden in the spring, he said he would loan Father some tools to help me get started.

He also had much useful advice on when to begin digging and when to plant, and what to plant where. I tried to write down as much of it as I could. It will be interesting to see if I, a privileged city lady who had not so much as seen a lump of dirt until six months ago, will be able to conjure up a productive garden from the patch of wilderness outside our door. Perhaps the Beast was kind enough to send me magic seeds I cannot kill.

"Despite my misgivings, I admit I am eager for the spring to come so I might try my hand at growing things. Claude is already so immersed in the principal of her new chores—ridding the house of dirt—she cannot see what is so appealing about dirt that I must go and dig in it. And I have been very severely warned against bringing any of it back into the house.

"In any case, my day was long, and I am very tired. So I must go to my bed now. But I will seal this up and keep it safe against your return, for I feel it in my heart that we will see each other again."

So saying, Marie signed the letter and folded it, then stopped to press tears from her eyes with the heel of her hand. She gathered her things and went into the little bare room they called their parlor. The casket with Isabeau's name on it had been placed on the mantelpiece. Taking a deep breath, Marie lifted it down and opened it. It was empty. She stood looking into it for a moment, then placed the letter inside, and returned the box to its place. Then she turned away toward the staircase.

The mirror began to grow dim again and I stepped back, pulling the drapes to. I returned to my chair by the fire, where a glass of wine awaited me. Marie's letter filled me with a tremulous anticipation. Dare I hope the de la Noue family fortunes were at last turning?

As I sat musing on Marie's letter and her family's mysterious past, I noticed something. Isabeau usually spent the evenings in her rooms, but tonight she was wandering around my house. She did not seem to be coming to see me. She was moving slowly, hesitating at each new turn. *Perhaps*, I thought, *she is just curious to see what this place is like at night*. It was so obviously deeply steeped in magic that, for all she knew, some magical transformation may occur at midnight.

My own curiosity was too strong to resist. When the candles in the hall flared into light as I left my study, I muttered an order to quench them and made my way in darkness. *What does she make of my house?* I wondered.

As I drew closer to her, I realized she must now be in the portrait gallery I had myself visited only that evening. I entered an anteroom leading to one end of the gallery and saw only a dim light through the other door. Like the hall behind me, the gallery was dark and no candles sprang into luminescence to light her way as she stole down the room. Hoping she would not see me in the darkness, I positioned myself where I could watch her.

She was perhaps halfway down the gallery, carrying a branch of candles that shed a nimbus of light directly around her. She stood, candles raised, intently observing the portrait before her. I think it may have been one of my great grandmothers. I was rather too entranced by her to take much notice of the picture she looked at. She had obviously readied herself for bed before deciding on her night-time tour of the house, as she was wearing her nightgown and a robe, and her beautiful hair was loose, falling down her back and over her shoulders in long tumbled curls. I found myself holding my breath.

After a minute or two she moved on to the next portrait and so proceeded down the gallery, taking time to scrutinize each painting. She had started at the end with the oldest works and was slowly but surely progressing toward the blank wall where my portrait had once hung. A strange anxiety began pressing on me and I nervously looked from her to the empty wall.

As I have said, there were no accidents in this house. The invisible attendants were well able to keep things immaculate. Yet, at the far end of the gallery, the shutters to one of the tall windows had come slightly ajar, admitting a ray of moonlight through the gap. The moon was setting lower in the sky now and the silvery swath struck across the gallery, and illuminated the bare wall with its naked hook. As I stared, it became apparent the space had caught Isabeau's attention, too. She walked straight past the last few paintings toward it. The moonlight was so bright that, from where I stood, I could see the large rectangular shadow my portrait had left on the wall.

She stood for a long time in front of the wall, her brow creased in a puzzled frown. Eventually a clock in a nearby room rang out a late hour—I didn't count the chimes—and recalled her from her reverie. She shivered, pulling her robe close around herself, and left the gallery in the direction of her chambers. I, too, went to my bed, and all that night I dreamed I was the haunted young man in my portrait, winding soft curls of honey hair around my human fingers.

CHAPTER XII

$\mathcal{T}$he next morning, Isabeau did not appear downstairs at the usual time. After waiting for her in the music room for an hour or more, I grew worried. Eventually I summoned the courage to go and knock on her bedroom door.

"Isabeau," I called through the door, "are you well?"

After a few moments and a flurry of soft sounds, the door opened partway and revealed Isabeau, wrapped in a dressing gown. She looked tired, and her eyes were a little red, but she appeared otherwise whole and hale.

"I'm sorry," I said, "did I wake you?"

"No, I was awake," said Isabeau, stifling a yawn. She hesitated and did not meet my eyes. "I stayed up longer than usual last night and slept late. I did not think I would be very good company this morning, so I dawdled. I can dress now and come down, if you like."

"No, no," I said quickly, stepping back from her door. "I was only concerned when you didn't come down. Please, take your time. There is no need to dress if you would rather stay in." I bowed and meant to go, but she stepped forward and laid her hand on my sleeve.

"No, I think I will come down," she said. "I feel like a walk. Would you like to come? Perhaps we could try to find the rabbits again."

I looked at her closely. Despite the tiredness in her face, there was a lightness to her voice.

"I should like that very much," I said. "Shall I wait for you outside?" She nodded and went back inside her bedroom.

As I waited outside on the steps, I noted the chill in the air from the previous evening had not dissipated. Within moments of formulating this thought, a cloak appeared from nowhere and enveloped me in its warm, woolen folds. A short time later, Isabeau appeared at the front door. She stepped out into the sunshine and when she saw me she *smiled*.

"Good morning, Beast," she said. "It is rather late, isn't it?"

"You have only yourself to please," I said, "and no appointments to keep."

"True," said Isabeau and covered another yawn with both hands. "Therefore, I think I will prescribe myself a day of complete indolence and spend the afternoon asleep." We started down the front steps, making for the snow-covered side of the house where Isabeau had seen the rabbits.

"Did you not sleep at all?" I asked, puzzled at this onset of insomnia.

"I . . . stayed awake reading," she said, not meeting my eyes. My puzzlement grew. I could understand she wanted to keep her tour of the portrait gallery private, but surely it could not have accounted for an entire night of wakefulness.

"Oh, you found something to your liking in the library,

then," I said lightly, looking away from her and becoming absorbed in scanning the snow ahead for signs of animal life.

"Mmmm" was all the response I received. It then became very easy to let this conversation drop, as a rabbit suddenly burst out from the hedge some way ahead of us, ran several meters, and froze.

"Look!" I breathed, barely able to believe my eyes. Isabeau turned to see and, as she moved, the rabbit leaped back into life and streaked off, vanishing into the hedge once more.

"There! I told you," said Isabeau, in a satisfied tone. "Let us see if we can find his brothers and sisters."

We walked along the hedge for some time, and while I did not get another view of a rabbit quite so clear as the first, we saw a number of tracks and had another glimpse of a tail disappearing into the dark tangle of leaves and twigs standing between us and the forest. I also found my beast's senses could detect a lingering odor I identified as rabbit in the places where we found marks. I had not smelled another animal for so long, I had forgotten this ability of mine. It was not a comfortable sensation, for it stirred up memories of the time I had lived in the forest.

Eventually Isabeau began to yawn again in earnest and when I pressed her she confessed to growing weary once more. I offered her my arm to lean on, in returning to the house, and she accepted with what appeared to be genuine gratitude. My satisfaction with our walk was made in all ways complete when we heard a twittering trill and a flash of red darted across the path in front of us. We turned and saw a robin alighted on a nearby bush. It watched us carefully for a few moments, then flew off again, disappearing over the hedge.

"She is probably looking for a snug place to rear her brood in your hedge," Isabeau observed.

My heart was too full to reply.

The next few days passed very pleasantly. Isabeau's family seemed to be almost happy, which did much to relieve my guilt over the removal of their youngest member. Neither sister was as miserable as they had been the first day I saw them.

Isabeau's music proved a welcome source of diversion for the both of us. Initially she spent all her time at the virginal and it was not many days before her hands became noticeably more nimble and the music more fluid. Then she began to dabble on the other instruments, but the virginal remained her favorite. She thanked me very prettily for the music I gave her and was good enough to start learning several of the pieces straightaway. It seemed she liked them, too, for she played them often and seemed as happily transported by these as by her other favorites.

She suffered me to sit quietly in the room and listen to her play, but she would not sing if I was there. After a few days I came to the conclusion she was a little shy of her playing as well and made more wrong notes if she observed me watching her too closely. She insisted I was welcome in the music room, though, so I began to take a book with me. Often I merely held it open in front of me and pretended to read, but even if Isabeau detected the ruse, it appeared to make her more comfortable.

One morning I heard her begin to play and went to take my customary seat in the corner. Given my general disinclination to read at these times, I had with me a small volume of poetry that was a favorite of mine, on the basis that I found poetry easier to pick up and leave off than prose.

Isabeau was somewhat restless and indeed, after only half an hour at the virginal, the melody trailed away half-heartedly. I raised my eyes from my book, wondering what was wrong. She was leaning forward on the stool with her elbow resting on the edge of the instrument and her chin in her hand. She appeared to be gazing out the window, but as I looked up she turned to look at me.

"You are not inclined to play today?" I asked.

Isabeau shook her head ruefully. "No. You see what a poor student I am? I am now paying for my earlier enthusiasm. I confess today I am weary of my music."

"That is a shame," I said.

"It's kind of you to say so." She smiled in a self-deprecating way. Then she knitted her brows thoughtfully and asked, "What do you do to entertain yourself? I mean when you are not listening to me play. What did you do before I came?"

What a question! What could I tell her about the wretched daze of my life in the château before she came? Of staggering about in an attempt to walk like a man and the dreamlike strangeness of holding such familiar things as a cup, a knife or a sword in my ungainly paws and being unable to use them? Of howling my loneliness to a blank and unsympathetic moon?

"I mostly read" was the answer I eventually gave, looking down at the book I had laid down on my knee.

"Then I imagine you have done quite a bit of reading in your time," she said quietly.

"Yes," I said, "I have read most of the books I possess."

Isabeau raised her eyebrows. "I have seen your library!" she exclaimed. "So many books!"

"I cannot take the credit for it," I admitted. "I have never added to its collection. It was amassed by others."

Isabeau frowned as though this had given her something curious to think about. Then she asked, "So what would you recommend to a young lady who doesn't wish to apply herself to anything too serious?"

Never before having had to make a recommendation to young ladies wishing to apply themselves to anything at all, I was somewhat taken aback.

"I have no idea," I said. "All I can do is tell you which ones I have enjoyed the most. They will be easy enough to identify," I said with a wry smile, holding out my hairy paws. "Those I have read often are rather battered, you see."

Isabeau smiled. "I can see you would use your books rather hard," she said. "What are you reading today? Would you mind very much reading some of it to me?"

Once again the conversation had taken a turn that left me more than uncomfortable. I tried desperately to think of a way to politely decline and couldn't. She must have seen my amazement in my face and misinterpreted its cause.

"My elder sister used to read to me often," she explained. "Papa was mostly too busy for such things and my mother passed away while I was still in leading strings. As you see with my music, I never had enough self-discipline to truly apply myself to any kind of studious pursuit. Marie used to read to me in the hope I would grow interested enough to do it more often on my own. Or, failing that, that I would glean some sort of education."

"I could," I said doubtfully. "I have never read aloud to anyone. I don't know if I would be worth listening to."

"Please?" she asked, a little more hesitantly now. "I promise to be as impressed with your reading as you were with my playing."

I tried to swallow my apprehension. It was the first request she had actually made of *me*. How could I deny her this simple thing?

"Very well," I said gruffly, feeling excruciatingly self-conscious. I picked the book up and Isabeau left her seat at the virginal and settled herself in a chair near mine. I cleared my throat and looked up and saw her large, liquid eyes fixed expectantly upon me.

"Would you mind . . . not looking at me, perhaps?" I said, and if a dark, hairy beast could have blushed I would have been the color of a beetroot.

Isabeau looked somewhat surprised, but said, "Of course," most contritely. She resettled herself in a different chair with a view out the window. I cleared my throat again and began to read.

Initially I must have sounded somewhat hoarse and halting, but I tried not to think of her sitting there listening intently, and concentrated on the verses before me. It grew a little easier and at one point when I dared to raise my eyes a little, while I could not see her face, her posture was relaxed. She had tucked up her feet underneath her and was leaning her cheek on her hand. At that point my throat had begun to grow dry and I was going to ask her if she had had enough. But, seeing how comfortable she looked, I determined to continue. No sooner had I formed this resolve, than a glass of water appeared at my elbow. Gratefully I drank it down and continued.

I must have read to her for more than an hour, because by the time I had finished the little volume, the sun had climbed high in the sky. As I closed the book and put it down, I wondered if perhaps Isabeau had fallen asleep. But she gave a happy sigh and turned around.

"I love those poems," she said blissfully. "Marie used to read me those very verses. They were some of my favorites."

"Really?" I asked, momentarily forgetting my discomfiture. "They are mine as well." She gave me a radiant smile.

"Really," she answered. "Thank you, Beast, that was very pleasant. You read very well."

"I am much obliged," I muttered gruffly, a good deal of my initial embarrassment returning. "I am glad you enjoyed it."

"Would you be kind enough to read to me again, sometime?" she asked.

I looked at her carefully to see whether she was just being polite, or whether she had genuinely enjoyed it. She seemed in earnest.

"If you will consent to continue to play for me, as you have been, I will read to you whenever you wish," I said boldly.

"That sounds like a fair exchange," said Isabeau, rising from her seat. "Shall we shake on it?" And she held out her hand. I stood to take it in my massive paw and we shook. Again I was glad beasts do not blush, for at her touch my palm quickened.

"Isabeau, would you dine with me again tonight?" I asked impulsively.

"Certainly," she said and, with her hand still in my paw, she dropped a brief curtsey. "Until this evening, then."

I bowed to her. "This evening," I said.

She left the room and my palm continued to tingle for the rest of the day.

CHAPTER XIII

$\mathcal{O}$nce again dressed with more than my usual care (and I had been dressing with extreme care since Isabeau arrived), I awaited her at the bottom of the grand staircase. I had ventured out onto the summer terrace, but an inexplicable chill in the air had driven me indoors. I puzzled over this briefly while I waited for her. My magical weather was not usually so capricious. Once I saw her on the stairs, however, all thought of weather was driven from my mind.

She was dressed again in a gown of fine brocaded silk, this time in that same pale pink that made her seem like a flower out of my rose garden. The full skirts swelled out around her and she appeared to float down the stairs. Her hair was elaborately dressed and threaded with pearls, and there were more jewels at her throat. The clothes she habitually wore during the day had continued to be very plain, almost common. The difference was enchanting.

I tried not to stare as I stood at the bottom of the stairs, but it is unlikely I achieved any measure of success because as she reached the last few steps, she gave me a sharp look and said,

"Clearly dinner is something of a grand affair, here," in an irritated voice.

"You did not wish to dress?" I asked, taken aback. I was more than surprised. My dismay must have been as evident as my admiration, because she immediately relented.

"No, no, I intended to," she assured me, "just not in anything so fine. But when I went to my wardrobe, this was apparently the only item of clothing I possessed. And the amount of grooming I was subjected to, you would not believe."

"I see," I said gravely, thinking this over. It occurred to me I had been looking forward to seeing her in just such finery this evening. I had grown very used to my own wishes being responded to almost before they were formed. Perhaps the magic had allowed me to somehow impose this wish on Isabeau? I uttered a low growl, appalled at the thought. In another time I might not have thought twice about insisting upon my own preferences, but now I was mortified at the thought. I looked at Isabeau, standing on the bottom step, staring at me, her eyes wide. I made my thoughts as clear as I could and directed them at the magic surrounding us.

From now on, I determined, *my wishes will* not *take precedence over Isabeau's. She will be accorded the same courtesy and obedience I have been shown. If a choice must be made,* her *comfort and needs are of greater importance than mine.*

There was a sharp crack, quite close by, as though a pane of glass had just splintered. This time I caught a clear, sudden scent of magic.

"What was that?" asked Isabeau, startled.

I offered her my arm. "I think perhaps it was old magic bending in a new way," I said, as she came forward and laid her hand hesitantly on my forearm. "You will not have a problem with your wardrobe again. You shall wear whatever you wish."

Isabeau looked around curiously, as though expecting to see someone else nearby. Then she looked back at me.

"Truly, I do not mind very much," she said. "I just never had occasion to wear anything so grand before. It seems a little too much just for dinner. And . . ." She hesitated a moment and looked uncomfortable, her cheeks turning pink.

"Is there something else?" I asked.

For a moment she looked as though she was trying to find a way to avoid the question. Then she closed her eyes and said in an embarrassed voice, "I am not used to being looked at."

"I see," I said, not sure what I could say to repair this awkwardness. "I'm very sorry if I embarrassed you. You do look very nice." It was hardly adequate praise and I was not sure if a compliment was really going to make the situation any better. However, to my relief she opened her eyes and managed a self-conscious smile.

"Thank you. Did you choose this dress?"

Now it was my turn to feel uncomfortable. "No," I said, searching for words to explain my suspicions. "Well, it was not my intention. But I think the magic in this place has grown accustomed to arranging things to please me. That may have influenced what you were offered to wear this evening. I apologize. It will not be so again."

Once more the small dining room yielded a feast of bewildering proportions and variety. As usual there was far more than even I, at my most ravenous, could have hoped to consume. I was searching for something to say by way of conversation, when Isabeau gave a low cry of pleasure.

"Oh, look!" she exclaimed as an elegant silver dish filled with something pale pink and creamy paraded before her. "This is Claude's favorite!" She smiled shyly at me and offered me the dish. "It's a kind of mousse made with smoked trout. You must try some, it's really very good. She never could resist it."

Obediently I took some. "It's very rich," I offered.

"Yes," said Isabeau. "I could never eat much of it. And it's terribly detrimental to one's waistline. Claude always used to moan over that. But she could never help herself. If it was on offer, she'd eat so much she would be in danger of making herself ill. It's what she asked Father to bring back when he left last autumn. That and ropes of pearls."

"What do you mean?" I asked, puzzled. Isabeau put the mousse down, realizing how cryptic she had sounded.

"She didn't mean it literally," she said. "Of course, even if Papa had been able to afford it, he could not have brought something like that all the way back from Rouen. It would have spoiled, even in winter. She just wanted Papa to come back and tell her she could have her old life back." Isabeau shook her head sadly. "Even if his journey hadn't been in vain, I doubt he could ever have offered us that." She sighed. "We all want something more than what our lives offer us now. But Claude would have done better not to draw his attention to it."

"Would you mind," I said hesitantly, "telling me why your father was traveling through my forest in deep winter, when no one else had dared enter it for so long?"

Isabeau looked down at her lap. For a moment I thought she was going to refuse.

"My father used to be quite a wealthy merchant," she said, her voice breaking ever so slightly. "We lived in a very beautiful house in the best part of Rouen. We did not want for anything money could provide. It started when there were problems with the supply of goods he used to trade, I think. He would have rallied, but then there was a terrible storm that destroyed some ships. There should have been some sort of insurance against this kind of calamity, but it turned out someone my father had trusted in this regard had cheated him—with disastrous results. My father didn't worry us with details. But one day he was bankrupt and his fortune gone. We had no choice but to sell our house. When there were rumors of sickness in Rouen, we left the city and set up house in a little cottage by the edge of your forest. That was a little less than a year ago.

"Then, in autumn, Papa received word that one of his ships had returned to port. He left straightaway to see what could be done about restoring at least some of our prospects. He thought he could salvage something, so he jumped at the chance, despite the lateness of the season.

"I gather whatever happened, it has had very little impact on our circumstances. When he returned, he was a little too pre-occupied with the bargain he had made with you to tell us much about what had occurred with his ship," she said somewhat bleakly.

I thought it was as well to remain silent, and she continued without pause.

"After concluding his business, he realized he had left his three daughters alone, in winter, and thought of nothing else but to return to us as quickly as possible, although he could not bring us any comfort other than his presence."

At this point she stopped and picked up her wine glass, and drank. I thought she had concluded her story, but when she put it down she looked up at me again and I could see she was making an effort to contain tears.

"Before he left he asked us if he could bring us anything back, if it was within his power," she said. "Claude asked for this," she waved a hand at the silver dish, "and ropes of pearls for her dowry. Marie, who wanted nothing more than her books back, and who knew Papa was unlikely to be able to give her that, asked for gold and jewels. They were only joking. I just wanted something I thought he would be able to get, something that would add a little beauty to our otherwise unlovely house. I asked him to bring me a rose."

She blotted her eyes with the heel of her hand. And I? I sat silent and appalled, convinced the legs of my chair would splinter and collapse under the groaning weight of the guilt I felt for adding to the burden of her family's pitiable situation.

"I just worry about them," she said, wiping her eyes again. "Claude was making herself ill. She was nearly engaged, you see."

Isabeau sat up straighter in her chair. "We all considered it a certain thing. But he . . ." Now I heard an edge of anger enter her voice. "When I think of how kind we were to him, how we welcomed him into our family, and how Claude doted on him! I can understand how the change in our circumstances may have made the match impossible. But—the expectations he had given her! And to break it off without a word, let alone a kind one. His behavior was despicable."

Now Isabeau's beautiful eyes were flashing. Her hands clenched the tablecloth with such ferocity I thought she may have been in danger of pulling her meal into her lap.

"You know," she said to me directly, "after our situation became known, we did not see or hear from him once. No fond good-bye to Claude, no note to Papa explaining he would be unable to continue his attentions to his daughter. And that would have been a barely acceptable minimum if it was supposed it was

simply a match of convenience and not affection! We were all led
to believe it was a love match, especially poor Claude! She grew
so ill from pining for him we were afraid she would not be able
to travel when it came time to remove ourselves to the country.
And she still tells herself he will come for her! She refuses to hear
the reports of him courting other women and makes excuses for
his continued estrangement. He is heartless."

Now I understood Claude's sighs after the mysterious Gilles.

"Of course my heart breaks for poor Claude, but," and here
she violently speared a morsel of food with her knife, "we are
thankful she escaped being wed to such a heartless cad. Thankful, that is, provided she doesn't die of grief as a result. I could
not bear watching her languish."

I frowned, thinking of Claude's considerable improvement
in spirits and wondering if I should show her the mirror. If I did
that, I would feel bound to relinquish it to her entirely, as they
were, after all, her family. She had a greater right to watch over
them than I did. And what if, as I dreaded, watching them from
afar was more than she could bear? A cold little fear wriggled
through my heart.

"Would you tell me about Marie? Why do you worry about
her?" I asked to distract myself from such disquieting thoughts.
For a moment Isabeau continued to scowl at her plate, then she
relaxed her grip on her knife.

"She is my eldest sister," she said at last, settling back in her
chair. "She didn't lose a lover when my father lost his fortune,
but I think she thought she lost all her prospects of a comfortable future." She lifted her gaze to meet mine once more. "Money
is a great comfort, you know. If you have money and you choose
to marry, you can always attract a variety of suitors and take
your pick. Or if you choose not to marry, you can still live well.

If you have no money, you cannot remain single and live at all comfortably, but you have greatly reduced chances of attracting a tolerable husband. At least that's what Marie said to me."

"Did she not have any suitors?" I asked, surprised.

"Oh, some," replied Isabeau, "but none she really cared for. I think she always compared herself too much to Claude and made herself a little jealous. Marie considers herself to be reserved and doesn't think she is as pretty as Claude. I think she believes someone like Claude will always be able to find a husband. Claude had dozens of beaus in the city, but her affair with Gilles was rather flamboyant. Everyone talked about it. Of course, this made it doubly humiliating when suddenly he wanted nothing to do with her, but Marie chooses not to think of this and only remembers how glamorous it all was. Poor Marie has worked herself into a state where she believes that money was her sole attraction." Isabeau shook her head sadly. "I wish I could make her see any amount of money was only the least of her virtues."

She was silent for a while after this, and I do not doubt she was thinking about the state she had left her family in and how they had been faring since. Eventually I summoned the courage to ask her a question that had occurred to me as she was describing her father taking leave of them last autumn.

"And you?" I asked curiously. "What do you miss most about your life before?"

"Me?" she asked, surprised. Then she frowned. "I'm not sure." She cupped her chin in her hand, obviously considering the question. "I think," she said slowly, "what I miss most is just my family's happiness. Papa looks so old and tired now, and Marie is so bitter and Claude is so ill. That is the thing about money. When you are comfortable, and all the little things are taken care of, it is very easy to be happy. Although . . ." She straightened and looked around the room, then back at the table, which was now striving to present her with the most inviting array of desserts imaginable. Then she looked up at me and her smile was wry. "You can attest to the fact luxury alone does not happiness make."

"Hmm," I responded, the sound coming out more like a growl than I had intended. "And what of the city?" I asked, trying to divert her to a less distressing topic for both of us. "Do you miss that?"

Isabeau's face grew thoughtful again and she helped herself to a dish almost absentmindedly. I was relieved to see the worried lines vanish from her forehead.

"I never cared much for parties and balls," she said. She looked up at me and gave me a small smile. "Too crowded. I should have been making the rounds of society with Claude, but I did not like to and Papa never pushed me."

Her expression changed, as though she was now looking at something far, far away.

"A few years ago, Papa took us to a party where there were fireworks," she said. "I would like to see that again. I'm afraid there isn't much hope of seeing fireworks in our little village." She sighed. "I suppose at least I can say I have seen them once."

I smiled to myself, feeling very satisfied.

"Well," I said, "I can offer you no balls and parties, but fireworks I can certainly manage. Are you finished with your meal?" She looked at me, her eyes full of surprised delight. I stood.

"Come with me," I said.

CHAPTER XIV

*I*sabeau dropped her spoon into her dish with a clatter and rose, her chair sliding back gracefully of its own accord.

"You can conjure fireworks?" she exclaimed, hurrying around the table to take my offered arm.

"But of course," I said, smiling down at her. "There have been fireworks here before. Why not tonight?" Isabeau gave me a searching look, and a tiny crease appeared between her brows, but she said nothing further.

As we stepped out into the hall, two heavy cloaks hung in the air, waiting for us. The one clearly intended for Isabeau was lined and trimmed with silver-gray fur. Mine was plain black wool.

"Ah," I said, remembering the chill in the air earlier. "It is rather cold outside, tonight." I helped Isabeau into hers and mine dropped around my shoulders.

As we made our way up the stairs, she asked, "Beast?"

"Yes?"

"Is there anywhere in the house where you would rather I did not go?" she asked quickly.

The only secret I was truly keeping from her was the mirror

in my study, and if she was supposed to find it, I did not think there was anything I could do to stop the house from showing it to her. In fact, as it had certainly not existed in the house before she arrived, there was no reason why one should not simply appear in her own bedroom if it came to that.

"No," I said eventually. "I cannot think of any reason why you should not go where you like."

"Are you sure?" she asked, sounding surprised. I could not help but smile, albeit a little grimly.

"You will find no forbidden chambers awash with blood in this house," I growled, and was instantly ashamed when she flushed bright scarlet. "The invisible servants would ensure anything of that sort was cleaned up instantly," I said hurriedly, in a feeble attempt to mitigate my lapse into bitterness.

"I didn't mean . . ." she started to say, clearly struggling to find the words for an apology.

"No, of course not," I said. "And now I have embarrassed you. Please forgive my thoughtless attempt at humor. You may go where you wish. There is nothing hidden here you must not find."

She nodded at that, but still looked uncomfortable. I gestured for her to proceed up the grand staircase and she walked ahead of me, following the lamps flaring into life to show her the way up to the roof. We made our way thus, in less than companionable silence, until we reached the final staircase. This was not long, but was so steep a person ascending it could almost reach out and touch the tread level with their nose. Isabeau regarded it with dismay.

"Are we going up there?" she asked, peering upward. I realized it would be difficult indeed for her to make her way up in the dress she was wearing.

"Ah," I said, understanding the predicament, and once again cursing my thoughtlessness. "I had intended we should. Perhaps we could . . ."

There was no other way up to the rooftop balcony I wanted to show her. I racked my brains, trying to think of another place that was easier to reach from which we might have such a view.

"No, I will chance it," said Isabeau uncertainly, gathering her skirts around her.

She began to climb. I waited until she was a few steps ahead, then followed her up. There was a twist in the staircase about halfway up and she paused here to look over her shoulder at me.

"You see, I haven't sent us both tumbling to the bottom yet," she said breathlessly.

"If you fell, I should catch you," I assured her. She gave me a nervous smile and continued upward. She did not stumble, however, and we both reached the top unscathed.

"This way." I gestured to a door that led out onto a balcony, set in among the pitched rooftops and turrets at the back of my house. It had a clear, uninterrupted view out over the gardens. It was usually bare when I came up here on my own to howl, but now, of course, a small brazier provided warmth in the chilly air and a pair of comfortable chairs offered a place to sit if we were so inclined. Isabeau walked straight past the chairs and went to stand by the balustrade.

"We're so high!" she exclaimed and pulled her cloak a little tighter around herself. Suddenly the first firework exploded before our eyes and we both jumped in surprise. A moment later the sky above us erupted into showers of gold and silver stars. It was hard not to duck as thousands of sparks rained down toward us, but they vanished into nothingness before they ever got truly close. For a few minutes I watched, rapt, as the brilliant colors dazzled the night sky and then Isabeau laughed out loud beside me. I turned to stare at her. She was leaning forward over the stone railing as far as she possibly could. Her face was entirely hidden by the hood of her cloak, but then she turned to face me. Once more I caught my breath as I saw her eyes, wide and dark, reflecting the night and the fireworks. I had not seen her look this happy and carefree since she had arrived.

"Thank you, Beast!" she cried above the screech, as another rocket shot upward, followed by a trail of smoke and sparks, erupting into a shower of pink and gold above us. "It's lovely!"

I smiled down at her and she smiled back and turned away again to watch a new series of fireworks blossom in shades of silver, blue and lavender across the sky.

I stood for a while longer by her side, then when I grew tired of watching the fireworks, I retired to one of the chairs and watched Isabeau watching the fireworks instead. Despite the chill, something warm glowed within me, as if I had drunk mulled wine, but more precarious and trembling. The comparison stirred an idea, however, and a moment later a steaming jug and two silver goblets appeared on a tray by my elbow. The jug lifted and poured itself into the goblets, then settled back down on the small table that had materialized to receive it. I took one over to Isabeau, who accepted it gratefully.

Eventually the show ended with dozens of gigantic silver fountains sprouting up from the gardens below.

"That was beautiful," Isabeau said with a sigh, turning to lean back against the balustrade.

"I'm glad you enjoyed it," I said. "You may have fireworks every night if you wish. Of course, if you don't want to come all the way up here every night, I can arrange for you to enjoy them from your bedroom window."

Isabeau gave a soft chuckle. "You are too kind," she said, shaking her head. "But if I had fireworks every night, they wouldn't be such a treat."

With no more fireworks to entertain us, the chill soon drove us indoors. When we came to the narrow staircase again we stopped and Isabeau looked down at it doubtfully.

"Perhaps you should go first," she said.

Indeed, her voluminous skirts seemed to give her more trouble descending than they had in the ascent. I tried to stay only a few steps ahead in case she needed assistance and it was well that I did. As I reached the lowest stairs I heard a gasp from behind me and swung about to see Isabeau pitching toward me from above. We were so close to the bottom she would not have had far to fall, but I instantly reached out to catch her. She fell into my arms with no more noise than the sound of air rushing past silk. My strength was more than equal to her weight, but I staggered back against the wall and took a moment to be certain of my balance. She was clutching my jacket with both hands, looking up at me, her eyes wide with fright. She gave another gasp and I could feel her shudder against me. I hoped it was the shock of the fall that bothered her more than the prospect of being held by a beast. But as I set her back on her feet, I saw her eyes flicker across my claws. We both flinched when one talon snagged in the fine fabric of her bodice.

"I promised I would catch you," I said lightly, as I moved away. She took a deep breath and put one hand on the wall. She looked so shaken I braved rejection and held out my hand to assist her down the last few steps. She took it without looking at me.

When we came out onto the landing, she stepped away from me quickly, self-consciously straightening her skirts. The ease of our companionship on the roof had vanished. We barely spoke as I walked her back to the hallway leading to her room. We bid each other goodnight and I watched her walk away down the hall, the memory of her enjoyment now nothing but a strange, twisting ache in my belly.

CHAPTER XV

$\mathscr{I}$ didn't want to retire straightaway. If nothing else, my cursed Beast's senses could discern the ghost of her sweet scent on my own clothes and I couldn't bring myself to change. So I went to my study. I pushed the door open to find the room almost in darkness. Only one candle was alight, set into a heavy silver candlestick on the mantelpiece under the curtained mirror. This was a sure sign something of interest was about to be shown to me, so moving the candlestick aside, I drew the curtains.

The mirror cleared and showed me Marie in her night-clothes, sitting at the kitchen table, preparing to write another letter to Isabeau. She had evidently been writing in her book as well, for it was open beside her, with two pages covered in her elegant script. As I watched, she finished sharpening her pen and took up a sheet of paper. As before, I could hear her voice, as though she were reading to me.

"Dear Isabeau, I am writing again to give you an account of how we are faring, as I promised. The last week has been significantly more bearable than the previous one. Do not mistake me—we are all working hard and thoroughly worn out by the end of each day, and both Claude and I have certainly found a share of chores we would be happy to never do again. But it seems we have both found our place in the house and are now able to be—dare I say it—cheerful about even the most disagreeable of tasks. Even Papa has rediscovered some forgotten carpentry skills and declares he will build me a henhouse. Although, the other day, he hit his thumb so badly with his hammer his thumbnail has turned all black. Before that, however, he had managed to dig me two beds, which are to be the beginning of my new garden!

"You see, my new friend was as good as his word. I have been back to Madame Minou's several times now. She is glad of the help I can offer and her advice on cooking has been invaluable. I must tell you I find cooking immeasurably rewarding. There is something almost alchemical about taking all those raw ingredients and turning them into something that sets the mouth watering and the stomach growling.

"Of course, I cannot pretend it is anywhere near as elegant as those pursuits I used to enjoy. But it is a different kind of accomplishment, when we have all been working hard all day, to have created something Papa and Claude find so satisfying and delicious. I get a warm glow when I see them stretch out after dinner, as full and sated as your old cat used to get. And there is the other piece of news you will welcome—Claude is eating properly again, thank heaven. And I have not heard her mention you-know-who for days.

"But I digress. A few days after I met Monsieur Dufour he returned to Madame Minou's with the tools he had offered me. He was very kind—he said if I had not been at his sister's inn that day, he would have driven out to the cottage to deliver the tools for me! As it was, he insisted on driving me home. He said

I could not possibly walk and carry all the tools. It was a very pleasant drive, and so much faster than walking! Especially now that the snow is becoming thick along parts of the way.

"When we arrived at the cottage he spent some time with Papa, discussing the best place to put my garden beds, and exactly how to dig them. He is a very gentlemanly man, and he and Papa struck up a friendship almost immediately. It is most amusing, I had planned one or two beds, but Monsieur Dufour and Papa pegged out markings for four vegetable beds and an herb garden!

"Monsieur Dufour then presented me with some pots of herbs he had brought me as a gift to start my garden, although he says to keep them by the kitchen door for now and plant them in the spring. I cannot remember them all, but I have among them rosemary, sage, marjoram and thyme to name a few. I have written tags for them all to remind myself what they are. Most of them are little more than bare twigs, but Monsieur Dufour says they are all hardy and will begin to grow again at the end of winter. He is very good, and I am at something of a loss to know how to thank him.

"So you see we are all busy now. I think I can say Claude has stopped moping, and Papa certainly doesn't stamp around looking like a thundercloud anymore. I am so pleased to think he may finally have found a friend in Monsieur Dufour who may distract him from his worries. Although there are times when I have caught him staring at your chair, or off into the distance with such a look of sadness on his face.

"Dearest Isabeau, I pray the Beast is as good as his word and you are safe and happy. I must live as though you are, because I cannot bear the alternative. We have not yet told anyone the particulars of your departure. What would we say? And if anyone were to shake their head and presume the worst for you, I fear my own resolve to think the best might be weakened. I must go to my bed now and lay my head on the new pillowcase Claude presented me with today. We all have them and I own it is very pleasant to be sleeping on fine linen again."

Marie signed her name at the bottom of the last page and folded the pages away. Then she went into the parlor and over to Isabeau's box on the mantelpiece. She pressed the letter to her lips for a moment, then opened the box to place it with the first.

The box was empty.

Marie's brow creased into a puzzled frown, and she took up the box to peer into it more closely. Thoughtfully she tapped the folded letter against the side of the box as she considered this new mystery. Eventually she placed the new letter inside the box and snapped it shut. She set it back on the mantelpiece and, glancing around as though she was half-afraid of being observed, she pulled out a hair from her head and wound it once carefully around the latch of the box. She stepped back and gave the box a hard look. Then she turned to leave the room. The image in the mirror faded.

Now it was my turn to frown. Clearly Marie had expected the first letter to still be in the box. Who could have removed it? And for what reason?

The next day I witnessed an interesting exchange between Marie and Claude. With the exception of Marie's letters, the mirror had mostly shown me images of them going about their chores, as this was how they spent the greater part of their time. Apart from the years I spent in the forest, I had never done without servants, magical or otherwise, and it soon dawned on me just how much work there was in keeping a family of three. My dismay deepened when I recalled the first unhappy conversation I witnessed between Marie and Claude, in which it had become apparent that before she left them, Isabeau did most of the work looking after her sisters. No wonder Isabeau had thanked me for giving her a holiday.

I looked in on them to see Claude busily turning out the bedroom she shared with her sister. There was considerably more color in her face now than when I had first seen her. I watched her attempting to plump the thin pillows and shaking a threadbare carpet out the window for a few minutes. There was a knock on the door and Marie entered the room, something almost surreptitious about her movement.

Claude turned from the window to look at her.

"Your boots?" Claude asked sharply. In answer Marie made an irritated face and lifted the hem of her skirt. I saw she wore only socks. Claude frowned at the dirt smeared around the bottom of her petticoat. Then she looked up at Marie's face.

"Why are you creeping about like that?" she asked, giving way to curiosity.

"I wanted to ask . . ." Marie stopped, hesitating, then plowed on. "Did you ever open Isabeau's box? The one we got from the Beast?"

Claude's mouth opened in surprise. She turned to look out of the window for a moment, as though making sure she and Marie would not be overheard, and stepped closer to her sister.

"No," she said. "Why?"

Marie bit her lip.

"I did," she said quietly.

I heard Claude's sharp intake of breath.

"What was in it?" she asked.

"Nothing," said Marie, sounding puzzled, "but, that is not the strangest thing."

"What do you mean?" asked Claude.

"I decided to write Isabeau a letter," said Marie, with the air of someone admitting to something slightly foolish. Claude nodded. The expression on her face was one of sympathetic understanding, as though she, too, subscribed to Marie's belief Isabeau would return, but also knew it was not a belief that would stand up to scrutiny.

"I wrote one a week ago," Marie continued, "and another last night. I thought to put them in the box with her name on it. When I first opened it, the box had nothing in it."

Claude raised her eyebrows.

"When I went to put last night's letter in the box," said Marie, her voice sinking to a whisper, "the first was gone."

Claude put her hand over her mouth.

"I put the second letter in anyway and tied a hair around the latch. I checked it again just now and the hair was still there, but my letter is not. Again!"

"No!" breathed Claude.

"You didn't take them out," said Marie, shaking her head. It was a statement rather than a question. "Do you think Papa might have taken it?"

Now Claude shook her head. "He won't even look at the box, if he can help it. What could have happened to them?"

"Do you think," began Marie hesitantly, as though reluctant to speak her thoughts, "perhaps the Beast has somehow taken them? Maybe he has given them to Isabeau?"

I straightened up in my chair, staring at the mirror in amazement. Claude put her head on one side, considering this possibility.

"How could that be?" she asked doubtfully.

"It can only be magic," said Marie, still whispering. "Think of Papa's saddlebags. They were not that large. How could so much have been inside them?"

Claude nodded in agreement. "Perhaps it was the Beast. What will you do?"

"I thought I would keep writing," said Marie, looking to her sister for approval. "Just in case . . ."

Claude reached out and clasped Marie's hand.

"I think you should," she said. "If he truly is a benevolent creature, then they will comfort her. If not, they will let him know she has a family who loves her and perhaps that will stir some pity in his heart."

The image in the glass faded and I leaned back in my chair. I found the substance of their worst fears depressing, but it was only to be expected, and I was resigned to it. Conversely, I was somewhat amused by their assumption I was in complete control of the magic at work here.

Mostly, however, I was intrigued by the thought Marie's first letter had been delivered to Isabeau. The more I thought on it, the more I was sure this was the case. I remembered how she had slept late the morning after Marie had written for the first time, and that she had told me she had *stayed awake reading*. I wondered if Isabeau was even now reading over Marie's second letter. A sensation of something like relief came over me. If Isabeau did indeed have Marie's letters, then she knew how her family fared and there was no need, surely, for me to reveal to her the existence of the mirror in my study.

CHAPTER XVI

*I*sabeau and I developed something of a pattern to our lives over the next few weeks. Most mornings she would rise early and take her walk in the gardens. I, too, began to rise early, and while I did not usually leave the house during this time, wherever I was I would station myself by a window so I might see her pass if she happened to walk close by. The warm glow of pleasure I felt at the sight of her in my gardens never failed. After this she would usually repair to the music room, where I would go and listen as she played. Often in the afternoons she would seek me out in the library and I would read to her. Every now and then she would spend an hour or two wandering over the house. She seemed particularly interested by the portrait gallery, but she never asked me any questions about the paintings there. She also repeated her midnight rambles several times, but never mentioned these to me either.

Her family also grew more settled as I watched them. Marie, in particular, appeared to be more than satisfied with her new life. Her garden, with an initial helping hand from the obliging René Dufour, flourished as much as a garden can in winter. She was clearly finding some satisfaction in her duties as the family cook. So much so, she continued to spend at least one day a week in Madame Minou's kitchen, assisting her with the labors of cooking for the popular local inn. When Claude pointed out she was fortuitously always there on the day Dufour made his delivery to his sister, Marie looked surprised and insisted this was one of the busiest cooking days. Claude then congratulated her sister on the convenience of this arrangement, as he always offered to drive her home afterward.

Claude herself, while I never saw her again as miserable as she had been in the first week after Isabeau left, still seemed to be quietly pining, although now she did her best to hide it from her family. There were times when I watched her by herself, when she would pause in her work and sigh, and sometimes rub tears from her eyes. I determined this private grief was more likely to be due to the villainous Gilles than concern over Isabeau, as the sisters continued to freely share *this* between themselves.

Isabeau's father was by far the least comfortable of the trio. While his relief at the equilibrium his elder daughters had found was obvious, the fate of his youngest continued to eat at him. Also, oddly, he was now the least useful member of the household, which came as a severe blow to his already battered pride. His daughters were now managing the household reasonably efficiently and while Marie and Claude had private concerns about how they would manage once the money I had gifted them ran out, their situation was by no means as desperate as it had been when Isabeau first left.

Monsieur de la Noue's practical skills were basic at best, and unfortunately he also proved to be somewhat accident-prone. In one letter to Isabeau, Marie described the progress of the henhouse as slower than expected. In the end, for fear the structure would end by collapsing and killing her new hens, and possibly her father, she secretly enlisted the help of Dufour, who I must say carried off his part in the deception with tact and subtlety. He planted ideas in Monsieur de la Noue's mind in a way that made him think them his own, and spoke at length about the problems—real or imaginary, I know not—he had experienced in constructing a similar structure. In the end, Marie was the proud owner of a very sturdy new henhouse and it only remained for Dufour to promise her the delivery of half a dozen hens in spring to finish it off.

All in all, I had never been so nearly contented. My main source of discomfort now was the continuing concern I caused Isabeau's family. My bitter consolation for this, though, was that their worry would eventually be relieved when her year with me was up and she returned to them. Naturally I did my best to avoid thinking about this event.

One morning, while Isabeau was taking her walk, I went to the library to search out more books to set aside to read to her. One end of the library looked out over a walk through lawns ornamented with fantastically shaped yews. The walk was bordered with particularly fine trees, all clipped to form columns of precise geometric shapes. They had been shrouded in snow when Isabeau arrived, and as my interest had been diverted away from my gardens since then, they had remained that way.

It was a beautiful scene, in its own stark, eerie way. The dark green of the yew trees was so deep it looked black against the snow. It was not so much an uplifting beauty—I had been used to wandering there when I was particularly despondent. It was a very still and quiet place, and I found it easy to wallow in my loneliness there. I had not paid much attention to this part of the garden at all of late, but now as I looked out on it, something caught my attention. Far away down at the end of the walk, close to where it ended against the hedge, the mantle of snow was dark and discolored. Curious, I put my books aside and went outside to investigate.

As I drew close, I realized it was simply mud. The snow was melting. Puzzled, I looked around. There was certainly something different. I took a deep breath. A certain scent in the air. I could not see through the hedge into the forest, but it came from there.

I heard a shout. I turned to see Isabeau waving at me from some distance away. It took her a few minutes to walk through the remaining snow to me, and when she arrived she was slightly out of breath. She was dressed in a heavy cloak, and wore mittens and a shawl that may have been tied over her head at some stage, but now her hair was uncovered. For the most part it was tidily pulled into a braid and wound around her head, but wisps and tendrils had escaped and formed curls at her temples and the nape of her neck. Her face was rosy from cold and exertion.

"Beast!" she cried when she drew close, and I felt a warm flush of pleasure at the friendliness of her tone. "You rarely leave the house so early! What has brought you outside this morning?"

"This snow is melting," I said, pointing to the enigma of the bare earth showing through the icy mush.

"Yes," she said, clearly puzzled by my own confusion. "Spring is coming."

I was about to protest that the seasons on the other side of the hedge had never yet affected my gardens, when I recalled the rabbit and the robin and suddenly understood what they signified.

"Ah, of course," I said quietly. Spring was leaking in through the hedge, and eroding the magical winter this part of the garden had been held under for so long. I turned back to look down the walk to the house. Now that I knew to search for them underneath the great yews closest to me, I could see green spikes pushing up through the earth.

I was visited by an unexpected memory of the yew walk lush with twenty different colors of green in a springtime long ago. When I was a child it had been a favorite place to play; I remembered running down the wide walks and across the lawns, in and out of the twisting paths through the maze of hedges. The giant clipped trees offered perfect places from which to ambush my grandmother and my nurse. I recalled, too, searching out the snowdrops as they began to flower at the feet of the yews.

I looked back up at the forest trees visible over the top of the hedge. Why now? First an unchanging limbo, then my own magically imposed seasons—why were my gardens now beginning to again respond to the vast wheel of the seasons moving over all the rest of the earth?

Suddenly I knew.

I turned to stare at Isabeau. It was her. She was the key. Since she had arrived, the magic that held this place had started to weaken. First the birds and animals had begun to come back to the forest; now the seasons were returning to my garden. If this curse could be broken, she could do it. I didn't know how. I just felt that if, when her year was up, she chose to go back to her family, as of course she would, any hope I ever had of returning to my former shape was lost. This thought made me frown. Did I truly entertain any hope of becoming human once again?

Yes, I realized, I did. I had hoped, and hidden this hope far, far down in the depths of my consciousness for fear that any exposure to rational thought would kill it. This hope, I further apprehended, was what had kept me from starving away in the forest and had spurred me on to make myself into my current, pathetic parody of humanity.

"Beast?" asked Isabeau uncertainly.

"I beg your pardon," I said, pulling my glance away from her. I needed to think about this. "Please excuse me." I bowed and strode back up the yew walk to the house.

Once inside, I went to my study and shut the door. For the first time since Isabeau had arrived, I did not want her company. I needed to be alone and undisturbed. I did not sit. I could not sit! A strange energy was burning in my limbs and my heart beat fast with excitement and fear, so I paced about.

It was Isabeau. She was the key to the ending of this spell. But how? I struggled to remember the Fairy's words. *Let all who look upon you see the nature of the heart beating in your breast.* That had been the curse. Those were the words that had condemned me to this beastly form.

And after the cursing, what then? I pressed my knuckles to my temples, trying to draw out the memories by force. Memories I had not revisited for obvious, painful reasons.

I recalled a strange haze, as though a veil had been thrown up between me and the rest of the world. Pain. A horrible cramping and stretching in all my bones and sinews as the magic had forced me into a new and terrible shape. The faces of the people around me changing from dismay to open fear. Lashing out and seeing only fur and claw, and then flight. Pure terror and the urge to flee overtaking my shaken reasoning mind. Did the Fairy speak any more words? Was there an "Until . . ."? I shook my head in frustration. I had not stayed to hear and those who may have done were long gone from this world.

It was no good. I could not recall anything further of the curse. *But why did she curse you?* a little voice in my heart whispered. My gut twisted and my heart began to pound. I did not want to think on that. *What is to be gained?* I thought desperately. *Why torment myself with those memories now?*

If you want to know how to end the curse, you need to understand why she cursed you, the little voice persisted. *And if you want to understand why she cursed you, look to your life before the curse.* I stumbled to my desk and dropped into the chair, lowering my head into my hands.

For some reason, the insistent little voice urging me to think on my old life was my grandmother's. She herself had passed away not twelve months after my father died, and the grief I felt at her passing was comparable only to the relief I felt at his. At the very last, she had fretted over the hatred I bore for him.

"He is dead and gone," she had said to me, as I held her frail hands in mine at the last. "Do not live your life to spite him. Free yourself from him."

At the time, her words had angered me. I had been a young man of barely eighteen, and with all the conviction of youth I was certain I had cast off his yoke when he breathed his last. Now, as I sat slumped in my study, recalling my life as a man and the raging anger that had sustained me in the forest, I had to concede the truth. The very thought of him still stirred the old resentment in my blood.

My hatred of him and all he had stood for had governed my every action. I had tried to make myself into his antithesis. In the face of his dissipation and licentiousness, I had modeled myself on hard work and restraint. Where he neglected his duties, his lands and his tenants, I saw to them rigorously, in a fever of righteousness and exactitude. No frivolity was permitted, no lapse went unpunished. Where he neglected himself, I made my appearance a point of fastidious pride. And where his lasciviousness and reputation for lechery had made him a figure of terror for every young woman in the vicinity, I eschewed the company and the advances of all women.

I had struggled to prove myself a different man, to deny the taint of his blood. But now, as I sat in my study, I wondered. He had been cruel and violent, and his ungoverned lusts had certainly caused the death of my mother and the misery of countless other women. But in all my anger and hatred, if the Fairy had not removed me from society with her curse, would I have turned out so unlike him? I began to tremble. To think on his worst excesses made me sick with repugnance. His undisciplined rage and increasing derangement were but the least of his vices. As a youth, I saw the hunted look in the eyes of our maidservants whenever he was near. I had pulled my pillow over my ears at night so I might not hear their sobbing. And I noticed when they began to look warily at me.

I did all I could. I swore a private oath I would never treat any woman the way my father had. I turned my eyes from anything, and avoided any situation, that might test my resolve. But nothing tempered the anger seething in my veins. I tried to turn it to good effect, to channel it into my duties and to use it to bolster my indifference to the society of other human beings. Still it consumed me.

I know this grieved my grandmother. She had been bitterly disappointed in her own son, but I know she loved me and would have given much to have seen me happy. In particular, I remember her counseling me on more than one occasion to exert myself to discover someone in whose love and companionship I might find comfort. It was something that certainly troubled her in her last days.

"If you could only know," she had said to me, her gnarled hands restless in mine, "how it changes everything. How anything may be endured when you know there is another whose heart beats in accord with your own. You must find someone who understands you, *chéri*."

I admit this puzzled me. I could not fathom why she should speak of such companionship when, to my knowledge, neither she nor any of my family had ever experienced it.

My parents' marriage had been an exercise in wretchedness and heartache, ending with my mother's miserable demise from the ravages of disease visited upon her by my faithless father. And my knowledge of my grandfather was such that I could not suppose my grandparents' marriage to have been a happy one— indeed, while his reputation was not so diabolical as my father's, he was known as a cold, hard man. I cannot think it was anything other than a relief to my grandmother when he relinquished his life.

So I dismissed my grandmother's earnest plea for me to find a companion as nothing but the fanciful ramblings of a dying woman.

I could hardly dismiss them now. Not when the thought of such companionship occasioned visions of gray eyes and honey hair and an ache beneath my breastbone I could not assuage. I did not know what to think. After my grandmother's death I had locked away my heart entirely, for fear of what it might contain. Then the Fairy's curse had condemned me to a form that gave substance to those fears. Yet . . . my heart, my monstrous heart, was still capable of such yearning.

A creeping realization stole over me. I had thought I was lonely, locked behind my iron gate and surrounded by the wall of the forest separating me from the world. But, until Isabeau arrived, my enforced isolation here was little different from the isolation I had imposed upon myself in my last life.

Isabeau.

The key.

My reveries were abruptly interrupted as a moth flew out of nowhere and blundered into my face. As I batted it away, I saw the curtains covering the mirror had been drawn. I rose and went toward it reluctantly, wondering with some annoyance what event in the de la Noue household I was going to be shown now. Whenever the drapes were drawn of their own accord, there was something important and fascinating to be seen, and I knew I would not be able to help myself from watching. *But why now, when I so desperately needed to think?*

I looked in to catch the now familiar glimpse of my own hideous visage. This time, however, instead of my face fading away and being replaced by a different scene, I continued to stare into my own reflection. I frowned, wondering what could be the meaning I was meant to divine from this, and the creature in the mirror scowled back. Suddenly, a slight movement caught my eye and I saw a person sitting in the chair behind me.

I whirled around, but my chair stood by the fire, as empty as it had been a moment before. I turned back to the mirror. In the world reflected by this magic glass, my chair was not empty. A woman sat there, reclining back and watching me with an air of relaxed patience, as though my reaction to her presence in the reflection was nothing more than she had expected. I took one more quick glance at my own empty chair to confirm the situation, then peered into the mirror at her as closely as she stared at me.

She wore a gown of some intricately patterned green material, but the style was difficult to tell while she remained seated. As I stared at her, however, I became convinced the fabric was in fact formed of thousands of tiny leaves stitched together.

Her hair was long and loose and fell in thick russet waves over her shoulders. She wore no visible jewelry. Her face was an enigma. She was not young, but she did not look particularly old, either. There was something very familiar about her, yet I could not recall ever having seen her before. Her lips were curved in a smile with a mocking quality to it and her eyes . . . They were as green as a cat's and twice as brilliant. I found her eyes more disconcerting to look at than my own. Indeed, while my eyes remained the only clue to my lost humanity, as I looked into her eyes I became convinced this woman was not and never had been human. My hackles rose and my paws clenched into fists.

The Fairy.

CHAPTER XVII

*Y*ou want to break my curse," she said after we had stared at each other for some time through the glass.

Her voice was deep and melodic, not cracked with age. And in all other respects there was nothing crone-like about her. But I had no doubt it was the same Fairy that had laid the curse so long ago.

"I do," I managed to say, my own voice coming out as a growl. I took a breath through my nose in an effort to be calm. I cleared my throat and swallowed and tried again. "Is there a way?"

"Of course," she said, still smiling that secret, superior smile. "There is always a way to break a curse."

Somehow her tone of voice left me far more discomforted than I would have expected on hearing those longed-for words.

"How?" I asked, then realizing how blunt I sounded, I added, "If you please."

She brushed aside my polite addendum, and leaned forward, as if to take my measure. Then she sat back in the chair again.

"I will tell you," she said, apparently amused at the idea of telling me how to break the curse she had laid herself. Then her face became serious, and a spark of something like anger flickered in her eyes. "I will tell you, as long as you understand that just because there is a way to break a curse, it does not follow that you will be able to do so."

I nodded, my mouth now dry.

"Still," she said, suddenly philosophical, "curses have a way of breaking when it is time." Our eyes locked. "Is it time?"

"I don't know," I answered, barely able to whisper. "It is your curse, Lady. Can you tell me?"

"Oh no," she said, looking slightly shocked. "That is up to you." She settled down into the chair, folded her hands into her lap and assumed an instructional air.

"You must find the woman you truly love," she said, "and inspire her to love you in return. When she agrees to marry you, the curse will be broken. Those are the terms." She was watching for my reaction again, and now her expression contained a challenge. "Of course, you may not tell her you are cursed, or that if she agrees to marry you, you will regain your human form."

I stared at her in despair.

"How—" I started to say, but she waved me silent.

"The how is up to you. If you want to break it, you must find the how." She smiled again, but this time it was a little wry, and a little sad. "You see, it is still about the nature of your heart. You cannot hide your true self behind appearances forever." She stopped and frowned. "Well, you can. If you fail to break the curse and die here in solitude, no one will ever know the man behind the monster." She shrugged, and the coldness of her green gaze gave me a sudden thrill of fear.

"Why did you not make this known to me before?" I asked heavily.

Her expression became prim.

"I could not have you contriving to kidnap any maiden that happened inside your domain in the hope you might be able to convince her to marry you," she said priggishly.

I stared at her in amazement.

"But," I managed, "that is essentially how Isabeau came to be here."

"Ah," she said, frowning again. She considered this for a moment and shrugged again. Then she fixed me with another piercing stare. She was angry with me. I could not doubt that. But there was something else in her gaze as well.

"Is she the one?" she asked. "Do you truly love her?" An image of Isabeau flashed into my mind. My heart thudded.

The expression on the Fairy's face changed again, growing inexplicably tender.

"You have your grandmother's eyes," she said. And then she was gone. The room reflected in the mirror was once more the perfect reverse of the one in which I stood.

After a moment I reached up to draw the drapes, but then a familiar haze began to cloud the glass and I stayed my hand. The scene it revealed surprised me. I was looking, not at one of Isabeau's sisters or her father, but at Isabeau. She was seated at the virginal in the music room. She was playing as I watched, but trailed off into silence after only a few bars. She stood and went to the doorway of the room in which I usually sat when I was hoping to hear her sing. She looked in and stood for a moment with her hand on the door frame staring into the empty room. Then, chewing her lip, she went back to the virginal and sat down again. She played another few bars, but stopped once more, staring down at her hands. Then she rose and, hugging herself thoughtfully, left the room. The image faded and again I was looking into my own study, inhabited only by myself. I closed the curtains and began to pace.

Was Isabeau the one? Did I truly love her?

I had to stop and grasp the back of the chair by the fire as it abruptly became difficult to breathe. The prospect of closely examining my feelings for Isabeau was less attractive than trying to remember the details of the cursing.

I took a deep, shaking breath. I had to answer this, and answer as honestly as I could. I knew myself to be infatuated with her. That I could admit. She was the first woman I had seen in all the countless years I had lived here and was at the very least—all bias aside—a very attractive one. Of course I was infatuated.

So, how am I to tell whether what I feel is infatuation or love? My grandmother's plea echoed in my head. *Does Isabeau understand me?* I asked myself. *Does her heart beat in accord with mine? How can I know that? I can only answer for how I feel!* But what was that? I searched through my memories of all the books and poems I had ever read that dealt with love.

Most of them spoke at length about their beloved's beauty and charm, but I brushed such considerations aside impatiently. Isabeau could never not be beautiful. Even with her hair blown awry by the wind, and her nose red from the cold. *Especially then.* As for *charm*, how inadequate a word to describe Isabeau's unforced passion and honesty, her strength, her courage, her compassion and the unfeigned delight she had shown at the things I had contrived to please her. *Of course,* the voice of reason in my head insisted, *any drowning man will think the log that saves him the most beautiful and charming object he has ever seen.* I tried a different tack.

What if she left at the end of her year and I did not see her again? I forced myself to consider this very real prospect—after all, what possible inducement was there for her to stay beyond the year? Could I wait for another maiden and try to woo her? I tugged at my collar; it felt suddenly tight and my study strangely airless. Was there another woman like Isabeau in all the world? How long would I have to wait before I found someone in whose company I felt so at home? With a pang I recalled the scene I had just witnessed in the mirror; I was sure she had missed me this morning, also.

Then, an image rose in my mind of Isabeau covered in roses: my dream. I remembered how, before ever I met her, I dreamed of her lifting a white rose to her lips, and then giving it to me, suffused with crimson. When I had awoken, the sense my dream was some sort of portent had been irresistible.

My fur prickled. Of course: the magic.

Nothing random ever happened here. I had no way of knowing the reach of this curse—if somehow Isabeau had been searched out and brought here. The Fairy had said herself: curses have a way of breaking when the time comes.

So was it time? For so many years, my quest to assert my humanity had been all for myself. Now I had a new object and that was Isabeau. She made me want to be a better person, even if it was only to be worthy of her friendship. If she was to leave me, Beast or human, I would be desolate.

I looked down at my hideous, beastly paws. Thickly furred on the back; black, leathery palms; and those terrible claws I could not sheathe. I was overcome with shame. *Who am I to love such a one as her?*

Just as quickly, my shame turned to anger. My talons sank into the back of the chair. *My heart is human!* I cried in my mind.

In a moment I was decided. If I could not win Isabeau's heart, remaining in this beastly form was only a darker shadow over an already bleak and intolerable future. This was my chance. Now I just had to hope that somehow the impossible would occur, and Isabeau would grow to love me, too.

CHAPTER XVIII

*A*nyone who has ever fallen in love will know that when the realization strikes—that you love that person above all others and want to spend all the rest of your days by their side—this is accompanied by an urge to run and shout it from the mountain-tops. Discovering you are in love is by no means an everyday experience, and when you do it feels inconceivable that the rest of the world will not notice the sudden, significant shift in the quality of the light, the bouquet of the air, the increased beauty of everything, and come to a realization of the underlying cause. Thus, it was very difficult for me to refrain from running to find Isabeau to acquaint her with the details of my revelation.

I could hardly expect her to feel anything for me at present other than, perhaps, friendship. But I knew I could not sit idly by and just hope for more. If I wanted her to love me in return, it would take some kind of action on my part—but what? I did not want to offend her, nor—God forbid—make her feel hunted and afraid. Perhaps it would be best to lay my cards on the table, as it were, and leave her to think it over. At least if she knew what my intentions were, she would not feel as though she had been tricked or manipulated.

I looked out of the window and the light told me it was now early afternoon. This was normally the time I would meet Isabeau in the library if she had asked me to read to her that day. My sixth sense immediately told me this was where she was. Waiting for me, perhaps? I rose from my chair and started toward the door, then froze. What would I say to her? Could I blithely walk in and take up a book and begin reading, as if nothing of significance had happened today? My courage failed me and I backed into my chair and sat down again. I needed time to prepare myself.

I took a few deep breaths. Perhaps . . . perhaps I could tell her at dinner, tonight. It had to be today, I told myself. I could give myself the rest of the day to think on this, but I only had what remained of the year to win her over. This was precious little when the better part of a century had not been enough time to reconcile me to myself. Dinner then. All that remained was for me to invite her.

Isabeau had now left the library, apparently having given up on meeting me there. As I sat in my chair and procrastinated, she went on one of her rambles through my vast and sprawling house. I tracked her for some time, until she reached the portrait gallery. At that point I gathered what I could of my unreliable courage and determined I would meet her in the anteroom at the far end. I left my study and went there to wait.

Isabeau's progress along the gallery was always slow and at first I thought this would give me time to further compose myself. However, I entered the anteroom when she was but halfway along, and the many minutes I had to wait soon turned into a kind of torture. I had to keep reminding myself I was only asking her to dine with me; the real test was to be met this evening. Eventually she came to the end of the gallery, spending, as she always did, a few minutes contemplating the blank wall where my own portrait should have appeared. I went to stand by the window, where she would see me directly as she came in.

A few moments later she entered, and while she had evidently not been expecting me, her face broke into a smile.

"Beast!" she exclaimed. "You did not come to the music room today. Or the library."

"I apologize," I said, bowing. "I . . . had some things to attend to."

"I missed you," she said, smiling.

A tingling warmth spread throughout my body. I felt almost giddy and when I spoke, I could not keep my intense pleasure from my voice.

"You missed me?" I asked, hardly daring to believe I had heard her correctly. It was one thing to watch her leave the music room in apparent disappointment, but quite another to hear the words from her own lips.

"Well, yes," she said, looking slightly embarrassed now. "I can't shower myself with praise like you do," she added lightly. I could not help but smile.

"I will not stay away again," I promised her. There was a slight pause and I took a deep breath. "I apologize for leaving you alone for so much of the day, Isabeau. I was wondering if you would like to dine with me again this evening?"

"Of course," said Isabeau, looking puzzled at the gravity of my air.

"Thank you," I said and bowed and turned to go.

"Beast!" said Isabeau again and I halted. She hesitated, as

though she, too, was gathering her courage to ask her question. "Could you tell me . . . there is a space at the end of the gallery where another painting once hung. What happened to it?"

It was now my turn to hesitate. How much could I tell her without breaching the Fairy's condition of secrecy?

"There was," I said carefully. "I had it taken down."

Isabeau frowned. "Why?"

"It disturbed me," I said eventually.

"May I ask where it is now?" said Isabeau, looking at me searchingly.

"It is in the attic," I said quietly, half wanting her to find it and see it, and half afraid she would. "You may go and look at it if you like."

"You would not mind?" she asked, curiously.

"Of course not," I said. "There is nowhere here you may not go."

She thanked me and I took my leave of her. As I went, Isabeau stared after me with a puzzled expression on her face. I hoped I had not been too abrupt.

I retreated once more to my study and attempted to compose how I would address Isabeau that evening. I remembered how I had upset her the first time we had dined together, when in something of a passion I had demanded she tell me if she considered me fit to marry. Naturally I did not want to repeat that scene. I wanted to go gently, prepare her for something uncomfortable, but assure her no reprisal would follow the refusal she would of course give me. I wrote out words and threw them into the fire. I paced about, rehearsing speeches. Once more I shredded the fabric covering the arms of my favorite chair. Eventually I decided I was trying far too hard and, desperate for some distraction to bring some peace to my buzzing brain, I went to the mirror again to see what Isabeau's family was up to.

This time I saw not their house, but a muddy street in what must have been the village nearby. On the opposite side was an inn, the painted sign hanging over the door declaring it to be the Crossed Keys. Claude was hurrying along, wrapped in a heavy shawl and trying to avoid the mud and icy puddles. Beside the inn was a small field, dotted with trees currently bare of leaves. A few stout wooden tables under the trees closest to the inn indicated its use as additional seating in a more clement season.

Claude entered the inn and the image of the street faded, replaced by what was evidently the interior of the tavern. A sturdy, rosy-cheeked woman hailed her and bid her take a seat, then disappeared through a door behind the counter. Shortly Marie appeared, dressed in a large apron.

"Have you eaten?" she called across the largely empty room. Claude shook her head. "One moment!" cried Marie and vanished again. She reappeared carrying a bowl of stew and some bread on a plate. She made her way over to Claude and kissed her, then put the bowl in front of her sister with a strange smile.

"You must be frozen," said Marie. "Try this, it will warm you."

Claude protested at first, saying she was not so hungry, but Marie insisted. Eventually she relented and Marie watched her carefully as she took a spoonful. At first I thought the attention she focused on her sister meant Marie was still worried about Claude eating enough, but as Claude tasted the stew her eyebrows rose and she looked up in surprise.

"Marie, this is so good!" she exclaimed. "It is just like Loussard used to make!"

Marie broke into a delighted grin.

"Well, the cuts of meat are perhaps not so choice," she said with an attempt at modesty, "but I think I have cracked his secret for the flavoring of it!"

"Well done!" said Claude, taking another mouthful and clearly savoring the taste. "I hope you wrote it down. Will you bring some back for dinner tonight? Papa would love it."

"Yes, I'll bring some," said Marie, sitting back in her chair. "But I have tasted it so often this afternoon, I think my tongue is numb."

Just then the door of the inn opened and a gentleman walked in, followed by a manservant. He wore clothes that were evidently fine, without being at all ostentatious. He went and stood by the fire to warm himself, passing Marie and Claude on his way. As he passed, Claude followed him with her eyes, although very demurely, and I doubt he noticed her watching him.

"Who is that?" she asked, after he had gone by.

"I think," said Marie uncertainly, "it must be the Vicomte de Villemont. He has an estate hereabouts where he spends a lot of time. I heard he grew up there. Madame Minou speaks very highly of him. He is apparently very generous to his tenants and is well liked around here."

"He is very handsome," said Claude sadly, returning to her stew.

"Yes, he is," said Marie in a knowing tone.

Claude raised mournful eyes to her sister.

"Please don't tease me," she begged. "I have had enough of handsome, rich men, no matter how good they are. My heart has been broken once and that was enough. I just want to live with you and Papa until I die." She looked down at her plate again, her lip trembling.

Unseen, Marie rolled her eyes, but then relented and reached over and patted her sister's hand.

"Come now," she said soothingly.

Behind them, the gentleman, having chased the chill from his bones, went to sit at a table not far away. He had noticed the sisters and was now watching them intently, but in a way that suggested he would prefer them not to notice him. As Claude finished her lunch in silence, Madame Minou appeared with a tray of food and wine for the gentleman. As she set it down she said something to him, smiling, and then placed the bowl of what looked very like Marie's stew before him. He looked at it with interest and tasted it, and evidently found it to his liking. Madame Minou laughed and indicated Marie. They continued to speak for a few minutes, and I thought perhaps, from the way they frequently looked over at Marie and Claude, he questioned her about the sisters.

"Ah!" exclaimed Claude, pulling my attention back from the newcomer. "But I almost forgot!" She bent down to lift her basket onto the bench beside her. "You are going to say I am extravagant, but I could not resist, and it was only a few copper coins." She pulled an object wrapped in a plain handkerchief from the basket and set it before Marie. Marie looked at her wonderingly and unwrapped it. It was a carved wooden dog. It sat up on its hind legs, its paws raised, an eager expression on its endearing little face. As Marie turned it over, it became apparent a handle set into its back opened the jaws of its pointed muzzle.

"Oh, Claude," she said.

"You know why I had to have it," said Claude defensively, taking back the wooden dog. She looked fondly at it, her broken heart apparently forgotten. Marie shook her head.

"You goose," she said.

I stared at the little dog in Marie's hand and wondered what its significance was.

"Do you think Papa will mind very much if I put it on the mantelpiece?" Claude asked, her hands in her lap and her attention on the carving. Marie shrugged and a wry look crossed her face.

"He spends so much time avoiding looking at Isabeau's box," she said, "I doubt he'd notice if we mounted a boar's head above the fireplace."

"Oh, Marie!" said Claude, shuddering, by which I understood hearths ornamented by boars' heads to be worse than passé. Then she looked about the inn with interest, her glance resting only momentarily on the newcomer. She smiled politely as her eye caught his, but she did not pay any more attention to him.

"Monsieur Dufour has not come yet?" she asked.

"He was here early," said Marie, "but is returning this afternoon."

"And will you ride home with him again today?" Claude asked, her voice a little *too* carefully neutral.

"Yes, he promised to bring me my hens today," said Marie, hurrying to explain.

"Ah, the hens," said Claude, and this time she could not keep the mischief from her voice.

"I can hardly carry the cages home myself!" protested Marie.

"But if it were not for the hens, you would surely walk home," returned Claude saucily.

"Really, Claude," said Marie, giving in to exasperation, her cheeks pink. "I may not tease you, yet I have to endure such insinuations!"

"Your lover has not broken your heart and turned you away

without a word," said Claude primly, taking back the dog and rewrapping it in its kerchief.

"He is hardly my lover!" exclaimed Marie in an embarrassed whisper. Claude waved a hand impatiently.

"*And*, lover or not, this is the first time I have ever had the opportunity to tease you about such things, whereas you have been taking liberties with me for years. And while I will admit the argument you are about to make, that your teasing was not unfounded, I will point out that therefore you have to bow to my greater experience in these matters when I declare him to be your beau!"

Claude stood up, smiling triumphantly, pushing her empty bowl away. She picked up her basket and returned the wooden dog to it.

"Why don't you bring home enough of your ragout for four and ask him to dinner?" she asked. "It is about time he had a meal with us—at the very least so he does not have to drive all the way home again on an empty belly, after so kindly filling the henhouse *he* built for you."

With that she left. Marie stood, staring after her with a look on her face of utter confusion. This was very shortly replaced by one of real pleasure when the door of the inn opened again and another young man walked in. His clothes were rather plainer than the gentleman's and more suited to practical, physical work. But they were well cut and spoke of a man who had resources enough to employ a good tailor. When he saw Marie his own broad, handsome face lit up with delight.

"Mademoiselle de la Noue!" he said happily. "I hoped to find you here. Minou said I should this afternoon."

Marie went very red, looking considerably less sure of herself than I had hitherto seen her.

"I have your hens," he added.

"Thank you kindly," Marie replied, standing up hurriedly. "I confess I hoped you would bring them this week."

"Ah, I promised, did I not?" asked the man who could only be René Dufour.

"I didn't like to presume," she responded, looking down at her hands. At this point, Dufour caught sight of the gentleman sitting at the table behind Marie.

"Sir! Good afternoon to you!" he cried, bowing to him.

"Monsieur Dufour, how do you do?" asked the gentleman, rising from his seat. He sounded genuinely pleased to see Dufour, although also slightly abashed, as though he was naturally rather shy. Dufour made his way over and the two shook hands.

"Will you introduce your friend to me?" the gentleman asked, looking at Marie.

Dufour turned to beckon her and said, "Sir, may I present to you Mademoiselle Marie de la Noue? Her family has only recently moved into this area. Mademoiselle, this is the Vicomte de Villemont. You will have heard of his good works from my sister."

Marie went forward and curtsied to him, and he bowed politely to her.

"Er, that was your sister, whom you spoke with earlier?" asked Villemont. He sounded anxious, whether because he found making conversation with strangers trying, or because he was very eager to know the answer. Possibly it was a little of both.

"Yes, sir," said Marie. "My sister Claude. My youngest sister Isabeau is currently away from home." I felt a guilty jolt and saw a tiny crease appear between Dufour's eyebrows. *Does he know?* I wondered sadly.

"And you live in the old cottage out by the forest?" asked Villemont, frowning.

"Yes, sir," replied Marie.

"That is a long distance for your sister to walk, is it not?" asked Villemont, sounding genuinely concerned. "If she is walking home," he added.

"It is quite a distance," said Marie in a tone that made me think she was now trying to set the young Vicomte at his ease, "but we are growing used to it." She curtsied again and, with another smile at Dufour, she returned to the kitchen.

Unwilling to draw the curtains on the scene at the inn and return to my own troubled thoughts, I continued to watch the two men as they had a short discussion about what the Vicomte could best do with a particular piece of land on his estate. It was an ordinary enough topic, but it held me enraptured. Once, I had held such conversations with my fellow men. Now I grew rose gardens in a night and no one cared where I put them or what other uses I might make of my grounds. When they had done, the Vicomte hesitatingly asked Dufour if it was correct Isabeau's father was previously in business in the city. Dufour replied he had been and gave the Vicomte a description of what he understood his interests to have been, based on what Marie had told him. The Vicomte thanked him and after Dufour had taken his leave of him, he remained staring at his empty plate with a thoughtful expression for some minutes. Eventually his manservant returned to tell him his horse was ready and he left.

The glass had little of interest to show me after that and I found myself in a quandary, wondering how I might spend the time until dinner. I was filled with a nervous restlessness, and decided physical activity was warranted. I went to the dusty gallery upstairs where I usually went to fence with shadows and phantoms and spent an hour trying to work off the strange energy consuming me.

Eventually, I determined I ought to dress for dinner. I lingered and dawdled on my way to my rooms and fussed over the clothes that appeared for me to wear, but still I was ready early. I was also still restless and perhaps my invisible servants recognized this. For, when no more could be done to make me any more presentable, I turned to find a cup of chamomile tea sitting on the small table at my elbow. This made me laugh, as I could not remember having tasted it since childhood. I sat myself down on the edge of my armchair and drank half of it very quickly, despite its heat. Then I took some deep breaths and settled more comfortably into the chair, forcing myself to drink the remainder of the tea more slowly. Something had a good effect because by the time I had finished it, some knot of tension had loosened, and I felt calmer. It was not as though I did not know what answer to expect from Isabeau, I told myself. I was quite prepared for that. I just hoped what I was about to do would not completely ruin the tenuous friendship we had established.

CHAPTER XIX

After the tea was gone, I went downstairs to wait for Isabeau in my usual place by the stairs. Although I was still earlier than usual, I did not have long to wait at all.

There was another pleasant surprise in her appearance. Since the evening when I conjured fireworks for her, Isabeau had been wearing much simpler attire to dinner, as she had expressed a wish to do. But tonight, if the dress she wore was not as fine as the one she had worn on the night of the fireworks, it was very nearly so. This time she looked like a queen in gold silk and velvet the color of amber, with a wreath of glittering golden gems at her throat. Her heavy, honey-colored hair was caught back in a net of gold threads, scattered with pearls. Her face told me she was feeling self-conscious, but her jaw was set in a way that suggested she was determined to overcome this. As she arrived at the bottom of the staircase, I offered her my arm.

"You decided to dress up again tonight?" I asked her, looking down at her. Isabeau kept looking straight ahead.

"Yes," she said, offering no explanation. I felt a compliment was in order, but did not want to overdo it and embarrass her.

"That color becomes you very well," I said at last and was justly rewarded when her shoulders relaxed a fraction and she smiled up at me. I have to admit, at that moment, I very nearly decided to abandon my determination to propose to her. She looked so very lovely, and as I glanced down at her slender white hand resting on the velvet sleeve above my own hairy paw, I cringed at my audacity. To pair such a one as her with a creature like myself seemed very wrong. A heavy sigh escaped me and Isabeau looked up at me again in alarm.

"Beast, is something wrong?" she asked.

"No," I replied, shaking my head—as much to disperse my misgivings as to emphasize the negative. "Forgive me, my mind was elsewhere."

Isabeau's brow creased in a puzzled frown, but she said nothing.

As we entered the dining room and saw the banquet laid out for the two of us, I became conscious of an unusual and entirely delicious aroma. Isabeau noticed it, too, and she looked around at the array of dishes.

"Is that . . . ?" she asked, but left the question hanging. We sat down and Isabeau, her face expectant, uncovered the dish closest to her. It became immediately apparent this was where the aroma issued from and Isabeau laughed in delight.

"It is!" she cried, revealing a dish remarkably similar to that which Marie had served up to Claude that afternoon. "I don't believe it. Here, Beast, you must try some." Curiosity reignited the appetite nerves had previously dispensed with and I assented, a silver ladle moving of its own to serve me.

"What is it?" I asked.

"Mm!" murmured Isabeau, savoring the first mouthful from her plate. "My father employed a rather brilliant chef when we lived in the city. This was his signature dish, and he made a great to-do about never revealing the secret of the ingredients. He claimed the recipe had been passed to him in the strictest confidence by his master when he had finally mastered his trade. We were never sure whether to believe him or not."

I wondered to myself at this dish turning up on our dinner table on the very night Isabeau's family was apparently sitting down to the same meal. As well as tasting very good, it had the pleasant effect of causing Isabeau to become very talkative, reminiscing about Loussard the chef and his idiosyncrasies for some time. This was very convenient for me, as I did not feel up to making conversation that evening. I was content to listen.

Eventually, though, Isabeau ceased talking, and after we had been sitting in silence for a few minutes, she said, "Beast, have I done something to upset you?"

"No," I said, surprised. "Not at all. Why do you ask?"

"You have been so quiet tonight and I have barely seen you all day." She set her spoon aside and looked at me carefully. "I confess my story about the meringue tower disaster usually makes most people smile at least. You look so very grim. Are you sure there is nothing wrong?"

"I am sorry. I am just distracted," I said, realizing the time had come. I took up my wine glass and looked down at it, dreading to look up into her face. When I did, I saw that same look of concern.

"Isabeau, forgive me, I must ask you a question," I said heavily.

"Of course," she said curiously.

"Please understand I need you to give me an honest answer," I said, looking directly into her eyes so she might know I meant it. "There will be no reprisals for giving me an answer you think I may not like."

She nodded and I was relieved to see she did not appear afraid, but the worried expression remained on her face. "I also . . ." I stopped. This was the part it had been so hard to find words for.

"It is an uncomfortable question, I am afraid," I said, "but I do hope it will not make things uncomfortable between us for long."

Isabeau sat looking at me, waiting for the terrible question.

"Isabeau," I said, unable to meet her gaze, "will you marry me?"

I heard her shocked intake of breath and raised my eyes. Her mouth was open and she looked nothing so much as surprised. She stared at me for a few moments and then slowly her cheeks began to grow pink.

"You are serious," she stated, as she realized I was.

"I am," I said quietly.

"Oh, Beast," she said in a choked voice, "what can I tell you?"

"Just give me the answer your heart tells you," I said bravely. She looked quite shocked.

"Oh no, Beast, I couldn't," she said, having the decency to try to hide the horror building in her voice. "I can't, I have to go home to my family, I—"

I held up my hand to quiet her.

"I understand, Isabeau," I said, unable to keep the sadness from my voice. "I expected nothing else."

Isabeau put her hand over her mouth, on the verge of tears.

"Please forgive me for upsetting you. It is not at all what I would wish," I said. And although her answer was exactly as I had expected, a great sorrow settled over my heart. I stood to leave and remembered one more thing.

"Again, I must ask you to forgive me," I said, "but I will have to ask you this question again. I am sorry."

"Must you?" she asked, sounding panicked. "I will never be able to give you a different answer."

"I am afraid so," I answered, remembering the Fairy's words: my only chance. And if she was truly resolved against me, then in less than a year she would be back with her father and sisters and this would only be an unhappy memory. I bowed and left the room.

I did not return to my study, though. It was too familiar, too comfortable, too human. What I wanted was to hide myself and my horrible, beastly form away somewhere dark, in some unlit corner where I truly belonged. And so I ended up in the curtained musician's gallery where I had hidden to spy on Isabeau's father. Here, with the thick crimson drapes pulled close and no lamps to illuminate the space, I could barely see my talons if I held my paw before my face. Here I sat and wept for some time.

Eventually my sobs ceased and in the quiet I heard a noise. My grief exhausted for the present, I pushed aside the heavy velvet drapes the merest crack. Looking down I could see Isabeau, only now returning from the direction of the dining room. She walked quickly, one hand pressed to her bodice, the other to her temple. As she mounted the stairs, she leaned heavily on the banister and when she reached the top, she paused, bending forward as though struggling for breath. She gave a small hiccoughing sob and picked up her skirts and hurried away in the direction of her bedchamber.

I shook my head in dismay, my own feelings suddenly immaterial. I had not wanted to upset her this much. Could I do anything to repair the damage? I stood and made my way back to my study, trying to think of how I could make it up to her. Gifts of any magnitude were largely meaningless in this house, owing to one's ability to conjure just about anything from thin air. But something small, perhaps, just a token to help my apology? And it would also serve to reassure her I meant what I said about there being no punishment for refusing me.

She had often shown a preference for chocolate in selecting desserts. Perhaps I could send something to her room? It seemed fitting as I had all but ruined our dessert this evening.

I arrived at my study and went to my desk. Some elegant notepaper was already placed on the blotter, with a newly sharpened pen beside it. For some reason this made me feel as though my plan had some sort of approval. From whom, I couldn't say.

I seated myself and wrote:

Dear Isabeau,
   Again I apologize for causing you so much distress. Please accept this in the hope it will revive your spirits. I want you to be comfortable in this house

I paused, then added:

   for the duration of your stay.
   Kind regards,

I stopped again, wondering how to sign myself. Eventually I wrote:

   Your friend, the Beast

I folded it neatly and a small silver tray appeared in front of me. I set it on this. Now, what to send her? I decided on a cup of hot chocolate and the tray vanished. A minute or two later I heard, by that strange magical echo in my house, a soft sigh and Isabeau's voice saying quietly, "Thank you, Beast."

I smiled to myself, relieved my gift had been accepted in the spirit in which it was given.

CHAPTER XX

With my breach with Isabeau mended, I decided I would look in on Isabeau's family again—just to see whether or not Marie did invite Dufour to dine with them that evening. I turned from my desk to find my easy chair had moved a little away from the fire to the best position to view the mirror and, as I went and settled into it, the curtains moved aside, revealing the de la Noues' parlor. Dufour and Isabeau's father were seated in two chairs close to the fire, with Claude engaged in some sort of sewing activity on a bench by the wall. Marie was bending down by the hearth, swirling something in a heavy earthenware jug. I noticed Claude's mysterious wooden dog had now joined Isabeau's box on the mantelpiece, as promised.

"Now if I just had some orange peel," Marie murmured, "that would be the very thing."

"The only place you might find oranges around here is in the Vicomte's hothouses—if indeed he has any," said Dufour doubtfully. "What do you want oranges for?"

"I'm sure Loussard used oranges," said Marie wistfully. "It

would just set the other flavors off so nicely." She peered into the jug. "Oh well, shall I pour?"

"Yes, please," said Claude, looking up briefly from her work. "I can smell it from here. Oranges or none, it smells lovely."

"I shall ask the Vicomte if he grows oranges when I see him next," said Dufour, frowning. He leaned forward, his elbows on his knees. "May I be of assistance?"

Marie gave him a self-conscious smile. "No," she said, covering her confusion by handing him a pewter cup filled with mulled wine. "Papa, for you?"

Without waiting for a reply, she poured some gently steaming wine from the jug into another cup and pressed it into her father's hands. She took a third cup over to Claude, who set aside her sewing to take it. Then Marie poured one for herself and sat down on a low stool by her father's chair. Dufour frowned again.

"Are you sure you will not take this chair?" he asked, making as though to rise.

"I will not," Marie demurred. "You will have had enough of hard, uncomfortable wooden seats by the time you arrive home. And yours will not be so warm as mine."

Dufour's frown twitched and became a smile. "You do me no favors," he said. "The seat in my rig will be all the colder and harder now when I go."

I watched them talking easily together for another hour or so. Their poor parlor had nothing like the comfort of any one of the rooms in my house—but I knew where Isabeau would prefer to be at this time. Eventually Dufour rose from his seat. He made his good-byes, regretfully saying he required a certain amount of sleep to be able to fulfill his duties the next day. He bowed to Claude and shook hands with their father, but when it came to Marie, he took her hand and kissed it. Marie went pink and I had to smile at the surprise on her face. Even her father looked pleased, trying to hide his own satisfied smile.

At the door, Claude handed Marie a heavy shawl and blandly suggested she go out with Dufour to light his way to the tumbledown shelter beside the cottage where his horse was stabled.

"Please, do not trouble yourself," said Dufour instantly. "It is far too cold!"

"Don't be silly," said Marie, looking self-conscious. "It is far too dark!" She gave Claude a furious glare as she turned to take the lamp from her.

However, after Dufour had harnessed his horse and ridden out through the gate looking perfectly content with life, Marie stood outside in the cold, looking after him for quite some time.

When she arrived back inside, Claude was pouring her father more wine.

"I like that young man," Isabeau's father announced to Marie as she replaced the lamp on its hook. Marie looked pleased and became very busy divesting herself of her shawl. Claude watched her with a smug smile on her face.

"He has been very kind to us," said Marie, a little too blandly.

Isabeau's father took several more sips of his wine, then drained the remainder in one draft.

"Well, I, too, must go to my bed," he said, rising. Claude began to fold away her sewing.

"And I," she agreed. "Will you come up now, Marie?" she asked.

"Not just yet," said Marie. "I have a few things to do before I go to bed. I will be along shortly."

When her father and sister had left, she went and fetched her pen and paper from the kitchen and, taking her book to lean on, settled herself with a self-conscious smile into the chair Dufour had only recently vacated. Then she began to write to her sister.

"Dear Isabeau, we have just passed the most pleasant evening," she began. "Today Claude insisted I invite Monsieur Dufour to dine with us this evening. She made it sound as though it would be the height of rudeness not to, given he brought me a present of three hens for my new henhouse. So I did, and how glad I am! We have all of us talked the evening away as though we are old friends and even Papa took the trouble to say how much he liked him. I am so comforted he has found a friend with whom he can talk with such ease!"

Here she stopped for a moment and her smile became a disconcerted frown.

"I now have only one problem," she wrote, her cheeks growing pink. "Claude has begun declaring he is my beau. I do not know what to say to her. I do like Monsieur Dufour very much, but I dare not contemplate anything of the sort. I cannot begin to think he might have any particular affection for me. The very thought is ridiculous."

She stopped and looked down at what she had written, frowning.

"Still, I would very much like for you to meet him so I might hear your opinion of him. He is kind and good and amusing. He manages Papa very well and he is even gallant enough to say he likes my cooking. I would never tell Claude in a hundred years, but if you will keep my secret, I will own he is very handsome.

"Isabeau, you will think me such a goose!"

Marie stopped and spent a good minute staring thoughtfully into the fire. Then she remembered her letter and dipped her pen once more in her inkpot.

"Speaking of my cooking, can you guess what we had for dinner tonight? I believe I have found out the much-guarded secret of our friend Loussard's special ragout. I was at the Crossed Keys again today and, as I was making up the normal pot of stew for the evening's dinner, I thought to make it a little more interesting with some of the ingredients from my spice chest. I was trying to decide which to put in and as I sniffed at one (a curious little star-shaped nut with a pungent odor) the combination of its scent and the aromas from the stew reminded me of Loussard's ragout. I thought it would be fun to try to recreate it. It isn't quite the same, but it was so nearly right both Claude and Papa recognized it at once. And Minou said she thought it was quite the best stew she'd ever tasted! I also received a number of compliments from the people who came to the inn for dinner before I left. So of course I am feeling very satisfied with myself. My only misgiving is—what if Loussard himself should ever find out his own ragout is being served without his permission at a simple country inn somewhere? I've had nightmarish visions of him looking fierce and pulling on that terrifying mustache of his and banging his pans at me!

"I also met the local Vicomte today. He came to the inn while I was there. He is tolerably good-looking—at least Claude thought so. I tried to tease her about him, but she reproached me on the grounds of insensitivity to her broken heart and I couldn't in conscience continue. According to Minou, he asked a great many questions about us and, although I didn't feel it was perhaps quite necessary, had our entire history related to him by her. Minou seems to think it *was* necessary, however. He was apparently greatly saddened to hear the tale of our being reduced to our current situation. He has a notoriously soft heart and Minou is sure he intends to try to find something he can do to assist us in our present difficulties. I know Minou meant well, but I have not told Papa or Claude of this as I'm sure they would not be at all comfortable knowing our difficulties are being so discussed. (I am not sure I am so very comfortable about it either.)

"On a more amusing note, do you know what Claude has done? Today she bought a carved wooden nutcracker in the shape of a dog. While I will own a nutcracker is a very practical thing, I do not think she was thinking of cracking nuts with it. No. She bought it because its dear little face has something in it of your darling Bijou. She has put it up on the mantelpiece. Dear Claude, I am certain whenever she looks at it she doesn't see a wooden nutcracker on a shelf in our poor bare parlor, she sees Joujou sitting on a velvet cushion in the morning room of our old house, with a satin bow about her neck.

"That is something very particular to our Claude, I find: the ability to treasure an object for the beauty it implies rather than for just itself. Perhaps that is why she is able to glean such satisfaction from a newly swept floor, or a well-hemmed kerchief. I believe you and she are similar in that way, only your talent lies more with people. For example, you were the only one of us who was never terrified of Loussard. This gives me some hope you will perhaps find something worthy in the Beast that Papa was not able to discern. Perhaps he is truly a lamb in wolves' clothing?

"At least he appears to be a generous Beast. Truly, due to him we are a household of the strangest contrasts! We have a rustic wooden nutcracker to decorate our mantelpiece, while upstairs in our bedrooms both Claude and I have caskets overflowing with jewels. We dine off the ugliest pottery imaginable, and our pillows are thin and flat, yet our bedlinen is of the finest quality. And this is to say nothing of the comparison between our poor, plain, patched daywear, and the luxurious ball gowns we hide in our chests.

"My final piece of news is that spring is truly arriving now. I wonder if you will notice in the Beast's enchanted gardens. I remember Papa describing flowers and sunlight when he had just come there from a fierce midwinter storm. I have found some clumps of daffodils that must flower soon. I am especially eager for spring to arrive, not just for the greater warmth and fewer drafts it will bring to our poor house, but because Monsieur Dufour has cautioned me against planting my first lot of seeds too early. I anxiously await his instruction to begin poking around in my mostly bare patch of dirt. My only misgiving is I know the warmer weather will make the journey from here to the village that much muddier. Oh well."

Here Marie paused again and her face broke into a mischievous smile.

"I am going now to sleep and dream some dreams of handsome farmers (I hope)," she wrote. "Au revoir!"

Marie signed her name and folded the letter, then sat looking at it for a few moments, her smile gone and her brow creased in a worried frown.

"Oh, Isabeau," she whispered in the dark. "I hope he is good. I hope his intentions are noble." For a moment I thought she was entertaining inexplicable doubts about Dufour, and then I realized: she meant me. Clearly she put only her most positive thoughts about Isabeau's situation into her letters, and that despite her continued outward optimism, she was still troubled by doubts. *Why would she not be?* I wondered bitterly.

I watched her place the letter in Isabeau's box, then bank the fire. As she gathered her book and writing implements, my view of the parlor began to fade. *At least*, I thought, trying to find something to lift my spirits, *Marie could not have written kinder words about me to Isabeau, or words that might better further my suit, if I had asked her.*

CHAPTER XXI

When I awoke the next morning, after more sleep than I had anticipated, but less than was really pleasant, I remembered with mixed relief and regret my promise to Isabeau not to miss another session in the music room. If I had not promised her, I do not know if I could have brought myself to attend. I was not sure if she would come down, or how she would feel about playing to me this morning, so I found a seat in the room next door.

A short time later, my heart lurched as I heard her enter the music room. There were a few more small sounds, then some moments of quiet, and then Isabeau appeared in the doorway. She looked anxious, but when she saw I was there, she managed to smile.

"Beast," she said, "you did come after all."

"I did promise," I said, standing up, "but I can leave again if you wish."

"Not at all," she said and paused, coloring slightly. "But I do not think I will sing today, so you may sit inside if you wish. I mean, I would be pleased if you would."

"That would give me very great pleasure," I said, relieved. She turned back into the music room and I followed her, seating my-self near a window where I could see her clearly. She walked to the virginal, but just as she reached it, she turned back to face me.

"Thank you very much for the chocolate last night," she said, still sounding self-conscious. "It was very kind, after . . ." She swallowed her words, but before I could speak she plowed ahead. "I regret the pain my answer must have caused you."

"Do not concern yourself," I answered, overwhelmingly grateful she clearly had.

"I do hope you will continue to think of me as your friend," she said anxiously. I had the sense there was still some remaining point of concern for her she had not yet voiced.

"Of course," I said. She was silent for another few moments, looking down at her hands, twisting her fingers together.

"Beast," she said at last, "I, too, have no wish to make things between us uncomfortable. Yesterday I questioned you about that missing painting. I had thought I would go and look at it, but then I thought if you would rather I didn't—"

"No," I interrupted her and rushed on before any of my own misgivings about the portrait could assert themselves. "Isabeau, you should go and look at it. Then perhaps you could give me your opinion of it."

She looked at me as though to gauge my sincerity.

"I am aware my feelings about the painting may not be en-tirely rational," I confessed.

Isabeau smiled. "Fancy, a great Beast like you, afraid of a little painting," she said, finally seating herself at the virginal.

"Oh, it's not little," I replied, more pleased than I could say by her teasing. "It's quite enormous."

"That will never do," said Isabeau, shaking her head and

playing a chord. She gave me a look of mock severity. "I will brook no excuses."

She began to play in earnest and I settled into my chair to listen, happier and more at ease than I dreamed possible after the fiasco of my proposal the previous night. Isabeau played on, but after a time I noticed her playing began to slow and she adopted a more thoughtful tone. Eventually she stopped and was silent for a minute. Then she looked up at me.

"If I went to look at it now," she asked, "would you come with me?"

"If you wished it," I answered, trying to ignore an over-whelming sense of dismay. The hair at the back of my neck prickled at the thought of confronting my portrait again, with Isabeau as a witness. Viewing it was like undertaking a personal pilgrimage—intensely private and not to be embarked upon lightly. And to tell the truth, I had not anticipated seeing it again so soon. But Isabeau had asked me to go with her. Of course I would accompany her. Before she could be put off by my an-tipathy, I rose and went to her, offering my arm.

"You will be pleased to know this attic is somewhat more accessible than the roof," I said to her, by way of preventing any misgivings on her part. Still, she looked at me doubtfully as though my bravado was completely transparent. "Although there is at least one set of very steep stairs."

"Are you—?" she began, but I cut her off.

"As you say," I told her, "it is only a painting."

She gave me another searching look, but then rose and took my arm. I led her through the house to the steps ascending to the attic, wondering if I would indeed have the courage to go in with her.

"Beast," Isabeau asked as we walked, "what sort of painting is it?"

"It is a portrait like the others," I answered, shortly. To tell the truth I was now beginning to be apprehensive she would ask me who it was in the picture, or what his relationship was to me—or worse, she might recognize my eyes and guess the rest. I was beginning to become afraid I was too close to revealing the curse and its nature to Isabeau.

"I guessed as much," said Isabeau wryly.

"Forgive me," I said, trying to compose myself. "It is a portrait of a young man. But, rather than have me describe it to you, perhaps it might be best for you to wait until you see it. I *did* say my response to it is not entirely rational."

I shrugged, trying to smile. She raised her eyebrows at me, but did not ask me any further questions.

Eventually we came to the narrow flight of stairs leading up to the attic. Isabeau peered up at them cautiously, and I asked her, "Will you be able to manage these?"

"I should think so," she said, and gathered up her skirts. I watched her ascend for a moment, then took a deep breath and followed her. She waited for me inside the door of the attic room, even though she no longer needed me as a guide. We could see the painting from where we stood. Isabeau looked at me as I stood inside the door, but when I made no move to approach the painting, she left my side and went over to it by herself.

I looked everywhere but at the portrait itself. It was quite obvious I had visited the portrait in the not-too-distant past. It was the only uncovered object in the room without a mantle of dust, and a set of large footprints also tracked across the dusty floor. Isabeau noticed these upon reaching the painting and glanced back at me, but she still did not say anything. Then she turned to scrutinize the painting itself. She spent some time looking up into my painted human face. So much time, in fact, I began to wonder what she was thinking. Eventually, she bent down to examine the tiny gilded plate at the base of the frame where the words *Julien Courseilles, Marquis de la Tour*, were inscribed. Then she rose and came away, with a thoughtful expression on her face.

"Well?" I managed, gruffly.

She looked up at me and shook her head. "I am afraid I see nothing sinister, Beast," she said. "I cannot account for your reaction." Then she walked ahead of me out of the attic and picked her way back down the stairs.

As I came behind her, I was assailed by a curious mix of thoughts and emotions. Primarily I was grateful she had made no teasing remarks about him being handsome or otherwise, in comparison to my own horrid appearance. However, a strange curiosity began to assert itself. Did she find the man in the portrait handsome? What did she think of my human face? I could not bear to dwell on this question, but it lodged in my mind like a burr in my pelt. All in all, I was now so unsettled and out of sorts I made my excuses to her and turned to go.

"Beast," she called out, as I walked away. I stopped. "I am sorry if that discomforted you. Do you think you can bring yourself to read to me this afternoon?"

I got the distinct impression she was doing her best to avoid any continuation of the awkwardness that had plagued our relations of late.

"Of course," I said, offering a short bow. "I would be pleased to."

She smiled at me radiantly and now it was my turn to stand and watch her walk away, smitten to helpless immobility as I was.

CHAPTER XXII

Usually when we met in the library of an afternoon, I arrived some minutes before Isabeau. That afternoon, however, Isabeau was there first. She was leaning on her elbows over a desk, immersed in a large folio. There were several others spread out over the desk as well. She looked up and smiled as I entered and on approaching her I found all the books she was examining were volumes of botanical illustrations.

"Ah, Beast," she said, straightening up, "you see me trying to find inspiration to fuel my new resolution."

Whether or not she was persisting with her efforts to avoid any further discomfort between us, I was grateful she had initiated a conversation I could join with relative ease.

"Will you tell me what it is?" I asked.

"Of course," she answered. "Looking at all your beautiful paintings has inspired me to try my hand at drawing again, now I have the leisure."

"Again?" I asked.

"Oh yes, a drawing master is an indispensible part of the education of all young ladies," said Isabeau, with a sardonic twist to her mouth. "Even those who haven't the slightest inclination. I'm thinking of my sisters," she added. "They both hated it."

She smiled again. "I can't offer you any comment on the quality of my work, but I did enjoy it. Although," she added somewhat quickly, "I have never pretended to be any good at drawing likenesses of people. I have always been happy to confine myself to studies of flowers and other things that don't move, and won't get offended if my pictures don't end up looking precisely like the subject."

"I am glad of that," I said, a small twinge of anxiety evaporating, "as you would find subjects for portraits sadly lacking here. Flowers I have in abundance."

She laughed and indicated the folios before her.

"I thought, as I also lack a drawing master, I might refer to these," she said, then looked at me expectantly. "Unless, of course, this is one of your own talents?"

I shook my head. "Alas, no. I never picked up a pen to sketch in my life, even—" I stopped abruptly. I had been about to say "even before I had these accursed claws," which would of course have been disastrous. Isabeau looked at me curiously, but when I did not continue she turned back to the books.

"Your library is very obliging," she said. "I had no idea where to look for these, or even if you had any such volumes. But all I had to do was voice my wish and they came flying around the corner and even thoughtfully opened themselves to the most beautiful pages."

"Mmm-hmm," I answered, still distracted by my near-blunder. I heard her sigh and recalled myself. "What shall I read to you today?"

"I found this, too," she said, handing me a volume bound in leather tooled with floral motifs. On inspection it appeared to be the published journal of a lady botanist, describing her ramblings over the countryside and the discoveries she had made thereon. "I thought it was topical, especially if I am going to begin searching your grounds for subjects. I might as well try to increase my knowledge as well as my sense of the aesthetic."

I went and seated myself on a couch by the window, so the light from behind me fell upon the pages. Isabeau found an easy chair a little distance away and settled her feet on a stool that slid across the floor especially for that purpose. I began to read.

I have to admit the journal was not the most scintillating of subject matters and I was unequal to sharing in many of the raptures expressed by the author over her discoveries of certain plants. It was no surprise to me, then, when I looked up at one point to see Isabeau, her cheek resting on her shoulder and her eyes closed. Feeling somehow easier, now that I had gained this advantage over her, I smiled in amusement and continued reading, thinking of how I could tease her when she awoke.

After perhaps half an hour, she began to stir. I waited until she yawned and opened her eyes before I closed the book and laid it aside.

"Did you enjoy that, then?" I asked archly.

"Beast?" she asked wonderingly, straightening up in her chair. There was something strange in her tone, so I rose and went over to her.

"Beast?" she asked again, shrinking into her chair.

"Isabeau, is all well?" I asked, but as I drew close, her expression changed to one of recognition and she relaxed.

"Beast," she said, passing her hand over her eyes, "I must have been . . . the strangest dream . . ." She made to rise and I offered her my arm. She put her hand in my paw and stood.

"Can I get you anything?" I asked.

Isabeau shook her head. "I'm sorry," she said. "I could not see you properly against the light and it seemed you had changed . . ." She frowned and shook herself as though trying to dispel a lingering, unsettling vision. A little prickle of cold ran lightly over my skin, turning it to gooseflesh and lifting my fur.

"Changed?" I asked cautiously, wanting to know more but not wanting to appear too eager. To my disappointment Isabeau shook her head more firmly.

"It is gone. You are here. All is well," she said, then she yawned. "I am afraid if that example is to be taken as a general indication, botanists are not the most interesting of people. You may want to make me promise not to regale you with tales of my own forays into the meadows."

"You know I listen with pleasure to anything you have to tell me," I said sincerely.

Isabeau colored slightly and looked away. "All you have to do now," she said lightly, "is receive my attempts at sketching with the same unstinting praise as you have received my attempts at music and you will be perfect. Indeed, as a consequence, my own opinion of myself will become so inflated that you, so good-natured as you are, will be the only being alive able to tolerate me."

Now it was my turn to look abashed.

"I think I can safely promise you to be just as harsh a critic of your artwork as of your playing," I agreed.

Thus it was on these good terms we parted. As I made my way down to the music room again the next day, as promised, I felt only the pleasantest sense of anticipation at seeing Isabeau. Isabeau, however, when she arrived, looked tired and distracted, as though she had slept badly. She did not play for long, pleading a headache as her excuse, and as she closed up her instrument she declared her intention to walk it off.

"Are you well enough to walk out by yourself?" I pressed.

"Beast, you are overanxious for my health," she said in a way that made me think she was trying to hold her annoyance in check. "If I so much as yawn you ask if I am well. I am not *such* a delicate flower. Until six weeks ago I had managed for a year on an average of five hours' sleep a night and I was spending my days doing all manner of heavy work to boot. I assure you I will survive the odd sleepless night in this haven of leisure."

"Of course," I said, bowing my head in consternation.

Isabeau made an explosive noise and came around the virginal toward me.

"Beast," she said sternly, her hands on her hips, "don't—" She stopped and closed her eyes, took a deep breath and opened them again. "I will only be cross with myself if I think I've gone and hurt your feelings, so please don't take what I just said too much to heart. Friends?" She held out her hand to me. I took it and she covered my paw with her other hand.

"Good," she said firmly. "Now, I just need to clear my head."

I remained in the music room for a while after she left, wondering what I should do now that my usual morning activity had been cut short. In the end, I did as I usually did and went to my study to see what Isabeau's family was doing.

Given the different nature of our lives, Isabeau's sisters and her father naturally rose much earlier in the morning than we did in our "haven of leisure." This morning the view in my mirror showed me Claude, with a basket over her arm walking about a market that had sprung up in the main street of the village near their home. There were a number of parcels and food items already in the basket, which, by the way she kept shifting it on her arm, was heavy enough. As I watched, she concluded a transaction that ended in her becoming the owner of a large, dead goose. The proprietor of the stall expertly unhooked the cord suspending the bird from the rack above and looped it over Claude's wrist, uttering an unkind bark of laughter when she nearly dropped it in the mud, clearly not anticipating the weight. With an expression of determined dignity, Claude left the poultry stall and hesitated before another displaying a range of dress materials. She spent a few moments browsing, but when the dead goose proved too unwieldy and any further burden untenable, she turned away and began to walk down the main street. As she left the village, I realized with some alarm she intended to walk the entire distance home with her goose and her heavy basket.

Indeed, she had not gone far before she put her basket down on a log and changed the goose to her left wrist, the right displaying a series of painful red lines where the cord had dug into her skin. She hoisted her basket up and set off again, frowning as the goose, with its wings open, banged uncomfortably against her legs as she walked. She managed to trudge for a further few minutes before stopping once more to put the basket down again. This time she tried to fit the bird into the basket, on top of her other purchases, but the basket was already mostly full and it was an awkward fit at best. She was so involved in trying to arrange her burden so it would become manageable, she did not notice a horse and rider approaching her from the direction of the village. Just as she uttered a suppressed shriek of frustration, the gentleman pulled his mount up behind her and called out, "Hello, mademoiselle!"

I recognized him as the Vicomte de Villemont. Claude started upright and spun around, shading her eyes against the sparkling morning sunshine.

"Good morning, sir!" she stuttered, clearly feeling herself to be at a disadvantage. The man sat looking at her for a few moments, then recollected himself and dismounted. Claude took a step back, realizing who he was.

"Excuse me, Vicomte," she said, sounding mortified, and dropped an elegant curtsey. Villemont seemed to be embarrassed and momentarily at a loss for something to say. Claude stood with her head respectfully bowed, and in the end I think it might have been a sort of desperation to make her look at him that spurred him on to speak.

"Ah, you don't know me," he started awkwardly, "that is, we have not met, but I believe I was introduced to your sister the other day. You are Mademoiselle Claude de la Noue?"

"Yes, Vicomte," murmured Claude, not looking up.

"Please, allow me to introduce myself. I am Henri Desmarteaux, Vicomte de Villemont. I . . . ah . . ." He trailed off, staring at her hopelessly. She still had not looked up.

"It is an honor, Vicomte," said Claude demurely.

"Have you been at the markets?" he asked after a pause, his expression changing to reflect a level of mortification as he saw what an artless question it was. As Claude opened her mouth to answer he plowed on. "I ask, mademoiselle, because I, ah, observe you are somewhat overburdened. I would be pleased to offer you any assistance I may." Now he was becoming a little more sure of himself.

Claude looked up at him in dismay.

"Oh, no, sir," she said, apparently trying to keep the goose off the ground with one hand and smooth her hair with the other. "Please do not trouble yourself."

"But I insist," he said, a note of desperation creeping into his voice again. "Please, let me at least take the bird from you. I can easily tie it to my saddle."

"No, really, sir," said Claude firmly, giving him a polite but resolute smile. "I am sure your path lies not at all close to my own. I assure you I will manage." At this she bent down to pick up her basket again. This spurred Villemont into his own resolution.

"Don't be ridiculous," he cried. "I absolutely insist." And he bent forward and lifted the goose off her wrist. Evidently he, too, was surprised by its weight, but he went around to the other side of his horse and tied the bird on. He stepped back and viewed the opened wings with some consternation, and conducted a brief search of his pockets and saddlebags for something, and pulled out a linen kerchief. This proved inadequate to the task, however, only making it part of the way about the goose. He stood looking about himself for a few moments more, then struck by inspiration, removed the garter tied just below his right knee, knotted it together with the kerchief and strapped the bird's wings closed. On seeing this, Claude's face broke into a delighted smile, which caused a similar, if not greater reaction in the young man. I had to chuckle. If he had been merely interested before, I was sure he was lost to her now. He ducked back around under the nose of his horse, but by this time Claude had schooled her face into a cooler, more detached expression and she stood demurely looking down again, her basket over her arm. Nevertheless, this seemed to be enough for the Vicomte for now.

"There," he said, still sounding delighted, plucking the basket away from her before she could object. "Much better." He gathered the reins of his horse in his spare hand and they walked on, the basket and a foot or two of space between them. Claude folded her hands in front of her and continued to look modestly at the road beneath her feet.

After a few moments of silence, Villemont, unwilling to lose what he had gained, cleared his throat and said, "Do you usually come to the markets?"

"No, sir," said Claude, looking up at him briefly, "usually my sister comes. But today she had some work she needed to do in her garden and I was hoping to buy some fabric for a dress, but . . ." She mentioned the fabric wistfully, but then seemed to decide, in spite of his obvious interest, the Vicomte could not possibly be concerned with such things. I observed, however, Villemont was suddenly paying attention to the worn state of Claude's clothing. Claude remained supremely impervious to the scrutiny.

"And where are you riding to today, sir?" asked Claude innocently.

Villemont flushed a dark red and I apprehended the object of this little jaunt must have been to see if he might encounter her coming to or from the markets.

"Oh, I just thought to take the air," he stammered. "It's such a fine day, isn't it? Spring so nearly here."

Claude continued on her way serenely, oblivious to his discomfort.

They continued in this manner, with Villemont trying to pique Claude's interest and engage her in conversation, while Claude maintained her untouched, but extremely interesting, politeness, until they reached the small rise over which I knew the cottage lay. At this point Claude stopped and simply refused to let Villemont escort her any farther, stating she had already taken him far too far out of his way. He argued with her as gallantly as he could, but she remained steadfast. Eventually he was resigned to watching her struggle up and over the hill, stopping at the rise for a brief curtsey, while he chewed his lip in a mixture of frustration and exaltation. Finally, when at last her head, with its honey hair so similar to Isabeau's, dipped below the hilltop, he remounted his horse and turned to leave. At this point he realized his garter was still wrapped around the goose. For a few moments he sat, apparently considering whether or not he should retrieve it, but eventually he decided against it and turned his horse and rode slowly away.

That evening, Marie wrote the following letter to Isabeau:

"My dearest Isabeau, I know this is my second letter in a very few days, but today something occurred that I may not discuss with anyone else, and it is so very interesting I could not help but unburden myself to you. But, before I go on, having piqued your curiosity unpardonably I'm sure, I must tell you the suspicions I will now relate may be completely unfounded, the product only of a fond sister's mind.

"Do you remember in my last letter, I told you of the Vicomte de Villemont and how I thought Claude found him handsome? Well, I will now relate to you some other circumstances, most likely quite trivial and innocent. Sadly, however, I cannot help my mischievous mind drawing them together in a more significant relationship.

"Today Claude went to the markets to buy a few things, but I had particularly requested she purchase some kind of bird I might roast for Papa (his appetite has been a little wanting of late and I thought a roast bird might tempt him more than salt pork, but you are not to concern yourself). She came home with the most enormous, fat goose, which was amusing in itself as I had been expecting a duck or chicken, perhaps. However, the most interesting thing was its wings were bound to its body (to prevent them dragging in the dirt and to make it easier to carry) by an elegant kerchief of the snowiest linen imaginable and a silken garter. The story was not easily extracted from our sister, as to how the bird came to be tied up so handsomely, but eventually I managed to elicit the following information: the Vicomte de Villemont happened upon our sister struggling home from the market with a heavy and unwieldy bird and was overcome with compassion. He then insisted upon tying it up with his own kerchief and, when that proved insufficient (it is a *very* fat goose), his garter as well. He then determined it was far too heavy a burden for poor Claude and escorted her most of the way home, carrying the goose! (You will acknowledge my heroic effort to refrain from embroidering this tale with all the romantic language it deserves.)

"In a separate, unrelated and completely unremarkable incident, I'm sure, I will only tell you that this afternoon Claude was heard humming. I note this for two reasons, the first being I have not heard her do this since the serious consequences of the state of Papa's financial affairs became known to us. The second reason it was interesting to me, which again may be put down to an overactive imagination, is, as I recall, Claude used to most frequently hum when she was thinking of a certain undeserving individual, either having recently spent time with him or in anticipation of doing so. At this time I cannot believe she is either thinking of Monsieur le Rat or, even if she were, the thoughts would induce her to resume humming. So my poor susceptible brain is reduced to making up my own reasons for her musical behavior and I confess I cannot help but link it to the incident of the Handsome Young Vicomte and the Heavy Goose.

"My last trivial and probably insignificant observation for the day is, this evening after our meal, when we were all sitting comfortably in the parlor, Claude, who had been humming again while doing her needlepoint, was heard to say what a fine thing for our evenings it would be if she once more had our old virginal at her disposal. Again, I am sure it is nothing and I am jumping to unsupportable conclusions, however, it seemed to only confirm my suppositions from earlier in the day. I confess, while I cannot think of any truly rational reason for him riding in this direction, I am now in hourly expectation of an impromptu visit from the Vicomte on the basis 'he was just riding past.'

"Dear Isabeau, I can see you shaking your head in patient amusement, and I am well aware of the irony of this. I can remember doing such to you when you brought me your fantasies of Claude's wedding. In any case, I have revealed to you the direction of my wild imaginings, so now I can be calm and go to my bed.

"Au revoir, my beloved sister!"

As was usual, I tried to follow Marie's example. However, my own retirement that evening was not to be accomplished in such a pleasant reverie as hers. Rather, I went to bed in a somewhat fretful mood. I had not seen Isabeau again that day. She had spent the morning as promised, walking over the castle grounds. At lunchtime she had then gone back to her rooms and had not left them again. I had waited hopelessly in the library, looking over some rough sketches of flowers and leaves she had left on her desk, but she had not come. When the sun dropped below the dark of the forest, I had dined alone in my study, then spent the early evening taking my discontent out on the straw-stuffed leather targets in my fencing gallery. Marie's thoughts on Claude's possible feelings for the Vicomte were the only glimmer of satisfying interest I had all day and they only put my own sad prospects into sharp, unflattering relief.

CHAPTER XXIII

$\mathcal{I}$f I was worried that evening, by the next I was beside myself and by the end of the week I was completely despondent. After that day, my only conversation with Isabeau was the following morning. Again I took myself faithfully to the music room and awaited her there. When she did come, she was very late and she did not stay and play.

I was anxiously pacing in the adjoining room when I heard her soft step and spun around to see her. If she had looked tired the day before, today she looked gray. There were distinct shadows under her eyes and even her beautiful hair was less brilliant. She was hunched beneath a large shawl she had wrapped around her shoulders and clasped against her chest like an old woman. Most worrying, however, was the strange light burning in her eyes.

"Beast, I'm so sorry to have kept you waiting," she said in a thin, hushed voice.

"Isabeau . . ." I started, then stopped, thinking of her earlier rebuke. She was quite clearly unwell, however. I pushed aside my hesitation with an impatient gesture. "Isabeau, you are ill. What ails you?" I strode forward and, taking her arm, propelled her into a chair.

"Beast," she said almost sulkily, "please don't."

"Isabeau, this is not simply gallant solicitude. You look ill," I said. "Have you seen yourself in the glass?" She stared at me somewhat reproachfully.

"There is no glass in my room," she said. "I did not think there were any in the house."

I blinked. "No," I said guiltily, "of course not."

"Beast, really," she said, laying her hand on my arm, "please do not concern yourself. I may look ill—I'm sure I do, but I assure you I am not. It is simply that I have barely slept these last two nights. My dreams have been so odd . . ." She paused, presumably lost in thoughts of these dreams. I searched her face for some clue as to their nature, but found none.

"They are so real . . ." she said quietly, almost as though she had forgotten I was there, "then I wake and . . ." She paused again and pressed the fingertips of one hand to her temple. "When I wake I cannot fall back to sleep for thinking on them. I . . ." She seemed to remember me at this point and stopped, coloring slightly. Then she gave me a wan smile, as though trying to dispel my concern. "So you see," she said lightly, "no illness, just phantoms in the night. I will go for another walk and try again to rest this afternoon."

I tried to curb my questions, for she clearly did not want to discuss the content of her dreams, but my curiosity was inflamed. Naturally my mind recalled the vivid dream I myself had dreamed the night her father stayed. What manner of dreams were keeping my Isabeau awake?

"Would you like some company on your walk?" I asked, trying to keep the desperation from my voice.

"No, thank you, Beast," she said sorrowfully. "Forgive me, but I would like to be alone."

Instinctively I felt solitude was not the answer to what ailed her. But how could I protest, given my own interest in her choosing company? So I stood, silent, and watched her go.

The next day she did not emerge from her room until well after midmorning. She did not seek me out at my sad, self-imposed station near the music room, where I noticed cobwebs gathering in the corners of the room. Instead she went, of all places, to visit my portrait. This time she spent almost an hour with it. Strange as this was, even stranger was the fact she visited it again, the next evening, and again in the small, dark hours of the next night. That time I woke in my bed to the sensation of her moving about the house, and if her journey afforded her any further rest that night, I lay awake and wondering in my own bed until dawn.

There followed two very bleak weeks indeed, where I might have been living with a ghost. There were days when the only evidence I had of her continuing presence in the house was her footsteps in the film of dust beginning to thicken upon the polished floorboards of the hallways. She had left her room only a few times, either in the very early morning to go walking outside, or at other points to visit my portrait again and again. Her early morning sojourns woke me—as did her midnight jaunts—and several times I stood at my window to observe her slight form, wrapped and clenched against the early chill, make its solitary way across the misty lawns and disappear among the yews.

She passed close by me several times in the house, too. For it soon became apparent that, when she left her room, if she was not going outside she was going up to the attic. Thus it became easy for me to place myself somewhere along her route so I might have a glimpse of her as she went. The candles lighting my hallways began to burn low and then go out. In the dim, flickering light, she never saw me, even when she passed by quite close.

I even went so far as to make my own way up to the portrait after she had gone away, to see if I could discern for myself what fascination it could possibly hold for her. That it had something to do with her dreams, I doubted not, but exactly *what* was the constant blank all my ponderings led me to.

When I went to see it, her visits had made a clear trail in the dust and debris on the attic floor. The floor directly in front of the painting was also bare, so it was obvious she had several times stood very close to it. The dust sheet was now entirely pulled clear of the frame and a trunk had been dragged across to provide a convenient seat for its solitary audience. I stood where she had stood, looking into the face of the man I had once been, and wondered with a curiosity as bright and sharp as a knife wound, what she saw and what she thought of when she looked.

Did she look with the eyes of a lover? Did she touch the curls around his face, imagining what they might feel like in life under her white fingers? Did she ache for those blue eyes to shift their distant gaze and see her before them? Did she, in short, harbor all the feelings about this painting that I held in my own great breast for her? And if she did, what could that possibly mean for my suit, in this giant, fanged and furred body I now inhabited?

Or did she look with the eyes of a judge? Were the dreams that stole her sleep and her peace a catalog of my father's sins? Did she avoid me because she had heard the Fairy cry out against me and understood the warning my beastly form represented?

These were all questions I could not answer myself. But even though I had no right to ask her to satisfy my curiosity, it remained that whatever it was that plagued her dreams and sent her into the attic to pace before my portrait, was also stealing away her health. Every day she grew a little grayer, a little more shadowy.

In the end it was the Vicomte de Villemont who inspired me to act. I had a lot of sympathy for that young man. Although he was trying much harder to gain his lady's attention than I, and reasonably stood a greater chance of succeeding, Claude was proving as elusive to him as Isabeau was to me. After what Marie christened "the Incident of the Handsome Young Vicomte and the Heavy Goose," he returned two days later to reclaim his belongings. Both sisters and their father were home, although Claude appeared to grow shy on Villemont's entering through their gate and did not come out to greet him. Isabeau's father's reaction was one of mortification over not being able to receive the Vicomte as his rank deserved. Marie, however, welcomed him politely and cordially and invited him in for a cool drink. I thought she kept her countenance very well considering her predictions in her last letter to Isabeau. Villemont declined the offer and explained the reason for his visit.

"Of course," said Marie smoothly. "Claude washed them herself and put them by to return to you. I shall ask her to bring them out." And she went back inside to summon Claude. Claude declared herself to be far too busy to come out to give them to the Vicomte herself, but Marie scolded her into compliance. Once again in his presence, however, the normally chatty and teasing Claude became silent and demure, offering the folded kerchief and garter back to the Vicomte with downcast eyes, only glancing up once, quickly, before looking down again. Villemont was, by all appearances, enchanted and frustrated in equal part. When she disappeared inside again he looked wistfully after her, as though wishing he had accepted the offer of a cool drink in the de la Noues' kitchen after all, even though it was hardly a fit place for a Vicomte.

A few days later he was back again. This time Marie was out in her garden, digging away happily and cosseting the seedlings that had sprung up over the last few weeks. Villemont rode up and dismounted outside the gate, begging Marie's pardon for disturbing her.

"No, do not think of it!" Marie exclaimed, trying to wipe her hands on her apron.

"It is only that Monsieur Dufour told me you had a particular wish for oranges some weeks ago," Villemont stammered bashfully. "I have a hothouse full of them, you see, but I use so few. I thought your family might accept a present of them." Marie smiled at the thought they were a present for her *family* and thanked him prettily.

"We have not had such a treat for some time," she said gratefully. "Please, will you allow me to offer you a drink this time?" When he appeared on the verge of refusing again, she held out her muddy hands and said, "Please, do not let my disheveled state put you off. I will ask Claude to bring something out. What will you have, wine or ale?" The prospect of seeing Claude again seemed to sway the young man and he assented to a draft of cool water from the well. Marie then went to call Claude, who came out looking unusually subdued again. When she emerged, Marie disappeared on the pretext of washing her hands, and the two young people were left in silence: the one trying to do his utmost to think of a way to dispel it, the other doing her utmost to avoid its being broken.

"Thank you for laundering my kerchief," said Villemont desperately. "You did not have to do that."

"It was no trouble," murmured Claude and fell silent again.

"I brought you some oranges," said Villemont, remembering the pretext for his visit. "Monsieur Dufour said your sister wanted some. That is, I thought you might like them, too." He untied a bag from his horse's saddle and held it out to Claude. She raised her eyes to him this time, looking quite delighted as she took them, then looked down again and bobbed an elegant little curtsey.

"I thank you, sir," she said modestly.

Villemont looked momentarily stunned by the beautiful smile she had turned on him as she took the oranges and stood staring at her for a few moments. Then it became apparent Claude was not going to say any more and, having discharged his purpose for coming, he could not seem to think of anything further to say either. With a frown of frustration, he bowed to Claude and asked her to pass on his adieus to her sister, then he remounted and rode off, looking back over his shoulder several times. After the second time, however, Claude had vanished into the house again and he would not have been able to spy her peeping through the window.

Another week passed, and this time he happened upon her walking home from buying some cloth in the village. Although "happened upon" is perhaps a misleading term to use. I believe he had, in fact, been riding back and forth for an hour across a particular section of the way between the cottage and the village in anticipation of her arrival.

On seeing her he instantly sprang from his mount and made his way toward her, while she stopped in surprise and then ducked her head and walked determinedly on as though she thought he had mistaken her for someone else.

"Mademoiselle de la Noue!" he cried out. This time she did stop.

"Vicomte!" she responded. "Good day to you." And she swept into a curtsey far more elegant than one would have thought possible in plain homespun.

"How do you do?" he asked politely.

"Very well, sir, and you?" asked Claude, just as politely.

"Yes, very well, thank you," he replied and I feared the conversation had come to an end. There were, indeed, several long moments of silence.

"Well . . ." began Claude, clearly preparing her exit. This inspired Villemont to speak.

"I give a dance for the village every summer," he burst out, "and it is to be held next month. Will you come?"

Claude looked quite startled. "A dance?" she said, then remembered to be reticent. "I thank you, sir," she said demurely, "but I do not know if I can. My father does not go out into society much and my sister . . ." She stopped, clearly trying to think of some way in which Marie might prevent her from attending.

"Your sister?" asked Villemont, in puzzlement. "No, she must come, too. René Dufour is quite counting upon it. And it may be just what your father needs. He is too hard upon himself. Think of the good it would do him to see his daughters dancing and happy. Please, will you come?"

"Well," said Claude uncertainly, clearly unprepared for his urging. But, confronted with the great benefits it would have for the happiness of both her sister and father, she began to be swayed. "I will speak to Father," she conceded.

"Splendid!" he cried, then he sobered and swallowed visibly. "And, may I ask, if it is not too presumptuous, if you come, would you be so good as to—that is, I would particularly like to dance with you. Would you dance with me?"

"Of course," murmured Claude, looking down at the ground again, her cheeks growing pink.

"I am honored," said Villemont, bowing low. Claude curtsied again and bid him good day, hurrying away clutching her basket. Villemont stood in the shaded lane watching her go. When she had vanished from his view, he leaped into his saddle and, to my amusement, let out a whoop and galloped off toward the village.

The mirror now showed me Claude, almost running in her haste to be home. I watched her rush along the muddy track across the field to the cottage. Marie, who now spent almost all her daylight hours in her formative garden, also watched Claude's hurried approach, putting down her tools and going to stand by the gate, her face showing the beginnings of alarm.

"Claude!" she cried, when her sister was only twenty yards or so from their gate. "Claude, what is it? What is wrong?"

"Oh, Marie," gasped Claude, clearly distressed and out of breath. "Marie, what shall I do?"

"What? What has happened?" cried Marie, growing more concerned.

"The Vicomte de Villemont!" wailed Claude. "He is giving a dance, he wants us to go! He has asked me to dance with him!"

Marie's mouth dropped open. It was a few moments before she spoke. Her voice, when it came, was grown calmer and now hovered somewhere between irritation and amusement.

"I can see your great calamity," she said wryly. "A handsome, rich, young nobleman of unexceptional character has expressed a clear interest in you. We must flee the country at once."

"Marie!" shrieked Claude. "I have nothing to wear!" And she stormed past Marie into the house, pausing only long enough to wrench off her muddy boots. Marie stared after her in amazement, then raised her eyes to the sky in exasperation. She took a deep breath, and when she had composed herself she turned sharply on her heel and followed her sister inside.

Claude was at the kitchen table, her head buried in her arms. Marie entered quietly and rinsed her hands in a bowl of water, then dried them, watching Claude's bowed head. When she finished she went and sat on the bench next to Claude and placed her hands gently on her sister's shoulders.

"Claude," she murmured, "please forgive me. It was very wrong of me to tease you just now."

Claude gave a great shuddering sob and lifted her tear-stained face. Almost straightaway she buried it on Marie's shoulder and gave another sob.

"Claude!" chided Marie, starting to look worried. "Please, don't cry so!"

Claude cried into Marie's shoulder for a few more minutes, then managed to sit up, a little quieter, and dab at her eyes.

"Now," said Marie, firmly, "please, Claude, you cannot be this upset over not having a dress for the dance. We have the Beast's finery, after all. It may not be exactly suitable, but we can alter it. What is it that troubles you, really?"

Claude sniffed and new tears welled up.

"I hardly know," she said unevenly. "It is as you say. He is kind and thoughtful, everyone speaks well of him . . ." She paused uncomfortably. "And he is handsome enough," she said defensively, "and most assuredly rich. Why do I feel like running away when I see him?"

Marie frowned. "Do you not like him?" she asked.

"No, no! It is not that." She looked beseechingly at Marie.

"I will never tease you about him again," said Marie solemnly. "And at your word, his name will never pass my lips in your presence again."

Claude relaxed a little.

"I don't ask that," she said. She took a deep breath. "The truth is, I do think of him sometimes. And I do think him very handsome." Another tear found its way past her lashes. "I might like him, but I'm so afraid!" She gasped again and covered her face with her hands. Marie wrapped her arms around her sister and held her close.

"Little Claude," she murmured. "My poor darling." After a time Claude's shoulders stopped shaking and Marie took Claude's hands from her face and looked directly into her eyes.

"Here is what you must do," she said. "If you think it will be too difficult for you, then I will do it, if you like. At the dance—or before—you must tell him about Gilles. You must tell him you are not yet ready to lose yourself to another. You must tell him he must be patient and wait for you."

Claude looked up at Marie, her eyes wide and fearful.

"But would that not be presumptuous?" she stammered.

"Sister," said Marie, more serious than ever, "the Vicomte is an honest man. If he has particularly asked you to dance with him, he has declared his interest. You must be honest with him. And so I counsel you, if you do not think he can win your heart, do not give him false hope. Tell him you wish only to be his friend. He is an honorable man. He cannot fault you for that."

The mirror grew dim at this point, then returned to reflecting the scene of my study. I was conscious of feeling a certain resentment toward the mirror. Why did I witness that scene? What lesson was I to take from it? On the one hand, Villemont's active pursuit of Claude inspired me. It had won him a place in her thoughts, at least, if not yet her heart. But she seemed well disposed toward him and I could only think that once the doubts sown by the faithless Gilles were overcome, he would rapidly gain her heart as well.

On the other hand, as Marie had so clearly pointed out, it was impossible for Claude to enter into another romance at this time. She was still bruised from the broken engagement and if Villemont truly wanted to win her, he would have to give her time to heal first.

Isabeau had no heart wound I knew of, but surely the obstacle of my hideousness could only be overcome with time.

Time. Again, time. Alone, it had been mine in abundance. Isabeau had promised me just one short year. And so many weeks had now slipped past while I stood by, pining for her from the shadows. I did not have time. When she had walked out that morning she had looked thinner than ever, and her movements were slow, as though she was in pain, or very tired. Whatever was troubling her would be the end of her. The very thought filled me with horror. And I was not the only one who loved her and would be distraught at her destruction. What of her family? Her father, surely, would die of guilt and grief.

I vacillated for a few more days. Should I take my inspiration from Villemont, and pursue a course of action? Or should I follow Marie's counsel and give her time? As I wavered, long rents appeared in the drapes at my bedroom windows, and whenever I sat at my desk, I had to brush it free of a scattering of mouse dirt and dead moths.

In the end, as I said, I chose the Vicomte's way. As for Marie's wise words, I told myself if I truly thought that in *time* Isabeau might come to accept my awful countenance and my suit, then she must spend *time* with me. She would not grow to love me if she never saw me, never spoke to me.

CHAPTER XXIV

So, one morning, as Isabeau left her room, I waited for her by the foot of the grand staircase. I watched her descend, slowly and haltingly, so absorbed in whatever troubled her, she did not notice me until she was nearly at the bottom.

"Isabeau," I said softly, holding her cloak out to her. She stopped in surprise, clutching the railing.

"Beast!" she gasped.

"Our paths have not crossed for so long," I said. "I miss your company and your music. Will you not allow me to accompany you today? Even if only for a short while?" But my heart shrank within me at the look on her face. It was almost as though somewhere behind her eyes she was drawing away from me, closing me out of her mind.

"I'm sorry, Beast," she replied woodenly. "I really would prefer to be alone."

"Please?" I begged, and I could not help the note of desperation that crept into my voice. "Will you not talk to me for just a few minutes? You look so ill, it pains me to see you this way. I beg you to tell me what has upset you!"

"Beast," she said, taking a step back. "You will suffocate me with your solicitude. I just want some peace."

"Of course," I said, holding out her cloak. "Forgive me. Perhaps later." She took the cloak with unwilling fingers and trudged out of the hall. I stayed until she returned, looking weary and not at all at peace. When she saw me again, however, a frown of exasperation crossed her face.

"Not now, Beast," she snapped at me, pushing past me up the stairs. I watched her go with dismay. This was not going to be easy. But her ill looks strengthened my resolve. I would pester her to speak to me, walk with me, eat with me, *something*. Until there was some change to her health, until I saw her happy and hale again, or at least on her way, I would dog her footsteps like the faithful animal I was.

So I lurked. Pacing in the entrance hall, wandering listlessly through the library, prowling down the portrait gallery. I couldn't sit still. I had to move. But, wherever I went, I remained alert to any stirring that would signal another opportunity to speak to her.

That afternoon she stayed in her room. I'm not sure if she slept again or not, but her door remained closed as I roved over the house, seeing new signs of decrepitude wherever I looked and trying to think of what might tempt her to become herself again. The sun was beginning to sink below the horizon, turning the light a deep bronze and lengthening the shadows of the yews outside, when she again emerged. From across the other side of the house I heard her door open. This time she moved quickly and her destination soon became apparent. She was going up to the attic again.

I met her on the third floor. My heart lurched to see her, she was so clearly distraught. Her hair was disordered, her eyes red and her face streaked with tears. She had her skirts gathered up and she was almost running. When she saw me she gasped and stared at me in consternation.

"Isabeau, won't you tell me what ails you?" I cried, stepping forward. I put a hand out toward her to stay her flight, but she brushed it away angrily.

"Not now!" she cried out. "I must . . ." But what she must do I never knew, for she fled away from me down the corridor. I heard a distant door slam and knew she had taken the stairs up to the attic. There was nothing else to do but wait. So I sat by the bottom stair where I knew she must come down and contemplated the large holes forming in the threadbare carpet.

By the time I heard her subdued steps upon the narrow stairs, the sun had long gone, and the crescent moon ruled alone in the sky, winking at me through the cracked window at the end of the hall. I got up stiffly from my lowly seat and went and leaned wearily on the opposite wall. Eventually the door pushed open and Isabeau emerged. She stopped again when she saw me, but the sight of me did not alarm her as it had before.

"Beast . . ." she said, in a broken little voice. But she stopped there and it did not seem as if she had any more to say. Slowly I straightened up and went over to her. I gently took her arm and began to bring her away. We walked in silence down the corridor.

I took her to her rooms, but did not leave her at the door. Instead I took her into her private sitting room and sat her in an easy chair by the fire. A tray with a bowl of warm broth and some fresh bread was waiting. I placed it on her lap and hunkered down beside the chair.

"Eat," I said. She looked as though she might refuse, but I

said, "Eat!" again, more firmly and she took up her spoon. When she had taken several mouthfuls, I had thought of what I wanted to say.

"Isabeau," I began, "I don't know what is troubling you. And I am not asking you for confidences you are not willing to give. But, please, I am your friend."

Isabeau put down her spoon and looked at me with tear-filled eyes.

"Whatever it is," I went on, "it is making you ill. You are not eating, you are not sleeping, and I have not spoken to you for two weeks together. I miss you. You can impute me with wholly selfish motives for wishing you well. I have no one else in this lonely place. But I care for you and I want to see you better for yourself.

"And if you cannot exert yourself for your own sake, or for mine, think of your family. They could not bear the loss of you a second time." I stopped. I had reached the end of my selflessness. I really could not speak of her going home to them without sacrificing my composure.

Perhaps it was the thought of her family, but her tears overflowed and she lowered her face to stare at the bowl on her lap.

"Eat," I reminded her, determined to stay at least until I had seen the bowl empty. She gave a little hiccoughing sob and took up her spoon again.

Although my heart still hurt to look upon her, I felt a little better. She was eating. And even though she had not said a word to me since she came down from the attic, her face was no longer closed to me.

When the bowl had naught but a puddle left at the bottom and Isabeau had even taken a few small bites of the bread, she put the tray aside and sat up a little straighter.

"Can I get you anything else?" I asked, realizing it was time for me to leave and that if I could do some small service for her, the moment of my departure might be delayed a fraction. Isabeau shook her head.

"No, Beast," she said in a low voice. "I thank you for your kindness tonight. You are a true friend."

I bowed to her, partly to hide my disappointment at her dismissal. But I managed a civil "Goodnight, Isabeau," and left her, looking small and fragile in her chair.

I was still restless with worry for Isabeau. I did not sleep until the small hours of the morning and even then I awoke when it was still early and the light was fresh and new. I lay sprawled in my bed, feeling the silence of the great house around me. Then I noticed it. The house was not just silent, but quiet. Some tension had gone from the atmosphere, leaving it calm and restful. I stayed in my bed, absorbing the change for several long minutes. It was almost like listening to the slow, measured breathing of some deeply slumbering animal.

What had changed? My thoughts flew to Isabeau and our small but hopeful exchange last night. Perhaps she had exorcised something of the demon stealing away her serenity. She was still in her room, and if the hush over the house was anything to go by, sleeping peacefully. I dearly wanted to see if she had, in fact, improved over the night, and my anxiety to see her well was filling me with a fitful energy. I decided that rather than roam the house and risk waking her with my own restlessness, I would take a leaf from her book and walk in the gardens.

I conducted something of a tour, taking myself all over the

grounds and seeing for myself the signs that spring was here and casting its own brand of magic over the landscape. Even in the orchards I had habitually kept in perpetual fruit, there was the occasional rogue blossom. My autumn display was looking sadly colorless, with a distinct haze of pale green touching the boughs of those trees closest to the forest. The rose arbor, perhaps because it had been brought entirely into being by magic and had never formed part of the original grounds, was the only section of the garden still wholly and defiantly in high summer.

Somewhere toward midmorning I felt a stirring in the house and wondered if Isabeau was waking. By then my explorations had taken me to the side of the house where her rooms were. Her window looked over a pond, framed by gravel paths and low hedges clipped into patterns. I skirted the far edge of this garden. Her curtains were closed and a sense of despondency settled over me for no real reason other than that I missed her terribly. I paced my way to the end of the path, hands clasped behind my back, staring down at the toes of my black leather boots. When I reached the arched doorway in the hedge at the end, I allowed myself one last glance at her window before leaving this part of the garden. I stopped.

The curtains were now drawn and I could see Isabeau framed in the window. She briefly lifted her hand to me, then vanished from view. Was she summoning me? I hurried through the archway and back toward the house, but in vain. Despite this fleeting moment of hope, she had not left her rooms by the time I reached the door to the entrance hall. I ate a late breakfast in the small dining room slowly, hoping she might join me, but she did not. I was left to myself again and to the fever of desperation growing in my breast.

*   *   *

After my breakfast, I set up a lonely, sentimental station in the music room. I was reading there on the pretext of being tired of the view from my study, but if I am honest it was merely an attempt to try to glean the dregs of her presence from a place she had visited often. Even so, it was not a cheerful place to be. Instead of music, all I could hear were mice scratching behind the wainscoting. The flowers that had appeared for Isabeau had withered and died in their vases and the whole room had begun to smell faintly of mold.

I was contemplating a new tracery of cracks spreading across the ceiling when the sound of a door being unlatched echoed quietly through the music room. I realized she was leaving her chamber.

I left my book and went to the entrance hall and took up my position by the stairs. This time she was watching for me and halted at the top when she saw me. Again she came down slowly, but it was as though she was delaying the moment when she must speak to me, rather than because her pace was dictated by infirmity.

She was already wearing her cloak (no excuse for me to halt her, then) and had the hood drawn up around her face. But, today, when she came to the foot of the stairs, she did not try to avoid me. Rather she looked directly into my face and nodded gravely.

"Good morning, Isabeau," I said, bowing politely.

"Good morning, Beast," she replied. Her voice was still low, but it was steady.

"Would you like some company on your walk today?" I ventured.

Isabeau's face grew sad. "Please forgive me, Beast," she said, "but once again I would beg your patience and ask for solitude."

My heart sank with disappointment.

"Isabeau," I said quietly, trying to keep my voice even, "will you not let me try to help you? Do your dreams still trouble you? Will you not tell me something of what ails you?"

Isabeau looked down at her feet, her face now entirely hidden by her hood.

"I am sorry, Beast," she said. "I cannot tell you." She looked up again at me and her eyes slid to the side. When she spoke again it was in that same soft, faraway tone she had used when she first spoke of her dreams. "I hardly know how to explain it to myself. I dream these dreams and they are so real, and when I wake I am not rested, and all I want to do is fall back into them, but sleep won't come. All I seem to do is sleep and try to fall asleep."

I waited, hardly breathing, trying to will myself into invisibility. I felt as though a rare and timid bird had alighted on the banister beside me and the slightest quiver would send it back into flight. But she turned her eyes back to me at this point.

"I do thank you for your care of me last night. I slept better for it and am much more myself this morning."

"Have you eaten?" I interrupted, somewhat roughly. She managed the ghost of a smile.

"Always anxious for my health," she said in a tone that would have been almost fond if there had not been a sense of absence, as though her mind had already moved on from me. "Yes, Beast, I ate a little breakfast today."

She pulled her cloak closer about herself and looked up into my face once more.

"I am sorry, Beast. I know this is poor fulfillment of my part of our bargain. But, please, I must be alone with my thoughts now."

"I have no thoughts of our *bargain*," I said stiffly, stung she had reduced my concern to merely getting my value out of a transaction. "My concern is all for you." At this she looked guilty, as though my reproach had found its mark.

"I am sorry," she said again, and turned to go.

"As you wish," I growled to her retreating back.

She left and I was confronted by an overwhelming sense of helplessness. Instead of sinking beneath the weight of it, however, something inside me ignited. My belly burned. I leaned forward and gripped the banister with both hands, sinking my talons deep into the polished wood. I closed my eyes, trying to contain my growing rage, but a low growl escaped between my clenched teeth.

At that moment, I had the sudden sense Isabeau had stopped in the doorway. I straightened up and opened my eyes. She was not there.

All my anger and impotence and anguish condensed in a ball in my chest. It gathered in my throat and erupted in a great roar of pain. The banister splintered beneath my claws and I tore the wood away. I hurled it to the floor and raised my face and howled again. The sound swelled and echoed and the dusty chandelier above me gave a nervous tinkle as it rocked on its anchor. Crumbs of plaster tumbled down from the ceiling. Somewhere far away, I heard the birds calling in alarm. The sound left me and I staggered backward unsteadily.

She had gone. She did not want my company. She would not let me help her.

I went upstairs to my fencing gallery and worked until my fur was sodden with sweat and my shirt clung to me. I abandoned technique and precision and savaged my targets, slashing at them until they burst apart. A dummy with one wooden arm disintegrated into splinters. When my chest was heaving and the room littered with wreckage, I dropped my abused blade on the floor and swiped the sweat from my eyes. I did not feel better.

Exhausted, I went to sit in my study and lost myself in morose contemplation of my misery and Isabeau's plight for perhaps an hour. I racked my brain, trying to hit upon some new strategy to bring Isabeau back to herself, but no revelations were forthcoming. Isabeau was still out walking in the gardens. In fact, my strange sixth sense told me she was just now pacing the walks of the rose garden.

Determined, though, to set a good example and rouse myself out of my low mood, I picked up a half-read book sitting on my desk. Silverfish scurried away from where I had disturbed them and I had to open the book carefully as the binding disintegrated in my hands. I ignored all this and began to read. Through sheer force of will I made my way through its fragile, water-stained pages until the early afternoon, when I sensed Isabeau making her way back to the house.

I almost didn't go down to meet her. Having suffered so many frustrating rebuffs, I was in no mood to open myself to yet more. But I did go and I was waiting in the hall like a footman as she entered.

The doors opened for her and she stepped in across the cracked tiles accompanied by a fall of golden afternoon sunlight. Her hood was thrown back off her face and her hair was lit up like molten gold. All my gruff irritation disappeared in that instant and the only sensation I was conscious of was my heart throbbing in my chest.

"Beast!" she said, and—oh joy!—her voice contained no irritation or wariness, but something of pleasure and even relief.

I went forward to her and offered to take her cloak, but instead of giving it to me, she abandoned her attempts to undo the clasp and took up my paws in her hands.

"Beast," she said again, looking anxiously up into my eyes. "Are you well?" For a moment I was speechless. Then a surge of laughter rose in my throat I could not contain.

"Me?" I gasped.

Now her beautiful eyes dropped away from my face.

"When I left you this morning," Isabeau said contritely, "you looked so despondent. Then . . ." She stopped and looked up at me. I realized she must have heard me and I could not meet her gaze. I looked away and my eyes came to rest on the ruined banister and the splinters of wood still scattered over the floor.

"Beast," said Isabeau, a catch in her voice. I looked back at her and saw she, too, was looking at the destruction I had wrought that morning. She glanced down at where my huge, black paws rested in her hands. For a moment I was suffused with shame at my outburst, certain she could feel nothing but fear and disgust at such violence. But then her hands tightened about mine.

"I know I have caused you a great deal of worry," she said. "I am so very sorry for it. Truly, I am more myself today." Then, in a gesture that removed any power of speech I might have been about to regain, she lifted my paws and pressed them to one of her cheeks.

"Dear Beast," she said in that same low, sad voice, "you are so patient." Then she relinquished my paws and gave me a watery smile, before moving off up the staircase.

* * *

My meal that evening was a lonely one again, but this time I had more stomach for my meat. Isabeau, it seemed, had turned some sort of corner. While she still did not want my company to any great degree, at least now she was accepting my comfort and was even concerned for my well-being. I had more work to do, to be sure, but her progress gave me hope.

CHAPTER XXV

A solid night's rest was not to be mine that night, however. At some small, dark hour, I was woken from my slumber by the sound of sobs echoing through the house. I was instantly awake and shrugging into my dressing gown. Somewhere, for some reason, something was breaking Isabeau's heart. I did not stop to think, but fled through the shadowy passages of the house to her door. I ran so fast the candles did not have time to spring awake to light my way, but sputtered into flame behind me.

I had barely raised my hand to knock upon her door when it swung open. The scene that greeted me wrung my heart sorely. Isabeau was on her knees in the middle of the floor, her hair falling disheveled about her face and her nightgown pooling around her. Her face was in her hands and she was weeping.

"Isabeau!" I cried and she looked up at me from where she knelt. The only light in the room came from the lit hallway behind me and from the guttering fire in her grate. Her eyes looked huge in the gloaming and her face, as she raised it to me, was white and shocked.

"Beast!" she cried out as she looked up. "My Beast, I'm so sorry!"

The next I knew, I, too, was on my knees beside her, taking her into my arms. No conscious thought entered my brain. She was in need and she reached out to me, so I went to her. And she clung to me. She held on to me as though she were shipwrecked and I her lifeline. All the time she wept into the brocade of my dressing gown, "I'm sorry! I'm so sorry!" I could do nothing but hold her and stroke her hair until she calmed.

When the storm of her weeping had subsided, I whispered back to her, "Do not fret, my Isabeau! All is well." She heaved a deep breath and hid her face farther into the folds of my gown. There were a few moments of peace. Then, as I felt her once again able to govern herself, I lifted her and took her to her chair by the fire. As I set her down gently, there was a moment (the merest instant!) where she did not seem to want to relinquish her hold on my gown. But release me she did, and settled with a troubled sigh into the velvet cushions of her chair. I stepped away and then seated myself on the footstool, watching her closely.

Her eyes were shut. Her tears still clung to her lashes and I could trace their journey down her pale cheeks. We sat in silence for a few moments.

"Beast, are you there?" she asked, eventually.

"I am," I answered quietly.

"Thank you," she whispered.

"Do you want me to go now?" I asked her.

"Not yet," she said, but she did not open her eyes. I sat and waited in silence, not knowing what to say to her. The minutes passed. I was beginning to wonder if she had fallen asleep when she spoke again.

"Have you been very unhappy?" she asked, more tears emerging from under her closed lids. It was another moment before I could answer.

"Yes," I said, then I could say no more.

Her mouth twitched miserably and a fresh flood of tears escaped.

"I'm so sorry I made you sad," she said after a while.

"Do not think of it," I answered her. "If you would only be well, I would be satisfied." With her eyes still closed, a small, tight smile crossed her face.

"Give me your hand," she said, her voice low. Tentatively I put my dark, hairy paw into her slender fingers. She held it for a moment, then softly, so softly, stroked down its length with her other hand, her fingers sinking into the thick fur covering the skin on the back of my hand and eventually finding the smooth, cruel points of my talons. New tears slipped out from under her eyelids. Then she opened her eyes.

"Dear Beast," she said, relinquishing my hand and pushing herself up straighter in her chair. The mood of exquisite intimacy evaporated. Banished, I understood, by my unfortunate countenance.

"Thank you for coming to my rescue," she said, bravely looking into my face.

"I cannot be easy if you are unhappy," I said truthfully.

She bowed her head.

"May I give you counsel?" I asked tentatively.

She looked up at me again and smiled ruefully. "Of course," she said. "And I promise to try to value it as I should."

"These dreams you have," I said hesitatingly, "they seem to enthrall you, to make you want to live in them and not the world. If you try to do that, I fear you will fade away to nothing.

Should you want my advice, I would urge you to try to live in the world. Perhaps if you do not allow them to encroach upon your daylight hours, they will cease to trouble you so." I fell silent, having said my piece.

Isabeau frowned and considered my words. For a few minutes she was quiet, not looking at me. Then finally, she spoke.

"I think you may be right," she said. "My dreams, for all that they are seductive, only grow more unhappy as I try to enter further into them." She paused, before looking up at me and smiling sadly. "After all," she continued, "are not our experiences in the world the basis for our dreams? If I forsake the world for my dreams, they will have nothing new to feed upon and can only grow more stale and unsatisfying."

I did not know what to make of this, so I tried a change of tack.

"Tomorrow," I urged, "will you come down to the music room and play again for me?" I hurried on, seeing the reluctance in her face. "Please, just for half an hour?" She thought this over for a moment, then nodded.

"I will," she said. "But, Beast, it may not be much."

"For you, perhaps," I said lightly. Then, more seriously, "Do I have your solemn promise to attend me in the music room tomorrow?"

She laughed at this and a little more worry melted away in my heart.

"I give you my most solemn promise," she said. Then raising her voice and her eyes to the darkened room, she called out, "There! House! Do you hear me? On no account am I to renege on my promise or keep the Beast waiting for even half a minute! I must keep my promise and you must help, do you hear?" Her only response was silence, but she seemed satisfied with that.

I gazed at her for a few more moments, then rose from my footstool.

"Will you be able to sleep again tonight?" I asked.

She gave me a curious searching look, then replied, "Oh yes, most assuredly."

I hesitated a moment, then I took her hand from where it rested on the arm of her chair, raised it to my beast's muzzle, and placed it gently in her lap. She watched me with a curious expression on her face: wariness, curiosity, anticipation. To her credit I did not detect revulsion.

"Goodnight, Beast," she said.

"Goodnight, Isabeau," I replied and left her, sitting in the firelight.

When I awoke the next morning, I discovered in myself a greater sympathy for Isabeau's longing to live in the world of her dreams. I did not know what formed the substance of the fantasies luring her away from wakefulness and life, but for the remainder of the night my own phantasms were constructed entirely of the sensation of her in my arms, clinging to me, crying out, "My Beast!" It was with a very great reluctance I allowed my eyelids to open and admit the day. But her solemn promise to meet me again in the music room spurred me to rouse myself and thus, I was there, at the appointed hour. To my relief, it was a cleaner and brighter place than it had been of late, and even the flowers had been refreshed.

True to her own word, Isabeau did not keep me waiting for any more than half a minute. If she still looked thin and worn, at least today that strange light was not in her eyes, and she greeted me like a friend and not an imposition. Either she or her invisible servants had taken care with her wardrobe today; she wore a gown of the muted pink that suited her so well and her hair was dressed in a manner both soft and elegant.

I suspected she may well have shed more tears that morning, for her eyes were a little red and her lashes still damp. But she appeared to be at least trying to hold herself together.

I stood as she entered. She came toward me and gave me her hands and again I brought them to my mouth in my own sad imitation of a gallant's kiss.

"Will I sit in the other room today?" I asked tentatively, not wanting to overwhelm her.

She shook her head. "No," she said ruefully, "I have been too long alone. I will probably not play much today—just a few scales to warm my hands up. But I would be grateful for your presence."

I nodded and seated myself in my usual chair. In the event, she played to me for over an hour. Certainly the first half was largely made up of uninspiring exercises to help her fingers back to nimbleness, but after that she decided she did not want to stop and continued on to run over some of her favorite pieces. I certainly had not spent a more satisfying morning for some weeks.

When she finally confessed herself tired of playing, she asked me if I would mind very much if she took her morning walk alone again today.

"Of course not," I said. "You only promised me this morning and you have given me twice the time you pledged. How could I begrudge you a solitary walk now?"

"Thank you, Beast," she said, smiling at me from over the virginal. "I believe you are good for me, after all. I need a walk by myself now, to think on some things, but do you think . . ." Her voice trailed off uncertainly.

"Anything you wish is yours for the asking," I said, trying not to sound as serious as I felt. Isabeau laughed.

"All I wish, Beast, is . . . well, would you be so good as to meet me in the library this afternoon and read to me again?"

Joy flooded my breast.

"You see," she continued, with an air of self-deprecation, "I fear if I wait until tomorrow to meet with you once more, I might be carried off again by my dreams." She laughed nervously and I could see she really *did* fear it.

"Of course," I said. "It will be my pleasure."

"Thank you, Beast," she said, and I could hear the true gratitude in her voice.

After she left me, I went to my study with a much lighter heart than I had known for nearly three weeks. I had thought to try to while away the morning by reading, or perhaps looking in upon the de la Noues. But I found a much more satisfying pastime awaited me. Isabeau had today chosen not to take to the yew walks and the orchards as she had customarily done over the past few unhappy weeks. Instead, as I looked out of my study across the pleasure gardens below, I saw her walking there in view of my own window. It was a pretty scene of neat pathways, garden beds and hedges forming patterns, showing to advantage from the height of my window. I found it was very easy for me to while away my morning by simply leaning my head upon one paw and watching Isabeau wander about.

It was quite late in the morning when she stopped to admire a particularly elegant flower bed close to the house. She stood with her back to me looking at it for some time, then suddenly she turned and looked directly up at me in my window.

I experienced a strange shock of warmth—not unlike being caught in the pantry with my fingers in a jug of cream as a child.

Isabeau smiled and lifted her hand in greeting. I waved back, then retired shyly from where she could see me in my window. I felt slightly giddy and shaken and could not bring myself to go near my window again for nearly half an hour.

In the afternoon I went down to await her in the library. I was relieved to find today it did not smell so strongly of mice. I had only just selected a book from my collection when she entered at the door. I could not immediately greet her; my breath caught at her loveliness, for she was smiling and her arms were full of flowers.

"Good afternoon, Beast," she said and if the brightness in her voice sounded a little forced, at least she was trying.

"You see, I mean to pick up my new hobby where I left off," she explained, putting the blooms into a vase of water on the desk, apparently sitting there just for that purpose. "Will you read to me while I draw?"

"Of course," I said, bowing and settling myself into my chair by the window. The sheer pleasure of reading to her again was only very slightly compromised by the frustration of having to look at the page instead of gazing upon her as she worked.

I read to her until the light began to fail and the shadows lengthened and stretched across the garden outside. Then at last, she laid down her pencils and paints and thanked me.

"Perhaps I have given you fodder for some new dreams?" I asked her, putting aside the book. A look of startled guilt crossed her face, but then she smiled at me ruefully.

"I hope so," she said. "Anything is better than the grief of the old ones." With that curious utterance she went away, leaving me to wait out the evening and the night.

CHAPTER XXVI

$\mathscr{I}$t was probably as well for me I was able to distract myself by looking in on the de la Noues that night. Upon drawing the velvet drapes, my mirror instantly showed me a view into their parlor. Monsieur de la Noue was seated in his chair closest to the fire, watching his daughters with a curious expression of affection and longing on his face. His daughters were engaged thus: Claude was standing in the middle of the room dressed in one of the garments from her father's saddlebags. Marie was kneeling at her feet, engaged in unpicking an extravagant flounce from around the hem of the gown. Claude was looking slightly forlornly at a pile of silk roses and gilt ribbons lying upon the floor.

I could not help suppress a groan at the outrageous inappropriateness of the gifts of clothing I had sent. At once, the flounce suddenly unraveled and fell into the astonished Marie's hands. Claude began to giggle at the look on her face.

"What did you do?" she asked.

"I have not the least idea," said Marie, completely puzzled.

I, too, had to laugh. I wondered if the dress Marie had set

aside for herself to wear might be found to have shed a large proportion of its finery.

De la Noue coughed and shifted in his chair.

"Ah, my angels," he said, "I had never thought to see you dance again!"

"Father!" protested Marie fondly. "You still look so darkly on everything! Our lives are not so bad! We no longer live in luxury, surely, but we are comfortable and lack nothing truly essential! Indeed, I think we have been fortunate to find our-selves among such people as we have . . ." Her voice trailed off, for her father was looking thunderous.

"Fortunate?" he spat. "Lacking in nothing? When your own sister's bones might lie in some dungeon in that castle, picked clean of flesh—"

"For pity's sake, control yourself!" cried Marie, the sharpness of the grief in her tone cutting her father's words off cleanly. "If you want us to sink under the weight of our sister's fate . . . !" Her words were swallowed up by a sob. She looked down and when she had mastered herself, she looked back up into her father's shocked, white face. "I cannot live thinking Isabeau has sacrificed herself. Until I know otherwise, I will hope for her return. Please do not try to take that from me, Father. If you do, I will never have any joy in this new life we have forged." She looked back down and began to fuss with some imaginary fault in the hem of Claude's dress. Claude, also pale and distressed, glanced from father to sister and back. Marie's words found their mark, for her father sat in his chair for some minutes, anxiously plucking at the arm of it, his countenance gradually crumpling in shame and dismay.

"I am so sorry," he finally said, in a distracted voice. With that he rose and made his way across the room to the door. As he passed, Marie reached out and caught her father's hand and pressed it to her lips. He stopped for a moment, but then tugged his hand out of her clasp and left the room.

The two sisters were silent for a space of time, then Marie spoke. She did not look up at her sister and her voice was almost lost in the folds of silk she held in her hands.

"I still write to her," she said, "and every time I place a new letter in her box, the last is gone. I have to believe she receives them. I cannot think why else they go."

At this Claude bent down and clasped her sister's hands.

"You are right, Papa is not. He just feels so sad and so guilty. The Beast will look after our Isabeau. He cannot help but love her as we do!"

Marie laughed shakily. "Sometimes that is what I pray for," she confessed. "But then I think perhaps it is best if he does not love her so well. Then he might grow tired of her and send her back to us!"

How can I describe how such scenes made me feel? Miserable with guilt; terrified at the thought of her departure. At least now, though, I was confident she would last the year and not sink away into her mysterious dreams and be lost to us all.

In the mirror, Marie sat back and looked up at Claude, an expression of critical assessment on her face.

"Yes," she said at last, "I think you will do very well. The dress has survived its de-beautification very nicely. You look not so grand that people will start to believe Papa has played his creditors falsely, but quite lovely enough to dance with a Vicomte."

Claude bit her lip and smoothed the skirt of her dress nervously, but said nothing.

"Have you spoken to him yet?" asked Marie.

Claude shook her head.

"Come to the Crossed Keys tomorrow around midday," said Marie. "I believe he is meeting Monsieur Dufour there in the afternoon. He is bound to take his luncheon there first. You will have the opportunity for a private word with him. Unless you would prefer me to take a message."

"No, no!" said Claude quickly, going very red. "I will come. Will you be there?"

"Yes," said Marie. "Madame Minou has asked me to help her there tomorrow afternoon. And Monsieur Dufour said he would bring us some more meat from his farm. He will bring me home."

The sisters were silent for a minute and Marie stood up and began to undo the lacings at Claude's back. Gradually the anxious look faded from Claude's face and she began to look more thoughtful.

"Monsieur Dufour is very generous," she said archly.

Now it was Marie's turn to go red and she ducked her head to hide her face. "Do not be unkind," she said. "I have promised not to tease you. Why should you tease me? Monsieur Dufour has not asked me to dance with him, in particular."

Virtuously, Claude refrained from responding, but she was not above raising her eyes to the ceiling in exasperation.

The next morning, Isabeau did, indeed, look much improved. To be sure, she was not as vibrant as I had sometimes seen her, but she looked as though she had passed a peaceful night. More importantly, she was *happy*.

"I can see you slept well," I commented after I had greeted her.

"Yes, Beast, I thank you, I did!" she said, smiling.

"Only pleasant dreams?" I tentatively queried.

Intriguingly, she flushed. "Yes, only pleasant dreams," she said, becoming absorbed in arranging the music on the stand.

I swallowed my burning curiosity and forbore to inquire any further, settling down to listen to her play. After warming up, she chose a number of extremely pretty, cheerful pieces to play, which I enjoyed immensely. I wondered if she had chosen them for my benefit, because as she played she glanced over at me often. Usually she became absorbed in her playing and would forget me, so the attention was unnerving.

Eventually, when she stopped to change her music at one point, I asked, "Isabeau, am I disturbing you today? Should I go away?"

"Oh no!" she exclaimed. "Not at all!"

"But," I said nervously, "I seem to be distracting you."

Isabeau went pink again. "No," she said, fussing with her sheet music, "it's just nice to have you there. Listening to me."

"Oh!" I responded, somewhat gracelessly. A warm glow spread through my chest, and I fear I smiled quite ridiculously. From then on, when she looked up at me she smiled.

When she finished playing, she actually gave me her hand before she left the room to go out on her walk. She didn't ask me to accompany her and I didn't offer, thinking she had already given me so much that morning. I hoped eventually she might ask for my company. But it was hard to be disheartened by her disappearance into the garden alone when she had again begged me to read to her in the library that afternoon. Thus it was with a light and happy heart that I repaired to my study to see if Claude would go to the Crossed Keys to speak to the Vicomte.

It was an extremely pleasant spring day and my mirror

showed me the Vicomte de Villemont seated at one of the tables in the orchard beside the Crossed Keys. The trees were a riot of pale pink blossoms, and clumps of golden daffodils littered the grass, which had brightened from tawny brown to green. On the table before him was a plate of bread, cheese and pâté, and a large tankard of ale, to which he was only paying the barest attention. What distracted him so, I could not at first see, but presently the form of a young woman came into the frame of the mirror and I realized he had been watching Claude approach up the roadway. The hem of her dress and boots showed the mud from her path across the fields, but the walk had brought color into her cheeks and disordered her hair in quite a charming manner. As she passed by the Vicomte's table, he sprang to his feet and bowed, saying, "Mademoiselle!" in an eager voice. Claude stopped, and curtsied.

"Sir, may I speak to you for a moment?" she asked hesitantly.

"Of course," said Villemont, coming forward to place a bench for her to sit on. Claude went pink, but sat down gracefully, placing her basket on the ground.

"Can I get something for you? A drink, or something to eat?" Villemont asked, anxious to please.

"Oh, no!" said Claude and indeed, she looked far too nervous to eat. Her hands were twisting in her lap.

"I mean, no thank you, sir!" she amended quickly. "I want to say something very particular to you, but . . ." If possible she went even redder.

The Vicomte looked extremely concerned. "You do not mean to withdraw from the dance?" he asked fearfully.

"No, no!" she said. She took a deep breath. "I fear I may be about to be very presumptuous, but if I am, I hope you will forgive me and not think very ill of me for it!" She looked at him beseechingly and I was amused to see Villemont look shocked at the idea of thinking ill of Claude.

"Of course I will!" he cried. "I mean—I could not think ill of you! Pray, speak, mademoiselle! I am honored by your confidence."

Claude nodded and looked down. "I was very honored when you asked me to dance with you," she said, speaking into her lap. "And very happy, too!" she added. "But my sister said I must speak to you about . . . I must tell you . . ."

"Go on, mademoiselle," urged the Vicomte, beginning to look seriously alarmed.

"When we lived in Rouen," Claude said, her voice trembling slightly, "I was very nearly engaged to a young man there. When Papa was ruined, he cast me off."

A large tear rolled down her cheek and fell onto her tightly clasped hands. The Vicomte managed to look relieved and appalled at the same time.

"I was very unhappy for a long time," Claude continued, her voice growing stronger, "but I hope—I believe—I have put him behind me now. But if you mean to . . . if you . . ." She stopped and gave a little hiccough, unable to go on.

I watched the light in the Vicomte's eyes change as he comprehended what she was asking of him. For a young man who had been so at a loss as to how to approach the object of his interest, he now did everything perfectly. He reached out and lifted Claude's hands from her lap and brought them to his lips, then placed them back on the table. Claude was surprised into looking up at him.

"Mademoiselle de la Noue," he said earnestly, "I can think of nothing more abhorrent than toying with the affections of someone as lovely and as gently reared as you. I wish for nothing more than that you will trust me with your broken heart, but I see that trust must be earned. Just give me leave to try."

Color flooded her face, but Claude nodded her head bravely.

"I am satisfied with that, for now," he said, looking quite radiantly happy.

"I thank you, sir," said Claude, rising to her feet. The Vicomte also stood, and she darted another quick look up at him from her tear-stained blue eyes. She dropped a quick little curtsey, then took up her basket and scurried away, leaving the Vicomte staring after her.

My attention was almost immediately distracted from the happy Vicomte, however, by the sound of Isabeau calling my name. I turned away from the mirror and quickly made my way into the entrance hall, and was just in time to see her running up the front steps.

"Beast," she cried out when she saw me, excitement filling her voice. "Come with me this instant!"

"What is it?" I asked, hurrying forward.

"Oh, it would spoil the surprise if I told you!" she cried, and turned and ran out the door again. I hurried after her, the length of my stride allowing me to catch her without difficulty.

"I have something to show you," she said, looking up at me as I drew close. "I think you will like it." After this she would not say any more, but just shook her head at me, smiling.

She led me into the rose garden. As we entered the gates, she laid her finger over her lips. Then, impulsively, she took my paw in her hand and led me down one of the paths following the wall. A little way along she stopped and pointed with her free hand into a thick tangle of climbing rose. For a moment I saw nothing, then there was a flash of brilliant red and a robin flew out of the briar and up onto the wall. He lighted there and filled the air with a merry trill, before darting off again out of the garden.

"Stay," whispered Isabeau, pressing my hand with hers.

In a short time, we saw him dart back again, this time with his beak full of something that wriggled. He disappeared back into the briar. After a few moments he emerged again and was off to forage for more.

We stood, watching him for some time. I was rooted to the spot, overcome by the presence of something more truly and more deeply magical than anything I had yet experienced in my enchanted house. Isabeau stood beside me, her warm hand clasped in my black paw and together we watched a tiny robin bring home food for his family. Rabbits venturing into my life-less realm had been one thing. But robins choosing my garden as a fit place to rear their chicks! I was humbled and elated.

Eventually Isabeau tugged at my hand and drew me away. Instead of relinquishing her hold, however, she tucked her arm cozily through mine.

"Thank you," I whispered, as we made our way out of the arbor.

"I thought you would be pleased," she said happily, as we strolled back toward the house.

"More than I can say," I acknowledged gruffly.

Isabeau turned her face up to mine and favored me with the most enchanting smile.

"First rabbits, now robins. Your domain is coming alive again, my lord!" she said, a hint of mischief in her voice.

I assented, but in my heart I wondered whether, if I could not convince Isabeau to stay, the new denizens of my domain would also leave at the year's end.

CHAPTER XXVII

*A*fter that day, Isabeau did not again give me true cause to worry for her health. If she still preferred to take her morning ramble in solitude, she spent much of the rest of her day in my company. And indeed, to my intense pleasure, she now adopted the habit of passing under my study window at least once during her walk, at which point she always waved to me and waited for me to do so in return.

Her dreams seemed to recede somewhat, although I do not think they stopped. I would sometimes catch her with a wistful, faraway look on her face. Or, if she had been dozing or day-dreaming in my presence, when she woke I would see, in that brief moment when a slumberer must reacquaint themselves with the world, an infinitesimal expression of loss cross her face. But, if the sadness that had almost consumed her before remained at all, it was much abated, and was locked away in some secret part of her heart. She clearly did not mean it to trouble her waking hours, so I tried not to let it trouble mine.

Now that the weather had settled and warmed away the last vestiges of winter chill, we began to move our reading sessions outside. Sometimes we sat in chairs set up on my terrace, or on the lawns. Then, one afternoon, when the weather began to grow hot, Isabeau came running into the library where I was choosing a book, greatly excited over a marquee that had materialized on our favorite lawn by the house. It had not been my idea, so I, too, was pleasantly surprised by its appearance. It stirred memories of elegant, lazy summer parties from very long ago that, if I did not scrutinize my recollection too deeply, were largely happy. Isabeau also moved her drawing materials out to the marquee. Thereafter, whenever we repaired there, its comfort was augmented with lavish floral arrangements—which Isabeau usually dismembered to find the objects she wished to sketch that day. I would lie back in my chair watching her pull them apart, perfectly satisfied.

Sometimes, beautiful as the marquee was, we took our books to one of the orchards and lay in the thick grass under the cool green leaves. I think those times may have given me the closest thing to a feeling of complete happiness I could remember.

The first time I sat down under those twisted boughs with Isabeau, I looked up to see the signs of the bounty to come in the small, hard, green apples still in miniature form and was instantly reminded of my time spent in the orchard as a child.

That Isabeau was there with me now, her back set against the same gnarled apple tree, set those precious hours apart as true havens of bliss. I could even forget at such times that the year must roll on and come winter, I might find myself shut indoors, surrounded by snow and with no one to read to.

Hope was all I had and hope was what I clung to. Happily, there were occasional things—little things—that let me fuel my small flame, although it never grew very large.

One afternoon, we settled down against our usual tree to

read that day's selection. But, soon after I began, Isabeau complained her side of the tree was unaccountably knotty that day and she could not get comfortable.

"Move over, Beast!" she begged.

"On no account!" I retorted, being in fine humor that day. "I am most comfortable. If I move *I* will end up against the knots and have to go and lie in the grass. And I cannot read to you like that."

Isabeau flashed me a delighted smile—she seemed to enjoy being crossed every now and then—and went to lie in the grass at my feet. But a few minutes later she was sitting up again, scowling, complaining the grass was full of tussocks.

"Beast," she said winningly, "might I lay my head against your leg? You will not mind? I promise not to wriggle."

Of course, what could I do but capitulate instantly? She rearranged herself with her head against my calf. I completely forgot about the book in my hands and sat simply staring at her in adoration until she turned her face up at me again and said, "Much better! This is the softest patch of grass I have ever encountered, I do declare. You make a perfect pillow, Beast. I am ready now—you may continue!"

Somewhat flustered, I managed to relocate my place on the page and began reading, although I have no recollection of what part of the story I related to her that day. After this, Isabeau would often lay her head on my knee as we sat under my apple trees, reading in the dappled sunshine.

All in all, the spring and the summer months passed in perfect contentment, but for one remaining point of tension between us. I mourned that, but as it was of my own creation, I could not resent it. It was, of course, my proposals of marriage to Isabeau.

After she had finally emerged from her sadness, I was at first reluctant to recommence my suit to her so blatantly, afraid she would retreat back into her bedroom and her sinister world of dreams. But then something occurred to remind me that time was not on my side, and I could not hope to win her heart by waiting for it to fall into my lap. In a way, it was again Claude's Vicomte who inspired me to action.

The night of the Vicomte de Villemont's summer dance drew near. This promised a rare treat not just for Marie and Claude, but also for myself, as the unknown spectator. René Dufour had offered to bring the de la Noues to the dance. Claude had expressed some misgivings about traveling there in a farm cart, but at the appointed time it became apparent Dufour had made some effort to ensure his passengers' comfort by sweeping it out thoroughly and providing such luxuries as cushions and blankets for the ladies to sit upon in the back. The cart may still not have approached anything like a fashionable vehicle, but Claude's relief at not being obliged to hold her dress up out of the way of sawdust and chicken feathers found voice in such charming expressions of joy, Dufour would have been forgiven for checking to see if he had in fact brought his own carriage and not, by some strange mistake, one belonging to the Vicomte.

My mirror showed me a merry party making its way out past the other side of the village to the Vicomte's estates. If I was curious to see them, this was nothing to the expression of attentiveness on the faces of Isabeau's sisters. Dufour, knowing the area so well as he did, was a perfect guide, pointing out various landmarks and halting his cart in several places to allow his guests to enjoy some truly beautiful views.

Marie was most entertaining to watch. René Dufour's farm
lay not far from the Vicomte's estate, and she tried once or twice
to encourage Dufour to talk about his own home. However, it
became clear Dufour was making far more of an effort to high-
light those aspects of the countryside pertaining to the Vicomte's
estate than his own farming interests. After Dufour expertly
used several of her questions as opportunities to talk further
about the Vicomte rather than himself, a look of sudden com-
prehension crossed Marie's face. She turned a secret, delighted
smile upon her friend, who smiled broadly back and gave her a
conspiratorial wink. After that Marie was inspired to ask many
questions about the exact extent and the particular virtues of the
Vicomte's lands.

Claude, bless her, remained oblivious to the current of amusement between her sister and Dufour, and continued to look about
herself in enraptured interest. Their father simply sat upon the
front bench beside Dufour as complacent as I had seen him yet.

When they arrived at the Château Villemont, the Vicomte
himself was waiting upon the steps to greet them. It may be that
he did so for most of his guests that evening. However, for this
particular party he descended and escorted them personally to
the area of his lawns set up for the evening's frivolities.

It was entirely charming. Lines of paper lanterns on strings
delineated the area set aside for dancing, and a merry band of
players was set up on a small stage at one end. Around and about
the dancing square, trestle tables had been erected and a little
farther off were tents. Some were well stocked with kegs of ale
and boxes filled with bottles of wine. In other tents, platters of
bread and cheese and other comestibles were set out. The Vicomte saw his guests seated at a table with a good view of the
musicians and then, after renewing his request to Claude to grant

him the first of the evening's dances, he left to fulfill his duties in welcoming other guests.

The Vicomte's lawns were crowded well before sunset. I marked a number of people who appeared to be other local gentry, but the only lady present who was clearly not a matron looked to be in the advanced stages of impending motherhood. So there was no one to take the least offense when the Vicomte appeared to bid the band strike up and then promptly made his way over to Claude and bowed, holding out his hand. Claude blushed fierily, but let him lead her out into the center of the square, where they were joined by a crowd of other revelers so quickly her discomfort at being the center of attention cannot have lasted long.

It was something of a bittersweet exercise, watching the Vicomte's festivities. The music was lively and well played, and if the dancers were generally more eager than accomplished, their enthusiasm for the sport made them a pleasure to watch. But, of course, it is always more pleasant to participate in such amusements than to watch them from the sidelines.

Predictably, René Dufour led Marie out to dance. Afterward, there were enough young men hovering about Isabeau's sisters I did not think either of them would be in any danger of being left without a partner that evening.

After they had danced a number of dances, the last one being quite energetic, the Vicomte approached Claude again as she was being led from the dance floor, flushed pink with her exertions.

"Mademoiselle," said the Vicomte, as Claude's dance partner retired from the scene with good, if resigned, grace. "Would you like to rest for a while? May I offer you refreshment?"

"Oh yes," said Claude with every appearance of eagerness,

and away they went to sit by her father. He had not danced at all, but appeared to be very well satisfied with watching his daughters. Most of the other revelers had to line up at the tents to get their meals; however, at the Vicomte's bidding, a servant brought over platters of food for the de la Noue family. The Vicomte stayed to drink a cup of wine with them, during which he made Claude promise to dance with him again, before he was called away on other duties as the host. Before he rose to leave, however, he leaned forward to get Monsieur de la Noue's attention.

"Monsieur," he said, having to speak loudly on account of the noise of the music and revelry, "I have a matter I would consult with you about." Beside her father, Marie went very still and Claude jerked her head around to stare at him in alarm.

"Of course," said Monsieur de la Noue, looking surprised and quite oblivious to his daughters' attention.

"It is a business matter," Henri clarified.

Both Marie and Claude visibly relaxed.

"When shall I come to you, sir?" asked Monsieur de la Noue, still looking puzzled.

"No, no, monsieur," cried Henri above the racket. "Do not trouble yourself, I will come to you." At that he rose from his seat, bowed and left the group.

"What do you think he could be about?" I heard Claude ask Marie, but Marie shook her head, looking almost as puzzled as her father.

After their meal Dufour returned to carry Marie off for another dance and one of the young men from the village blushingly sought out Claude. Monsieur de la Noue was left alone once more. I found myself gazing at him as he watched his daughters and I wished the mirror would show me the dancing. It may have been my imagination, but despite the contentment in his thin face, I still fancied I could see a deep sadness lurking in his eyes and I could not help but feel responsible.

I did not have to sit looking at Isabeau's father for long. A sound intruded over the gaiety of the Vicomte's spring dance. Oddly, it was the sound of Isabeau's virginal.

It was not late. The western sky still held the faded flush of the departed sun. I, myself, had only just finished my own meal, eaten in lonely solitude in my study, while watching the lives of Isabeau's family. If Isabeau and I had dined together, as we used to do, we would most likely still be lingering over dessert, while I gathered my courage to ask for her hand once again. So my surprise was not so much that she was awake, but that she was in the music room.

Of course I left the de la Noues to their dancing and made my way there. I did not go inside—I wasn't sure yet if she wanted my company. But I hovered in the doorway.

She was not playing the usual parlor music she most often chose in the mornings. Tonight she was playing lively tunes akin to those being performed by the musicians at the Vicomte's dance.

She finished a piece shortly after I arrived and although I swear I had not made a noise, she turned toward me with a sheepish smile on her face.

"Good evening, Beast," she said. "I hope I'm not disturbing you."

"Never," I said.

She made a droll face and I laughed.

"I swear I heard music floating through my bedroom window this evening," she said musingly, flicking through the pages of music on the virginal before her. I stared.

"Perhaps there is some country dance being held somewhere

not too far away," she continued. She looked up at me again. "Have you never heard such music floating to you from over the forest?" she asked.

I shook my head. "I never listened for it, at any rate," I told her.

"Well, if you were going to hear it, this is the season for it," she said. She put her head on one side and her face grew sad and serious. "Whatever did you do here, all alone for so long?" she asked. "Especially at night. I never knew how long an evening could be."

"Are you very lonely, here?" I choked out, more than a little taken aback by her line of thought.

A smile twitched up one side of her mouth. "Not when you are about, Beast," she said teasingly. "But I cannot be bothering you all the time."

"It is no bother," I insisted.

"I knew you would say that, of course," she said, turning back to her music. "Will you stay and listen to me? We can't have dancing, I suppose, but I can supply the music."

I went and sat in my accustomed chair by the window and Isabeau began to play once more. After a few minutes, however, my gaze was distracted from Isabeau by some glimmering light in the garden outside. I turned in my seat to see what it could be. What I saw made me spring out of my chair.

"Isabeau!" I cried, holding out my paw toward her. "Come quickly!"

"Whatever is it?" she asked, stopping in the middle of the piece she was playing.

"Just come," I insisted.

She was at my side in an instant, and with her hand in my

paw we hurried through the house, through one of the down-stairs salons and out on to the terrace. The moment we stepped through the doors, Isabeau gasped.

"Oh my!" she breathed.

Even though I had seen it from above, I was also enchanted into temporary wordlessness. To one side of us, the yew walk marched away toward the boundary hedge, and on the other my bedraggled autumn grove stood. Before us, a green lawn sloped away to the flat space usually inhabited by the marquee that had recently appeared. But now it was decked out in a very similar fashion to the lawns of the Château Villemont—only in sub-stantially more lavish style. There were strings of paper lanterns hung upon poles, but these poles were garlanded with ribbons and flowers. Between them, great basins had been placed in which floated tiny candles among a scattering of rose petals and camellias. The space was further decorated with urns of box and ivy clipped into spheres and obelisks. On the other side of the dance floor stood a tiered marble fountain I had never before seen, the light catching in the falling drops of water.

"That's . . ." murmured Isabeau, also, it seemed, speechless.

"Outrageous," I muttered. But Isabeau looked up at me and laughed and pulled me forward for a closer look. As we hurried down the slope, I fancied I *could* hear the far-off fiddles and flutes of the dance at the Château Villemont out here in the warm sum-mer air. Then, as Isabeau and I stepped under the first string of lanterns marking out the square, the music rose around us.

"Oh, listen," cried Isabeau, peering up at the sky in delight, as though the musicians were to be found there. She pulled at my arm again.

"Come *on*, Beast," she laughed, "we *must* dance!"

"I don't know these dances!" I cried in panic—and I didn't.

I had only learned those dreadful courtly dances, where everyone steps solemnly around each other like the figures on a cuckoo clock.

"It's easy!" she cried, still laughing. "Just go around in circles!" She linked her arm through mine and started dragging me about in dizzy spirals. For a few moments I felt like the hulking, awkward beast I was, but then I looked down into her laughing face and something else in me awoke. I couldn't help but laugh back at her.

"Is that all there is to it?" I asked. "Well, then!" And, clasping her arm firmly in mine I began to swing her about even faster. For once my superior size and strength came in handy, and within moments she was shrieking in delight. We capered around in this fashion until we were both so dizzy we began to stumble and nearly ended up in the fountain.

"Oh dear," Isabeau gasped, hanging on to a pole in an effort to stay upright, while I simply gave in and dropped to my knees. "I don't think that's quite how it's done."

"No," I confessed, "I suppose not."

The music continued going around and around, however, in joyful repetition, so when she had caught her breath, Isabeau held out her hand to me once more.

"Shall we try again?" she asked. "With a little more decorum this time?"

How could I resist? This time, however, I tried my best to remember some of the dance steps I had seen earlier in the evening. I very much doubt there is any country dance anywhere in the world quite like what Isabeau and I ended up doing together that night, but as the only people present we were both very well pleased with our performance, so I do not suppose it matters.

When we were really too tired to dance another step, we

turned to find a table and chairs set out by the fountain with a bowl of cold punch ready for us to drink. I had served Isabeau her drink, and was just ladling some into my own glass, when a loud bang sounded nearby and in shock I dropped my glass. It hit the edge of the fountain as it fell and shattered spectacularly. I stared at it in dismay.

"Ohhh!" breathed Isabeau, beside me. Her upturned face was spangled with light. I followed her gaze skyward and saw the fading blooms of fireworks falling through the night. We watched in silent delight for a few minutes as new bursts of pink and gold lit up the sky.

"Thank you, Beast," said Isabeau, looking over at me with shining eyes.

"If I had planned it I would by all means take the credit," I said, my heart skipping at the look on her face. "But I confess I had no thought but to be content with listening to you playing in the music room."

"What happened to your glass?" she asked, seeing my empty hands.

"I dropped it and it broke," I said, puzzled no replacement had materialized.

"Here," she said, refilling her own glass and handing it to me.

"Thank you," I said gravely, trying to stop my hand trembling as I took it from her.

"Pour me another when you are finished," she said artlessly, putting her chin in her hand and looking up at the latest burst of fireworks overhead. A satisfaction that was almost painful welled in my breast. I was almost afraid to think on how perfect this moment was. She had told me her evenings were lonely without my company; we had danced; and now we sat, watching fireworks and drinking punch from the same glass. If it had been pure brandy I could not have felt more intoxicated.

But, as I put the refilled glass down in front of her and she threw me a happy glance as she took it, I understood how the evening would end. A chill weight settled in my stomach.

Almost as though the magic had been awaiting my unpleasant revelation and did not mean to allow a moment for my courage to desert me, the fireworks erupted in one last spectacular explosion of color and then fell away into darkness. Even the lights around us had grown softer and the music faded once more to distant strains.

"That was beautiful, Beast," Isabeau sighed.

"Isabeau, will you marry me?" I blurted out painfully, realizing the evening had now come to a close.

Isabeau sat very still for a moment, then swallowed visibly. She turned to me, her eyes wide. "No," she said carefully, "but I would be very pleased if you would invite me to dine with you again tomorrow night."

"Will you dine with me tomorrow night?" I asked obediently, trying to keep my voice calm.

"Yes, thank you, Beast. I will," she replied cordially.

CHAPTER XXVIII

$\mathscr{O}$ur meeting in the music room the next day, to my regret, did not have the same sense of easy familiarity that had been building between us of late. But I was determined, and Isabeau seemed equally so, not to let the awkwardness of my most recent proposal sour our relations.

So she played to me, and I did my part by listening and basking in the pleasure of her company. When she went out for her walk she made sure I would meet her in the library that afternoon. And when she had had her fill of sketching and being read to, she mentioned how she was looking forward to our evening meal.

"For I am tired of dining alone," she added, putting her pencils away. "Will you meet me in the entrance hall again tonight, Beast?"

"Yes, if it pleases you," I said, laying aside my book.

Isabeau nodded. "I will see you then," she said and, favoring me with a last smile, she left the library.

The hour arrived and found me at my station at the foot of the stairs. She did not keep me waiting. I caught my breath as she appeared at the top of the staircase. Once more she had dressed for dinner as though attending some function of regal proportions. This time her gown was of pale, sea-green silk, with some floral pattern worked in gold, echoing the color of her honey curls. A collar of aquamarine jewels glittered about her throat.

"Good evening," I said, bowing as she descended.

"Good evening, Beast," she replied, a glint of mischief in her eyes. "Am I grand enough for you tonight?"

"Perhaps," I said airily, trying to conceal my pleasure and offering her my arm. My answer must have pleased her for she gave me an amused smile and tucked her hand through my elbow.

The meal was superb. It even surpassed the meal Isabeau and I had been served the first evening she had dined with me. A centerpiece of ice carved in the shape of a giant cockleshell contained numerous Venetian glass bowls of ices in a variety of flavors, and in the end Isabeau abandoned all interest in the other dishes and concentrated on sampling as many of these as she could manage.

I sat back, drinking a delicious, pale golden wine and watched her, trying to stave off the inevitable. But, at last, she laid down her spoon and pushed her bowl away and propped her elbows on the table.

"That was delicious," she said contentedly.

"Isabeau," I said, "will you marry me?"

The happy, relaxed expression on her face froze. She closed her eyes. I waited. She opened them again and tried to smile at me.

"I had hoped the after-dinner conversation would last a little longer before we reached this point," she said in an attempt at a light tone.

"I must ask," I said.

"No, Beast," she said. "I cannot."

We sat in silence, looking at each other across the table.

"I am sorry," she said sorrowfully.

I shook my head. "You are honest," I said.

"I really am sorry," she repeated.

I nodded and rose from my seat.

"Can we not just be friends, Beast?" she asked, pleading.

"We are always friends, I hope," I answered. As usual, my question had killed the conversation, so there seemed little point in prolonging the awkwardness between us and I left. As I stepped through the door, though, I thought I heard her catch her breath as though to speak to me. But she did not and I gently pulled it closed behind me.

It had all happened just as I'd thought it would. I had asked, she had refused. Still, I could not help the disappointment and hopelessness that rose within me. I thought of going straight to bed, but I feared in my present mood I would just toss and turn. So, instead, I went to my study to see if I might distract myself by looking in on the de la Noues.

They were a quiet family party that night, sitting peacefully around the fire. Isabeau's father was reading, Marie was writing in her book and Claude was sewing. They spoke little, but de la Noue would cough every now and then and Claude was humming ever so quietly as she worked. The melody was familiar and after a moment I recognized it as one of the tunes from the Vicomte's dance. As I watched, Marie glanced up at her sister and a knowing smile twitched at her lips.

This was not much, but it was enough to turn my thoughts from hopeless contemplation of the impossible task of winning Isabeau's hand back to the successes I had most recently gained in restoring her to the land of the living. Thus I was able to go to my bed with a tolerably peaceful mind.

If the worst of my disappointment was soothed by witnessing this vignette, all the old fears for Isabeau's health sprang back into life when, some hours later, I was awoken by the whispering echo of Isabeau weeping. These were not the desperate, heartbroken sobs that had drawn me from my bed some weeks earlier. But it was not possible for me to hear her in any kind of grief without attempting to somehow ease it.

As I drew on my robe and hurried through the house, the sounds stopped and started again several times. But when I stood outside her door at last, I could still hear the hushed, sad noises issuing from the other side.

Hesitantly I knocked upon the door and called, "Isabeau! Can I help?"

There was a brief silence, then the handle turned and the door opened. Isabeau stood there in her nightgown with a shawl wrapped around her shoulders.

"Beast," she murmured, wiping the tears from her eyes with the heel of her hand. "How is it you always know when I want you?" She gave me a watery smile and stepped away from the door, inviting me in.

"I—I heard you," I confessed uneasily. "I don't want to intrude. But . . . is there something I can do to help?"

She gave me another sad smile. "If you would just sit with me awhile, I would be grateful," she said uncertainly.

"Of course," I said, the constriction about my heart easing a little. "May I get you anything?"

"No, no." She shook her head and turned back toward the fire. I took a step to follow her, then stopped. There were two chairs now, where there had only been one before. Isabeau seated herself.

"You were expecting me?" I asked as she sat down. Another shawl was lying on the end of the bed, so I took it up and spread it over her knees. She gave me a far more convincing smile at this and I sat down, warmer than simple proximity to her small bed-chamber fire could account for.

"It has been here since the morning after you last visited me in the middle of the night," she explained, a hint of amusement in her smile. "It is just as well really. For you are far too big to sit hunched up on the footstool like you did last time. And I know you too well to think I might have any hope of convincing you to take this chair, while *I* sat on the footstool."

I had to smile at this.

"Are you sure you do not want anything?" I asked.

Isabeau made a face. "Oh dear," she said. "I *do* make a poor hostess. Beast, surely *I* should be offering hospitality to *you*, don't you think? Do *you* want anything?"

I made a thoughtful noise deep in my chest. Isabeau looked delighted.

"Did you just growl at me?" she asked.

"No!" I said, offended. "But as it happens, since you have woken me in the dead of night, and I presume my task is to get us both back to sleep, I consider some mulled wine is in order."

"That is a superb idea!" she said and clapped her hands imperiously. "House!" she cried. "Mulled wine for two, please."

Immediately a pewter jug and two tankards appeared by the fender.

"Very good!" cried Isabeau and she took up the jug and poured a tankard for me. It reminded me of Marie serving mulled wine to Dufour and her family and I must have stared a little, for Isabeau frowned at me.

"Beast?" she asked. "Is something amiss?"

"No, no," I answered. "I was just thinking you reminded me of someone."

She poured a cup for herself and we drank in silence for a minute or two.

"Isabeau," I said eventually, "will you tell me what upset you so?"

A shadow fell across her face and she gave me a quick, guilty glance, then looked moodily into the fire.

"You don't—" I began, not wanting to pry. But she waved a hand at me and I fell silent.

"I . . ." she began, then stopped. She took a deep breath and started again.

"I'll tell you, Beast," she said, her chin lifted obstinately. "But only on condition you pretend to be someone else!"

"I beg your pardon?" I asked, startled.

"Can you do that?" she persisted stubbornly.

"I'm not sure," I confessed.

Isabeau gave an exasperated sigh and closed her eyes. "Just try," she said, with her eyes still closed.

"Very well," I said, still puzzled.

"I have a friend," she said, keeping her eyes shut. "Today he asked me something, and I did not give him the answer he wanted."

My heart lurched within me, but I stayed silent.

"My answer made him sad. I know it did. And so I was upset. But—" Here she opened one eye and glared at me. I sat very still, staring at her in dismay.

"My friend has a tendency toward despondency," Isabeau said, an edge of severity in her voice. "If he knew I had been upset, he would be sad. And then I would be more upset and he would grow sadder and—" She paused and opened her other eye, fixing me with a very direct stare. "Do you see my dilemma?"

"I do indeed," I said, trying to keep my voice neutral. "Perhaps . . ."

"Yes?" asked Isabeau, an edge to her voice.

"Are you quite recovered?" I asked.

"A little better," said Isabeau.

"Then perhaps if you were to get a good night's sleep and show him a cheerful face on the morrow, he will have no cause to be despondent," I finished awkwardly.

I was rewarded with a droll smile from Isabeau. I smiled nervously back. In response she reached out with one bare foot and nudged my leg sharply. We looked at each other and she giggled. My small smile became a grin and she grinned back at me happily.

"I suppose that is a hint for me to turn you out and go back to bed, then?" she asked, stifling a yawn.

I drained my cup. "Yes," I said, firmly suppressing my strong inclination to sit here, drinking mulled wine with her until dawn. *Really, it wouldn't do.* I stood up and she stood, too.

"Goodnight, Beast," she said, holding out her hand.

"Goodnight, Isabeau," I said, taking it and kissing the back of it with more confidence than I felt. She smiled at me again.

When I returned to my own bed, sleep came to me instantly and I do not think I ever slept so deeply or so well as I did for the remainder of that night.

*　*　*

The next day passed pleasantly enough. In the afternoon, as Isabeau was putting her brushes and pencils away, she said, without looking at me, "Do we dine together again tonight, Beast?"

"Certainly," I said, a happy warmth flushing my body.

Again, I met her at the stairs, and again we dined, and again, when we had eaten our fill and Isabeau laid down her spoon, I asked her the question I had to ask.

"Isabeau, will you marry me?" I begged.

The light went out of her face.

"No, Beast, I cannot," she replied sorrowfully, looking down at her lap.

"Then," I said, choosing my words carefully, "will you consider indulging me in a game of chess, perhaps?"

She lifted her face to look at me and the shadows receded from her eyes.

"Of course," she said, her voice warm with relief.

So we took ourselves back to the library, where we found two comfortable chairs and a chess set all ready for us by a good fire, and played until it was very late indeed.

CHAPTER XXIX

$\mathcal{I}$n the absence of Isabeau fully and freely returning my regard, I was now as content with my life as it was possible to be. We dined together daily. And, while on the nights I chanced to make my proposal that same haunted look came into her eyes, instead of fleeing from her with my tail between my legs, I would offer her my arm and we would go together to the library to play at chess, or drafts, or fox-and-hounds, or some other such game, until it was time to retire.

My time to look in upon Isabeau's family became fairly well restricted to the mornings, when Isabeau took her walk, or the late afternoon when we parted from reading in the library. However, the de la Noue household was also enjoying a similar period of contentment and prosperity. René Dufour continued his quiet, modest courtship of Marie and the Vicomte once more took a direct hand in steering the course of his own path to happiness in securing the affections of the fair Claude.

He scarcely waited a week after the summer dance before waylaying Claude on her return from the markets. "Waylaying" is perhaps an unfortunate term to use, but this time Claude did not look at all disconcerted, only pleased at the happy "chance" that saw him cross her path.

He greeted her and instantly dismounted, and was readily granted the favor of walking with her for a short time. Claude was even so good as to overlook the further coincidence that he happened to be carrying with him a small bag once more filled with oranges from his hothouse that he thought the sisters would be happy to make use of.

"For now it is summer, I simply cannot use them all," he insisted, handing it to her as she blushed.

I am happy to say there was no want of conversation on this occasion and it was only as they were drawing close to the hill over which the cottage lay, when the Vicomte suddenly said, "Stay! I had forgotten!"

"What?" asked Claude, her face glowing and a curl of hair, dislodged during her walk, lying most becomingly across her cheek.

"I meant to ask—that is, I do not know if you overheard me mention to your father I wished to consult with him on a matter of business?" Henri asked.

"Oh, yes," said Claude.

"I had a man who managed certain interests for me," Henri explained. "One Monsieur Beautin. However, he sadly passed away some weeks ago and I was wondering if your father might favor me with some advice?"

Claude opened her eyes wide in surprise. "I do not know," she said uncertainly. "I mean, I am sure—" She stopped.

Henri looked at her, his face also uncertain. "I confess," he said tentatively, "I made some inquiries as to his reputation and I am assured your father can provide me with the counsel I need. I must tell you I heard nothing but good about him."

Claude's face brightened at this reassurance.

"Thank you," she said. She dropped her eyes to the ground. "I understand our current straitened circumstances are as a result of Father insisting on meeting his commitments."

Henri nodded sympathetically, a warm light in his eyes.

"Do you think it would be convenient," he said, "if I were to call on Monsieur de la Noue tomorrow? At about ten o'clock, perhaps?"

"I do not believe he has any engagements," answered Claude. "If by some chance he does, I can leave word at the Crossed Keys."

Henri nodded. "Thank you, mademoiselle," he said, bowing elegantly. Claude gave him her hand and dropped a neat little curtsey, and they parted. This time Claude did not seem to mind when he stayed to watch her over the hill, or, indeed, that he was able to witness the several shy glances she cast over her shoulder at him as she went.

Claude did not tell her father about the Vicomte's request to meet with him when she arrived home. Rather, she waited until the evening when Marie returned, driven home by René Dufour. The moment she heard the wheels of Dufour's cart she ran out to the gate, and after waiting decorously until her sister's good-byes were done, she hurriedly explained the Vicomte's request, before the two of them reached the front door. Marie halted on the path and turned to Claude.

"Indeed?" she asked in some surprise. "This may be just what he needs!"

"Yes," agreed Claude, "but will he consent to it? I think it a perfectly wonderful idea myself, but Papa's confidence is so shattered."

"Yes," said Marie thoughtfully, her face grave. She stood in silence for a few moments.

"Oh, do say you can think of a way to manage him," pleaded Claude fretfully.

"I think I may have a way," said Marie slowly. She gave Claude a sharp look. "Can you bear the indignity of my mentioning the Vicomte's interest in you to Papa?"

Claude bit her lip, but nodded.

"Then leave it to me," said Marie, more firmly now. "And I suppose," she added, adopting a resigned demeanor, "I will have to concoct some sort of delicacy fit for offering to his Excellency by way of refreshment."

"Oh, I was so hoping you would agree to that," confessed Claude, as the two of them went arm in arm into the house.

The next day the Vicomte de Villemont arrived faithfully at the de la Noues' cottage. This time, however, instead of having to wait for a glimpse of Claude, it was she who came out to greet him and open the little wicket gate.

"Vicomte," she said shyly as he dismounted and led his horse through into their small front yard. He bowed, and she curtsied, and then they stood there for a moment, he looking delighted, she looking charming. It took a moment for Villemont to realize he was staring, at which point he recovered himself and looked about for somewhere to tie up his horse. This done, he followed Claude into the cottage.

The Vicomte was a tall man and had to stoop a little to enter the doorway into the de la Noues' parlor, which lent his demeanor something more than his usual air of self-effacement. But Monsieur de la Noue, who appeared to be thoroughly overcome at the thought of the Vicomte coming to wait upon him, was so deferential in his welcome, it fell to Villemont to take charge of the pleasantries, otherwise the conversation would have stalled entirely.

Once her father and Villemont had shaken hands, Claude very prettily asked if she could fetch them some refreshment. It looked as though Villemont might decline on account of it being any trouble whatsoever, but Monsieur de la Noue at last seemed to recall what it meant to be a host.

"Thank you, my dear," he said firmly to Claude. "That would be kind. Sir, what will you have? Wine or ale?"

"Ah," said the Vicomte, caught between not wanting to draw unnecessarily on his host's scant resources and not wanting to offend.

"If I might make a suggestion," said Claude, "Madame Minou's brother has been so kind as to stock our cellar with a dozen or so bottles from his own vineyard. It is very good wine."

"Oh yes," said Villemont, looking pleased. "Well, that would be lovely, thank you."

With Claude absent, the two men spoke briefly about mundane things such as the warming summer and Villemont's own local farming concerns. Then Claude returned with the wine and some slices of cake she pressed upon the Vicomte.

"You must, for it is made with your own oranges," she said, smiling. Of course, Henri accepted and was even happy to own it was very good cake indeed. When Claude had left the room again, Monsieur de la Noue bid Villemont to a seat.

"You said you wished to consult with me on some matter?" he asked uncertainly. The Vicomte was silent for a few moments as he finished his mouthful, then he cleared his throat.

"Sir," he began, "I have a business proposition to make to you."

Monsieur de la Noue's look of curiosity and concern gave way to one of surprise.

"I have recently had the misfortune to lose an old friend who I was in the habit of going to for business advice of a certain nature," the Vicomte continued. "His son has now taken over his legal practice, and is very capable in his way, but himself owns he does not have the depth of experience his father had in these matters. The advice I require relates to investments I have abroad, and I understand you have considerable experience in these matters."

Monsieur de la Noue, who had been staring at Villemont incredulously, was overcome by a fit of coughing. He turned away for a moment, until he was able to catch his breath.

"Vicomte," said Monsieur de la Noue when he was able to speak at last, clearly trying to keep the bitterness from his voice, "I thank you for your compassion toward a man in my reduced circumstances, but you can see for yourself what all my experience and knowledge has brought me to."

"Sir," countered Villemont, "I understood your misfortunes were largely of a nature that was beyond your own control."

"Again, I thank you," said Monsieur de la Noue, "and I can honestly say that was the case. However, I do not hold myself blameless." He coughed again and took a drink from the cup Claude had poured for him.

"Here is my proposal," said Villemont, leaning forward in his chair, an expression of the utmost seriousness on his face. "Will you come and consult with me, Tuesday next, and give me your advice? I will then consult with Monsieur Beautin before I decide to take it. If I take it and it proves good, I will then pay you at your terms. Then we may discuss doing business again. Will you agree to that?" He rose and approached Monsieur de la Noue, holding out his hand.

"I will agree," said Monsieur de la Noue, also rising and still looking faintly bewildered, "with one addition. You only pay my terms if you find them fair and reasonable."

"I am confident of finding them so," said Villemont, grasping Monsieur de la Noue's hand and shaking it firmly.

I did not see the following meeting between Villemont and Isabeau's father, as it occurred in the afternoon, and as usual I was occupied with reading to Isabeau. But it seemed each of them was pleased with the outcome, for, not a fortnight later, Monsieur de la Noue was again called to attend the Vicomte. And a week later he was summoned a third time. After that, Isabeau's father and Villemont must have come to some arrangement, for every Tuesday morning, promptly at ten, a carriage would arrive at the de la Noues' door and Monsieur de la Noue would enter it and leave the cottage to go and meet with Villemont.

This new enterprise was treated with some suppressed joy by his daughters, who—in his absence—danced for joy in their kitchen the day the carriage first arrived to collect him. When he returned from that meeting carrying a purse full of the Vicomte's gold, Marie had to take herself off to her bedroom, she was so overcome with tears of joy.

And so the summer passed away in a sort of happy dream. Isabeau and I were on the best of terms and, discounting any concern for Isabeau herself, her sisters were each in a fair way to finding their own personal fulfillment. Even her father seemed better placed to regain his shattered confidence than ever before. But the year marched on and all too soon the days began to grow shorter and the flowers in my summer gardens began to fade. At the same time, my autumn grove, which had become a verdant, shaded shelter from the summer heat, began to show hints of gold and vermilion once more.

I had never felt the turn of the season to be less welcome than it was that year. There was nothing that served as such a sharp reminder that my time with Isabeau was coming to an end, as the reversion of my magical summer paradise to the natural cycle of the seasons. Autumn was here. Winter was on its way.

CHAPTER XXX

*I*t was no easy task to contain the desperation that surged in my heart each time Isabeau cast down her eyes and told me "No," she could not be my wife. I tried very hard not to let my sadness color my demeanor toward her. But then something occurred that, ironically enough, resulted in somewhat lowered spirits for us both. I say it was ironic, for this event, of itself, was reason for much joy for Isabeau's family and anyone that loved them.

The day on which it occurred began to sour early. After Isabeau played to me in the music room, she left for her walk. But she returned early, on account of the weather, which that morning was cold and gray. The heavy clouds were as good as their promise and sent down a chill shower Isabeau was forced to escape by running back indoors with her shawl over her head. So I did not get to see her pass under my window as usual. It made me realize I had been neglecting the enchantments controlling the climate in my gardens. But, even as I tried to send the shower away, I found this part of the magic had grown vague and elusive. Eventually I gave up in irritation.

The summer marquee had been taken down some weeks earlier and while we still went to the orchard some afternoons to sit and read under trees heavy with apples, today was so dreary there was no question of conducting our usual afternoon activities anywhere but the library. However, when I went to meet her there, instead of finding her busy with arranging leaves and flowers for drawing, I found her standing by the window, looking pensively out at the far-off treetops of the forest, visible over the hedge. She did not hear me come in and it was not until I came to stand beside her that she noticed I was there. Many of the forest trees were already in the full panoply of autumn splendor; some, indeed, were already starting to lose their topmost leaves. Most of the green now to be seen on the other side of my hedge was that of the evergreen trees. Tall, somber spikes that would provide the only hint of color out there once the snows fell.

For a moment, as I looked at Isabeau staring out at the trees, I thought perhaps the advancing of the season was as little welcome to her as it was to me. Then she turned and saw me and a shadow of such guilty sorrow passed across her face, I realized she must have been thinking of her family and how long it was since she had seen them. And perhaps counting how many weeks it would be until she could be with them once more.

She didn't draw that day, but chose to curl up in a chair close by as I read to her. After a while, I looked up to see her staring at me, her chin in her hand. She smiled as my eyes met hers, as though she had been waiting for me to pause, so I laid the book aside.

"This is very pleasant, Beast, is it not?" she asked a little wistfully.

"Yes, indeed," I replied.

"So why is it I am so gray and out of sorts today?" she asked.

"The weather?" I suggested.

She sighed. "Is it always so temperamental here, in autumn?" she asked. "Last year at the cottage the weather was quite glorious, I remember. It grew cold, but the sun was still warm."

"I hardly know," I confessed. "I have not had a true autumn here for so long. Parts of my gardens have lived in autumn the year around, but I wouldn't think the weather they experienced was necessarily representative of the natural climate here."

Isabeau frowned. "Yes," she said thoughtfully. "I suppose that's true. The gardens were quite different when I came here. Why did you change them?"

"I didn't," I said, slightly embarrassed. "They have themselves slipped back into the natural way of things."

"Now why would they do that?" Isabeau mused.

Because you came, I wanted to say, but my tongue cleaved to the roof of my mouth.

"Do you not like them this way?" I asked after a moment, trying to direct the conversation to subjects I could actually discuss. Isabeau looked thoughtful again.

"Yes," she said at last, "I think I do. The strangeness of it all was very pretty when I arrived. But I think I am more comfortable with gardens that flower and fruit and change in the more ordinary way."

"Well, there you have it," I said. "If that is what you prefer, then of course my gardens will have changed to accommodate you."

"I see," said Isabeau, sinking back into her chair. It seemed for a moment she was about to ask me something else, but she remained silent.

Perhaps, I thought, *she was going to ask if I will rearrange things when she is gone.*

We met again at the usual time for dinner. This time, however, when the meal ended, her eyes were brighter than usual and I saw her blink several times. *Could she be crying?* I wondered. I forbore to press my blighted suit and humbly asked if she would favor me with her company in the library instead. But this time, she declined.

"I am sorry, Beast," she said, "but I have something of a headache tonight. Would you mind very much if I went straight to bed?"

"Of course not," I said gallantly. "May I walk you to the stairs?"

"Thank you," she said and put her slender hand confidently upon my hairy, black paw. I stood at the foot of the stairs and watched her ascend, then wandered despondently to my study.

I had not looked in upon Isabeau's family at this time of day for many weeks now, but it was an attractive proposition compared to the alternative of sitting and contemplating my solitude for the remainder of the evening.

I pushed aside the drape covering the mirror and was greeted with the sight of Isabeau's family sitting down at their kitchen table, having just finished their dinner. René Dufour was again there as their guest.

"That was excellent," said Dufour seriously. "I never eat so well as when I come here."

Marie laughed. "Do not let your sister hear you say such things!" she warned, but her face was pink and she looked well pleased with his compliment.

"She has said herself her cooking is not equal to yours," said Dufour, smiling at Marie.

"Oh, stop!" she said, blushing even more. "Will you gentlemen take your ease in the parlor?"

"Thank you, my dear," said Monsieur de la Noue, rising slowly.

"Will there be mulled wine?" asked Dufour, a twinkle in his eye.

Marie rolled her eyes at him and Claude hid a small, satisfied smile behind her hand.

"I only ask because it is grown so cold now!" cried Dufour in defense. Then he turned his knowing smile on Claude.

"And if I am not mistaken, those are the Vicomte's oranges there, on the sill, and I know what wizardry your sister can do with those, mademoiselle."

There was indeed a bowl on the sill with three oranges in it. I smiled to myself. At this season Villemont could hardly still be using the excuse his poor trees were groaning under the weight of excess fruit he could not use.

"The same wizardry she can turn upon an entire barrelful of apples, I suppose," returned Claude. And now it was Dufour's turn to look abashed and I saw a bowl on the table brimming with crisp, red apples, and beside it a dish containing the remains of a pie.

"Go and sit," said Marie, flapping her hands. "I will bring the wine."

Dufour and Isabeau's father retired to the parlor, while Marie and Claude cleared the kitchen, each pair talking together with the ease of familiarity. Eventually Marie went in with the wine to set it to warm by the fire, and Claude soon followed. I noticed another chair had been added to the scanty collection of parlor furniture, which meant Marie could now eschew the stool and sit by Dufour in relative comfort. Claude still elected to take her seat by the window where the lamp was, so she could do her needlework.

They sat and talked and drank Marie's wine when it was ready, until at last Dufour rose from his chair, saying he had to go. Claude and Monsieur de la Noue said their good-byes there in the parlor, but Marie went to hold the lamp while Dufour readied his cart.

Just before he climbed up onto the driver's bench, he turned to Marie, his face resolute.

"Mademoiselle," he said, "I must ask you something."

Marie stared up into his serious face, and her lips parted in an expression of surprise.

"I have known you only since the spring," he said urgently, "and I know I cannot offer you anything like the life you used to lead. But I beg you will consider my poor offer kindly when I ask if you will accept my hand and my heart in marriage."

Marie said nothing, but her eyes filled with sudden tears and she lifted her hand to her mouth.

"Do not answer me now," said Dufour, a little breathlessly. "Think on it for a day. Your father might well still turn his fortunes around—I know the Vicomte has employed his services. It might not be wise to settle yourself if there is a chance of something better."

"You want me?" Marie whispered, sounding shocked.

"With all my heart," said Dufour, his voice catching. He looked worried.

"But—" said Marie, disbelievingly. She took a shaking breath. "You love me?"

Dufour nodded. "Think on it," he begged. "I know I cannot expect—"

"René," interrupted Marie, putting her hand on his arm. "I don't need a day. Or a moment. Yes! My answer is yes!"

Dufour's eyes lit up and he let out a great sigh of relief. He took up Marie's hand and kissed it fervently. Then his face became serious again.

"Marie," he said in a voice that trembled ever so slightly. "I insist you sleep on it. I will come again tomorrow and if your answer is still yes, I will speak to your father."

Marie drew his hand to her lips and kissed it just as ardently as Dufour had kissed hers a moment before.

"If you like," she said. "It will not change."

"I hope not," said Dufour, trying to look serious, but unable to hide his delight. "I will come to the Crossed Keys to bring you home tomorrow."

He lifted her hand to kiss it again, but Marie tugged it aside, tilting up her face. Dufour's face broke into a foolish smile and he took her face in his hands. Their lips met.

Long moments passed.

Eventually he let her go, grinning sheepishly. Marie's face was radiant. Dufour clambered reluctantly up into the cart, still holding her hand.

"*À bientôt,*" she whispered.

He bent and kissed her hand once more before urging his horse forward. Marie watched until he was out of the reach of her small lantern and went inside, covering her smile with her hand.

For some reason she chose not to share her news with Claude or her father that night. But, after they had gone up the bare, wooden stairs to bed, she sat down in the kitchen with her pen and some paper.

"Dear Isabeau," she wrote, "I have some news. It is so momentous and so delightful, perversely I must keep it to myself for just tonight. I don't know why. For it will make Papa and Claude so very happy. But, just for tonight, it is my secret.

"Which does not offer any rational explanation for why I am now about to tell you my news. Happiness has made me capricious. You see, darling Isabeau, tonight René asked me to marry him. Now, this next part is the most irrational of all. You see, I tried to say yes. Even now, every part of me is thrumming with the chant of 'Yes and yes and yes again!' But, perverse man, he would not let me. He said I must think on it for a day and give him my answer tomorrow. His excuse was Papa might yet right his fortunes and then I could do better for myself! Obscene! Outrageous! Unthinkable! I stamp my foot!

"If Papa won every cent of his fortune back tomorrow, I would gladly turn my back upon all of it for the chance to be a farmer's wife. A *particular* farmer's wife. Ah! My darling René!

"Wish me happy, dear Isabeau! Perhaps you will receive my letter tomorrow morning, with your breakfast, and you can feel smug that you, of all my family, knew it first."

Marie sealed up the letter and went and put it in Isabeau's box upon the mantelpiece. Then, before she went up to bed, she did a little dance about the empty parlor by the light of the glowing embers in the fireplace.

I watched her go, a curious mix of conflicting emotions stirring in my breast. I was very happy for her. I was. It was most satisfying to see that courtship come to its desired conclusion. But, even so, I knew a pang of envy for Dufour, who had asked and been answered upon the instant, with such perfect frankness and affection, even while he sought to delay Marie giving him her answer!

All this and, once more, I was beset by doubts at having never shown Isabeau the glass in my study. Indeed, she had not been inside this room since the first night she spent in my house. I knew what happiness it would mean to her to know Marie was going to be married. I felt a sudden, sharp guilt for having wit-nessed that private moment between Marie and Dufour, when even today I had seen Isabeau staring out over the forest in ap-parent homesickness.

But I still did not want to think about relinquishing the glass to Isabeau. I did not know if it would cure or quicken her homesickness. I did not know what she would think of me for using it for so long without her knowledge. So I took the only course of action open to me and stumped, growling, off to bed.

CHAPTER XXXI

$\mathcal{I}$ had expected Isabeau to show some elation at her sister's news. However, when I met her in the music room the following day she was subdued and the music she chose reflected a somewhat somber turn of mind. It suited my own mood, which had not improved overmuch since the previous evening, but I was puzzled at hers.

When she finished, she sat staring into space for a moment, then threw me a quick, darting look.

"Do you walk out this morning?" I asked. The weather was significantly improved upon the day before.

"Yes," she said, somewhat unenthusiastically. Then she surprised me. "Beast, would you mind very much coming with me?"

"Of course," I said, laying aside my book instantly. "I would be happy to."

She gave me a little wry smile.

"You are very good to me," she said lightly, but there was something of a catch in her voice that made me wonder. "Solitude when I want it, company when I choose."

I stood and offered her my arm.

"Who else have I to please?" I asked her. "I have been here for so long, I am done with pleasing just myself."

Again, that little shadow I had started to notice lately crossed her face. But then she smiled and rose from her seat, taking my arm.

"Thank you," she said.

In the hall we paused to don the cloaks laid out for us, side by side, before going into the gardens. The air was crisp, but after the previous day's showers, the clouds had vanished and the sunlight shining down upon us was clear and warm. The dissatisfaction I had mysteriously experienced on Marie's betrothal also vanished—or at least it became obscured by my happiness at Isabeau leaning close upon me as we walked.

We walked in silence for some time, Isabeau choosing our path until, suddenly, she burst out, "I cannot account for it!"

Startled, I stopped.

"Account for what?" I asked.

She looked up at me, then away, until eventually she said, "I want to tell you."

"Shall I pretend to be someone else again?" I asked. That drew a quick laugh from her.

"No." She smiled. "Dear Beast. No, it is just . . ." She paused again, then drew a breath and continued. "It means I must tell you something I perhaps should have told you some time ago. I can't think now why I haven't."

"I see," I said carefully, a suspicion of where this was leading forming in my mind. She gave me another of those quick, searching looks.

"It may be you know already!" she said accusingly.

"Will you tell me?" I pleaded.

She cast me a look that started in exasperation and ended in a smile.

"For some time now," she said slowly, looking down and toying with the lace of my cuff where she held my arm, "I have been receiving letters from my eldest sister, Marie. She gives me all the news of my family I could wish for."

I held my breath. After a moment she looked up again, her eyes searching my face for my reaction.

"I knew she wrote to you," I said. "I hoped you received the letters."

Isabeau let out a sigh as though she, too, had been holding her breath.

"This morning I received a letter from her saying she has accepted a proposal of marriage," said Isabeau. "From a good man—a farmer. I know him a little. They have been friends for some time. And he has been very kind and helpful to my family."

"You don't seem very happy," I observed.

"That's just it!" cried Isabeau, stopping abruptly. "Why am I not overjoyed? She loves him! She has said so! And even if she hadn't, I can tell from the way she writes about him. He will be able to provide for her very well. And if it's nothing like what we were used to before Papa's fortunes were ruined, it's nothing like the good fortune any of us ever expected to meet with again! And she is *so* happy! So why can I not be happy for her?"

By now our path had taken us up to the gate of my magical rose garden. It was the only part of the garden still in full bloom, although I noticed, even here, there was the odd yellowing leaf, or scarlet hip, among the summer abundance. I led Isabeau inside and we found a seat in a patch of sun, the air around us filled with perfume.

"Are you really not happy for her?" I asked her carefully.

Isabeau looked down and scuffed one toe along the ground.

"Of course I am," she said after a moment. "I am very happy for her. But then," she exploded again, "why do I feel so cross?"

She made an inarticulate noise of frustration and buried her face in her hands. A moment later a shudder ran through her and I realized she was trying not to cry.

I was at an utter loss as to what to do. What I wanted was to put my arms around her and hold her. Instead I patted her ineffectually once or twice on the hand. I was completely stunned when she turned and buried her face in my shoulder.

After a minute or two her shoulders stopped shaking and she sat up straight again, scrubbing the tears from her cheeks with the backs of her hands.

"So silly," she chastised herself fiercely. I sat by in silence.

"Perhaps it's pure jealousy," she said after a while.

"Jealousy?" I asked.

"After we moved to the cottage," Isabeau sniffed, "they relied on me for everything. At home, I was always the *extra* sister, the one in the background. But at the cottage they were both so miserable, they couldn't do anything for themselves. Now Claude has found happiness in keeping the house neat and pretty, and Marie has a garden and hens. And she's getting *married*. They don't *need* me anymore!" She sniffed again and new tears welled up.

"Isabeau," I said, a little hoarse from the intense emotion closing my throat. "Anyone who loves you will always *need* you."

She threw me a little doubtful glance, then her shoulders sagged.

"Yes," she acknowledged. "You are right, as usual." She paused, frowning.

"It is so nice to feel you have some purpose, some sort of contribution to make," she said eventually. "From what Marie says, Claude has made that cottage far more homely than I ever could. They have curtains and posies of flowers and carved wooden animals ornamenting the mantelpiece!"

I had to suppress a smile, remembering Claude's nutcracker.

"And Marie! They all think she's a most brilliant cook and now she's going to be *married*." Isabeau let out another frustrated huff of air and looked up at the sky, blinking away more angry tears. "I am such a horrible sister," she whispered.

"Isabeau," I said, trying to coax her into better humor. In response to my tone she gave me a sad little grimace of a smile and I reached out to touch her shoulder again. But, as I lifted my arm, she moved toward me and I found myself with my arm about her as she leaned into my side. I could barely hear anything for the blood thundering in my ears. I was too afraid to move, in case she would suddenly fly away.

We sat there together for several minutes until, just as my heart finally began to slow, she sat up straight, looking around, a puzzled expression on her face.

"What was that?" she asked.

"What?" I asked her.

"I heard something," she said, frowning. I shook my head. I had heard nothing but the pounding in my ears. After a moment, she looked back at me and smiled, a little more happily this time.

"Thank you, Beast," she said. "I always feel so much better for talking to you."

"It is always my pleasure," I said, trying to master my voice. But the moment was broken and a short while later we walked back to the house and went our separate ways.

* * *

Typically, after spending an hour floating in a pleasurable dream, chiefly made up of my remembrance of the warm weight of Isabeau resting against my side, I was beset by a fit of despondence.

Perhaps her frustration and distress was the result of seeing her two sisters a fair way to being in love and married, while she remained here, with me for a suitor. She'd told me she'd had no sweetheart when she first came here. But reading her sister's letters, filled with tales of Dufour and Villemont and the sisters' growing affections for their beaux . . . Why would she not be out of sorts over yearning for something she did not have herself?

Of course, I only succeeded in making myself perfectly miserable and jealous following this train of thought. I could not sit still. My enthusiasm for watching over the daily lives of the de la Noues had evaporated for the time being. To make matters worse, the thought of the mirror remaining a secret from Isabeau was tormenting me. She had now confessed to me her own secret—Marie's letters. I knew the right thing to do would be to show her the mirror. Yet, still, I hesitated.

That afternoon we met in the library and again Isabeau chose to sit by me, rather than draw. I had no idea where the flowers now came from that stood in the vase on the desk, for almost the only flowers left in the gardens were the roses. But she showed no interest in the unseasonal splendor on her drawing desk, instead coming to sit by me on the couch under the window, she at one end and I at the other.

I read to her for a short while, but I was not much in the mood for it and Isabeau, too, seemed to have her mind on other things. Every time I looked up she was staring out the window, her eyes once more on the far-off treetops of the forest over the hedge. My ill humor began to swell as I imagined her once more thinking of her home and how it was only a matter of weeks now, really, until she would be back there.

I paused, thinking to perhaps finish early, and she spoke.

"Autumn is such a sad, dreary season this year." Her expression matched her solemn tone. "I usually like autumn. I like the change of the season, when you first start to smell the chill in the air. And the scent of fallen leaves. And the colors, of course. But this year I find I just cannot like it." She leaned back in the chair and looked at me mournfully.

"We are a pair, aren't we?" she asked.

I frowned. "What do you mean?" A little, painful ache throbbed somewhere in my chest. She shrugged, giving me one of those smiles that never failed to make me catch my breath.

"We two—we are both miserable today," she pointed out. "What ails you, Beast? You are not often so glum in the afternoons."

I looked out the window. I could hardly tell her the thoughts weighing on my heart today.

"Perhaps I, too, miss the summer," I said evasively.

Isabeau gave me a long look. "It was a lovely summer," she said at last. "I miss being able to go and lie out in the orchard together. There was never anything more charming. How many books do you think we read, in all?"

I smiled a little, unable to resist the pleasure of those memories. "Perhaps fifty?" I suggested.

Isabeau laughed and reached out with her foot and poked me in the leg. "Fifty?" she asked incredulously. "Ridiculous, Beast."

"Perhaps not fifty," I conceded.

Isabeau smiled at me happily. "There," she said, sounding self-satisfied. "I have lifted the cloud from your brow for a moment."

I was struck by inspiration and, setting aside the book in my hand, I stood up. Isabeau looked up at me in surprise.

"You are not going to read any more?" she asked, and I was gratified by the disappointment in her voice.

"No," I said, glancing out the window again. "I have another idea. Will you come outside with me?" She put her hand into my paw, and I led her out through the hall, where we collected warm clothing and gloves. There was a definite nip in the air outside, but any unpleasantness this may have created was entirely dispensed with when Isabeau responded to the chill by taking my arm and huddling against me.

"What scheme have you concocted today?" she asked, looking up at me with a gleam of excitement in her eyes.

"Come," I said. I led her down the steps and through the gardens to the lawn where the marquee had sat. Instead of a marquee, however, there were now archery targets set up against the hedge.

"What is this?" asked Isabeau, puzzled.

"Do you know how to shoot?" I asked her.

"No," she said doubtfully.

"Ah!" I said. "Then today you will learn."

I was perhaps not the most adept of teachers. Archery was something I had been able to practice on my own, but as a solitary pastime it offered far less satisfaction than it did with companions. So, of course, I had not practiced and my skill was sadly dulled. Still, even though I did not hit my targets with anything like the accuracy I would have liked, I could teach Isabeau how to draw a bow. And she was very willing to learn. If the sight of the bare branches in the forest was a reminder of the short time I had left with her, it was easy to banish the specter of my impending misery from my mind when I had to stand so close to her, my hands on hers, assisting her to hold the bow steady and draw it back. She was apparently content with my company also, her earlier dissatisfaction entirely gone. She happily allowed me to correct and support her grip and leaned back into me as we watched her arrows fly across the verge. Even as the cold crabbed our fingers and reddened her cheeks, it was Isabeau who called for warm cider to dispel the chill rather than return indoors.

Indeed, it was not until the light turned thick and coppery and we had to strain to see where our shafts flew, that she reluctantly allowed me to lay aside the bow.

"Have you not had enough of this?" I asked her. "Are your hands not sore?"

"Perhaps," she admitted. "I shall probably find my fingers stiff tomorrow morning." She held out her gloved hands to me and I took them, rubbing her fingers to dispel any lingering aches.

She sighed happily. "Thank you, Beast," she said. "That was a lovely way to spend an afternoon. You have entirely done away with my ill temper. I could not want for a more ideal companion." She smiled up at me and I flushed warm with pleasure.

We walked together back through the twilight gardens to the house. Once inside the hall we stopped and I helped her off with her coat.

"Well," she said, "shall I see you at dinner?"

"Of course," I said.

I walked her to the staircase, my heart beating fast. Such a lovely afternoon. After such a morning. She had sought my company all day. She had leaned on me; she had put her hands in mine. She had told me how much she enjoyed my company. A bout of nervousness possessed me. Would she, perhaps, be minded to accept my proposal tonight?

No.

I dressed with care. The meal was delicious. Isabeau was more beautiful than ever. But the moment her name crossed my lips after she had pushed her plate away, she seemed to freeze and her eyes fluttered closed.

"Will you marry me?" I asked, my voice turning to lead.

There was a long moment of silence.

Isabeau, her eyes still closed, opened her lips.

For the briefest moment I thought perhaps they formed the sound that began the word I most wanted to hear in all the world.

But then her eyes opened again and filled with tears.

"No, Beast," she choked, "I cannot."

I was growing used to the devastation by now. The next words I would have uttered would have smoothed over the new crack between us, would have been a tactful request for her to join me in a hand of piquet or some such. But as I drew breath to invite her, she rose from her chair.

"Excuse me," she said quickly. And before I could say a thing she had rushed from the room.

CHAPTER XXXII

*W*e plunged once more into frustrating awkwardness. Isabeau met me in the music room and played for me the next day, but she did not ask me to accompany her on her walk. She appeared in the library at our appointed meeting time, but became once more absorbed in her drawing and did not talk much to me. Dinner was downright painful. We chatted about the weather and the next book we might choose for our afternoon reading, but I began to resign myself to another lonely evening.

For dessert that evening we had been offered a selection of little flavored crèmes. They sat in pretty pastel-colored rows on a long silver tray and wobbled gently as we moved them. But, even though she chose three, Isabeau did not eat them. Rather, she merely toyed with her spoon.

"Isabeau," I began, but before I could even draw breath to utter my question she held up her hand.

"Why must you keep asking me to—" Her voice was angry and her eyes refused to meet mine. "It's not fair. You always give me everything I ask for. Yet, the one thing you've ever asked of me—the only thing you ever ask—*I just cannot give you.*"

She dropped her spoon into her plate, pushed back her chair and fled.

"Isabeau!" I called, but she had gone. I ran out into the hall after her, calling her name, but she left so quickly I did not even see a flicker of her skirt. She was running toward her rooms, so I did the only thing I could think of and followed her.

I arrived at her firmly closed bedroom door to the muffled sounds of weeping and paused for a moment. Her anger shook me. Why *did* I persist in asking her, when I was almost certain her answer would never change? *Because I don't know what else to do,* I thought despairingly. *I cannot invite her to dances, or bring her oranges or plants for her garden, or drive her home in the dark.* And what did she mean by saying I did not allow *her* to return *my* favors? Eventually I gathered the courage to knock on her door. Immediately the weeping ceased.

"Isabeau," I called through the door, "you are wrong. This is not the only thing I have ever asked. How could you forget? You agreed to give up a year of your life to spend here with me. How can I find any way to repay that gift after so many years of solitude here? The debt I owe to you far outweighs any obligation you should ever feel toward me. You may reject me as many times as you like and never tip those scales one whit."

All I received in response was silence and eventually, utterly dejected, I made my way to my study with the intention of drinking a glass of wine and contemplating the ruination of yet another dinner.

And that is exactly what I did there, for perhaps half an hour, at which time there came a knock on *my* door and Isabeau appeared there, standing quietly, half in shadow, half in candle-light. She looked so like she had the first night I met her, my heart lurched.

"May I come in?" she asked.

"Of course," I said, quickly rising from my chair. She pushed the door open a little farther and slipped in through the gap, almost as though she was trying to avoid being observed entering my study.

"Won't you sit down?" I asked, casting about for some way of setting her at ease. "A glass of wine?"

"Thank you," she said, accepting the glass that materialized upon the instant. To my surprise she turned and sat herself, not on the chair opposite mine, but on a low footstool closer to the fire. For a moment I stood there, unable to move, entranced at the charming picture she made, with her beautiful skirts all crumpled around her, holding her glass of ruby wine. Then she looked up and I collected myself, replacing the decanter on the side table and seating myself back in my chair. She was very close and my heart beat quickly at her nearness. I could not take my eyes off her. Then she looked up at me and gave me a small, sad smile.

"I'm sorry," she said. "Please forgive me."

"Please," I said, "you never need to apologize."

She gave me another sad smile. We sat in silence for a few moments, she gazing down at her glass and I gazing down at her. Eventually she looked back up at me again.

"I know it is highly unorthodox and out of all keeping with our usual routine," she said, "but would you mind very much if I asked you to read to me?"

"Of course not," I replied, feeling a fluttering hope. "Is there anything in particular you would like me to read?"

Isabeau shook her head. "Anything," she said, "just so I might rest my mind."

I put my glass down so that I might go and peruse my

shelves and saw a faded leather volume had appeared beside the decanter. When I picked it up I found it was a volume of poetry. The first poem was about the beauties of spring and seemed pretty enough, so I began to read. As I read the first line, Isabeau closed her eyes. After I had been reading for a few minutes, she put her glass down on the hearth and shifted so she was leaning against the arm of my chair. Her honey-blond hair now rested only an inch below my left paw.

I had read five or six poems and was several lines into the next before I realized the subject matter had changed from the beauties of nature to the beauties of the poet's beloved. I stopped in confusion, half expecting Isabeau to react with embarrassment. But to my surprise she did not stir, even to ask why I had stopped. I leaned forward and saw she had fallen asleep. I wondered what I should do—wake her and send her to bed, or perhaps engage the invisible servants to carry her away as she slumbered? But her face held such an expression of contentment I was reluctant to disturb her at all. I hesitated a moment more. *Should I keep reading?* Taking the trouble to find another book might end in disturbing her. But this poem . . . The words on the page were so close to my feelings for her. When else would I get such an opportunity to express them? She was asleep; if she heard me, it would only be in her dreams. I took a breath and went on.

I continued reading for perhaps an hour. Every now and then Isabeau sighed in her sleep, but otherwise she seemed perfectly at ease. Then, as I began to draw to the end of the slim volume, Isabeau shifted on her stool and her head slid to the side, coming to rest upon my knee. I caught my breath, but she did not wake. Her cheek was warm through the cloth of my breeches. One curl of her honey hair lay over the arm of my chair, caught upon the velvet. I could not help myself. I reached out and touched the silken strands.

Several things happened in quick succession.

As I stroked the lock of hair, I saw a tear slide out from beneath Isabeau's lashes and come to rest on her cheek. At almost the same moment I heard a sound like glass breaking. At this, Isabeau startled awake, sitting up straight with a gasp and turning to stare at me. I snatched my hand away.

"Beast," she said wildly, as though she had found herself somewhere unexpected.

I sat frozen, the book of love poetry in one hand and the other held guiltily in the air. "I . . ." I said stupidly, stricken.

But rather than call me to account for touching her hair, Isabeau rubbed her hands over her eyes and said, "I must have fallen asleep." The tone of her voice made me think something had confused her. She looked up at me and suddenly her eyes filled with tears and she looked quickly away.

"I must have been dreaming," she mumbled. She was breathing quickly. She stood up hastily and nervously began to smooth her skirts. I, too, rose.

"I must be tired, Beast," she said, not meeting my eyes. "I think I must go to bed. Thank you for reading to me." She held out her hand and I took it, and she gave me a brief curtsey. "It was lovely. Goodnight."

And she left so quickly I did not have time to utter another word. I was left standing by the fire clutching the book of poetry, staring after her for the second time that evening.

Now I was confused. Was her discomfort caused by the realization I was reading her love poetry? Or my touching her hair? But there had been no censure in her voice when she left.

Only . . . I stopped and thought about it. Disappointment? Grief? I frowned in puzzlement, trying to account for how I could have inspired those emotions.

Of course . . .

Grimly I imagined her dreaming of a handsome, whole *man* reading her those poems. In that case I could well understand a sense of disappointment upon waking. My good humor evaporating, I threw the book of poetry onto my desk and stalked out of my study to bed.

CHAPTER XXXIII

After that strange interlude in my study, the next morning I wondered if Isabeau would be distant again. To add to my sense of despondency, when I looked out of my bedroom window upon rising, I saw patches of frost riming the grass and fallen leaves. Time was marching on and it was so easy to be swallowed by despair each time I realized how far I was from winning her heart.

But she surprised me. She came to the music room and played. She kept glancing at me as she played and while she smiled at me each time she caught my eye, I could not shake the feeling her mind was occupied with serious thoughts. Still, she gave me no cause to think she wished me elsewhere.

When she finished, she did not get up immediately, but sat looking down and fiddling with something I could not see.

"Beast," she said eventually, "I feel I owe you an explanation for last night. I rushed out so rudely at dinner, and then ran away again from you in your study."

"Isabeau," I started, thinking guiltily of the touch of her hair under my paws.

"Beast," she said quickly, "it's my dreams. I have such vivid dreams. Sometimes I cannot tell if I am awake or dreaming. I think I was still half asleep when I left your study." She stopped abruptly. She looked down and took another breath.

"I do hate being at outs with you," she said, her cheeks growing pink.

"I hope we are never at outs," I said, finally having found something worth saying.

"Now you are just being gallant," said Isabeau, with something a little more like her usual spirit. "If you want to be really gallant, Beast, what you should do is change the subject to spare me any further awkwardness."

She fixed me with a very bright look.

"Perhaps you could ask me if I want to walk out this morning, or if I've had another letter from Marie."

"Which would you prefer me to ask?" I queried.

"Both," she said promptly. "No, wait. Perhaps if you ask me to go for a walk with you, then I can respond that I've had a letter and ask if you'd like me to read it to you?"

"Very much so," I answered, delighted.

Isabeau shook her head. "You're getting ahead of yourself," she chastised me. "You haven't asked me to go for a walk, yet."

We stopped in the entrance hall to don cloaks, given the frost I had seen earlier, then walked out, arm in arm. Isabeau drew out the letter she had in her pocket and read it to me as we strolled around the large pond filling the hedged garden beneath her window. As could be expected, it contained a large amount of discussion of the coming wedding. Dufour had sought the de la Noues' agreement to a wedding date at the beginning of winter. The reason, Marie explained, was because, as a farmer, autumn was one of his busiest times, especially if he was also to get his household in order to receive a new mistress. While in winter, he had told her, he was not so busy and indeed he rarely traveled to the village; if the snows were very deep, it would be impossible.

"We are both agreed it is simply unthinkable that either of us could last out the winter without seeing each other so regularly as we are accustomed to," Marie wrote. Isabeau paused here and for a moment I thought she was going to make a comment of her own. But she did not. "I know that is soon," she continued reading. "Claude says there is far too much to do and is in a state of anxiety lest none of it be done. But, I confess, it seems to me Father Time is dragging his feet in a most unreasonable manner. I cannot wait for the autumn to be over."

Despite the jubilance of Marie's words on the paper, Isabeau's tone was flat and we walked in silence for a few minutes.

"It is a dreary enough season, this year!" she burst out. "But winter is worse. Why hurry it?"

We were silent for a little longer. As Isabeau's words so clearly echoed my own sentiment, I wasn't able to immediately think of anything useful to add.

"What else does it say?" I prompted her eventually. She lifted the letter again, but did not read it out loud.

"Oh," she said after a few minutes.

"What is it?" I asked.

"I'm not sure," said Isabeau, sounding worried. "Marie says here Papa was not able to visit the Vicomte this week on account of a cough that kept him in his bed."

"Is he very ill?" I asked.

"She does not say," said Isabeau, scanning the lines of writing. "She says when the Vicomte heard of Papa's indisposition he sent over his own physician, which was very kind." She flipped the page over and stared at the words.

"Poor Papa," she murmured. "His chest was never very strong." She looked up at me with a strange intensity in her eyes.

"He told us of the desperate state he was in when he chanced upon your gates," she said. "I haven't told you, Beast. But I think that's why I thought I would be safe if I came here."

"What do you mean?" I asked uncertainly, my insides squirming to find myself discussing that shameful bargain.

"Several times in recent years Papa has had to take to his bed from an inflammation of the lungs," she said, shaking her head. "It was foolhardy in the extreme for him to take the route through the forest last winter. It is nothing short of a miracle he never sickened from it. I thought perhaps you had fed him some magical potion to keep him well.

"I thought if you had been kind enough to heal him," she continued, "perhaps you could not be quite the monster Papa described."

"I see," I said.

"You're not a monster at all," said Isabeau, a little severely.

"Ah," I said, thinking, *But you still won't marry me.*

I was growing increasingly desperate. By my reckoning, there was a little less than three months to go until I must open my gates and send Isabeau home. I had no doubt of her *friendship*. I was certain of her sincere regard for me and even that she would be sad to leave me when she went. Indeed, while to begin with I had thought the coming of autumn had made her think more of her home and her family, it was soon apparent that leaving was not actually a prospect she relished. I certainly never raised the subject of her return home, but neither did she. If she were indeed eager to be off back to her family, surely she would have talked of it a little. Perhaps she did not simply to spare my feelings. But, after hearing her decry her sister's yearning for winter to come, I became certain she was as reluctant for the season to advance as was I.

This puzzled me. I could not help but feel a glow of happiness that she looked upon the end of her year with me with so little enthusiasm. But, even so, all this was very, very far from returning my love and consenting to be my wife.

I was at a loss as to what else I could do. We spent so much of the day together, I could not very well sue for more of her time. It would have been entirely understandable if she had in fact grown weary of my company.

Each night that I made my proposal, she heard me and gave me her answer in the negative. She did not even look away from me now, she had grown so used to it. She would watch me with her large eyes dark with sorrow, her hands folded in her lap and her face pale. Then she would reply calmly. And then we would leave the room together and go to the library—or sometimes to my study now—and read or play some parlor game.

I had not shown her the mirror. In fact, I had barely looked into it myself for some weeks now. The last time I had done so, I had seen something that only served to impress upon me even more strongly my failure to inspire Isabeau's deepest affections.

The last time I had drawn apart the drapes, I had seen Claude walking in the market with her basket over one arm. As usual she stopped at her favorite stall—the one selling ribbons and laces—and was in the act of purchasing a length of heliotrope ribbon. She had just handed over her coins and was putting the little packet into her basket, when a young boy ran up to her and stopped beside her, his hands clasped behind his back.

"Excuse me," he cried, "are you Mademoiselle Claude de la Noue?"

"Why, yes," she said, puzzled.

The little boy drew his hands from behind his back and held out a neat posy of flowers to her.

"This is for you," he said, standing very straight.

"Me?" she asked, taking it nervously and glancing all around.

"There's a note," confided the boy, then added, in the manner of one who has had a particular instruction drummed into them, "and I'm to stay in case you've anything to send back."

A little awkwardly, on account of the basket, Claude managed to locate a folded strip of paper wrapped around the stems of the flowers. As she unwrapped it, I saw something glinting beneath it. Claude saw it, too, for she stood very still for a moment to stare at it. It was a small, golden, filigree heart on a length of delicate gold chain. There was only one person it could have come from.

Covering the jewelry carefully with her hand, Claude unfolded the note and smoothed it out. The image of the paper filled the glass. On it I saw in elegant handwriting the following message:

> *Dear Mademoiselle,*
> *I would say you had stolen my heart, except I give it freely to you. There is no one else I'd rather held it. If it is too heavy a burden to bear, please return it and we will part as friends. If you choose to keep it, I will have hope; hope that one day I will see you wear it. On that day I*

will know I may come and ask for your heart in
recompense for the heart you have captured. I hope I may
make it a fair exchange.
    Yours,
    HV

The note was suddenly folded away again and once more I beheld Claude, staring all around her with considerably heightened color, breathing quickly. She did not see what she was looking for, however, and once more her eyes fell on the child in front of her.

"Do you have anything to send back?" asked the little boy impatiently.

Claude looked down and opened her hand a little, looking again at the tiny golden heart glinting in her palm, the chain tangled among the flower stalks.

"No," she said shakily. She closed her hand again around the posy, hiding the chain, and walked back down the street. I watched her as she went, wondering if perhaps the Vicomte had overshot his mark. However, by the time Claude had reached the edge of the village and started back upon the path to the cottage, she was smiling softly and all but glowing, and I had to concede the Vicomte's aim was true.

How to similarly impress upon Isabeau the depth and sincerity of my own affection, I could not tell. Dufour had simply proposed to Marie. The Vicomte's path was a little more difficult, yet even he was making progress. I racked my brain for some strategy to further my suit with Isabeau. Some act that would inspire her to love me. Some *thing* I had overlooked.

Looking back now, it is easy to curse myself for my stupidity. Especially after I had witnessed Claude receive the Vicomte's letter. It was such a simple thing, after all. To do myself justice, though, at the time I had no notion of it being so important, nor did it seem as though it had any effect. But, knowing what I know now, I have a notion this *thing*, this very small *thing* I had so clumsily overlooked, was something akin to setting light to a wick that burns away with a tiny flame until it finally reaches the powder keg and sets the world on fire.

CHAPTER XXXIV

$\mathcal{D}$espite my fervent wishing for time to slow, the seasons continued to turn and soon I was waking up to frost upon the lawns every morning. Delicate ice flowers bloomed over the windows during the night and when we looked out through the misted panes we saw mostly bare branches, with only a few bright leaves clinging here and there. Isabeau had taken to wearing a shawl about the house and when we went out to walk in the gardens we needed thick cloaks and gloves against the cold.

I noticed more and more the songs Isabeau chose to play in the mornings were solemn, languid pieces. She drew less, preferring now to sit by me as I read, pretending—as she said—she was back lying in the long grass of the orchard under the trees. And my occasional proposals began to distress her once again.

With my increasing ambivalence toward entertaining myself by looking into the mirror in my study, I had to find other ways to keep myself busy when I was not with Isabeau. Sometimes I walked alone, sometimes I fenced alone and sometimes I read, but always I was conscious this would be my entire lot when she left.

One day I sat down to read in the velvet chair before the fire in my entrance hall—that same chair I had found myself lying beside when I first came back to the house—but my mood was bleak and I could not concentrate on the book in my hands. Instead I found myself staring into the fire, contemplating how very much more bleak it would be when Isabeau was gone. I was so deep in my thoughts I did not notice Isabeau had walked into the hall. When I finally became aware of the warmth of her presence, I turned to see her standing there with such a look of sadness on her face my heart stuttered. But then she recovered herself and said something bright and trivial and the moment passed.

The day after this I noticed a new catch in her voice when she said, "No, Beast, I cannot." A few days later when I chanced to make another proposal, she again ran from the room.

"Isabeau, I am sorry!" I cried out at her departing back. But she didn't stop. She came looking for me later and refused to hear my apologies, so I refused to hear hers and we both went to our beds that night feeling dissatisfied with ourselves. But the next morning she made me shake hands and played a selection of determinedly cheerful songs.

Two nights later it came to a head.

As the dessert plates began to vanish and small crystal glasses of liqueur appeared before us, the now-familiar air of uncomfortable expectation began to gather. Isabeau avoided looking at me and took small sips of her drink.

"Isabeau," I said, trying to keep my burgeoning disappointment from my voice, "will you marry me?"

"No, Beast," said Isabeau, sounding as upset as ever. "I cannot."

I nodded and put down my unfinished glass.

"Very well," I said sadly. I rose to offer her my arm so we

might remove to the library, but she looked up at me, clutching her glass so tightly I was afraid the stem might snap in her hand. Her face was pale and the very set of her shoulders radiated a brittle unhappiness. I felt wretched.

"Beast," she said desperately, "you know what my answer will always be. It only ever causes the both of us distress. Why must you keep asking me this?"

I was instantly assailed by the impossibility of ever finding a way to explain myself adequately. To tell her of the curse was not only expressly forbidden, it would also make my question—which came from the bottom of my heart—sound hopelessly mercenary. And in any case, how could I hope to put into words the vicious circle that confronted me? That I loved her, but to have any hope of winning her affection I knew I needed to regain my human form, yet to do that, I first had to win her affection and her promise to wed me. I wanted to beat my hands against the blank injustice of it.

Then, in that moment, something crystallized for me. I had to put my hand on my vacated chair to steady myself.

"Because I love you," I said.

Four simple words. And I had never thought to speak them to her.

She did not say anything, but sat, staring at me, her face white and shocked. She raised one trembling hand from her lap and pressed it to her mouth. At once I found I was trembling myself. Lowering my gaze to my black, hairy paw clutching at the gilt scroll of my chair, I said with as much gentleness and control as I could muster, "I am so very sorry to distress you again. Goodnight, Isabeau."

I left the room. But rather than hearing the door click shut behind me, as I expected, I heard the infinitely more painful sound of sobbing. I turned back to look at the door, which stayed open for another moment, as if to reproach me for upsetting her so much. Then it did close, with such a final and decided click, I wondered if I could have opened it again if I tried. Not having the courage to attempt it, I left; and not having the heart to think of anything else to occupy myself, I went straight to my bed.

Of course sleep proved elusive and for several hours I was tormented by visions of her distraught face, and the remembered sounds of her sobs. Did I really love her? I knew I did, but how could I keep asking her this terrible question when I knew the embarrassment it caused her? I tossed and turned trying to reconcile this selfishness on my part. Surely if I truly loved her, I would give up my hopes of returning to humanity and leave her in peace. Indeed, the only thing preventing us from being perfectly comfortable together was my obstinate insistence on proposing to her every few days. Why was I compelled to persist?

Then, somewhere in the very early hours of the morning, a new question emerged. If the Fairy had not told me how to break the curse, would I ever have had the courage to tell Isabeau how I felt?

That was an easy question to answer. Never. But it led to a new question. What was it I was offering her? The pillows I had thrown around in my restlessness returned to the bed, plumped and soft, and I settled into them to contemplate this new conundrum. What could I possibly offer Isabeau? Why should she accept me? Again I considered the lack of randomness in my cursed house and a tiny tingle wriggled down my spine, growing stronger as another new thought clarified itself. If Isabeau had been sent, or brought, because she was the one woman whom I could truly love, was it possible the reverse was true? Had I been kept imprisoned here for so long, waiting out the endless years, because I was the one for her? Every hair of my thick pelt stood upright with something like fear. I pressed my paws to my temples in consternation. *Me* make her happy?

In a terrifying flash, I realized that if I did not accept this was the case and I continued to pursue her, I was, in essentials, no better than my brutish father.

My heart was racing and a chill sweat settled about my neck and shoulders. This new thought triggered a reaction close to panic. I forced myself to confront the question: could I make her happy? I revisited memories of the happiest times we had spent together, when we were both comfortable and at ease. She found pleasure in my company—of this I was certain. An image arose in my mind, of Isabeau at the dining table, hearing my proposal with her eyes closed, her lips moving to form the longed-for words of assent—all my hopes falling to ashes when she opened her eyes.

I pressed the heels of my paws to my eyes. Given what I saw every time I stared into the mirror, I could hardly blame her for keeping any deeper feelings for me at bay. But what could I possibly do? If I had, indeed, managed to win her heart, however unwillingly, my mystification over how I had achieved *that* was no help in determining how I was to convince her to accept it.

Supposing I had in fact won her heart.

I would just have to continue as I had and perhaps some new strategy would suggest itself. I closed my eyes. I would just have to wait and see.

As it happened, I never got the chance.

CHAPTER XXXV

*M*y mind was just beginning to settle into a tenuous prelude to sleep after the previous whirlwind of thought, when I was startled out of all drowsiness by a sudden, thunderous hammering on my door.

"Beast! Beast!"

Isabeau's voice was high and shrill with desperation. I was instantly awake and struggling out of the bedclothes. I threw open the door as the candles in the nearby sconce flared dramatically into life. Isabeau practically fell into my arms.

"Isabeau," I said in consternation as I saw her face, white and wild-eyed.

"Beast, it's Claude! She is ill, she is dying," she cried, clearly distraught, grasping at my nightshirt.

"What?" I asked, confused.

"I had a dream," Isabeau sobbed, "she was wasting away. It was my fault! I left her to die. I must go home." With this, all strength seemed to leave her and she collapsed.

"Come and sit down," I said, trying to contain my own alarm. I half-led, half-carried her to an armchair and set her in it.

She was shivering, and had clearly left her room in such a panic she had forgotten her robe. Almost instantly a blanket appeared beside the chair. I covered her knees with it, then shrugged into my own robe and knelt beside her. A cup of chamomile tea appeared on a tray, hovering in the air. I took the cup and placed it in her hands. She did not seem to notice it and stared at me with wide, frightened eyes.

"Now tell me," I said, "what has happened."

Isabeau opened her mouth and gave a small hiccoughing sob, then swallowed and began again.

"I had a dream, Beast," she said in a shaking voice. "It was so real. I dreamed Claude was on the verge of death, wasting away. She was nothing more than skin over bones and her eyes held such reproach in them. I knew it was my fault!" She covered her eyes with one hand and began to sob in earnest. "I was the only one who could coax her to eat. She was pining away. And I left her to die."

"Isabeau," I said, putting my paw on her knee and shaking her gently, "it was a dream. Claude is well and happy. You know that from Marie's letters."

"What if the letters are not real?" sobbed Isabeau, not meeting my eyes.

I sat back a little to absorb what she had implied.

"They are true to my knowledge," I said after a moment. "If they are not, then I have not been a party to the deception. Indeed, I have been subject to it as well." Here I hesitated again, but in the face of her distress, my reluctance lasted less than a second.

"Let me show you something," I said. "It is the best I can offer to reassure you your sister is as the letters tell you."

Isabeau looked at me wonderingly, but her panic had subsided for the moment.

"Drink your tea," I said, and she gulped it down. I noticed what must have been Isabeau's own robe now lying across the foot of my bed. I helped her into it and took her hand as I led her out of my room toward my study. She followed meekly.

"Beast," she said in a very small voice as we walked, "I am sorry to wake you."

"Who else would you rouse at this hour?" I joked, trying to make her smile. I succeeded, although it was a very wan and tear-stained smile.

"Never mind it, I was not asleep," I said. Her fingers tightened their clasp on my hairy paw.

We came to my study and I steered her across the room until she was standing in front of the curtained mirror, then I pulled aside the drapes. At first she frowned in puzzlement, but then her mouth opened in amazement as her reflection began to grow hazy.

I stood to the side, looking on in a state of sick apprehension. How would she respond to the knowledge I had been keeping this from her all this time? Would she be angry I had essentially been eavesdropping on her family's private life?

The mirror cleared and—of course—showed us a picture of Claude, sleeping sweetly, curled on her side with one hand under her cheek, looking the picture of health and contentment. Isabeau stared at her for the longest time. Eventually she stretched out her hand to touch the glass and, as if in response, Claude shifted in her sleep and rolled over. As she did so her pillow moved and out fell the filigree heart Henri had given her. It hung there, dangling from its chain. Isabeau brought her hand to her mouth and I saw fresh tears welling in her eyes.

Then the mirror blurred again, and Isabeau uttered a small,

disappointed "Oh!" before it cleared and revealed Marie, asleep in her bed. She lay on her back, breathing evenly, her dark hair strewn across the pillow, so different from the way she usually wore it pulled neatly back. On the hand lying on top of the covers, she wore the ring René had given her. I turned my attention back to Isabeau, who now had her fist against her mouth, tears sliding down her cheeks. Then the mirror changed again.

This time the image was of Isabeau's father, asleep. Isabeau uttered another low cry and covered her mouth with both hands. He was propped up on several pillows and, unlike his daughters, he was not sleeping peacefully. He twitched and moved his head and hands, and muttered unintelligible syllables. The sight of her father affected Isabeau far more than had the images of either of her sisters and she began to shake her head.

"Oh, Papa," she moaned into her hands. Then the mirror began to cloud again and this time it returned to a simple reflection of my study. The curtains fell closed of their own accord. Isabeau turned to me.

"Beast, he is so ill," she said, clearly upset anew. "I dreamed it was Claude who was ill, but it was Papa, all this time."

"I never knew him before he came here," I said, "and I do not think he was ever well since that time. But you know him much better than I. Has he so declined since you left?"

Isabeau clasped her hands in front of her.

"I don't know," she said, worriedly. "Looking at him then I thought so. But perhaps it is the moonlight . . ." Her voice trailed off, as though she was trying to think of some other excuse for her father's poor appearance.

"I know he worries about you a great deal," I said heavily. "That is my fault."

Isabeau nodded silently. "Perhaps there is some way I could reassure him?" Isabeau wondered out loud. "Marie writes me letters. Could I write to Papa?"

"Would he credit it?" I asked her, knowing the answer.

Isabeau bit her lip and shook her head. "I . . ." she said and then fell silent.

"Isabeau?" I asked, an icy sense of expectation taking hold of me.

She looked at me and shook her head silently again. She looked away and said, "I can't ask it." She took another quick breath that sounded almost like a sob and then her eyes met mine and slid away.

"Beast," she began again, "could I go home for a visit? Just for a visit? Just to reassure Papa." She looked back up at me, her eyes pleading. "If I went tomorrow I could see Marie married."

She stopped abruptly as she saw the expression on my face.

"I mean just a visit," she said pleadingly. "Just for, say, a week. I would come back and see out the year. I promise. I would even stay an extra week, to make up for it." She came forward and took my paws in her hands.

"Please, Beast," she entreated.

I was frozen. I could not breathe. A huge weight had settled upon my chest and was suffocating me, pressing my heart in my chest so it could not beat and stopping the breath in my throat. For her sake I would have tried to school my face into a neutral expression, but I was frozen to the quick.

"Isabeau . . ." I managed to croak.

"Please, Beast," she begged, "at least think on it. Don't say no. Please say you'll think on it."

Stiffly I managed to nod. It was a reprieve.

"Thank you," she said earnestly. She held my paws for a moment more, then released me and stepped away. I tried to shake off my stupor and managed to take a new breath.

"You should go to bed," I managed to whisper. "You must get some rest."

Isabeau nodded, looking at me with concern.

"And you," she said.

"Of course," I lied. So she said her goodnights and thanked me again for my patience with her night terrors, then returned to her rooms.

It was only after she had left I realized she had not challenged me for keeping the mirror a secret for so long. This thought only distracted me for a moment, however, from the deeper disaster of her request to return home.

There was, of course, no more sleep destined for me that night. I did not even try to return to my bed. Although I did challenge sleep to take me unawares by sitting motionless in my chair, staring into the fire until the sun arrived and woke the world.

There was no true dilemma. She had asked; I could not refuse her. My contemplations were more selfish—how could I convince her to stay with *me*? How could I get her to change her mind? Oh, do not credit me with more nobility than is my due. From when she left me for her bed until I saw her again, my mind was busy concocting schemes by which I could convince her to stay.

In the end, when I felt her stirring, I returned to my rooms and dressed. While she rose and breakfasted, I ordered the air to pack trunks with more fabulous contents in readiness for her departure. When she emerged from her chamber and came down to the music room, I was there waiting.

Her trunks were there and when she entered and saw them, she looked over at me in surprise. I could only nod gravely and hand her the fur-lined cloak that lay across them, as though she were about to undertake a journey by more conventional means.

It was very early, far earlier than our usual meeting time in the music room. The winter sun was only just warming the eastern horizon.

"If you go quickly, you will be there when your family awakes," I said, not wanting to entertain any further questions about whether or not she should go.

"Beast," said Isabeau, her voice thick with some emotion. Gratitude, I supposed. Or overwhelmed at the thought of being once again with her dear Papa and sisters. I waved away her words irritably and helped her into her cloak. When she was ready I took a ring from my pocket and held it out to her. A twisted band of gold. She looked at me in puzzlement.

"Take it," I said. "Put it on. Twist it once, clockwise, and it will take you back to your family."

"Oh, Beast, thank you," she said, taking it from me and putting it on at once. "And to return?" she asked.

"Isabeau," I said, shaking my head, hoping to disguise the trembling that threatened to overwhelm me. Would she really?

"And to return?" she asked more firmly.

I shrugged.

"Twist it twice, in the other direction," I said, making it up on the spot. I'd made the ring up on the spot. But the idea of her wearing a ring I had given to her, whether she returned or no, had its appeal.

"Isabeau, you do not need to return," I said. The time had come for truths. "I release you from your promise."

"No!" she said sharply. "I did not ask you to release me. A promise is a promise. I will return in a week."

"A week then," I said, not wanting to hope too much.

She turned back around to face me then, her large gray eyes looking out at me beneath the silver fur of her hood.

"Isabeau, I will miss you!" I rasped out, unable to help myself. I wanted to embrace her and hold her to my heart.

She gave me a thin smile. "It is only that you are grown used to the company now," said Isabeau. Even though I knew she was only trying to lighten the mood, it wounded me she so easily dismissed my love for her.

"If it pleases you to think so," I said, trying to keep the hurt from my voice. I must not have succeeded, however, because Isabeau went red and looked away.

"Beast," she said uneasily, clearly trying to find some way of softening her tactless remark.

"Isabeau," I interrupted, "please believe I would never have asked for your hand if I did not truly love you. Were you gone for a week or forever—" I stopped. It would not do to try to make her feel guilty for leaving me. Even I must own she had a duty to her family, not to mention how she must miss them in any case.

"I will return, Beast," she said anxiously, looking me in the eye. "I promised you a year, and I have not yet fulfilled that."

I shrugged and tried to smile, though I wanted to weep.

"And I have released you from that promise," I said to her. "I will be most grateful if you return, but you are not bound to do so."

She looked at me with the strangest expression on her face. I could not read it.

"But I want to come back," she said earnestly.

As I looked at her, I could not help but reach out and touch her face; not with my shining, vicious talons, but with the back of my hairy black paw. To my surprise, Isabeau did not flinch, but put her own hand up to clasp mine to her cheek.

"I cannot tell you how grateful I am for everything you have done for me and my family," she said. "And your friendship means a great deal to me."

My surprise grew as tears welled in her eyes and one slid down her cheek, becoming lost in my coarse dark fur. I could only nod, too overwhelmed to speak. She stared at me for another long moment, as though waiting for something, before she released my hand and stepped back, laying a hand on her trunk.

"Good-bye, Beast," she said, her voice unsteady. "I will see you in a week."

Then she twisted the ring on her finger. There was a brief gust of wind from nowhere and she and her trunks vanished. I was left staring at nothing, in an empty room.

"Good-bye, Isabeau," I said hoarsely, my throat so strangled with grief I could barely speak the words. I looked down at the hand that tingled with the memory of her touch. The fur that had been wet by her tears was now a streak of silver in my otherwise coal-black pelt.

CHAPTER XXXVI

$\mathcal{I}$ only remained in that hateful place for a few seconds. I turned and left, striding through the house to my study, then running in my haste. I threw open the door and in three steps was before my mirror. The drapes were already cast back and it showed a tiny attic room in the cottage, furnished with a simple bed.

Isabeau was sitting on one of the trunks that now stood at the foot of her bed. Her expression was not one of overwhelming joy. In fact, as she looked around her old bedchamber, she looked decidedly forlorn. She sat there for some time, looking down at the ring on her finger and twisting it to and fro. But not twice, counterclockwise, all the way around.

There was a muffled thud from below, followed by more noises, and Isabeau looked up, listening. I was surprised to see the tracery of tears on her cheeks. My heart contracted with longing for her, but I instantly began to second-guess myself. Was she crying for me? Did she really miss me already? Or was she just overwhelmed to be back with her family?

There was the disappearing sound of footsteps on wooden stairs and I surmised Marie had risen and was making her way down to begin breakfast. Isabeau, finally starting to smile, lifted her hands to cover her mouth. A few moments later the sound of humming was heard from the room below.

"Claude!" whispered Isabeau, a delighted grin spreading across her face. But still she sat there. Then, from far below, came the muted rumble of a more masculine voice.

"Papa!" she gasped, and sprang to her feet. But, she did not rush out. She took off her cloak with trembling fingers and then went slowly down the stairs, letting the creak of her step announce her presence before the others saw her. The voices in the kitchen suddenly fell silent. Then, mischievous girl, she went through the doorway into the kitchen, stretching like she had only just awoken.

"Good morning," she yawned.

Marie found her voice first. "Isabeau!" she said weakly.

Then Claude shrieked out loud and flew across the kitchen to hug her younger sister.

"Isabeau?" asked de la Noue, sounding shocked. The look upon his face said he could not believe his eyes. Marie sat down on the bench by the table, looking very much as though her legs would not support her any longer.

"Hello," said Isabeau a little sheepishly, still wrapped in Claude's arms. "I came back."

What chaos there was then. Isabeau was hugged and kissed over and over by each member of her family so many times it was almost as though she had returned to an army of relatives, not just three. It seemed to take quite some time for her father and each of her sisters to be satisfied it was, indeed, Isabeau returned to them and not just some apparition.

"You really are back," said Marie wonderingly, once more sitting at the table, when all had quieted down again.

"Of course," beamed Isabeau, standing behind her father, who was sitting beside Marie. She wrapped her arms around his neck and leaned on him comfortably. "I had to come back to see my sister married."

"But how—" asked Claude, when she was interrupted by Marie, who gave a gasp of pleasure, her hands flying to her mouth.

"You have been receiving my letters?" she cried happily.

"Yes," said Isabeau. "I give you joy, Marie. I'm happy to see you so happy."

Entwined in Isabeau's arms, Monsieur de la Noue frowned, looking puzzled. Then he patted Isabeau's hand where it lay upon his shoulder.

"And are you well, child?" he asked hesitantly.

"Yes, Papa," said Isabeau, bending to lay her cheek against his. "I am very well. I am here among you again. I am very well indeed."

"Ah," he said, reaching up to press her more closely against his whiskered cheek. But the frown did not entirely leave his face.

Of course Isabeau's arrival put them all out of order for the morning, but eventually Claude remembered she needed to go into the village to run some errands that could not wait. As she left, Marie stopped her at the front door.

"Claude," she said in a low voice.

"Yes?" asked Claude, pausing in the door with her basket over her arm.

"When you go, be sure to tell someone we have had word Isabeau is returning and will be with us tonight," said Marie, peering over her shoulder.

"Of course," Claude whispered. "It would seem so odd, otherwise."

"It will probably look odd anyway," said Marie, grimacing. "But I cannot think of any other way to explain it."

Claude nodded, and was gone.

I sat by the mirror the whole day, watching Isabeau and her family. There were a few odd moments. The first occurred when Isabeau went to fetch the crock of butter from the pantry for Marie. She went directly to a corner as though expecting it to be there, but it was not, and she had to ask her sister where she had put it. Marie told her quickly enough, but I watched Isabeau pausing in the pantry, looking at the crock in her hands, then the place where she had first sought it, then at the shelf on which she found it, the tiniest of frowns upon her face.

Another moment came when Marie offered to brew coffee for them all. Isabeau went to get the cups, but Marie put one back and selected another, saying, "Papa always has this one."

She did not know where Claude kept the tablecloths and napkins, or where Marie had stored the wine gifted to them by Dufour. When her father went outside to see to some task, she went looking for his scarf at Marie's exhortation, but could not find that either. Each time I saw her look a little lost, I ached for her. I could see it written so clearly on her face: after all this time she felt like a stranger among her own family. My heart twisted. Isabeau did not feel herself to be home. A little flame of fierceness surged within me at that thought. I found myself thinking, *No. Her home is here!* But a moment later I sagged back into my chair, watching her set the table for her family's evening meal. It mattered no longer. Her home had been here. It should have been here. And perhaps she might return. But, for now, she was *home* with her family and I must bear it as best as I could.

As they ate, I grew conscious of a delicious aroma. I turned away from the mirror to see a table set beside me with all manner of good things to eat. A roasted fowl, a glass of wine, a silver dish of green beans topped with a curl of butter slowly melting away. There was a golden-crusted pie emitting a savory smell and some confection of cream and sugared fruit. My stomach clenched painfully and I remembered I had not eaten all day.

I took a slice of the pie and some of the fowl. I ate a few mouthfuls, watching Isabeau's family eating their somewhat plainer fare. Isabeau was very quiet, listening to her sisters talking over their plans for the wedding the next day. Their father sat, an odd smile on his face. I put my plate aside and leaned forward to look closer at him. Despite my expectations, despite the fact his youngest child sat by him, healthy, whole and apparently happy, the lurking grief had not been chased from his expression. Indeed, I fancied sometimes when he looked too long at Isabeau, his smile would waver and his eyes would grow bright.

At that point I comprehended another subtle awkwardness about the family in the glass. All day Isabeau had kept within sight of one or other of her sisters, offering to help with chores, chatting to them about the coming wedding or their acquaintances in the village. Each time any of the family sat down together—to eat a meal or drink a cup of coffee—Isabeau would sit by her father and hold his hand or tuck her arm through his. But she had not sought out his company alone and I began to be convinced he may have taken some pains to avoid being alone with her as well.

And now, as they all sat together, I noticed something else. They had talked almost exclusively of Marie's wedding, all through the meal. This would not, perhaps, have been so extraordinary, except their youngest member had just returned unexpectedly from an absence of some eleven months' imprisonment in the den of some monstrous beast. I grasped what was wrong as the sisters were discussing their arrival at the church the next day.

"And now I shall have *two* bridesmaids," said Marie happily.

"Oh," said Claude, frowning. "But, Isabeau, what shall you wear?"

Isabeau gave her an enigmatic smile.

"I am sure I will have something suitable," she said, a twinkle in her eye. "You should see the size of the trunks the Beast has sent home with me."

There was a sudden silence and the expression on her father's face froze.

"Excellent!" said Marie brightly, a heartbeat too late. "There is no need to worry over that, then."

The twinkle had vanished from Isabeau's face and she looked lost again.

"Well, is everyone finished?" asked Marie, blithely. "Papa, should you like to go and sit in the parlor now?"

My heart grew cold and heavy. Clearly there was to be no discussion of me or Isabeau's time here. She was back in the fold and they were happy, but there had been no questions about her life in my domain.

A gloom descended upon me. I sat staring despondently into the mirror. It took me some minutes to notice Isabeau, too, had realized the prohibition. She began to collect the plates into the washing basin, and when Marie tried to shoo her into the parlor to sit with her father, she shook her head and silently went about her chore. Marie stopped to watch her, frowning. I saw it immediately. It was as if a light inside Isabeau had been doused. She was holding her lips very tightly together, but every now and then they quivered.

I could not help myself—in a moment I was out of my chair

and standing beside the mirror. She needed comfort and I was so far away. I leaned my forehead against the wall so my muzzle was a mere inch from the image the mirror showed me. It was a hopeless, pointless thing. But I lifted my paw and laid it against the glass.

A tear slid down her cheek. She dashed it away, but another followed. She put her hand to her cheek, directly under my paw, as though she was trying to hide her tears. I seethed in impotent frustration. I could do nothing.

Then Marie came up behind Isabeau and put her arms around her younger sister.

"Shh," she said. "Depend upon it, Claude and I want to hear all about it. But perhaps not in front of Papa just yet."

Taking a sharp breath, Isabeau nodded, then managed to turn a watery smile upon her sister. Marie squeezed her tight again and kissed her cheek and left her to the washing.

At this, Isabeau rallied and I returned to my chair. But my meal was cold and I had lost my appetite, so I sent it away. I watched, a little resentfully, as Isabeau sat by her father for the remainder of the evening, touching his knee or his arm each time she spoke to him. Eventually, however, Monsieur de la Noue rose and kissed his children, saying he could barely keep his eyelids open.

After their father had retired, there was a tense silence, as Marie and Claude's sense of propriety warred with their curiosity and they tried to think of ways to delicately frame impertinent questions they were desperate to have answers to. After pretending to be distracted for a few minutes, Isabeau eventually began to laugh.

"You two look as though you are about to burst," she cried. "Ask me! Am I so changed you stand on politeness now?"

Marie and Claude hesitated for a heartbeat more, and then Marie smiled.

"Do you live in the lap of luxury?" she asked. "It is something I have imagined to myself after Papa's tales of the Beast's house. It made your fate more bearable."

"Oh yes," said Isabeau, smiling mischievously. "All the books and all the gowns and jewels I have."

Marie frowned as though this phrase had some meaning she could not quite catch.

"That's what you wrote in your first letter to me," explained Isabeau. "You said you imagined me living in luxury, surrounded by all the clothes and jewels and books you and Claude could desire between you. I've read it so many times."

Marie pulled Isabeau close and Isabeau rested in her sister's embrace for a moment. When she sat up, Marie brushed tears away from her own eyes and laughed to see the tears in Isabeau's.

"Well, my letters have done more good than I ever hoped," she said fondly. "For not only did they comfort us both, but they have brought you home on the eve of my wedding. I cannot tell you how happy I am you will be there."

"Marie, I am so glad for you!" said Isabeau in a voice very close to a sob. "I cannot tell you how happy I am you have found someone to love."

If Marie was surprised at her sister's sudden emotion, I remembered Isabeau's despondency when she first heard of Marie's engagement. I watched the sisters embracing and wondered if my epiphany of the previous night held any truth, if Isabeau had indeed found her own match in me and was breaking her own heart by failing to admit it.

"You will come to love him, too," Marie said. "Indeed, you must! For you are all to come and live with us, you know."

"Papa and Claude are leaving the cottage?" asked Isabeau, startled.

"Yes," replied Marie. "Have I not mentioned it in my letters?"

Isabeau shook her head.

"We are *all* to go and live with René," said Marie. "It is especially convenient now winter is coming on again. And there are other reasons." She looked significantly at Claude here, who presumably would therefore be closer to her lover. Claude's composure was not at all ruffled, however, and she completely ignored her sister's insinuation.

"Do not say you will miss this awful house?" she asked, seeing Isabeau's dismay.

"I suppose not," said Isabeau looking worried. "It will be harder to imagine you all somewhere I have not seen."

Marie's mouth dropped open.

"What do you mean 'imagine us'?" demanded Claude, sounding alarmed.

Isabeau looked at them, belatedly realizing she had revealed her return was not permanent. Her worried expression deepened.

"I didn't say before, when Papa was still here. I will tell him tomorrow, but I am going back."

I felt a warm shock of unexpected pleasure at this. She did mean to return!

"What?" demanded Claude, sounding angry now. "Did you not escape from him? Why would you want to go back?"

"I didn't escape," said Isabeau carefully. "He released me from our bargain."

Claude began to rise, exclaiming again, but Marie put out a hand to stay her.

"Your bargain?" she asked, just as carefully.

"Yes," said Isabeau, looking down at her hands in her lap.

"You made a bargain with the Beast?" repeated Marie. "And he released you from it to *visit* us?"

I could not tell from her tone what she made of this, whether she was outraged or had perceived some unexpected magnanimity.

"Yes," Isabeau said and looked up. "The day after I arrived, the Beast told me he had tricked Papa into bringing me because he was so lonely."

"Tricked?" asked Claude.

"Yes," said Isabeau firmly. "He told me he would never have harmed Papa."

I felt a surge of pride. She was defending me.

"He has been alone in his château for a very long time," she continued. "He was terribly lonely and just wanted to meet me. But the day after I arrived he told me I was free to leave. He begged me to stay for a year, as a favor to him, but he would not keep me against my will."

"And you chose to stay," said Marie flatly.

"It was only for a year, Marie," said Isabeau in a voice that begged for understanding.

"Do you know what Papa has been through in these last months?" asked Marie. She was clearly angry now. "Did you not think of us at all?"

Isabeau flinched.

"Of course," she whispered. Then in a stronger voice, "But I talked to Papa before I left. The Beast promised him—"

"He blames himself entirely," Marie interrupted, "for your premature death, torture, whatever." She waved a hand to indicate subjects that did not bear thinking of.

"I'm very sorry," said Isabeau tearfully. "The Beast is very sorry, too. And I was so tired. I could not bear to see you both so—"

There was another awkward silence.

"The Beast is sorry?" asked Claude eventually.

"Yes," cried Isabeau in a low voice, seizing on something positive. "Of course he is."

Marie and Claude looked at each other.

"You must talk to Papa," said Marie seriously. "And go gently. He can hardly bear to have the Beast mentioned in front of him."

"I will, tomorrow," promised Isabeau. She looked at her sisters, nervously twisting her hands in her lap. "After the year is up I will come home for good."

The pleasure I had felt before died and I was left feeling cold and sick.

"He is making himself ill," said Marie. "But only for love of you. Now you have come back and shown his fears to be groundless, he may be easier."

Isabeau nodded and Marie, giving in to her youngest sister's distress, put her arms around her again.

"And when I am married," Marie continued, "I am sure René will think of things to keep him from dwelling on his demons. He manages Papa very well, you know."

"Oh, don't let her get started," said Claude, rolling her eyes and clearly trying to lighten the mood once again. "We will hear of nothing but René for the rest of the evening. We want to hear about the Beast. Is he very ferocious?"

"Oh no," said Isabeau, and I was gratified to hear her sound shocked. "Not at all. He is very gentle. And so generous. I am completely spoiled." She told them about the invisible servants, the many-seasoned gardens, the music room and her wardrobe that produced whatever she had a whim to wear.

"And he reads to me, you know," she said, looking shyly at Marie. "Most afternoons."

Marie's eyebrows rose. "And does he read well?" she managed to ask.

"Very well," said Isabeau smiling. "I asked him to do it because it reminded me of you, you know."

"And what did you do to remind yourself of me?" asked Claude.

"I ate your favorite mousse," said Isabeau mischievously.

Claude cried out in mock frustration. "You did not! Oh, I do not believe it. I have a mind to come and visit you."

Isabeau frowned in thought.

"I wonder if you could?" she said thoughtfully.

Claude's face became a picture of dismay.

"Oh no, really I would be far too frightened," she said fearfully. "I am afraid of mice. Even your monkey used to make me nervous. I cannot conceive of confronting something man-sized."

"Oh, somewhat larger," said Isabeau teasingly. "He is far taller than any man I ever met."

My heart revived a little—was that a hint of pride in her voice?

"Is he not ugly?" asked Claude curiously. "Papa said he was hideous."

To my shock, Isabeau shook her head emphatically. "No, not ugly!" She hesitated. "There is something a little disconcerting about him at first. I'm not certain what—perhaps it is that despite his appearance he dresses and behaves as a man. Really, he is not frightening at all. He is very gentlemanly and kind."

Marie and Claude exchanged surprised looks. There was an awkward pause as the elder sisters tried to reconcile Isabeau's version of me with the tales told by their father.

"Why is he there?" asked Claude eventually.

Isabeau did not answer immediately. "I don't know," she said eventually, shaking her head. "I have wondered if he might have been a man once. But he says he used to live in the forest and terrorize all who entered it. It was certainly he who gave it its evil reputation. Perhaps he was just some forest Beast and someone imprisoned him to make the forest safe again. Perhaps the effect of the magic over all the years has made him become more like a man."

"But, then, why would the forest have kept its reputation?" asked Marie. "Surely if he was imprisoned to make it safe, whoever cast the spell would have made it known he was contained. And why imprison him? Why not just kill him?"

"I've wondered that, too," said Isabeau, still shaking her head. "I don't have answers."

"Have you asked him?" asked Claude timidly.

Isabeau uttered a humorless laugh. "That would be breaking with all propriety," she said.

"What do you mean?" asked Claude.

"Well, he never speaks of it, so I assume the subject is taboo," said Isabeau. Her expression became pensive and she opened her mouth as though about to say something else, but hesitated. I suddenly became afraid she was going to tell them about my proposals of marriage. I could not fully explain it, but I did not want her to share that with them. If she told them, they might urge her to continue to refuse me. I had no real hope of Isabeau ever accepting me now, but I wanted this to be her decision alone and not spurred on by her sisters' influence. And what could any responsible sister in their situation do, but try to prevent their youngest from being wed to a monster? I did not doubt even Marie, with all her attempts to think of me in a positive light, would balk at such a prospect.

Isabeau looked up at them. "He seems so sad," was all she said.

Soon after this, the sisters retired to bed. I watched them go, laughing and happy again, Marie insisting both Isabeau and Claude share her room, as she would not have the opportunity to sleep with her sisters again. I drew the drapes across the mirror and looked around my study—dark, save for a single candle. My large, empty house seemed larger and lonelier than ever before. But, as I lay down to sleep that night, rather than dwelling on my renewed solitude, my mind found comfort in the way Isabeau had spoken of me to her sisters. At least, if she could not love me, she felt kindly toward me. And she was clearly eager for her family to share her good opinion of me. Really, I could not ask for more.

CHAPTER XXXVII

*S*leep was a fey creature for me that night. Unable to lie still, I abandoned my bed to prowl the halls of my château at a very early hour. It may have been my imagination, but it seemed the shadowy corners were already filling with cobwebs and the paint beginning to peel from the walls, even though Isabeau had been absent for less than a day. Eventually, as the sun crested the edge of the forest, dusting the darkened treetops with gold, I threw myself into my chair in my study. I was exhausted, but burning with a feverish energy. I intended to remain in front of the mirror all day. It was the only means of escaping the terrible solitude of the house.

At first all I saw was the empty kitchen, cold and gray in the morning light. Even the coals of the fire were covered over with a soft layer of gray ash, hiding their burning hearts. But the ascending sun must have been the de la Noues' cue to rise, because it was not long before I began to hear muffled sounds, and only a little longer before Marie arrived in the kitchen. She moved purposefully about, rekindling the fire and setting the table. She stopped for a moment as she laid out the plates and utensils, then smiled happily and added an extra place.

Her father appeared a short time later, and then Claude. They greeted each other quietly and Marie served them slices of toasted bread and large cups of steaming milk, but neither of them paid much attention to the food. There was an air of anticipation in the room, and all of the family kept glancing toward the door. Finally Isabeau appeared, wrapped in a shawl and yawning hugely. The tension in the room eased palpably and Monsieur de la Noue's face lost its anxious expression as she went straightaway to kiss him.

"Is there anything I can do to help you?" she asked Marie, clearly pleasantly surprised by the scene of orderly domestic felicity before her. "It seems inappropriate for the bride to be serving us on her wedding day."

Marie laughed and shook her head. "Sit yourself down," she said. "I have to prove to you I can take care of you as well as you took care of me."

Isabeau snorted. "You need do no such thing," she said, sliding onto the bench beside her father. As she did so, however, I noticed she was pale, with shadowy smudges beneath her eyes. There was also something heavy about her movements. My heart lurched at the familiar signs; she had slept badly.

Marie also noticed this, for as she handed Isabeau an earthenware cup of something hot and steaming, she said to her, "You did not sleep well?"

Isabeau smiled up at her sister and shook her head.

"No," she said ruefully. "I fear I have grown too used to feather beds, pampered as I am."

I looked more carefully at her. It sounded feasible enough, but I was sure it was something of a white lie. I also noticed

Isabeau's father watching her closely, but I could not tell if he also thought this may not have been wholly true. Isabeau turned to her father as though she had sensed his scrutiny and took his hand.

"Do not think I would not give up all the feather beds in the world, though, to be here with you today," she said warmly.

De la Noue covered her hand with his own and smiled back, although his smile was weak and his eyes watery.

After they had eaten, Marie asked Isabeau what she would like to do in the next hour, before they had to begin making themselves ready for the wedding.

"Well," said Isabeau slyly, "I have spent most of yesterday admiring Claude's domain, perhaps it is time for me to see the garden and the fabled henhouse."

Both Claude and Marie laughed, and their father flushed with pleasure and sat up a little straighter on the bench.

"I am rather proud of it," said de la Noue, and I saw Claude lift a hand to cover a smile.

"I will show it to you directly," said Marie. "Just let me clear these dishes away first."

"By no means!" Claude cried out. "This is one thing you are not to do on your wedding day! What will René think if you arrive at the church with your hands all wrinkled from washing dishes?"

"He will be thankful he has chosen a bride who is not afraid of work," said Marie dismissively.

"But Marie," said Isabeau with a most mischievous twinkle in her eye, "cannot you see you are depriving Claude of the opportunity to greet the Vicomte with wrinkled hands? If he sees her in such a state, he will surely be inspired to rescue her from such a desperate situation and whisk her off to his château."

Claude blushed pink, but Marie laughed out loud.

"Oh, sister," she said to Claude, "I may have promised not to tease, but Isabeau has made no such pledge."

When it was finally time for Marie to begin readying herself for the church, the sisters all ascended together one last time to her room. There was a great deal of fuss as the wedding clothes were brought out along with all the other finery the sisters would wear. As Isabeau had predicted, a dress had been found in one of her trunks that was a perfect match to the one Claude had set by for herself. As Claude began to unhook the back of Marie's dress, I realized what was about to happen and leaped from my chair, vacating my study to pace the corridor outside until I heard Claude declare Marie was ready to have her hair done. I deemed it safe to return and seated myself once more in my chair as Isabeau claimed this duty for herself, and Claude agreeably ran outside to pick some late roses to add the final touches. She left and Isabeau picked up a comb and started to brush out Marie's long, dark tresses.

"Was it truly the bed?" asked Marie abruptly, into the silence.

Isabeau looked up at her reflection in the glass, frowning in confusion.

"You said you did not sleep well because of the bed," said Marie, "but I am wondering if that was the whole of it."

I sent a silent thank-you to Marie. Something was surely troubling Isabeau. Perhaps her sister could soothe away whatever it was.

"No," said Isabeau quietly, and she looked down, forgetting the curls of Marie's dark hair in her hands. When she looked up at Marie, her eyes were brimming with tears. My heart lurched to see her so sad.

"Marie, have you ever had a dream where someone appears to you, and you know they are a person you know well, but they wear a stranger's face?"

Marie frowned. "Yes, I think so," she said, "but not very often."

"I do," said Isabeau, as though she were giving up a secret. "Every night."

"What do you mean?" asked Marie.

Isabeau took a deep breath and again began winding curls into Marie's hair.

"In the Beast's château," she said, "he has a long gallery full of paintings—portraits of people. Some of them are very old. But at one end, there is a space where a painting used to hang. I asked the Beast about it and he showed me where it was. He said it disturbed him, so he had it taken away and put in an attic."

I leaned forward in my chair. Not even the house falling down around me could have distracted me from the mirror at that moment.

Isabeau shrugged.

"It was a picture of a young man. I could see nothing disturbing about it. He was handsome enough, well dressed, with the usual hound and horse. There was something rather arrogant about his air, but," she smiled wryly, "compared to the expressions on some of the faces in the gallery he looked quite amiable."

I could not but help utter a short bark of laughter. This was true.

"The only thing I thought a little odd was . . ." She stopped and thought for a few seconds. "I don't know," she eventually said. "Perhaps it is just hindsight, but I did think he looked somehow familiar."

My eyes, I thought. *You recognized my eyes.*

"The Beast clearly *was* disturbed by it, though. He did not approach it with me, although it looked as though he had been there recently. He was very quiet after we visited it. He never did tell me what upset him so about it. To be honest, I put his unease down to simple jealousy.

"Anyway, that night I dreamed about him—the man in the portrait. Only somehow it was my Beast as well. And I've been having such dreams ever since."

Her words struck me like a thunderbolt. I had never suspected *this*.

"Do they bother you? The dreams?" asked Marie. She turned around to face Isabeau, who backed away and sat on the edge of the bed.

"At first," said Isabeau, and I remembered the haunted look in her eyes during that time. "They were very unsettling, and sometimes . . ." Her voice trailed away and her cheeks grew pink. My heart all but turned a somersault. *What had she been about to say?*

"They were never unpleasant," she said more firmly, recovering her composure. "In fact, they often repeat the most agreeable things we've done." Her eyes lit up and my heart lifted to see it. "We watched fireworks together—twice. I've dreamed about that several times.

"But mostly they are almost mundane. I usually dream we are doing the same sorts of things the Beast and I usually do— playing music, walking in the garden, reading—except he wears the portrait's face. He wears the same clothes and speaks to me with the Beast's voice. He even says things to me the Beast has said that day." Her voice trailed to a halt and her eyes darkened. She lifted her eyes to meet her sister's again.

She shook her head. "All last night I dreamed of my Beast, with this man's face, pacing through the house alone. All the rooms were dark, and he was so terribly, terribly lonely. And so sad. And all I can think of is that I have left him in such a state."

Marie did not say anything to this at first. In fact, her attention appeared caught by the flame of a candle she had set on the dresser to light Isabeau's efforts with her hair. She stared at it as though it offered her some sort of revelation. My own head was reeling.

"Marie?" said Isabeau eventually.

Marie turned back to her.

"Isabeau," she said firmly, "you have promised us a week. I cannot think anything terrible will happen to your Beast in a week. Papa needs you here. Knowledge of your safety and well-being is what he needs to heal. I do not mean to upset you, but without that, I do not know if he would survive the coming winter. You must focus on Papa now."

Isabeau bit her lip and looked down. My gut squirmed in guilty horror.

"But, Isabeau," said Marie seriously, leaning forward and taking her sister's hands, "if you truly fear for your Beast, then I believe you must keep your promise and return in a week. I warn you, Papa will never want you to return and Claude will not think twice about trying to convince you to stay an extra day, or more. And I won't be here to help you stand firm, little sister."

Isabeau nodded, dismayed by her sister's sober tone.

I sat back in my chair, shaken. Truly, I was too overwhelmed to feel anything but numb. She said she'd dreamed of the fireworks. What else had she dreamed? Lounging in the orchard? Learning to shoot with bow and arrow? Dancing under the stars? Had she . . . My breath caught in my throat. Did she dream of my proposals coming from a man and not a monster?

In the mirror, Isabeau resumed arranging Marie's hair in silence. I could see Marie's face in *her* mirror, and again she was staring at her candle.

The bride and her sisters remained in Marie's bedchamber until Claude started up from her chair, crying, "I hear them!" and they all ran to the window. I could hear music, and the glass showed me a small procession coming over the hill toward the cottage, led by Dufour, striding along quickly and beaming like the sun. Behind him came a group of musicians, filling the air with a joyful melody. Following them came his sister and her husband, with a collection of children from the village trailing behind them. The three sisters ran down to the parlor, where their father was waiting. There was much kissing, and a little crying, and then Dufour was knocking upon the door.

De la Noue opened it and as he drew Marie forward, the small crowd of people at the gate let out a happy cheer. Dufour stood by as Marie was escorted out by her family, blushing furiously and turning her laughing eyes back to her intended amid the cheerful chaos. The wedding party stopped at the gate where some of the children had mischievously tied a garland of ribbons across it, as though to prevent her leaving. Laughing again, Marie took a pair of scissors Claude extracted from her pocket; the ribbons were cut and the procession moved off, following the musicians back to the village.

Now the musicians led them all, the fiddles and pipes spinning out a rousing tune that brought a spring to everyone's step and had the children dancing about. Marie and her father followed, with Isabeau and Claude close on either side. Dufour was left to follow behind with Madame Minou and her husband.

I observed the de la Noue family party with interest. Marie was a picture of happiness and excitement. Claude seemed in similar spirits, but her hand kept straying to her throat with a curiously nervous flutter. Eventually I spied the filigree heart hanging there upon its chain and understood. De la Noue largely looked quite satisfied, but every now and then his attention would come to rest upon his youngest child walking at his side, and the expression of contentment upon his face would slip. Isabeau seemed happy enough, but there was a wistful quality to her gaze that left me in a fever of frustrated speculation.

At the church, the rest of the family drew back, allowing Dufour to lead Marie through the small crowd of people waiting for them, up to the church door where the priest was waiting. They stood together, holding hands as the priest said the words over them, then blessed them. There was a burst of happy noise from those who had come to see them married and a brief shower of rice and wheat as some threw handfuls of grain at the couple. Laughing, Marie waved at her father and sisters, then let Dufour lead her inside for mass.

The church was almost full, and when Isabeau walked in behind the couple, it filled with a quiet murmuring. She glanced about shyly, aware of the wondering eyes turned her way. But then the priest entered and chivvied the stragglers into their seats, and all the congregation's attention turned to the sermon.

Well, almost all. The Vicomte sat in his family pew at the front of the church, staring at Claude as though she alone had just walked into the church. Claude was looking demurely down at her hands. But at one point she looked up at Villemont and caught his eye, before her cheeks grew pink and she quickly looked down again.

I threw myself back against my chair, trying to quell the rising bitterness within me. Was the whole world falling in love and finding happiness just to spite me? I glared at Isabeau and all my anger instantly evaporated in a fit of longing. She was looking at Marie, a wistful smile upon her face and her lovely eyes full of happy tears. What I would have given to have her look at me that way.

After the service, the couple ran through a renewed rain of rice and wheat to the Crossed Keys where a feast of food and drink had been set up. The musicians established themselves by the fire and began to play as the bridal couple were given a two-handled silver cup to drink from, and then everyone cheered as they kissed over a towering pile of sweet cakes.

It was close to midnight when the dancing finally ended and the last, most determined revelers began to drift away to their beds. Isabeau and Claude finally managed to convince de la Noue they must leave, and led him away, one on either side. The Vicomte insisted on escorting them home in his own carriage. There was little conversation to be had as they trotted steadily home in the moonlight. But each member of the party looked extremely satisfied and serene.

At the gate of the cottage the Vicomte helped each member of the de la Noue family from the carriage. Somehow Claude was the last to alight, which gave him the opportunity to kiss her hand while Isabeau was busied with escorting her father through the gate. I could tell Claude blushed even in the moonlight, but she did not pull her hand away. Instead she allowed the Vicomte to retain possession of it for a few moments more while she curtsied gracefully and thanked him most prettily for his trouble.

"There is never any trouble in any service I may be able to render you," he said before he let her go. He did not drive away until he had seen them all safely into the house and was rewarded for his patience by seeing Claude look back at him not once, but twice.

Inside the cottage, it was plain that each of the remaining members of the de la Noue family was making directly for their bed. Isabeau, however, did not go straight to sleep. She sat on the edge of her bed in her nightclothes for some time, once more toying with the ring on her finger. She looked serious and even a little sad, and I could not prevent myself from reaching out to touch the surface of the mirror. I was then startled to see her lift the ring to her mouth and for a wild moment I thought she kissed it. But then I saw her brow was creased and her mouth set in a frown and I realized she was merely deep in thought.

"Goodnight, Beast," I eventually heard her whisper. "Sleep well tonight." Then she climbed into her bed.

It took her a long time to fall asleep and I watched her until she did. I stayed until the crease faded from between her brows and her breast rose and fell with the deep, even breath of slumber. I watched her until the ache in my heart became too much to bear. Then, in desperation, seeking some way to bring her closer to me that night, I went to her rooms. I stood in her sitting room, breathing the vestiges of her scent and trying to recapture some of my dearest memories of her. It was the only room in the house that did not smell of damp and dust. Here, on this carpet, she had wept as I had knelt beside her and held her in my arms. There, on that chair, she had lain while we talked in the darkness.

It was to that chair I went and sat myself down. It could be but a poor substitute for Isabeau herself. But now, in the dark, exhausted by grief and longing and loneliness, surrounded by her fading scent and the things she had lived with while she stayed with me, I lay back in her chair and succumbed to a restless slumber.

CHAPTER XXXVIII

$\mathcal{T}$he first gleam of light on the eastern horizon woke me, and saw me hurrying back to my futile post before the mirror. It showed me almost the same sight as it had when I had left it: Isabeau asleep in her bed. Her beautiful honey hair was tumbled over the pillow and her cheeks were flushed. I reached out to touch the mirror, but as I stretched my paw forward, I saw how much it trembled and drew it back.

A moment later I heard a sound as though someone standing behind me had cleared their throat. When I whipped around, breakfast was laid out upon a tray on my desk. I turned away in disgust. Nothing could compel me to eat at this moment. My stomach rebelled at the thought of food.

I watched Isabeau until she woke. She did not sleep peacefully. Frowns tugged at the corners of her mouth and creases puckered her brow. When eventually she rolled over and opened her eyes, they were clouded with some anxiety.

"Beast," she murmured into the morning dimness and I sat forward in the chair. Was she really calling me?

"My Beast," she whispered again, and my heart stuttered. "Be well, my friend. I have not forgotten you."

This cast me into utter confusion. Part of my heart soared as she called me "My Beast," but the other half heard "my friend" and wanted to throw it back in her face. I did not want to be her friend. Could she not see she must love me as I loved her? Why did she dream of me, if she did not? *All this talk of "friends" and "friendship,"* I thought bitterly. I wanted none of it. It was just a guise, a veil she drew over the feelings she harbored for me that she could not bear to acknowledge.

I had a brief fantasy of meeting her at my gate on her return and sternly demanding she marry me or be gone. This bitter vision crumbled, of course, as I glanced again at the mirror and saw her sleepily rubbing her eyes. Then she sniffed hard, and I saw she was crying. A moment later sounds of movement came from below and Isabeau quickly wiped her eyes. She pressed the heels of her hands to them hard.

"Dear Beast," she said. Then, a wry smile twisting her lovely mouth, she muttered, "If you would only be well I would be satisfied."

Of course I felt the gentle sting of her words. I had said exactly that to her as I knelt before her on the hearth rug, the first time she had called out to me in the night. If she dreamed of me every night, then she knew of my restlessness, my grief. She must know how I had barely moved from this chair the day before, and how I had only been able to snatch some few hours of rest by sleeping in her chair last night.

"Be well," she had said. I turned to stare at the breakfast, cooling under its silver covers on my desk. For all I was not hungry, I could not recall the last time I had eaten. I went to my chair and managed half a piece of toasted bread and some gulps of tepid tea before my throat closed over again with grief.

I turned back to the mirror.

Isabeau had left her room and encountered Claude on the stairs.

"We will have to contrive something to eat, I suppose," Claude was saying resignedly. "Marie was such a good cook. To think we would never have known had we not come here. Even Madame Minou says she has a magical touch and that people come for miles for the dinners on the days when Marie is due to help her in the kitchen."

"Ah, yes," Isabeau said, sadly contemplating the prospect of the breakfast she now faced. "The food is incomparable at the Beast's house, although I would not have Loussard hear me say so!" Claude gave a gurgle of laughter at this. "I am so spoiled, I confess. Brioche and hot chocolate for breakfast every morning." She sighed and, quite comically, Claude sighed, too.

"Oh, I have not had brioche since we left Rouen!" she said plaintively.

At this I sat up straight, wondering if the reach of my magic was enough to grant the sisters' wishes. I did not have long to wait, and I was not disappointed. The two young women tripped down the last of the stairs and opened the door to the kitchen.

"What's this?" gasped Claude, walking in to find a pale blue earthenware bowl on the table, covered with a checkered red and white cloth. She lifted the cloth and looked almost afraid.

"What is it?" asked Isabeau.

"Brioche!" Claude whispered back, sounding shocked. Isabeau gave a little jump and clapped her hands.

"It is a gift from my Beast, to be sure." She looked around

at the stove. Sure enough, set upon the warmest part was a pot with a lid. Isabeau sniffed, then laughed. "And look!"

"From the Beast?" asked Claude anxiously.

"Of course," said Isabeau, fetching plates and cups from the shelf. "Where else are you going to get fresh-baked brioche and hot chocolate from in this place?"

Claude sat down and cautiously took one of the small, round loaves from the bowl. Isabeau deftly served her up a cup of chocolate, little curls of steam rising from the rich, brown liquid. Claude tasted them and looked impressed, but the worried frown did not leave her face.

"It's very good," she admitted, "but I think it will be best if we do not tell Papa you think they are from the Beast."

"Whyever not?" asked Isabeau, looking as crestfallen as I suddenly felt.

Claude made a face. "He will not eat them," she said. "He hates the Beast."

"But . . ." began Isabeau, but she did not finish her sentence. She pressed her lips together in an unhappy line.

"He is not able to be reasonable about the Beast," said Claude gently. "He thought all this time he had sent you to a hideous death, or at best a life of unmentionable misery. He has barely been able to live with himself. Marie has managed him very well, but"—she paused, then continued in a voice grown suddenly rough—"we have worried he would not last the winter. Indeed, now he has seen Marie safely married, knowing she and René would take care of me, I do not know whether he would have felt we needed him anymore. I think he would have just sunk away in shame."

Isabeau had gone quite pale.

"Oh God, what have I done?" she said. "I never meant to

hurt him so. I stayed with the Beast because he was so sad. He *promised* Papa I would not be hurt." She sank down into a heap on the table, her head buried in her arms.

Just then the creaking of the steps was heard as de la Noue came slowly down from his room. Isabeau rose hurriedly from the table, her eyes red.

"Dear God, he cannot see me like this," she cried and ran from the room.

Maddeningly, my view in the glass remained of the kitchen. De la Noue was bemused by Claude's information that Isabeau had gone for an early walk, and still more surprised by the gift of brioche and chocolate some kind soul had delivered from the village in honor of his eldest daughter's marriage. He sat chatting pleasantly with Claude for half an hour or so about the wedding and all there was to do before they left the cottage. He appeared to think the newlyweds needed more than a week on their own before Marie's family descended upon them, but Claude disagreed.

"No, Papa, Marie cannot do without you for so long. She has said so. And recall you will be so much closer to the Vicomte. He will not have to ride out to you so often—you may call on him."

De la Noue gave a chuckle that turned into a cough.

"Ah, yes," he said, a rare twinkle in his eye. "And you will be wanting me to bring you with me, no doubt."

"Papa!" exclaimed Claude, but she looked pleased.

"No, but there is also Isabeau to consider now," said de la Noue, shaking his head. "René had only thought to take in you and I. Perhaps we should stay here."

Claude bit her lip and was silent for some moments.

"Why don't you go and find her?" she suggested at last. "She did not finish her breakfast, and you two have had so little time together."

"Ah, that is a good idea," said de la Noue, but he looked anxious. He rose from the table, clearing his throat and brushing bread crumbs from his hands. He looked at Claude, who held out the blue bowl to him. He hesitated as his daughter looked at him pointedly, then his shoulders sagged the merest inch. "I will take her one of these. They were ever her favorite."

Isabeau was not hard to find. She was, in fact, seated on a rough little wooden bench up against the back wall of the house, watching Marie's chickens pecking at the ground around their henhouse. She did not notice her father at first, being deeply involved in her own thoughts. But as he approached her she looked up and her eyes brightened.

"Papa," she said, taking the brioche he offered her.

"Hello, my chick," said de la Noue, sitting down and taking up Isabeau's hand. Isabeau smiled at him fondly. To my eyes, however, her smile was strained and her face pale.

"At last I have you to myself," he said, patting the hand he held. "I cannot believe you are returned to me."

"Papa," said Isabeau unsteadily, "I have so many wonderful things to tell you."

Her father turned his face away from her and began to blink.

"It is enough for me to know that you are safe at last," he said gruffly.

"But it is not enough for me," said Isabeau.

I waited, on the edge of my seat with anxiety.

"I have always been safe, Papa," she said. "I was never in any danger. The Beast has been so good to me. I cannot tell you how good."

"I do not want to hear about the Beast," said de la Noue

roughly. He began to cough. For a moment Isabeau looked as though she wanted to argue with him, then she took a deep breath and waited until his coughing subsided.

"Then let me tell you about myself," she said. "Surely you will want to hear how I have been going on? I know all about you, you know. Marie has been writing me letters."

De la Noue turned to her, his face a picture of surprise and disbelief.

"Yes, really," said Isabeau, pressing on. "I have heard all about René and his kindness to her and how she loves him so. I think they will be very happy together. And she told me of the henhouse you built." Here she paused and I detected a devilish gleam in her eye. "She was so proud of that. And," her voice dropped to a hush, "she has told me all about Claude and her Vicomte. She is certain they will make a match of it. Do you think so?"

"Well, he has been very attentive," said de la Noue uncertainly.

"Marie thinks he is quite head over heels in love with her," said Isabeau in a conspiratorial tone. "And from what I have seen, I think he will suit her very well. Indeed, I cannot imagine her married to anyone less grandiose than a Vicomte. Yes, I think they will do very well. I think both my sisters will do very well."

"And you?" asked her father sharply.

At this, Isabeau's cheeks reddened slightly, but she affected an air of unconcern.

"Me?" she laughed. "Well, I have spent my days playing the piano, drawing, going for walks in the Beast's gardens, listening while he reads to me. He reads very well, you know."

De la Noue's face had also grown red. "I do not care to hear about the Beast," he growled.

"Papa," said Isabeau firmly, "I am afraid that if you want to hear about me, you will have to hear a little of the Beast. He is all I have for company, you know."

"You should have your family for company," snapped de la Noue, his anger bringing on another spasm of coughing.

"What I want to tell you," said Isabeau, her voice soft again, "is that you really have no cause to worry about me. The Beast is no tyrant. He doesn't make me do anything I do not want to do. Indeed, I rather think he indulges me too much. I live in the kind of comfort we used to know, in the city. I want for nothing."

Unfortunately, this was the wrong thing to say.

"Nothing?" spat de la Noue, red-faced. "Nothing? What of the society of human beings? The presence of those you love? So he keeps you in comfort, does he? Like a little caged bird to amuse him with your singing? This is not what I would have had for you. As you are so good to point out, I have one daughter well established and another in a fair way to be so. But what of you? What of *you*? Where are your suitors? What are your prospects? Do not ask me to be grateful to him. I am only grateful you have escaped him at last."

Having delivered this tirade he pushed himself up from the bench, but Isabeau was before him. She leaped up, as straight as a poker, her hands clenched by her sides. Her face was as flushed with anger as her father's and her eyes blazed. She was magnificent.

"I *do* ask you to be grateful!" she cried. Her father's mouth opened in shock. "Look at what we were when you left us last winter. Claude, wasting away from grief over Gilles. Marie in such deep despondency she never left her bed. And me! I was never so tired in my life from looking after you all.

"You cannot imagine the pleasure it is to me to see my sisters happy, busy and glowing with love. Without me they have each found tasks to keep them busy and to help them get on with their lives. I do *not* see Claude pining over her worthless lover, or her gowns or her balls, or Marie sighing for her books and a secure future.

"I've just seen the sister who thought her dowry was her only claim to attraction married to a man she loves and leaving us as eager for her life as a farmer's wife as she ever was for any new book of philosophical essays! And even you cannot doubt the happiness Claude will find with her Vicomte."

De la Noue opened his mouth to respond, but Isabeau continued, her voice high and angry.

"I spent nearly a year worried to death our reversal of fortune would be the end of each and every one of you and working myself to the bone to try to stave that off, and to do all the things that needed doing, which no one else would do. And now, to see my sisters as happy as they ever had a hope of being when we lived in the city! Papa, you cannot discount what a precious gift that is."

"Gift?" echoed de la Noue in furious amazement. "Gift? You are asking me to believe this is the Beast's gift?"

"Marie has written as much to me," Isabeau threw back at him. "She says if I had not suddenly gone away, and she and Claude had not had to shift for themselves, who knows but they might both still be lying about moaning over the life they used to lead. But instead Marie is married and Claude is receiving the attentions of a *Vicomte*."

De la Noue opened his mouth to retort, but Isabeau barreled on.

"And you, Papa, this is to say nothing of you! If you had not come upon his château in the forest, you would certainly be dead of cold. And if you had died then, where would the rest of us be now? He has given me you, Papa, and both my sisters' happiness. Papa—" The fire faded from Isabeau's eyes and her voice became warm and coaxing. "Cannot you bring yourself to feel a little more gently toward my Beast? And to cease to worry about me?"

De la Noue's expression did not soften. "*Your* Beast?" he asked, a dangerous tone in his voice. Isabeau flushed deep red. "And tell me, daughter, why should I *worry* about you, now you are home at last?"

Isabeau looked away, unable to meet his eyes.

"I have not *escaped*, Papa," she said sullenly. "I asked to come home to see you, and the Beast granted my request. And I am going back."

"You are not." De la Noue's voice was flat with anger. Simultaneously Isabeau and I both winced at his tone.

"I have given my word," said Isabeau, her face pale and set.

"Do you scruple to keep your word to such a creature?" said de la Noue bitterly.

"He is not a *creature*," Isabeau flashed back, her eyes beginning to flame once again. "He is a *good man*!"

CHAPTER XXXIX

$\mathcal{I}$ cannot tell you exactly what happened next between them. I was overcome, stars spinning across my vision and my heart leaping wildly. I barely registered both Isabeau and de la Noue's voices raised in anger and the sound of something breaking. When finally I could breathe again and my sight cleared, my mirror showed me only de la Noue standing by his cottage, his fists clenched in hopeless rage. Isabeau was nowhere to be seen.

I sat on the edge of the seat, gripping the arms of my chair, willing it to show me my Isabeau. As much as I wanted to find her in the mirror, however, it now grew cloudy, obstinately clearing to show me nothing but my own fearsome face. I turned away in frustration. Clearly I had seen what it wanted me to see and I would be shown no more for the present.

Suddenly possessed of an irresistible surge of energy, I leaped out of my chair and began to walk. I have no clear memory of where I ranged—over the house, over the grounds, along the hedge that sketched the limits of my existence. I paced restlessly everywhere I could, her words echoing in my brain: "a good man!"

Had she heard herself? Did she comprehend what she had said? I was convinced, now more than ever, her heart saw me clearly, if only she would listen to it.

I was recalled to myself only hours later, when I caught sight of my house from wherever it was I had roamed to and saw it lit up, its windows gleaming golden, the shape of its bulk black against the darkling sky. I looked down and could barely see the black of my paws in the dim light.

I made my way back to the house slowly, the memory of her words glowing within my heart, warming away the cold grief of her absence. As I entered the house I heard the chink of cutlery and saw the door to our dining room standing open. Within was all aglow with candles, and the repast set out to tempt me included all of my favorite dishes.

I turned my steps from the grand staircase toward the dining room and seated myself. The platters and dishes jostled each other in their attempt to serve me with their contents, and my wine was so eager to pour itself it even splashed a few droplets over the snowy linen. I was in humor enough to find amusement in the way the carafe, after so disgracing itself, retreated in a mortified fashion to the farthest corner of the table. However, I had not taken many mouthfuls before I realized my magic glass may now have relented and I leaped up, leaving it all uneaten, and raced off to my study.

As I opened the door it was all darkness within. However, the candles and fireplace sprang to life a moment later. They did not burn with the same merry intensity I was used to, but I ignored their reluctance and sat myself in my chair. The curtains to my mirror parted half-heartedly, and slowly the glass cleared to show me Isabeau seated in the parlor of the cottage with her father and sister.

There was little conversation occurring and I surmised that Isabeau and her father had not yet properly made up after their argument. De la Noue stared moodily into the fire and Isabeau stared moodily into space. Claude appeared to be trying to concentrate on her sewing, but kept darting anxious glances at each of them.

"I wonder if Marie is settled at the farm yet?" she inquired of no one in particular.

Isabeau glanced at her and smiled wanly. "Hardly, I should think," she answered. "I doubt you will find her settled when you go to her next week."

De la Noue made a bitter noise that sounded like "Pah."

"It is just as well for you, though, she has insisted on such a brief honeymoon," Isabeau continued, clearly intent on ignoring her father. "She has become such a delectable cook. I swear I have never had better than that terrine she left for us to eat today. To have to put up with my poor efforts in the kitchen after becoming used to her wizardry."

De la Noue turned his face away from his daughter and in the firelight I saw tears glinting in his eyes. But Claude bravely tried to carry the conversation forward.

"Nonsense," she said loyally, "although, speaking of magic, do you know, she did say she often thought cooking was a kind of alchemy."

"Yes!" exclaimed Isabeau. "She wrote that in one of her letters to me." She paused, then said in a wistful voice, "Do you suppose she will have time to write to me now she is married?"

"Oh, heart," said Claude, leaning over and clasping Isabeau's hand, "I am sure she will."

De la Noue stood up abruptly. "Goodnight," he said gruffly and stumped out of the room.

Claude made a face and set her sewing aside. "One moment, Father, I will light you up. There is something I need upstairs."

She hurried after him with her candle. For several minutes the mirror showed me only Isabeau, seated by the fire, alone with her thoughts. They were not happy ones, that much was evident. For no sooner had Claude left her to herself than Isabeau curled up in her chair and hid her face in her hands.

Wish as I might that she grieved for missing my own self, I was satisfied it was the breach with her father that was now causing her heartache. I could understand it well enough. To have forgone her beloved father's company for so long, only now to be at odds with him when she had only a few short days to spend with him. I wanted to comfort her somehow, to hold her close, or kiss her hands, but I was so far away and could do nothing but watch.

After several long minutes, Claude returned. At her light footstep on the stair, Isabeau straightened up in her chair. However, her efforts did not appear to fool Claude in the least. When she re-entered the room she stopped at the sight of her younger sister and exclaimed, "Oh!" before hurrying to her side and picking up her limp hands.

"Dear Isabeau," she said warmly as Isabeau's eyes began to overflow anew. "It is such a shame. I have just spoken with him as plainly as I dared and told him how senseless it is to be so cross when you are only here for a few days." She shook her head. "He shut his door in my face, so I had to say most of it through the keyhole, but I am sure he heard me."

At this, a breath of laughter left Isabeau's lips.

"Oh, Claude," she said, "how that must have infuriated him."

"I don't pretend to manage him anywhere near so well as

Marie does," said Claude, ruefully shaking her head. "But I certainly had to tell him how badly he is behaving tonight."

"I told him I was going back to stay my year out with the Beast," said Isabeau, looking apprehensively at her sister.

"I guessed," said Claude, going back to her chair and picking up her sewing.

"We fought about it," confessed Isabeau.

"Oh, I heard that," said Claude frankly.

Isabeau went pink. Then, frustration creeping back into her voice, she said, "Papa will hear not one good word about the Beast."

"I did warn you," said Claude, not unsympathetically.

"The shame of it," continued Isabeau, an edge of anger in her voice, "is the Beast is just the sort of man Papa would be sure to like, if he really knew him."

My skin tingled and all my fur was stood on end. She had done it again.

Claude noticed this as well, for she put down her sewing and looked searchingly into her sister's face.

"But he is not a man," she said.

Isabeau stared at her sister as though Claude had slapped her. Her face went very pink and she dropped her gaze in confusion. She murmured something indistinct into her lap, but when Claude begged her to repeat herself, Isabeau just shook her head and rose from her chair.

"I think I will go to bed, too," she said, not looking at her sister. "Tomorrow we should really begin to pack away the house. It will be best to get an early start."

She left quickly and hurried to her bed. But she did not sleep for a long time. Instead she lay looking out into the darkness, her large gray eyes open and staring at things only she could see. I watched her until eventually her eyelids fluttered down and she finally slept, all the while aching to be close to her, to offer her what comfort I might.

I did not go to my own bed that night, but sat for many hours in my chair, my chin in my hands, thinking about the words she had spoken that Claude had not heard. Somehow the magic of my mirror had picked up her whisper and delivered it to me as clearly as if she had spoken directly into my ear. All night those words echoed in my head and even when I finally dozed off in my chair, they repeated throughout my dreams.

"I had forgotten" were the words my Isabeau had said to no one in particular.

The next morning, I woke in my chair to see in my glass a vision of the de la Noue family at breakfast. Claude was the only one who looked as though the night had afforded her any rest. Indeed, the shadows under Isabeau's eyes were more deeply marked than the day before. She was so lost in her own thoughts she was barely conscious of her family around her. Her father, on the other hand, kept glancing anxiously at her with such a look of longing on his face I found myself in sympathy with him. Clearly Claude's words, spoken through the keyhole as they were, had been heard and heeded.

Claude herself bustled around, chatting brightly and trying to make up for the want of spirit in both father and sister. As Isabeau washed the breakfast things, Claude announced the two young women would walk into the village that day.

"For it is market day today," she said, "and for all that we will be moving to René's farm, there are a few things I want. In any case, we can get some fresh bread from Madame Minou and see if she has news of René and Marie." As she spoke I noticed the filigree heart was once more hanging about her neck.

The plan was agreed to and an hour or so later saw the sisters take leave of their father and walk toward the village. De la Noue hugged Isabeau particularly closely as she bid him good-bye. Although no words were exchanged between them, she kissed his hands fondly and left him looking much happier than she had done at breakfast.

"You see?" said Claude when they were out of earshot. "You two will make it up."

Isabeau smiled, and by the time they had reached the Crossed Keys she seemed more like her usual self.

They spent some time at the inn as Claude had planned, talking with Madame Minou of the wedding and asking after the happy couple. Minou said she had not seen René since the wedding, but one of his hands had been out to deliver some goods and reported his master was over the moon and Marie had made a singularly good impression on all the servants and work-ers on the farm. From his account she was as pleased with her new home as could be, and was in perfect accord with all the key farm and household staff about how the place should be man-aged. Minou promised to keep a pair of loaves of bread aside for them and the sisters went out to wander up and down the mar-ket stalls that had sprung up on the main street.

"Marie tells me," said Isabeau, with a familiar mischievous curl to her mouth, "the first time you went to the markets alone, you brought back an enormous goose all trussed up in the most elegant silk kerchief."

A flush rose to Claude's cheeks. "I had no idea they were so heavy," she said primly. "The Vicomte de Villemont came upon me struggling to get it home and was kind enough to assist me."

"Ah, the Vicomte," said Isabeau, as though this explained the whole story. "Does he own land out our way, I wonder? It must be a very troublesome piece of property. Marie says he is forever riding past the cottage."

Claude was bright pink now.

"Oh, do not tease me!" she begged, a hand involuntarily closing about the little pendant at her neck. "It is not . . . it is just . . ."

"What?" asked Isabeau innocently. Then she saw the expression on her sister's face and laughed.

"Oh, Claude, I am sorry," she giggled. "Really, though, he is the most elegant dancer, and his manners are just what they ought to be. It was so kind of him to take Papa home the other night. Marie says he is very well spoken of around here."

The color in Claude's face subsided, but did not fade away altogether. Isabeau's words were all she needed to launch into a catalog of the young Vicomte's graces.

"And he has indeed been so kind to Papa," she finished, as the two sisters were examining lengths of ribbon at Claude's favorite market stall. "He has sought out his advice several times now on matters of investment and so forth. Papa does what he can around the house, but it is not what he is good at, you know. When Henri began to seek him out for his advice, I believe Papa at last began to think himself truly useful once again."

Isabeau frowned.

"He has always been truly useful to *us*," she said irritably. "He does not value himself as he should. He is our father. We love him, and will always need him."

Claude cast her an anxious sideways look and did not reply. After a few moments, however, Isabeau recalled herself.

"Forgive me," she said ruefully, "we were talking of your Vicomte. Do you think I will get to meet him today?"

"Oh yes," breathed Claude, her eyes lighting on something farther up the street. Isabeau turned to see Henri riding slowly down the main street. His face came alive with joy when he spied Claude waiting demurely by the ribbon stall and he instantly dismounted and approached them. He was all that was polite to Isabeau; however, it could not be said that he let his eyes stray from Claude's face any more than was absolutely necessary, especially after he had spied his gift once more about her neck.

Alone in my study I watched them all stroll back down the street to partake of refreshment at the Crossed Keys, and then wander at an easy pace back to the cottage, Claude with no more to show for her trip to the markets than a better acquaintance between her younger sister and her beloved, and two loaves of bread.

Isabeau and her father did not repeat their tête-à-tête during the next two days. They were certainly making an effort to remain on good terms with each other. Indeed, Isabeau must have bestowed hundreds of kisses on the top of her father's head and de la Noue appeared happy to receive them. However, Isabeau was careful not to broach the topic of myself or her imminent departure, and de la Noue was just as happy to stay out of such dangerous territory.

To be sure, I did not spend quite every moment in my study, gazing into the glass. There were times when it refused to show me anything other than an ordinary mirror might. The sight of my own reflection was pathetic enough to spur me out of my chair in irritation, but I did little other than wander and reminisce, and prick myself against the keenness of the yearning that constantly devastated my peace.

The house was becoming less and less a place of comfort. Panes of glass cracked, letting in chill drafts, and I found mouse droppings scattered liberally over the shelves in the library. Dead moths lay upon the windowsills of my fencing gallery, and the shutters along the portrait gallery began to warp and rattle on their hinges.

I went several times to the shrine of Isabeau's chambers, but their emptiness rendered these visits ultimately unsatisfactory, leaving me feeling the desolation of my domain all the more.

I visited my painting and narrowly avoided destroying it in a rage. It was only saved from being torn to shreds when I recalled that I owed Isabeau's dreams of receiving my proposals from my human self to it.

I paced around and around the rose garden. Its winter garb was a perfect foil for my misery. Stripped of all color save the odd yellow leaf or vermilion hip, its bare brown thorns suited my mood as the bleak yew walk had also once done. Even the little robin's nest now stood empty and abandoned, exposed to the elements with the fall of the leaves and beginning to come apart.

The odd tray of food appeared on my desk, but I ate little. My dining room did not again try to tempt me in with a feast laid for one. I felt drained of all energy and exhausted all the time, but sleep remained an almost unattainable state. Many of my rambles and wanderings happened in the small hours of the night when the de la Noues all lay asleep in their beds and my chair grew diabolically uncomfortable. I did try, once or twice, to cast myself upon my bed and let sleep overtake me, but it did not come.

There were moments when I thought I would go mad from

the terrible emotions boiling in my breast. I flew into some black and violent rages—such as the one that nearly caused the destruction of my portrait. But each time I found myself standing amid some new scene of destruction, the heat fading from my blood, I was suffused with shame. I could not help but remember my father's drunken rampages and how they plagued my childhood.

I tried my old trick of howling my despair up at the moon. However, my throat now seemed to have become molded along more human lines and the sound that came out was so miserable, so like a human blubber, I slunk down from the rooftops in humiliation.

Always I would finish back in my study, sprawled in my chair, waiting for the first flush of dawn to wake the woman sleeping in the attic of the cottage just outside the borders of my forbidden forest. And always, when her eyes flickered open, I would see the pain that filled them and the shadows that grew darker by the day as Isabeau spent her first few waking minutes in her room, staring out at nothing. It racked me with guilt to think, in her dreams, she had seen me giving way to grief and desolation. But I did not know how to stop myself.

CHAPTER XL

❧

*T*hen came the last day of Isabeau's week. Sleep had not come to me at all that night. Weary as ever, I was yet filled with a nervous energy that would not let me sit still, much less rest. Would she really return? Could I even face her, having so comprehensively failed to fulfill her one request of me—to "be well"?

I stared at her hungrily in my mirror as she woke on that last day. I watched with more relief than I can describe as she folded her nightgown and placed it, not under her pillow, but in one of the trunks I had sent with her. She sat on her bed for a few minutes before going down to breakfast, twisting the ring on her finger to and fro. But not twice around. Not yet.

Breakfast was a subdued affair. As usual, Claude and Isabeau were up before their father and sat in the small kitchen for a few minutes, talking quietly over their morning meal.

"So many 'lasts,'" moaned Claude forlornly. "Today is your last day with us, our last night in this cottage."

"Surely you are not bemoaning leaving this house?" Isabeau asked, skirting the issue of her own departure. Claude made a face.

"I believe I am," she said wistfully. "It has grown so familiar. And it was *ours*. When we go to Marie, we will be living in *her* house. Hers and René's."

"She will not begrudge you keeping house for her," said Isabeau. "She will have so much to occupy her time."

Claude frowned. "I know, but I will feel obliged to ensure I am doing things to suit her, rather than myself."

Isabeau gave her sister a smile.

"I think you will be not long without your own domain to arrange as you wish," she said.

Claude went pink and ducked her head.

"I do not like to presume," she said primly.

"I believe it cost Marie quite a pang to leave her henhouse and her garden," said Isabeau. "I cannot believe how homely you two have made this place. *I* at least will be sad to quit it." A little break came into her voice as she spoke.

"Truly, do you have to return to your Beast?" asked Claude.

Isabeau nodded.

"I wish I could explain to you how much he needs me," she said. "I promised him a year, and I promised him I would return from this visit and stay out my pledge. He is *so* lonely in that house of his. And I will be back with you all by the end of winter."

The little glow that had begun to warm my cold, numb heart faded away.

"But, Isabeau," said Claude, frowning, "what of your Beast when you do return for good? Will he not be very lonely then, too?"

Isabeau looked down at her hands, her face pale.

"Yes, I suppose he will," she said as though this thought had never occurred to her. I waited to hear what she would say next. She turned to her sister.

"I have not thought on it," she said. "I don't know what to do!"

"Is he so very dear to you?" asked Claude carefully, not looking at her sister, but concentrating very hard on the cup of warm milk she held in both hands. A thin prickle of fear ran over my skin. Had Claude guessed? Would she try to prevent her sister from an alliance with a monster like me?

"He is a very dear *friend*," choked out Isabeau. "He has been so good to me, to us all. Why can't you see that?"

Claude's mouth fell open in astonishment and she watched, wordless, as Isabeau rose abruptly and stormed out of the kitchen. A moment later, though, she put down her cup and hurried after her sister.

I flung myself out of my chair at the mirror with a roar. I cannot tell what last-minute reflex saved the precious glass and had me pounding angrily upon the wall to either side of it. I stood for a moment, my forehead pressed to the cold, unyielding surface, then stormed out, half-afraid I would do something else to shatter it and deny myself any further sight of Isabeau.

"I am not just your *friend*!" I cried out at the empty corridor, hitting out at a wall and leaving a ragged line where my talons caught at the plaster. Then a memory flashed into my brain, of the note I had sent her after the very first time I had asked her to marry me. *Your friend, the Beast*, scrawled across my vision as though written in the air.

"*I am not your friend!*" I bellowed again, taking a stumbling step backward and crashing into the opposite wall. The knowledge that, whether she returned to me or not, she would likely witness this outburst in her dreams that night broke over me and I sat down suddenly, slumping against the wall. I could almost feel her presence, standing before me, an expression of horror on her face.

"We are more to each other than any mere *friend* ever was," I said brokenly to the air.

After that little episode, I could not bring myself to immediately return to the mirror, knowing the distress I would undoubtedly bring her that night. The house, and all its empty rooms, began to weigh heavily upon me once more and I left, striking out for the yew walk.

Out in the cold without a coat, I decided a bottle of brandy was an attractive solution to warding off the cold. But after several burning mouthfuls, my empty stomach protested at being doused with such stuff without the fortification of any food and my head began to spin. Despite my anger over Isabeau's continued denials, I did not want to be inebriated if—when—she returned home that day.

I reached the boundary hedge at the bottom of the lawn and turned aside to follow it to the great iron gate. When I reached it, I could not help but test it. Despite applying all my strength to trying to wrench it open, it remained resolutely shut against me. In a surge of rage I hurled the bottle of brandy at it and gained no satisfaction from watching the heavy glass burst apart against the implacable iron bars.

I nearly did not return to my station in front of the mirror. But, for all my sulky bravado, as I drew closer to the front door, the image of Isabeau grew clearer and clearer in my mind. By the time I reached the door, I could almost smell the scent of her hair. When I set my foot upon the bottom of the grand staircase, I was running.

Still, I doubt I had missed much of note during my angry wanderings. As I sank once more into my chair, the mirror showed me Isabeau and Claude being industrious. I surmised they had mended the morning's breach. Though Isabeau remained distracted, stopping to stare at nothing every now and then, the two were chatting quietly as they sorted and packed their family's meager belongings. In the corner of the parlor sat a rolled mattress, tied about with rope. Isabeau sat on the floor tying a stack of cooking pots together with string, and Claude was carefully packing their meager collection of stoneware cups and jugs and their four pewter plates into a box full of straw.

"It hardly seems worth bringing them," she sighed, holding the wooden dog from the mantelpiece in her hands a moment, before tenderly fitting it into place beside the plates. "I am sure René will have better."

Isabeau looked up at her.

"But, if you take our things, it might not feel quite so much that you are living in someone else's home," she suggested.

"True," said Claude, but she still sounded wistful.

"There," said Isabeau with some satisfaction, looking at the bundle of pots. "I have got them trussed up. There's only the food left in the pantry—which is probably best packed up tomorrow morning after you've eaten. It will be boiled eggs and bread and cheese for dinner tonight," she added with a wry twist to her mouth.

"Will you stay and eat with us?" asked Claude, watching her sister carefully. Isabeau looked away.

"Yes," she said reluctantly, as though forced to discuss something she'd rather not. "I thought I would."

Claude nodded a little sadly, her eyes still on her sister.

"Are you sure you want—" she began, and stopped as Isabeau threw her a furious look.

"Well," Claude said in a very neutral tone, "that's Marie's things and the pantry all packed away. Perhaps we could take these things out to the cart now?"

I watched them all afternoon as they worked, bundling things up, putting them in boxes, wrapping them in cloth. I wondered where de la Noue was, but he did not come back to the house until it was nearly sundown. He was wheezing and perspiring as though he had been exerting himself.

"The hens are in their cages," he said gruffly to Claude, who was setting the table, his eyes sliding over to where his youngest daughter stood by the stove.

"Oh good," said Claude with relief. "I was not looking forward to having to chase them tomorrow morning."

The plates were laid out and the bread cut. Isabeau put a bowl of cold boiled eggs onto the table.

"Oh dear," said Isabeau as the family seated themselves, "it's not quite what Marie would have conjured up, is it?"

Claude made a wry face, but de la Noue just made a noise in his throat and peeled his egg, still refusing to look at Isabeau. After an uncomfortable silence, in which Isabeau and Claude exchanged speaking, if hopeless, glances, Isabeau spoke.

"You know I am going back tonight, Papa?" she said tentatively.

Far away, in my dark, lonely study, I sat up a little straighter in my seat. I found I was shaking. Would she *really* be here soon?

In the kitchen, a few feet across the table from her, Isabeau's father finally raised his eyes to hers. His expression was thunderous.

"No, you are not," he said flatly. Then he dropped his eyes to his bread and butter again.

"Papa," said Isabeau, "I am going. I gave the Beast my word."

De la Noue's fist slammed down upon the table, making his daughters and all the cutlery jump.

"No!" he roared. "You are not! I forbid it! I forbade it last time and, God help me, you are not going again!"

Isabeau had gone white, her eyes large in her face. But she sat up straight and put her bread down on the plate, taking a deep breath.

"Papa," she said, "please don't worry about me. I want to go back! I *miss* the Beast. I—"

Whatever precious thing she was going to say next was lost as her father uttered a strangled bellow and leaped up from his seat, knocking the bench over backward. He slammed both hands upon the table this time, knocking over the bottle of wine, which was only saved by Claude's quick reflexes.

"I said no!" he cried, his face wild. "You will obey me in this. You *miss* the Beast? Are you mad?"

"No!" cried Isabeau. "I—" But he cut her off.

"What do you know of the world?" de la Noue spat at her. "Nothing! You know nothing. Clearly you know so little you think that monster a fit companion. No." He lifted a shaking hand and waved a finger at her. "No! You will stay here. You will come with your sister and me and you will have a life, and you will learn what it is to be *happy*!" He dissolved into a paroxysm of coughing.

Isabeau stared at him in dismay.

"Papa," she said in a choked voice. "I *was* happy. I want to go back. You cannot stop me."

"You are nothing but a child," de la Noue rasped out. "You do not know what you are saying."

"You think I am a child?" asked Isabeau, her voice high and angry once more. "Do you see a *child* before you?" She gestured to herself. "Is that what you see?" she pressed. She turned to Claude. "Is that what *you* see, sister?"

Claude put her hands up as though fending off the question.

Isabeau leaned forward over the table, glaring at her father. My heart was beating so fast I felt as though I were in the grip of some terrible fever. They stared at each other across the table, his dark eyes full of rage, hers full of indignation. Her mouth was set. I had seen that stubborn look before.

Apparently, so had he. His shoulders sagged and he turned his face away from her.

"Pah!" he said, shaking his head. Then, walking slowly and thumping his congested chest, he left the kitchen. I heard the creak of his feet upon the stairs.

Isabeau and Claude stared at each other, stricken. Claude recovered first.

"Give him some time," she said quickly. "In half an hour, go up to him. He is just worried."

Isabeau covered her face with her hands. At first I thought perhaps she was crying, but then she shook her head and looked up.

"Time," she said wearily, sitting down heavily. "I don't have any more time. Why won't he just listen to me? I don't know how else to make him understand. Time is running out. I must go."

"Just stay a little longer," pleaded Claude, reaching to clasp Isabeau's hand. "He will be so miserable if you go away again without repairing this breach with him."

"He'll never understand," said Isabeau, bowing her head and resting it on the table.

Half an hour later Isabeau took up a cup of warm chamomile tea. She sat outside her father's bedroom door and talked through it until the tea was grown cold. Then she went miserably back down to Claude in the kitchen.

"He won't answer the door," she sobbed into her sister's shoulder. Claude put her arms around Isabeau and held her, her own eyes full of worry.

"I promised the Beast so faithfully I would return today," Isabeau cried. "Now Papa is making it so hard. I don't know what to do."

Claude chewed her lip. "Could you stay just one more day?" she asked tentatively.

Isabeau shook her head hopelessly.

"The Beast is so lonely without me," she said wearily.

The scene in the mirror suddenly changed.

I was looking into the dim interior of de la Noue's room. He stood in the center of the floor, his head bowed and his shoulders hunched. There was something about his posture that sent a thrill of alarm through me and I sat up, the hair on the back of my neck prickling.

In his hands he held a length of rope and I frowned. What could he be doing? He moved slightly and I saw the noose around his neck.

I leaped from my chair, slamming my paws into the wall on either side of the mirror.

"*Isabeau!*" I roared.

In a flash, the mirror changed.

The sisters sat together in the kitchen, their arms around each other. But, as the last syllable of her name tore from my throat, Isabeau sprang up from the bench, her face a picture of shock.

"Your father!" I cried, without hope she would hear me.

"Papa!" gasped Isabeau. "Claude, did you hear that?"

"No," said Claude, looking at Isabeau, confused. But Isabeau clambered over the seat and ran from the kitchen. I heard her feet clattering up the stairs.

A moment later I was looking at her rattling at the handle of her father's bedchamber door.

"Papa!" she called urgently through the door. "Papa!" When he made no reply, she kicked and threw herself at it, but it did not give. I bared my teeth and snarled, my claws gouging chunks from the plastered walls beside the mirror. At her next kick, the door burst open.

De la Noue was standing upon a chair, trying to tie the rope over one of the beams above his head. Isabeau let out a terrified scream and rushed at him, throwing her arms around his thighs.

"Claude!" she cried out. Her sister followed her into the room and also let out a scream.

The next few minutes were awful. Isabeau's father seemed shocked at first, and struggled to push his youngest daughter away, but she hung on grimly. Then Claude was upon them, sobbing and clutching at her father. Between them, they somehow managed to get him down from the chair and pull the noose from around his neck. Eventually they brought him to sit upon the bed, where he dropped his face into his hands and began to sob: a hoarse and broken sound.

Isabeau and Claude sat on either side of him, their arms around him, and stared at each other, white-faced over his shaking shoulders, neither of them capable of speech.

Sometime later, Isabeau sat alone in the kitchen, staring at the little orange light winking through the door of the stove, her eyes wide in the dim light.

Together, she and Claude had dressed their father for bed,

and given him a large draft of brandy. Claude had been sure there was no brandy in the pantry, but Isabeau had, of course, found a bottle sitting in the middle of the kitchen table.

Isabeau had pressed him again and again to tell her why he had done it, but he had just looked away from her, his eyes full of tears, and shaken his head.

I felt cold to my core. I was certain I knew what black thoughts had driven him to such a desperate act. Isabeau had removed everything that could conceivably cause him harm from his bed-chamber and she and Claude had dragged Claude's mattress from her bed and placed it on the floor. Isabeau had left Claude sitting upon it, watching her father sleep and weeping quietly.

I didn't want to move. I felt almost as though I were in the same room as she, and that if I distracted her, something pre-cious might break. After a time she rose and went despondently up the stairs.

Once she stepped inside her bedroom, she stopped short, looking around at the packed boxes, the rolled mattress, the bedlinen stacked in a pile, the dismantled bed.

"Oh, Papa," she said in a low, unhappy voice. She held up her hand, looking at the slim band of gold on her finger. "Oh, Beast," she said. She touched the ring with a finger and a tear slid down her cheek. My entire body vibrated with tension. I found myself digging my claws into the arms of my chair again.

"Stop it!" she whispered fiercely. Guiltily I relaxed my hands, but she was talking to herself. It did no good, however. As quickly as she wiped one tear away, more flowed. She gave a little hiccoughing sob and turned about, walking angrily to the window. When she reached it, she turned about and paced back the way she had come.

For a few minutes I watched Isabeau stalking back and forth

in distress within the confines of her tiny room. She kept clench-
ing and unclenching her fists and occasionally raising a hand to
dash away the tears that kept welling up in her eyes. Eventually
she dropped onto the rolled-up mattress on the floor and lowered her head, pressing the heels of her hands against her eyes.
Every fiber of my body yearned to reach out and take her in my
arms, stroke her hair, kiss her cares away.

"Papa! Papa!" she moaned and began to sob in earnest. I had
no idea what to hope for. The window of her bedroom showed
the night was well advanced. There was only an hour or two left
of the day appointed for her return to me. Yet I knew it was
impossible for her to leave now. She would have no peace while
she stayed with me. And I could see now, with a shudder, I was
no less selfish in my desire for her company than her father was.

My paws clenched over the arms of my chair, my talons
rending the upholstery and scoring deep furrows in the wood. I
shut my eyes, threw back my head and let out a roar of grief.
After the sound had ripped out of me, I sagged back in the chair
and opened my eyes. Isabeau was still sitting on her mattress, her
hands over her face and her shoulders shaking.

"Isabeau," I croaked, my voice scratched and broken from
my fury. I had a desperate notion she might hear me.

Indeed, the instant her name left my lips she looked up as
though startled.

"Don't think of me," I went on, trying not to choke on the
bitterness that rose up with these words. "Heal the breach with
your father. I release you."

Isabeau remained sitting on her mattress for some moments,
her eyes wide, then she hit her knee with her fist.

"Dear, generous, *stupid* Beast," she said with a sob, then
jumped up and whirled around. She pulled off the rope tying up

the mattress, then turned to the trunk sitting in the middle of the floor. With some violence she threw open the lid and tore out her nightgown and cast it onto the mattress. She began to tear her clothes off with equal violence.

When she was dressed in her nightclothes, she threw a blanket onto the mattress, but instead of laying herself down, she sat in the middle of the makeshift bed, her knees drawn up to her chest. Far from being reconciled with her decision to stay, she still seemed agitated. As I watched, she leaped up again and disappeared down the stairs. The mirror changed to show me a view of the kitchen once more. Isabeau entered, moving quietly, but with a certain recklessness. She took up the bottle of brandy and to my shock began to drink it straight from the bottle.

After taking several long swallows, she stopped and wiped her mouth, panting.

"I am not going to be able to sleep, otherwise," she whispered apologetically into the dark empty room. "For worry over you, you know. As well as him." She took another draft. I sat forward in my chair. Was she talking to me?

"I heard you, Beast," she said decisively. "It was like a wind brought me your words from a distance. And I know you watch me. You have your mirror and I have my dreams. You know about them now." She took another mouthful of brandy and grimaced, then rested the bottle on the table.

"You don't know about all of them, though," she said, and for a moment she smiled a ghost of a smile. "I didn't tell Marie about the nicest ones." Then her lips quivered and she dashed her hand across her eyes again.

"Oh, Beast . . ."

She stood in silence for a long moment.

"I am going to go to my bed now," she said. "Please, dear

Beast, won't you go to yours tonight? Please let me dream of you asleep in your bed, not roaming your house or sitting sleepless in your chair or in my room. You can't know how hard that is to bear. Let me have that peace."

She let go of the bottle and then, curiously, kissed her fingertips and held her hand out to the air as if she was waving good-bye to someone she loved. Then she turned and went unsteadily from the room. The mirror did not change, and I was left staring at the empty darkness of the kitchen, with only the sounds of Isabeau's feet on the stairs.

What did she mean? What other dreams? Was that kiss a final good-bye, or a simple token of affection? I was frozen for a moment, wavering between despair and hope. But then her request asserted itself in my mind. I rose from my chair and went to my bedroom. I looked at my bed in distaste. I had not spent many hours in it at all since she had gone, and in truth it did not beckon me now. But she had asked, so I would try.

"Wine," I said roughly to my empty house. There was a silent pause, of the kind that occurs when a servant has been ordered to do something very much against their liking, so I repeated my command. This time a flagon of wine appeared by my bed. A goblet also accompanied it, but I chose to follow Isabeau's example and simply drink from the bottle.

CHAPTER XLI

$\mathcal{T}$he next morning I woke before the sun, feeling heavy and oppressed. Perhaps it was the quantity of red wine I had imbibed, but my sleep had not noticeably refreshed me. I shrugged into my clothes and staggered back to the mirror in my study. It was almost as if I had not left. It showed me an identical scene to that which I had left last night—the dim kitchen with the bottle of brandy on the table. I sank into my chair.

Perhaps I dozed again, I am not sure. But certainly my attention wandered. I grew aware of movement within the de la Noues' kitchen, and was conscious of a sense I had missed something. Then Claude moved back into my view. She was simply preparing breakfast.

A short while later a slow, heavy step was heard on the stairs and de la Noue entered the room. He mumbled a greeting at his daughter and sat down heavily at the table, clasping the warm drink Claude put into his hands. He looked sad, angry and old. Claude spoke softly to him, offering him breakfast and he barely responded.

At one point Claude went outside into the day that was just beginning to grow light. I heard her exclaim and she came tripping back inside calling, "Papa! Just look!" De la Noue half-turned in his seat, his face lightening.

"Papa, it has snowed!" announced Claude. "Not much, but it is the first fall of the season. Winter is truly here." De la Noue's face sank into gloom again and he turned back to his breakfast without a word. Claude bit her lip, her face dismayed. She did not seem to know what to say.

Then the both of them heard a muffled sound from the room above, and turned their heads to look up at the ceiling. I wished violently for the mirror to take me into Isabeau's bedroom so I could see her, but it remained steadfastly focused on the kitchen. There were more soft sounds and de la Noue turned to Claude.

"Did she not go?" he asked gruffly, barely covering his amazement.

"I don't know," said Claude wonderingly. "She said goodbye to me last night."

They had not many minutes to wait before another set of feet was heard upon the stairs and the kitchen door was pushed open to reveal Isabeau. She, too, looked as though the night had afforded her little rest. Her eyes were red and her lashes were wet. But she came into the room, smiling bravely.

"Isabeau," croaked her father, staring at her helplessly from his seat.

"Papa," said Isabeau simply and came behind him to wrap her arms about him. De la Noue was speechless and could only pat the arms now encircling his shoulders, but I saw tears leaking from his old eyes.

"You stayed," he said eventually.

"I could not leave you," she said.

At her words there was a sudden roaring in my ears and I hid my face. As she spoke, I had also seen fresh tears well up in Isabeau's eyes. Her tears—whatever they might signify—were not something I could easily watch. Her whispered words from the previous evening, *"I have my dreams,"* stung me into action. I did not want her to witness me weeping alone in my study over her reconciliation with her father. So I rose and made a bow to the mirror, saying quietly, "Well done, Isabeau." Then I left.

I went to the library, thinking perhaps to find some book to distract myself with, or perhaps one of her drawings I might pine over, or the ghost of the scent of the flowers she drew there. Of course, there was nothing but shelves of disintegrating volumes and the odor of mildew. I found myself staring out over the yew walk, its somber, formal grandeur a perfect foil for my bleak mood. The very early sun was only just beginning to show itself above the rim of the forest and its pale radiance showed me a light fall of snow had coated the grass in powdery white. Across the frozen lawn I could see the tall, impenetrable hedge walling me off from the world. The sight was unbearable and I turned away.

Several of Isabeau's volumes of botanical illustrations were still piled upon the table, their bindings growing loose and spotted with mold. I sat down and began to look through them, but I confess I saw little of what was in front of me. I must have spent a long time there, my vision obscured by the tears crowding my eyes and the thoughts crowding my mind. I tried to focus on memories happy and tender, but this was exhausting. No sooner had I called one up, but a miserable voice in my brain would whisper such would never be repeated. Drowning out this voice by conjuring more memories was wearying in the extreme.

Eventually I found I had grown so cold and stiff I could no longer force my paws to turn the pages over, and I noticed my breath forming frosted clouds in the air around me. Overcome by the misery of the derelict library, I left.

All the magic remaining in the house now seemed concentrated in my study. There, a roaring fire recalled sensation to my frozen paws. A soft rug lay over my chair and a steaming mug of some sort of tea stood on the table close by. But despite the ache in my belly that spoke of days without food and the shudders of cold convulsing my massive frame, there was only one object in the room that could hold my attention.

I staggered to the mirror and pushed the drapes aside. I saw the cottage, its poverty and disrepair made charming by the mantle of snow lying lightly, like lace, along the edges of its roof and the henhouse. I saw Dufour's work cart, stacked with a pitifully small load of belongings for a family of a man and his three grown daughters. Indeed, the bulk of the load consisted of the trunks Isabeau had taken from my house.

The cottage door opened and René Dufour exited, supporting de la Noue on his arm. Claude followed, locking the door behind herself, and placing the key upon the top of the door frame. She paused a moment, with her hand on the silvered wood, as though saying a fond good-bye to the house she had turned into a home. Then she followed her father.

Where was Isabeau?

At the gate, Claude stopped and turned back to the house.

"Isabeau!" she called out. "Isabeau, we are leaving now."

A few moments later—I could not stop my heart lurching

in my breast—Isabeau rounded the corner of the cottage, walking slowly. Her face was pale, and as she drew closer I could see her eyes were red. But she shed no tears and came to help Claude see her father settled comfortably in the front of the cart. The seat only had room for three, so a short dispute ensued between Claude and Isabeau about who would sit in the rear of the cart.

"Please, Claude," begged Isabeau, "I would so like some time alone with my thoughts. I've not had any time to myself since I returned." Her voice shook and the dispute was ended.

Isabeau settled herself in the back of the cart, as comfortably as she may. The last vision the mirror granted me of her showed her staring back at the forest behind the house as the cart began to move away. Her face was very white and the deep, dark green of the trees was reflected in her gray eyes. As I watched, they finally filled with tears and she dropped her face into her hands, her shoulders shaking with silent sobs.

I don't know if the mirror showed me any more of their journey, for my own eyes stung and blurred at seeing her so miserable. My poor Isabeau! What had I done to her? She loved me—I knew she loved me, even if she could not bear to know it. And I knew her heart was breaking just like mine as that cursed cart bore her farther and farther from my reach.

What joy could the future now hold? Whatever misery awaited me in this next eternity of loneliness was magnified a thousandfold by knowing Isabeau, too, was just as surely condemned to grief. I wondered how her father would be able to rejoice in her return to her family when he saw how unhappy she was. Perhaps when he was restored to health and he saw her continuing misery, he would let her come to me then?

A cold that had nothing to do with my prolonged sojourn in the library settled in my stomach. I had no real notion how far Dufour's farm was from the forest. Would my magic reach so far? What if, in some months' time, Isabeau twisted her ring and nothing happened? What if the distance was too great?

And then there were her dreams. The cold in my bowels deepened, solidified. She could see me in her dreams. She would see how miserable and hopeless I was. If she loved me, how could she bear that grief? I knew only too well how dearly her dreams had cost her last spring. Would each of us really be able to bear watching the other so unhappy?

I hit the mantelpiece below the mirror so hard the trinkets upon it jumped and jangled. Then I turned around and walked back out of my study, fire, tea and comfortable chair forgotten.

This time I left the house. Its empty hulk held nothing for me. On stepping out into that bleak, winter garden, some resolution crystallized within me, as though forming out of the frosty air. If Isabeau was going to watch over me in her dreams, I would give her as little to fret over as I could. I could not pretend to be carefree. But I would do my best to be calm, though my mind was crazed with grief; to eat, though the food turn to ashes in my mouth; to repair to my bed at night, though sleep may not come. I will not lie: the thought of ending my own life had occurred to me several times in the last few days. But now that I knew about her dreams, it was not an option. I would choose to live another century in solitude before I put her through what her father had subjected her to the previous night. I could not do that to her.

I went first to Isabeau's rose garden. The one part of my garden entirely brought into existence by magic, it had also been the last part of my gardens to resist the returning seasons. Now, however, new snow frosted the edges of the beds and lay in cold drifts in the shadows where the weak sunshine had not found it out. Only the merest rags of petals still clung here and there to dry flower heads and the few leaves scattered among the brambles were yellow and ill-looking. This fabulous garden, once so full of nodding blooms, was now cold, wet and colorless.

I walked slowly, clasping my cold paws behind my back to prevent them shaking, but I stopped when I saw the pavilion—a dim, unattractive place in this season. I could not help but picture her on our first meeting here. The sharp stab of sorrow accompanying this image was too much and I turned away. There was nothing left for me here in this garden but heartbreak.

Back outside the gray stone walls of Isabeau's rose garden, I turned toward the yew walk. An icy breeze dipped cold fingers beneath the collar of my coat and I shivered. I had not stayed long enough in my study to get truly warm. *Where is my cloak?* I wondered. But it did not appear and I had no inclination to insist.

Partway to the yew walk, I became conscious of something hovering at the edge of my vision. I turned and focused my gaze upon a dark shape in the hedge that had not been there before. It was an archway. Low and looking in danger of becoming imminently overgrown, or perhaps, rather, as though the tangle of branches threatening to obscure it had only just this minute begun to withdraw from each other.

There was something familiar about it, yet I could not recall ever having seen it before. There had been no hedge around the estate in my former life and I *knew* no breach had ever existed in it since it had come into being with the curse. I started toward it in confused fascination. For some reason I was certain it was not a way out of my ensorcelled realm. *Where might it lead?*

It didn't matter. It had appeared at this moment, when all hope had vanished from my heart. At the very least it offered me a certain refuge from rooms and gardens haunted by the absence of the woman I loved.

I crossed the hoar-whitened lawn and stepped beneath the rustic portal. Immediately, I was plunged into a lightless gloom. This was no door through the hedge, but some sort of tunnel, its walls as tangled and impenetrable as the hedge itself. I forced my frozen feet onward, my breath forming pale clouds before my face. My beast's nose scented cold, and earth, and the faintest tang of magic. Not the same magic that pervaded the house, or even the forest. This was something older and wilder, filled with sadness and decay. Yet . . . I breathed in deeply, the chill searing my lungs. I ignored the shudders gripping me and concentrated on the magic. At its core was something pure and clear, like the peal of a bell, or the heat of a burning ember. Or—

I stepped from the tunnel into an open space and came to a halt.

Or the color of a crimson rose.

I had entered a churchyard. The churchyard of the small chapel that had stood just outside the grounds of my house, a lifetime ago. To one side I could see the church itself, barely more than crumbling stone walls now. Around me the hedge rose up, encircling the churchyard as surely as it encircled my estate.

Before me, headstones reared like broken teeth through the unkempt, snow-dusted grass. The entire place was stark and colorless, save one leaning monument. I remembered that one. I did not remember the dark, thorny branches that tangled thickly over it, sprouting glossy leaves of deepest green and bloody blooms the color of my broken heart.

I stumbled forward and sank to my knees in front of it, reaching out to touch the fading words on the pitted stone.

Marguerite de Serres.

My grandmother.

Why this, here, now? I wondered. What cruelty was this? To distract me from the loss of Isabeau by reminding me of the loss of the only other person I had ever truly loved?

I stared at the headstone, caught in the embrace of the ancient roses. The vivid crimson blooms began to waver and blur as tears filled my eyes. My taloned paws curled into angry fists as bitter grief flooded my heart. Was I doomed, then, to such solitude? Condemned to nothing more than the unhappy contemplation of my lost loved ones for the remainder of my days?

Isabeau. I did not want her to see me weeping in her dreams. I dragged the back of my paw across my eyes. *"You have your grandmother's eyes,"* the Fairy had said. I took a ragged breath. She had known her. That much I knew.

It was here, by my grandmother's grave, that I had first met the Fairy. Then, the grave had been fresh, the soil newly turned and my grief for my grandmother raw and terrible. I had been young, and angry, and feeling more alone than ever before in my short life.

I had been standing, staring at the shallow heap of dirt that covered her, when someone stepped up beside me. I turned and saw an elderly woman. She was small and delicate in appearance and dressed in mourning weeds of considerable elegance. But she had not been among those who came to pay their respects at the funeral. I had no idea who she was.

"So she is gone and all is at an end," she said to me, and I was surprised at the strength of the bitterness in this stranger's voice. She was glaring fiercely at my grandmother's grave.

"All, madame?" I asked, offended anyone dared intrude

upon my grief. I was also affronted that she, whom I had never seen before in all my life, might think her sorrow for my grandmother was somehow greater than my own.

"Oh, I will endure for eons, yet," she said grimly. "But my heart lies bleeding in that grave."

She turned her gaze upon me and I was struck by the piercing brilliance of her ancient eyes. I could see the tracks of tears upon her lined cheeks.

"So, you are the grandson," she pronounced. "I see she was right to be concerned."

"I do not understand you," I said coldly.

"No," she agreed.

I scowled at her, waiting for her to explain herself, but she looked away from me and back down at the grave. Her expression wavered and such a look of rage came over her face, I knew a moment of true fear. Without looking at me, she lifted a finger, as crooked and bent as old wood, and pointed at me.

"His heart was rotten, but yours is frozen," she said. "It is as bad."

"Madame," I said through gritted teeth. "I cannot think what interest you should have in my heart."

"Between you, you very nearly broke the heart I treasured above all others," she said in a voice like a cold wind. "Marguerite wanted nothing else in life but to see you happy. Now she is gone from this world. Your blood is the only vestige of hers left in it. For that, I offer you this warning: *mend your ways.*"

I opened my mouth to make an angry retort, but before my eyes, she seemed to crumple. A moment later, a raven burst up into noisy flight from where she had been standing and I was alone.

*   *   *

A new draft of cold air recalled me to the present. It tore petals from one of the crimson roses and scattered them over the ragged grass. I looked at where my grandmother's name was inscribed on the old stone.

"I'm sorry, *Grand-mère*," I said brokenly. "I wish you could have met Isabeau."

I did wish it. I could picture each of them so clearly in my mind, I felt as though if I were to look over my shoulder, I would see them standing behind me. I bowed my head in sorrow. I was alone. My grandmother was dead and the closest I could come to Isabeau now was through my mirror and her dreams.

I imagined Isabeau seeing me visit this sad place in those dreams. She would worry about me. I was now so cold my jaws had locked together. Perhaps I should return to the house. I tried to stand and a wave of dizziness swept over me. Alarmed, I reached out to steady myself on my grandmother's gravestone. "No . . ." I muttered to myself. I did not want Isabeau to see me in this weakened state. I wanted her to see me trying to be well. Our exhortation to each other: "Be well."

I leaned on the cold stone, waiting for the spell to pass—the result, surely, of too little food and rest and too much grief over the last few days. A great tremor passed over me. *And the cold*, I thought. *I am so cold.*

I gathered my strength, thinking of my chair with its rug in my study, or the chair before the fire in the entrance hall. Even that would do as somewhere to rest my weary body, while I warmed myself and ate something. I would be well, and I would wait for Isabeau to come home. I may not be happy in her absence, but—I gave a snort of bitter laughter—I did not think I had ever been happy in my life before she came.

Bracing myself against the stone, I stood. It seemed a much harder thing to do than I remembered. But I was on my feet again. I took one careful step and then another toward the gap in the hedge and the path back out of the cemetery. Behind me, there was a sudden screech and I lurched around. A huge raven soared into the churchyard. Its violent wings beat up a small tempest of snow and rose petals and inky, flying feathers. My head reeled. A rushing in my ears rose up, my vision blackened and I fell away into nothingness.

CHAPTER XLII

I have no idea whether I lay there, asleep or unconscious, for an hour or a day. But eventually something roused me from my stupor. It was a voice, a cry, insinuating itself between myself and oblivion. For a moment my heart lifted, thinking Isabeau had somehow returned. Then I remembered: she had left the cottage to be with her family. I was so tired, my very bones weary. My heart was conjuring ghosts from memories. It had been a raven and nothing more.

I let myself sink back toward the comforting dark enveloping me. But the cry came again, louder and more insistent.

"Let me in!"

I tried to move, but I could not. My limbs were heavy with cold. There was a violent rustling. I tried again and flexed the claws of my right hand. There was the sound of branches breaking.

"Beast!"

That voice!

A moment later there were swift footsteps and something landed beside me and a warm weight fell across my chest.

"Beast!"

Isabeau's voice was urgent with some passionate grief. She was shaking me, dragging my head and shoulders into her arms. She murmured brokenly to herself and, as I struggled to open my eyes, her words began to filter through to my dull brain.

"Dear Beast, don't die! Don't die!"

I forced my eyelids apart enough to make sure she was really there.

Through my frozen lashes I could see her pale, pointed face leaning over me. I tried to move my hairy paw to touch her hand, but my limbs seemed frozen solid.

"Isabeau," I managed to whisper.

"Beast?" she cried in a low voice. She snatched up my paw, pressing it to her cheek. Like magic, a wave of warmth washed down my hand and spread through the rest of my body. "Are you alive? Please be alive, Beast! If you live I'll never leave again, I promise. I'll stay with you forever. I'll marry you, Beast, only don't die. I love you!"

Several things happened all at once.

First, with her words I experienced a moment of disbelief. Then came the joy. I thought my heart would burst as colors and stars bloomed before my eyes.

Second, there was an almighty crash as though something vast and brittle had shattered spectacularly, and for the briefest instant I thought it had to do with the explosion of color across my vision, but Isabeau cried out in fear and I knew she heard it, too.

Thirdly, my entire body was suddenly suffused with a brilliant white-gold light, so intense I felt myself burning up within it, and although I fought to stay and tell Isabeau I loved her, too, and that I was hers body and soul, it overwhelmed me and in one terrible, rending flash, everything I was tore apart and scattered to the fading stars.

When I came to myself again, it could only have been moments later, because I still lay with my head in Isabeau's lap. However, everything seemed subtly different. I was still light-headed, but instead of heaviness pervading my limbs, I now felt somehow weightless. Isabeau had found me in a garden just beginning to slide under winter's rule, the ground hard and crusted with frost. Yet I opened my eyes on melting snow and mud, and a golden gleam in the air that had not been there before. Then I lifted my eyes to Isabeau's face and the happiness that had warmed my whole body a moment ago faded abruptly, leaving a sinking coldness in my belly. She was staring at me, wide-eyed in horror, the hand that had held mine so recently now pulled away in shock.

She had not meant it. She could not pledge herself to a beast.

"You!" she gasped.

My throat was so thick with sadness I could barely speak, yet I managed to say, "Isabeau, I released you—"

But she interrupted me, her voice shaking with panic. "Where is my Beast? Where is he?"

"Isabeau—" I reached up to her and froze.

Stretched out toward her was a human hand.

It seemed as alien as if I had suddenly sprouted wings or scales, yet almost familiar. I flexed it and the fingers moved. I brought it back close to my face and stared at it—clean square nails in place of gleaming claws, no more hair than an ordinary man.

"Isabeau," I said again in wonder and noticed my voice, lighter and without the animal growl, "you broke the spell!"

"What do you mean?" she demanded. She still stared at me fearfully, with tear tracks down her face.

"I am—I was—the Beast." I couldn't help but keep looking first at her, then at my hands. "I never thought the spell would end."

"I don't understand," said Isabeau, looking as though she was on the verge of tears and doing her best not to succumb. The mud was becoming progressively worse. I hauled myself up and offered her my hand. (*Hand!*) She allowed me to help her to stand, but she was shaking, her gray eyes still wide with shock. Her lips moved as though she was trying to form words, but no sound came from them.

"I was a man once before, but I was enchanted—cursed," I said. My limbs were trembling and I had to reach out to steady myself against a nearby headstone. I could not tear my eyes from her beautiful face, still pale with distress. I wanted to touch her, to reach out to her, but all the old uncertainty came rushing back as I stared at her shocked expression.

"It may take some time to explain," I said desperately. "Please, Isabeau, you may not feel you know me at all, and you may want to take back the things you said to me just now—" She opened her mouth to say something, but I plowed on. "We are both of us tired and weary. Just please promise me you won't make up your mind about anything just yet. Wait until we have had a chance to talk."

Isabeau shook her head.

"Beast," she said, her voice unsteady. "I know you. You are the man in the painting. When I think of you, half the time I think of you with this face."

She stepped closer to me and reached up to touch my jaw. My head whirled and the world tilted. I gripped the headstone more tightly as she leaned back to take a better look at me. I stood motionless, hardly daring to breathe, as she ran her fingertips over the unshaven skin of my cheek.

"I've done this a hundred times in my dreams," she whispered so quietly I wondered if she realized she had spoken aloud. Then she looked into my eyes and said, "No wonder the picture disturbed you, *Julien*."

Hearing her say my name was a new kind of magic and for a moment there was nothing in the world but Isabeau's gray eyes. She stood so close to me, her hand cupping my jaw, her face turned up to mine. It would be so easy to . . .

"Your eyes," she said, "you always have your eyes."

My courage failed me.

"Please, will you come back to the house?" I asked, offering her my arm.

The state of the tunnel back through the hedge was such that it was not possible to walk through it together. Indeed, it was clear Isabeau had needed to fight her way through to me. However, once we were standing on the other side, she put her arm through mine again and looked up at me with a radiant smile.

"You are not so tall now," she observed, leaning close against me.

"No," I said, my throat tight. I could not stop looking at her.

The sensation of her beside me was the only thing that sustained me as we made our way up to the house. My heart was thundering and black spots danced before my eyes. *She said she would marry me. She said she loves me*, I thought, hardly daring to believe it. But, the curse had broken.

I darted another quick look at her and, with a thrill, found she was gazing up at me. She smiled. My heart tripped.

The front door stood ajar, sagging slightly upon its hinges, and I had to push it open so we could enter together. It creaked closed behind us. A fire burned in the hearth, but the house was somehow still and silent.

"I think the magic is dying," whispered Isabeau, clinging to my arm. Then she frowned up at me. All the consternation was gone from her face and a different light burned in her eyes now.

"You are shivering!" she accused me.

"I—I am," I admitted. My clothes were soaked with icy mud and I had been chilled before I had collapsed out in the garden.

"Oh! This is a fine time for your magical servants to vanish!" she exclaimed. She dragged me across the hall and up the stairs. I cast a longing look at the chair by the fire as we passed it, but Isabeau had apparently discounted it as a suitable resting place for my weary body.

"You need to get out of those wet clothes," she fretted. "And I know you've barely eaten in the last week. Where am I to find a hot meal now?"

"No idea," I confessed through teeth locked together with the cold.

When we reached my bedchamber, she threw open the door and pulled me inside, then momentarily abandoned me to shiver in the middle of the room while she pushed my chair close to the dying fire in the grate. She made impatient noises as she threw more logs onto the coals, and I stood, caught between disbelief and happiness that she was here with me again. She turned to look up at me and saw I had not moved. With a cry she leaped up and bustled me into the chair.

"Beast," she cried in frustration. "Sit. I won't have you perishing from the cold. I won't!"

She knelt at my feet and tugged off my boots, then turned her attention to my wet, dirty clothes.

"Take your coat off, Beast—Julien," she said decisively, pulling at my sodden garters. "Where are your clothes?"

Still shivering, I indicated a chest where my clothes were kept. She crossed to it and threw it open, pulling garments out apparently at random, while I struggled with the buttons on my coat. I still wondered at the sight of my pale fingers against the dark cloth, but, even human, they were clumsy with cold. Isabeau gave another impatient cry to see how little progress I was making, and flew back over to me. She knelt in front of me again, tearing at the buttons so ruthlessly it was a wonder some of them did not part company with my coat entirely.

"Careful," I admonished her, laughing breathlessly.

"Careful?" she asked, standing up and tugging me upright also, so she could strip my wet coat from me. "I am trying to save your life and you tell me to be careful?"

My coat went onto the floor in a crumpled pile. She dragged my wet shirt from my breeches and pulled at the laces at the neck. At that moment my skin turned to gooseflesh for reasons that had nothing to do with the cold. I froze, unable to move. But Isabeau was lifting my shirt over my belly, then over my head. Her hand grazed my chest. In a moment my shirt joined my coat.

Then, in the act of handing me the dry shirt hanging over her arm, Isabeau suddenly grew still. I heard her sharply indrawn breath and saw her cheeks grow warm. I was standing before her in nothing but my breeches. She was staring at my chest. Guiltily, she raised her eyes to my face and smiled.

"Your hair," she said, "it's so much longer than in the portrait."

"Isabeau, my shirt," I said, my jaw clenched with distress as much as the cold. For no reason I could name, I was terrified.

"Beast . . ." she said softly, stepping close. She laid a hand in the center of my chest. The heat from her palm was like a brand. I held up my own hand to ward her off, my fear tearing through me, making me unsteady on my feet. She caught my hand and began to kiss my fingers. The air rushed from my lungs in something very like a sob. A moment later, Isabeau was somehow in my arms, the silk of her hair soft against my bare skin.

"Beast!" she cried into my chest, and I couldn't tell if she was crying or laughing.

I was overwhelmed with memories and guilt. Images from the worst of my father's drunken routs rose up in my mind, along with all the old terror of what would happen if I allowed myself to feel even the smallest flush of desire. But Isabeau was so warm against my chilled flesh and I had been dreaming of holding her like this for so long, I couldn't push her away. Involuntarily, my arms moved around her.

"You're so warm," I said, my voice trembling. I could no longer tell whether I was cold or not.

"I've dreamed of this," she said. "I never told you."

"This?" I said shakily. "Me almost dead from cold?"

"No," she laughed. "Of holding you, like this."

She moved her hand over the skin of my chest and my whole body thrummed.

She glanced up at me shyly.

"And you kissing me," she said.

I could barely breathe. She wound an arm about my neck, tangling her fingers in my long, black curls.

"Did you ever dream of me?" she asked in a whisper.

"Did I—?" I asked, still breathless. That was when she kissed me for the first time.

It was nothing like I'd dreamed. It was so much better. Her mouth was sweet and warm, and for the longest time it was the only thing I knew. I even forgot to be afraid.

But, gradually, I became aware of other sensations. Her hand on my neck, tugging on my hair. The burning warmth of her, pressed up against the length of my chilled body. And other feelings, more base and visceral. My gut clenched in sudden terror and I broke away from her lips, lifting my head and struggling for breath. Isabeau looked up at me, concern filling her eyes.

"But you are still so cold! Here!" She pulled away and handed me my shirt. I pulled it over my head and she stepped close again, lifting my hair—which had indeed grown long and unruly—from my neck and smoothing the wide, lace-edged collar over my shoulders. I found I was shivering again. Isabeau fetched my robe from where it lay over the foot of my bed and held it out to me. I slid my arms into the sleeves and wrapped it around myself, as grateful for the modesty it offered as for the warmth.

"Now these," she said, handing me a pair of dry breeches.

"But—" I protested, looking at her in consternation.

She made a face at me.

"I won't look," she said, turning away.

I did not move.

"Although," she continued, "I *know* you watched me dressing through your mirror."

I was flooded with perishing shame. My face burned. "I am sorry," I whispered.

There was a long pause. She turned her face so I could see her profile. Her cheeks were pink again. "I don't mind," she said.

I could not look at her. My blood drummed in my ears and my belly curdled. The enormity of the dishonor I had done her threatened to overwhelm me. I was no different from him after all.

"I'm sorry," I choked out again.

"Beast. Julien," she said, her voice full of concern. She turned back to look at me. I stumbled backward away from her.

"What is it?" The worry in her voice was sharp. She was moving toward me. I held out my hands to stop her coming closer.

"Don't touch me," I said.

"Why not?" she asked. "What's wrong?"

"I can't—" I gasped.

"Can't what?" she asked. I twisted away. "What is wrong?"

"You don't know," I croaked, too many thoughts crowding into my head. I could hear her, feel her coming toward me again, and a terrible fear began to squeeze the air from my lungs.

"Tell me!" she begged.

Blindly I staggered away from her. I stumbled against the bed and fell at its foot. I heard her quick footsteps and a moment later her warm hands were upon me, brushing my hair back from my eyes, taking my face and turning it toward hers. A sob caught in my throat and I closed my eyes tightly in pain.

"Beast," she said, her voice gentle. "Julien, whatever it is, you can tell me."

I reached out to push her away, but somehow found my hands gripping her shoulders. I found I was as much terrified she would leave again as I was of what might happen if she stayed.

"Don't leave," I croaked, barely able to speak.

"I'm not leaving," she said. "I love you."

My eyes flew open. Her wide gray eyes were all I could see.

"I love you," she repeated.

She kissed me again. The pure magic of that sensation swept

over me, burning away all else for a few, blessed moments. Nothing mattered but that she was here with me and that she loved me. I pulled her close. My hands roved up her neck and into her hair. The blood was pounding in my ears and I shook all over, but, God help me, I did not want to stop.

When she eventually broke her lips from mine, with the smallest of sighs, she did not pull away from me. She stayed, kneeling on the floor in the circle of my arms, her forehead leaning against mine. As much as I had not wanted the kiss to end, I now found I could happily sit like this with her forever. But she must have noticed me trembling, for she brushed her hand against my face and frowned.

"You are not well," she said uncertainly. She turned around and looked searchingly at the air.

"House," she called out. "For the love of God, if you have any magic left, please, please get him some hot food and drink! If you let him die I'll tear you apart myself, brick by brick."

She turned back to me.

"Come," she said, finding my hand and tugging it. I let her help me up, then she pushed me toward the bed and put the crumpled breeches into my hands.

"Change," she said firmly. "Now." She turned her back upon me resolutely. I struggled out of the wet, dirty garment and hurriedly pulled on the dry pair. As I buttoned them, a new smell filled the air, savory and rich.

"Ah!" cried Isabeau, spinning about. A steaming bowl had appeared on my bedside table, accompanied by a large chunk of bread—fresh from the oven, if the smell was anything to judge by—and a pewter tankard of what could only be mulled wine. She bustled me into the bed and put the bowl into my hands, standing over me with her arms folded. She was wearing her stubborn face again.

"Eat," she commanded. "All of it."

"Will you sit with me?" I asked humbly, hoping now that she had seen me dry and fed she would not think of some vital task that might take her from my company. Her mouth twitched and her expression softened.

"I am not leaving you," she said. "I am far too terrified you are just a dream and I will wake up alone in the cottage once again." She leaned over and touched my face, a silly grin pulling at the corners of her mouth. I could hardly breathe.

"I don't think I am a dream," I said.

"Eat!" she repeated, pulling her hand away. She went to my chair and dragged it back beside the bed and sat down. It took me some moments to reaccustom myself to the sensation of holding a spoon in human fingers, and she watched me eat the rich broth, hiding her smile of amusement behind a hand. I confess I was so absorbed in her presence, I barely tasted it. When the bowl was half-empty, however, I became aware I was no longer trembling with cold.

"I believe I am warm again," I said, leaning back against my pillows.

She smiled, leaning her chin on one hand.

"I am glad to hear it," she said. "But I am not moving until you finish your meal."

"That is no incentive," I pointed out. "For I do not want you to go."

She gave me another brilliant smile.

"I might move closer if you were to finish your food," she said.

My face grew warm and my skin tingled. I still experienced a twist of uncertainty in the pit of my belly, but I applied myself anew to cleaning my bowl.

"There," she said, placing the empty bowl back upon the bedside table after I had done. "Now drink this!" She passed me the tankard of warm wine.

"If I drink that, I may fall asleep," I demurred. Indeed, after so many days without adequate food or rest, in my current state of satiation my limbs felt heavy as lead.

"I intend for you to do so," Isabeau said. "You have watched over me as I slept, these last few nights. Now let me keep watch over you."

"But—!" I protested. I did not want to fall asleep. I wanted to sit here with her and . . . I looked away from her, my face burning.

"You cannot know how hard it was to see you so restless and unhappy in my dreams," said Isabeau. Her voice caught, and when I looked back at her, the laughter had vanished from her eyes. I felt a stab of shame. But she reached out and twined her fingers through mine.

"You may make good your debt by letting me see you sleep peacefully, now," she said, lifting my hand to her mouth and kissing it. "Drink your wine."

How could I deny her? I drank and, with my hand still in Isabeau's, it was not very many minutes more before I slept.

CHAPTER XLIII

*S*omething was askew. It was as though a new scent hovered on the edge of detection, but my senses had grown unaccountably dulled and I could not pick it up. I swung my head to and fro, trying to catch it, but it vanished like a rabbit into a hedge. I growled.

The room was unfamiliar, shrouded in darkness. I did not want to be here. I could see a dim haze ahead of me, like the glow of reflected firelight. I tried to move toward it, but my body was sluggish and the effort was agonizing. Eventually the ruddy blur began to take form and I could see the silhouette of another person. The shape was unfamiliar, and all my fur stood on end in alarm. I inched closer, struggling against the torpor that threatened to overwhelm me.

I caught the gleam of his eyes in the gloom and a heartbeat later I realized I was standing before a mirror. I stared at myself, a disheveled echo of the image in my portrait, my heart thundering wildly in my chest. *Human*, I was *human*. I tried to lift my hand to touch the hairless skin beneath my eyes. But as I did so, the hair on my unshaven jaw began to thicken and spread up over my cheeks and I watched in horror as my fingers swelled into clumsy pads and sprouted wicked claws. The growth of cursed fur spread rapidly over my arms, becoming thick and shaggy in seconds. Then, in a burst of searing pain, the furred skin of my forehead split apart and a new pair of horns erupted from my skull. I cried out, throwing up my hands to cover my hideous face—

The movement jolted me awake.

I lay panting in terror in the darkness. Shaking, I lifted a hand to my face. The skin of my forehead was smooth and hairless. In the dim orange glow emitted by the coals in the fireplace, I could see my hand was human. Seeking reassurance, I glanced at Isabeau's chair. It was empty.

The sound of quiet, even breathing drew my attention to a warm presence at my other side. She was lying against me, curled upon the bedclothes and covered with a shawl. Her hair had come loose and lay tumbled over the pillow. My heart gave a familiar bound at the sight of her.

I wanted to reach out and touch her, but I hesitated. My mind was still reeling from my nightmare and I half expected at the least sign of impropriety I would see a black tide of animal fur surging over my skin. A fresh bout of fear gripped me. My chest seemed wrapped in bands of iron, growing tighter by the moment. What was I to do? She loved me enough to break the curse, but she couldn't possibly understand the horror of the monster I might yet become. I could not stomach the thought of hurting her.

Lying so close to her and not being able to touch her was unbearable. The ache it gave me was intimately familiar, but it had been easier to withstand when I had worn my Beast's skin. I resolved to move, to put some distance between us. I sat up, but at the movement she stirred and opened her eyes.

"Beast?" she murmured. She looked up at me sleepily and frowned. "It is still night." She reached out, but I jerked myself back away from her.

"Beast?" she said more sharply, pushing herself up onto her elbows. "Julien? What is it?"

I couldn't speak. My breath was frozen in my throat and the constriction around my chest stopped me from filling my lungs anew. I scrambled to my knees, ready to flee, but she reached out and caught hold of my shirt.

"Julien? Why are you so afraid of me?" Her voice was rising and all the soft sleepiness had fled from her eyes.

"I'm not afraid of you," I choked, resisting her hold. I *wanted* to pull her into my arms. "It's not you."

"Then what?" she cried, tightening her grip on my clothes. "There is something wrong! Won't you tell me?"

"I don't want to hurt you," I gasped.

"Hurt me?" she asked. "Why would you hurt me?"

I could not answer.

"Don't leave," she said, her voice trembling slightly. All my resolve to go evaporated instantly. She stared at me intently, her eyes huge in the darkness.

"Won't you tell me what it is? Is it the curse?"

I nodded, breathing heavily.

"Are you still cursed?" she asked apprehensively. "Are you going to turn back into a beast?"

"No," I whispered. "Not like I was. A different kind of monster. Like . . . *him*."

Isabeau inhaled sharply. I looked at her, my heart filling with hopelessness. "It is why the Fairy cursed me."

"Like who?" she asked resolutely. "Tell me."

"My father," I choked out, the words bitter in my mouth.

"He was a terrible man. His faithlessness brought nothing but misery and death upon my mother. He was vicious and cruel and—"

"But you're not like that," interrupted Isabeau.

"I might change," I protested miserably.

"Julien." Isabeau spoke my name slowly and deliberately. "You could never be like that. I know you. I've spent almost a year here by your side."

"I have a terrible temper, as did my father," I said, visions of his livid face rising up in my mind.

"You have a temper," Isabeau acknowledged, but she was smiling.

I shook my head, trying to make her understand.

"When he was in his cups he would fly into violent rages. He also . . ." I stopped. How could I tell her about the women?

"Is this why you were cursed?" asked Isabeau indignantly. "Because of your father?"

"No!" How could I explain the fear that had plagued my entire life? "No, because—because I may become him—"

A terrible shrieking noise filled the air. I was blasted by a sudden hurricane stinking of dust and ashes. Isabeau cried out in fright and I found myself clasping her tightly in my arms. A host of flying things erupted from the bed hangings; bats churned around us with a leathery clatter and tiny, soft-winged bodies battered my face.

An impossibly tall, gaunt figure loomed over us, amid a swirl of sparks being sucked from the fireplace.

"You fool!"

Through the wind-whipped hair streaming across my eyes I could see a pair of enormous, lambent green eyes glaring down at me from a face as white as bone.

"Have you learned nothing?" The Fairy's voice was an angry screech.

"What is that thing?" cried Isabeau, her voice high with fear. She was holding on to my shirt with both hands now. I clasped her tighter.

"You have paid for Marguerite's pain," said the Fairy, in a voice so filled with rage I felt as though she were battering me with her fists. "But I will curse you again, rather than see you perpetuate the misery that broke her heart!"

"No!" Isabeau shrieked.

"Lady," I cried. "Forgive me! I do not understand."

The maelstrom of flying things subsided and I was able to see the Fairy more clearly. She stood at the foot of the bed, in a gown like a tatter of gray cloud. Her pale hair was a tangle of cobweb, full of twigs and mummified insects. Isabeau was breathing quickly.

"Your heart is not his!" hissed the Fairy. "If you let it freeze again, you will become a monster of your own making. Do not blame him!"

"But—" I struggled to bend my mind to what she was saying.

The Fairy caught my gaze and held it. In her terrible eyes I saw the anger and sorrow I remembered from years before, but also a depth of pity.

"You are not just your father's son," the Fairy continued ruthlessly. "Other blood flows in your veins. Your vices and your choices are your own."

A light dawned in my brain, a revelation so simple and piercing it tore the breath from my lungs.

Your heart is not his . . . a monster of your own making . . . Do not . . .

. . . blame . . .

. . . him!

There was an abrupt change in the atmosphere of the room, as though the full moon was suddenly shining out from behind a cloud. Had I thought the Fairy's hair wild and unkempt? It was a gleaming fall of silver. Her gown was not rags, but surely silk, rich with moonlit iridescence. She was not at the foot of the bed, but beside me, leaning over to touch my face.

Isabeau drew in her breath sharply and pressed close against me. Through the fabric of my shirt I could feel her heartbeat, racing like mine. I tightened my arms around her as I felt the Fairy's cold fingertips on my cheek.

"You have your grandmother's eyes," said the Fairy. Her own eyes were bright and tears shone like stars upon her cheeks. "My Marguerite. For her sake, I would see you happy."

Isabeau shifted slightly and one of her hands searched out and found mine. I slid my fingers through hers.

"Ah," said the Fairy. And, with a sigh like the wind through trees, she vanished, leaving nothing but a shimmer of moonlight dancing over the walls.

I looked down at Isabeau.

Her face was tilted up to mine, the warm light of the slumbering coals touching the sweet curve of her cheek.

I was still terrified. My heart was pounding in my chest. But I gathered all my courage together and this time *I* kissed *her*.

We did not go back to sleep straightaway. We did not try. But, with everything we had to tell each other, Isabeau's first question surprised me.

"Who was Marguerite?" she asked. She was still curled upon the bed, wrapped in her shawl, watching me as I added more wood to the fire to drive off the night-time chill that hung in the air.

"My grandmother," I said.

"And who was *that*?"

I did not need to ask who she meant.

"She laid the curse," I said.

Isabeau nodded. "Well, I am grateful to her."

"Grateful?" I asked, startled.

"If she had not cursed you, I would never have known you," she said.

"No," I agreed.

I returned to the bed and sat down beside Isabeau. She reached over and took my hand, threading her fingers through mine.

"I still don't understand it," she said. I looked down at my human fingers, tangled so happily in hers.

"My father was a vile and violent man," I said, the words still difficult. "He was a lecher, and a violator and abuser of women." My throat closed over with the strength of my repugnance. I found I was trembling.

"After he died, I was so adamant I would *not* be my father," I said, "I fear I let my anger at him govern me. I first encountered the Fairy after my grandmother died. She rebuked me for causing my grandmother grief and told me to mend my ways, but I did not understand her."

Isabeau's hand tightened around mine.

"But, then, some seven years later, I was visited by a cousin of my mother's. He wanted money, which I refused to give him.

He grew angry and accused me of treating my mother's family ill, as my father had treated my mother. He said I was just like my father."

I had to stop and take a breath.

"I always feared I would prove susceptible to the same vices," I said. "We dueled and I nearly killed him. I destroyed my father's portrait that night and threatened to burn my cousin with it. The Fairy came back." I shuddered. "I always thought she had cursed me because my father's capacity for depravity and viciousness lurked in me."

Isabeau reached up and turned my face to hers. Her gaze found mine and held it.

"There is nothing of that in you," she said firmly.

"How can you be so sure?" I asked shakily.

"I know you, *Julien*," she said with conviction. "When I've needed you, you came whatever the hour. You have been nothing but gentle and gallant. I have sat with you, drinking mulled wine in my nightdress—" She went pink, and dropped her hand from my jaw.

I was momentarily robbed of speech, remembering the intimacy of those nights.

"You may not have been so polite in my dreams," said Isabeau, looking away and blushing furiously.

It took all the courage I had to overcome the trepidation that seized me. I lifted her hand and kissed it.

"Nor in mine," I confessed.

She smiled at me self-consciously. I put my arms around her and she leaned happily against me. I was dizzy with bliss, despite the edge of anxiety making my pulse race. Isabeau slid her hand under my robe to grasp at the neck of my shirt. Her fingers were warm against my chest.

"Your heart is beating so fast," she murmured.

I nodded and closed my hand over hers, holding it against me. I kissed the top of her head, breathing in the scent of her and she turned her face up to mine again.

"I am so glad I came back," she said.

"What changed?" I asked. "Why did you come back?"

Isabeau's eyes clouded.

"I saw you fall," she said, a catch in her voice. "I was sitting in René's cart and I closed my eyes. I don't know how, but I could see you. I wasn't dreaming, but I could see you so clearly. But I was so far away!" I pulled her closer.

"I didn't know if my ring would work," she continued. "I couldn't even see the trees of the forest anymore. We were over the hill. I saw Father and Claude turn to look at me, but then I was here, in the music room.

"I ran out, but none of the doors would open and nothing helped me. I didn't know where you were! And when I found the break in the hedge I thought I might never get inside to you!" She shuddered against me. "Beast, I have to apologize."

"What?" I asked. "Why?"

"For being so stubborn and refusing to see you clearly," she said, her voice quavering.

"Isabeau—" I protested.

"No!" she insisted. "If I had admitted it when I first began to love you—"

I laughed shakily.

"How could you?" I asked. "I was a beast."

"My Beast," she said passionately.

I could never hear those words without pleasure.

"I have always been yours," I said in a low voice, my throat tight. Isabeau hid her face in my chest.

"I thought when I went back to my family I would miss you a little, perhaps," she admitted. "But I kept seeing you in my dreams and I just wanted to come home." She swallowed and glanced up at me, as though looking for reassurance.

"Then, my father . . ." Her voice trailed off miserably. The room grew a shade darker.

"Ah," I said.

"I know it was you that warned me," she said. "Thank you."

"I owe him a great debt. I would mend the breach with him if I could."

Isabeau shifted in my arms, turning to take my face in her hands. "You will," she said seriously. "By showing him how happy you have made me."

"You will stay with me, then?" I said breathlessly.

"As much as I love my father and my sisters, my home is not with them anymore," she said.

"No," I agreed, lifting a stray curl from her cheek. "Your home is here."

Isabeau smiled at me in the dusky light. She brushed her fingers across my collarbone and over the curve of my shoulder. New warmth spread across my skin.

"This is like a gift I was not expecting," she murmured. "Although—" She paused, and her face broke into a smile that was positively devilish. "Oh! The trick I will be able to play upon Claude! I never did tell you about how I would torment her with my pet monkey, poor darling."

"You will marry me?" I asked, wanting to hear her say it again.

"As soon as I may," said Isabeau firmly. "And I am not leaving you again. I am too afraid I will wake up and find it all a dream."

"I confess I am a little afraid of that, too," I said, smiling, "but I will promise to come and present myself to you the moment I awake in the morning so you may reassure yourself as to the permanence of my transformation."

"You misunderstand me," said Isabeau. I heard the all-too-familiar stubborn note creeping back into her voice. "I am not leaving your bedchamber. I am going to sleep here, in your arms, for I will not dream of you alone again."

I stared at her in consternation.

"But—"

"You will have to get used to it," said Isabeau. "Especially if we are to be wed."

I could not think of a response. But a cold sweat pricked my skin and my mouth grew dry.

"You must trust yourself," said Isabeau firmly, "for I do. Now, lie down."

Haltingly, my face hot, I did as she instructed. Isabeau lay down beside me and dragged the covers over us. I did not know what to do, but Isabeau curled herself close beside me and laid her head upon my shoulder.

"There," she said, her hand settling into the center of my chest. "Does this not feel right?"

Racked by nerves and insecurities as I was, I could not deny it was more than pleasant to be lying in my bed with her in my arms.

"I could become reconciled to this situation," I said, attempting to disguise my unease. Isabeau giggled and a knot of tension unwound itself somewhere inside my belly. I was silent for a few minutes, listening to the quiet crackle of the fire, gradually losing myself to the sensation of her body against mine.

As we lay together Isabeau gave a melancholy sigh.

"You know, I will miss your Beastly face," she said sadly. "I believe I had grown quite fond of it."

"Really?" I asked, unable to disguise my surprise. She pushed herself up on an elbow and made a show of looking at me closely. She smiled.

"Well, perhaps not. Perhaps you don't look so different after all."

It was my turn to sigh.

"It is well that after so long as a beast, any shred of vanity I had is gone, and I am unable to be offended by that remark," I said sadly.

Isabeau laughed and buried her face in the crook of my shoulder. She sounded almost as happy as I.

I could not resist. Without hesitation, I drew her to me and kissed her. She wound one arm around my neck and kissed me back, meeting my passion unequivocally with her own. Every dark thought and creeping fear that had ever possessed me evaporated in the wave of intoxicating sweetness that engulfed me as I relinquished myself entirely to her.

And that moment of sweetness seems a fitting end to my tale. I could tell you about how the magic gradually faded from the house, how the forests receded a little, and how the gardens were never quite as fabulous again.

We do not miss the magic, though. For my château, so silent and empty for so long, is now full of human voices and human industry. It's true that sometimes I grow wistful for the time when it was just Isabeau and I. But we have our little sanctuaries, and they are the same as they have ever been. Her music room, my study, the library, the rose garden. And, of course, when the weather is fine and we have the time, you can still find us in the orchard beneath boughs heavy with blossoms or with fruit. We are no longer so young that we can lounge carelessly in the grass as we once did, but there is a bench in our favorite spot. We sit there together and Isabeau can still lean against me as I read to her.

I could tell you how we restored my portrait to its place. We have added several new paintings to the walls since. I am not alone in my new portrait and if I have any criticisms of this one, it is that I look a little too self-satisfied and the artist sadly failed to capture Isabeau's true radiance. Isabeau laughs at me and tells me I look happy and that her own likeness is very well. But neither of us spends much time contemplating portraits anymore, surrounded as we are by our living, breathing loved ones.

I could tell you of how Isabeau took me back to meet her family. She wrote to Marie first. The letter simply said:

I have freed him. I am bringing him to meet you.

I was terrified we would be met with spears and pitchforks but, as the cart we hired in the village rolled up to the farmhouse, it was Marie and René who came out to greet us, their faces alive with cautious curiosity. I cannot pretend those first few hours were comfortable, not least because René's farmhouse seemed to fairly throng with people. But Isabeau's family heard my petition for their forgiveness with grace and granted it in exactly the manner Isabeau predicted. Claude forgave me my trespass upon her father and sister on the instant and immediately set about making me feel welcome in the family. Marie was polite enough, but reserved her judgment until the following day, after I had undertaken that most important interview with her father and Isabeau and I could announce our betrothal. Since then, however, I can truly say I know what it is like to have an older sister who will not hesitate to give me her affection, her censure or her counsel, frequently in the same breath.

Monsieur de la Noue was the hardest to convince, having suffered the most harm at my hands. Oh, he said the words of forgiveness I begged him for and he granted us permission to wed readily enough. But it was a long, long time before he could look at me without a certain wariness in his gaze; and he did not come to the château again until there came a time when Isabeau herself could not leave it for the happiest of reasons.

I could tell you about all these things, and more, as we continue to write new chapters in our lives together.

But what I most want to tell you is this: the revelation of her trust that Isabeau granted to me was not the last of her gifts, by any means. And each new pinnacle of sweetness she brought me was as sharp and true as those that came before: the moment she pledged herself to me on the steps of the tiny village church; the moment I brought her home and together we stepped through the gates that had held me prisoner for so long; and of course the moments when she gave me our sons, Jean-Pierre and Louis, and our daughters, Marguerite, Marie-Claude and little Isabeau.

And after everything, I think in fact she loves me just as much as I love her, and gleans as much joy from our life as I do. Sometimes more so: of course it was she who gained the greatest satisfaction from watching our little firstborn son in her father's arms, pulling on his beard with impunity, and then in their turn his brother and sisters. Even now, while we both await the joy we brought to Isabeau's father, watching our own Marguerite approach motherhood, I believe it is my Isabeau who feels it most deeply.

And that never-ending joy, I think, is her overwhelming gift to me. My Isabeau. My font of sweetness. For her I would have endured another thousand years of solitude.

Ah yes. And the Fairy.

To this day there is always a vase of fresh flowers to be found beneath my grandmother's portrait, even in midwinter. And a single candle burning. But I never saw *her* again.

ACKNOWLEDGMENTS

*F*irst and foremost I have to thank Thorne Ryan and the team at Hodder & Stoughton for taking a chance on my story and for loving it as much as I do, and being such a dream to work with. I owe a debt of gratitude to Anne Perry, too, for pulling me out of the slush pile. Huge thanks also to my lovely editor at Berkley, Anne Sowards, and to the marketing and publicity team, Fareeda, Lauren and Alexis. And, of course, artist Lisa Perrin for creating such an exquisite cover for *The Beast's Heart*.

A big shout-out to the mighty hive mind of the Canberra Speculative Fiction Guild, the best writing tribe a starry-eyed, wannabe writer could ever fall in with. In particular I have to thank the novel-critiquing circle of 2012 who saw the very first, inadequate incarnation of this story. Ian McHugh, Robin Shortt, Chris Andrews, Alexa Shaw, David Beveridge, David Coleman, Robert Phillips: thank you for your insight, frank criticism and encouragement. Especially thanks to Ian for asking if it was ready when it really wasn't and Robin for letting me be part of his own first-novel journey. Thank you to Craig Cormick for his early encouragement in that first Year of the Novel course and for his ongoing mentorship, and a huge thank-you to Russell Kirkpatrick for incisive critique of the penultimate draft and knowing how to say exactly what I needed to hear. And to Robert Hood, who offered a second pair of eyes on the final proof: I owe you a drink.

Thank you to Fiona McIntosh for the crucible of her 2013 Masterclass, and the knowledge, friendships and opportunities I've gained through that. I also want to acknowledge Bernadette Foley, formerly of Hachette Australia, for her generous feedback and valuable advice on an early draft, and the wonderful Jane Ainslie, who also read an early draft and helped me pull it into much better shape.

I'm also grateful for the opportunity I had to participate in the ACT Writers Centre's HARDCOPY 2016 program, supported by the Australia Council for the Arts and convened by the delightful Nigel Featherstone, for fortifying me with some incredibly valuable industry knowledge and introducing me to another great bunch of Australian writers. Thank you to Alex Adsett, as well, for her assistance in negotiating the legal side of things.

Finally, to my beautiful family, who patiently listen to my tortured explanations of plot and point out the holes, leave me alone to write for hours on end while they all play computer games, bring me cups of tea and tell me they're proud of me: Dennis, Nyssa and Ronan, thanks, guys, I love you to bits.

Leife Shallcross lives at the foot of a mountain in Canberra, Australia, with her family and a small, scruffy creature who snores. She has a tendency to overindulge in reading fairy tales, then lie awake at night listening to trolls (or maybe possums) galloping over her tin roof. Ever since she can remember, she has been fascinated by stories about canny fairy godmothers, heroic goosegirls and handsome princes disguised as bears. She is particularly inspired by those characters that tend to fall into the cracks of the usual tales. She is the author of several short stories, including "Pretty Jennie Greenteeth," which won the 2016 Aurealis Award for Best Young Adult Short Story. *The Beast's Heart* is her first novel.

CONNECT ONLINE

leifeshallcross.com

Ready to find
your next great read?

Let us help.

Visit prh.com/nextread

Penguin
Random
House